Praise for D. Z. Church

Saving Calypso-- "This well constructed thriller provides plenty of action... The protagonists are unusual and compelling. Their mutual need to reinvent themselves in order to survive will resonate with readers as the double-crosses and questions pile up. **Great for fans of** James Patterson's *The 6th Target*, David Baldacci's *A Minute to Midnight*. *– Booklife Reviews*

Perfidia-- "In Church's debut thriller...Church manages, quite impressively, to maintain a sense of hidden but perpetual threat...Overpowering dread and a leery protagonist make this a suspenseful read." *--Kirkus Review, Indie Book Worth Discovering*

Cooper Vietnam Era Quartet:

Dead Legend— "Church writes in a muscular prose that never loses its noirish register...there's something compelling about the milieu and the language that keeps the reader engaged, particularly as the mysteries of Mac Cooper begin to unravel." *--Kirkus Reviews*

"Dead Legend is a taut thriller with a compelling plot and fascinating characters. Highly recommended." *--Janet Dawson, author of the Jeri Howard and California Zephyr series.*

Head First -- "This sequel continues the saga of the Coopers, a Navy family grappling with its past against the backdrop of the Vietnam War... Church's prose is precise an often subtly lyrical, asking readers to pause and sit with every scene...an intriguing family saga." *--Kirkus Reviews*

"(Head First) is moving
of a family living...und
Reedsy Discovery, Must

t

D0813942

Books by D. Z. Church:

Perfidia
Saving Calypso

Cooper Vietnam Era Quartet:

Dead Legend: 1967
Head First: 1972

Saving 🕐 Calypso

D. Z. Church

Bodie Blue Books
Alameda   Monterey

A Bodie Blue Books original

Cover design © 2019 D. Z. Church (using BookCreative)
Photographs: Shutterstock by Busko Oleksandr; Wallenrock; Mary
    Swift

Copyright © 2019 Dawn Zinser Church

Library of Congress Control Number: 2019951463

ISBN: 0-9983297-6-2
ISBN-13: 978-0-9983297-6-5

Dedication

For Janet Dawson,
met in the Broomfield High School Library,
another dreamer of dreams.

Contents

Four Years Ago

They were back.

Display advertisements in the San Francisco papers seeking Calypso Swale, a missing heiress, preceded the watchers by two weeks. Only six months before, Calypso was sunning herself on the deck of a borrowed villa in Mustique when she noticed binoculars trained on her. She disappeared with the help of friends, landing in San Francisco, clutching a passport bearing a new name and the take from her father's safe. She rented a house and found a job at the Dolce and Gabbana store on Grant Street. She loved working, she hadn't thought she would, but she did. She met the right people, many on the Social Register, wormed her way into their graces, and got paid for doing so.

Now, the watchers were back.

She spotted the first one gaping at her via her reflection in a store window as she passed. Every day since, she had been surveilled as she arrived for work and at the end of her shift as she trotted to catch the bus at the corner of Geary and Kearny. No matter which watcher it was, he wore casual dress clothes with sneakers. Who does that? Someone sent to return her to the East Coast to take her lumps, that's who.

She was prepared to run if need be, her camping gear, hatchet, just-in-case knapsack, and parka, all from REI, were in the trunk of her silver Lexus sedan. What remained of her father's cash and the envelope he handed her fourteen months ago were sewn in the lining of her purse. Not much of the money remained, she had wasted it on the feel of silk against her skin, cashmere over her shoulders, and chemicals which she kept dry in a tin lunchbox bearing a portrait of the young Captain James T. Kirk. The colorful box with the plastic handle was wrapped in lingerie from Victoria's Secret, stuffed in a tote, and tucked behind the front seat of her car.

She scurried through her workdays. At night, she prepared to be a bridesmaid for a co-worker's wedding at the Bellagio Casino in Las Vegas. She had her favorite Gucci dress cleaned at a laundry specializing in haute couture. The dress and the matching slingback Jimmy Choo shoes were boxed and on the backseat of her sedan. She dreamed of watching the Bellagio water jets at the front of the casino dance to soaring music while holding her dream man's hand, knowing it was a chimera. She would never make her friend's wedding. The tall, dark, and handsome dream man with his well-cut jaw and broad shoulders might never be. Still, she kept up pretenses, meeting with friends, speed dating guys, planning for the wedding and checking items off her get-out-of-town list.

The Thursday before the wedding, she hustled to her Muni stop, had her pass ready, then jammed herself up and into the bus before her watcher crossed Grant Street. She trotted from the bus stop to her rented home on Noe Street, changed into jeans, a heavy sweater, and hiking boots, grabbed her luggage, and rushed down the interior stairs to the street level garage.

A footstep, her name, her real name, a hand over her mouth. She spun kicking. The man stepped back. Her knee rammed home. The minute his hands lowered to his crotch, she slammed her elbow into the bridge of his nose. When his back met the garage wall, she climbed into her car and tore into the San Francisco night.

She drove as due east as she could, heading for a parcel of land bequeathed to her great-great-grandfather by his gold rush 49er mining father and so on down to her mother, Virginia Culhane. When her mother told her about the property, Calypso's imagination was piqued by the girlish romance of owning a piece of California Gold Country. When she checked, she found the property taxes were paid by a private holding company, the land's existence hidden in a folio of leases and mines that no longer produced.

Months ago, on a lark, she checked out the property. Thank heavens for Google maps, she had the GPS coordinates from the land records and nothing else. Google did the rest. Sending her through the town of Oakhurst in the foothills of the Sierra, then up one poorly maintained tarmac road after another before dumping her onto a deeded tire-track lane. A barbed-wire gate on rusty hinges marked the only entrance. Barbed wire fencing ringed the 2400-acre property. Red and white No Trespassing signs decorated the wire at thirty-foot intervals. Small tree branches, many with thorns, wove in and out of the wire, making the intent of the signs clear if bullet-riddled Trespassers Will Be Shot signs required clarification.

She ducked under the fence and hiked in a mile or so through heavy timber, fifteen minutes at a steady pace. A log cabin came into view. Reaching it, she stepped onto the covered porch and jiggled the wooden front door held closed by an oft-used padlock. She peered in the two front windows, for all she could see through the dust and grime there might have been six families of raccoons in residence. She sat on the porch, swung her legs, munched a sandwich bought in Oakhurst, and hydrated on fancy sparkling water. The tall trees sang. Gusts of wind whipped the grassy meadow fronting the cabin into kaleidoscopic designs. There was magic in the place.

Having finished lunch, she inspected the area around the cabin. The property included a shed, a broken-down windmill, a rusting stamp mill, a bumptious year-round brook, and the entrance to a long-abandoned mine with signs warning would-be prospectors of its dangers. She had never camped, never used an outhouse, never been more than five miles from a grocery store, yet the freedom represented by the property beckoned her. A person could disappear off the grid here, set up a lab, work in peace. Inspired, she took basic survival classes at an REI store on Brannan Street in San Francisco. She made lists based on her courses: lanterns, propane stove, cooking gear, propane bottles, warm socks, whatever made sense to her and purchased the brands her instructors recommended.

Now, she pelted out of the garage onto Noe Street, then across the Bay Bridge, took Highway 580, then down 99 to Madera. According to the National Weather Service app on her smartphone, a winter storm warning was in effect with the snow level as low as two thousand feet. Exiting at Madera, she checked her rearview mirror for followers, no one exited or joined her at the stoplight.

She wound through Madera to Highway 41 then turned toward Yosemite National Park. Snowflakes appeared mixed with the rain at an abandoned bar appropriately named Snowline outside of Oakhurst. At first, the snow slid off the window, nearer rain than snow. Then the rain bounced nearer ice than snow, finally settling into a wind-driven blizzard. The chain-in station at Big Cedar Springs, a broad curve in the road, was unmanned. She eased past, her windshield wipers smearing frozen snow. Her Lexus handled well on the plowed, sanded roads, but got progressively sloppy on each of the three roads to the property.

Between windshield wiper swipes, the window iced. Soon, only the bottom third of the window was clear. She dialed up the defroster then leaned forward to see. Nearly missing her turn, she skidded onto the rutted tire-track lane that swung through the neighboring parcel. The car slewed violently to the left. The passenger side slammed against the trunk of a tree. Glass shattered. The passenger door creaked inward. She kicked the driver's side door open and scrambled out. Six inches away, a cliff plunged two-hundred feet to a rumbling, leaping river. She pounded on the hood of her Lexus.

Vented, she took stock of her circumstances. She had to act fast, slight depressions in the snow marked the path to the property, soon the narrow parallel lines that defined it would be hidden under the deepening snow. She snuggled into her REI parka then slid around the car to the trunk for her hatchet. Hatchet in hand, she built a crude cache of small branches chinked with pine needles to keep her suitcases and her party clothes dry, at least until the next thaw, possibly the next day. The weather was fickle at this altitude.

After approving her work, she shrugged into the straps of her green camouflage print knapsack and hung her shoulder purse around her neck. The pack was stocked with freeze-dried foods, a backpacking stove, utensils, and other essential gear. With a backward glance, she started up the snowy lane. A moment later, she stopped. If the Lexus were found, she'd be tracked down in a matter of days. She trotted back to her car. She pulled one of those tools that include a spoon, scissors, a screwdriver, and knives from a side pocket of the knapsack. She fingered open a blade and slit the palm of her left hand.

When the blood flowed, she dabbed it on any surface that seemed logical, including the broken window. Satisfied, she started the car, turned the wheels sharply away from the tree, threw it into gear, pushed, and jumped back. The car bounded down the cliff into the icy stream below dislodging snow-capped rocks and thundering into the hush of snowfall. The car didn't explode. Instead, it nosed down into the water, its back wheels spinning. She wrapped a scarf around the cut in her hand and disappeared into the swirling wall of the storm, the wind wailing with her every step.

She awoke on a bed of pine boughs and gunny sacks, immobilized by hypothermia, bruised, and hungry, a man's hand clamped across her mouth. When asked who she was, the name Jessie Woods tumbled from her lips.

Now

Seated on a cushion in a room with carpeted walls, Grieg Washburn finalized explorations rights to a small Kenyan rift. The two-day trek to view the formation involved Land Rovers, guides, guns, and sleeping under the big stars of dark African nights. The first view of the promised geological formation rich in fluorspar made the safari worth the risk of disease and discovery.

Washburn Exploration, known as WashEx, had no immediate plans to mine the find, but the time would come when the current Mexican and Chinese supplies of fluorspar would be insufficient for the world's needs. Fluorspar was essential in the manufacture of open-hearth steel and aluminum, as a catalyst in high-octane fuels, and for apochromatic lenses to correct chromatic and spherical aberrations in cameras and microscopes. Grieg exhaled the moment the last signature swashed across the bottom of the contract. With the one-hundred-year lease, WashEx controlled one of the few remaining basins of fluorspar to their competitors' awe.

Grieg stood in the doorway of the hut letting the signatures dry on the multi-page agreement. Despite the phone call that morning, he wasn't walking out on this deal, no way, no how. His father, Ray Washburn, would have flailed him. Grieg took a deep breath lingering over the words; would have. Doug Purdy, Ray's Chief Operating Officer, had broken the news on the call. Doug currently waited for Grieg at Damascus

International Airport, clutching Ray Washburn's ashes in a stainless-steel box supplied by the Syrian government.

Grieg had spoken to his father via computer the day before; they'd laughed about the fluorspar. The Washburns, père et fils, were engaged in a game to lock in mineral rights for a specific set of rare chemicals. Rhodium was number one. On the call, Ray confirmed Grieg's prediction of an unclaimed rhodium outcropping in southern Turkey near Cizre. Now, Ray was dead.

It happened in an instant. A young man in jeans and a T-shirt rolled a bomb under Ray's rental car as Ray parked in front of a highly rated restaurant in Damascus. He was meeting Doug Purdy. The explosion blew Doug onto his back. Doug spent the night with Syrian officials, fighting for the release of Ray's body, followed by hours at the U.S. Embassy filing the papers to hand-carry Ray's remains home. Informed of his father's death, Grieg ordered Doug not to tell Delia Washburn that her husband of thirty-two years had been reduced to bone fragments and ashes. Besides, she wouldn't believe Ray was gone until Grieg placed Pops' wedding band in her outstretched hand. That had been Ray's only promise to his bride, no matter what she was told she wasn't to believe he was dead until she held his wedding ring.

Grieg hurried to the hired SUV. His current bodyguard made a wild dash for the Nairobi airport, skidding the car to a halt at the base of the stairs into WashEx's Cessna Citation X+ executive jet. The minute Washburn was aboard, the pilot taxied the jet then took off for Damascus, making the wheels-up time with a minute to spare.

Rolling to a stop at the Executive Airport at Damascus International Airport, Grieg lowered the stairs. A U.S. Embassy staff member handed Grieg an eight-inch square stainless-steel box. It was silky smooth. Grieg ran his left hand over his father's remains. Agitated, Doug was shouting at the Embassy official, his words blurred by the jet engine. Grieg watched the disagreement escalate, unable to comprehend how a man who had lived as large as Ray Washburn fit into the box Grieg held. Ray Washburn and Doug Purdy, friends as well as partners, had been shot at, trapped by landslides, taken hostage, ransomed, and cited as missing, but they'd never been dead. The bitter, contentious voices crescendoed as Doug rasped out a final barb, then pivoted and mounted the steps.

"Get the hell out of here," Doug snapped at the pilot. Snatching the box from Grieg, Doug shoved it under the first seat in the cabin and sat. "Now! Before they revoke our sojourn license."

Grieg pushed a button. The minute the door settled, he lowered the lock. Satisfied it was secured, he settled into the soft gray leather seat to the right of the pilot. Doug rotated his index fingers around each other, signaling the pilot to rush the pre-flight check. Doug's left foot tapped. The minute clearance was given, the pilot taxied onto the runway. An official vehicle, lights rotating, roared up the Executive Airport offices. The jet was wheels up, the airport miles behind, before the call to return squawked. Two Syrian Air Force fighters escorted them into international airspace.

They laid over in London to refuel, eat, and tap dance with customs. The WashEx jet was wheels up by 0200, a flight plan filed to Gabriskie Airport on Long Island. Shortly after take-off, Doug placed Ray's remains on the next seat over. One hand on the box, Doug stared out a starboard window, his lips moving from time to time, having one last conversation with his old friend.

"Got any coffee back there?" Grieg called from the cockpit.

Doug patted Ray's box then went to the small galley. Ten minutes later, he offered Grieg and the pilot brewed coffee. "I don't suppose you had time to warn your mother?" Doug asked.

"I don't suppose you thought to get Pops' wedding ring?"

Doug shook his head.

Pops and Moms were everything to each other. Everything. Thirty-two years after they eloped, they still held hands and whispered sweet nothings. Grieg's mother, Delia, was Ray's second in any duel. A Bronx girl, and an ex-Rockette, she was a dazzler who controlled any room she walked into with her verve. She'd bounce back, maybe maniacally at first. Grieg was counting on her moxie to nudge him into the leadership of Washburn Exploration.

In the purple twilight, the pilot taxied the executive jet up to the WashEx hangar at the Frances X. Gabriskie Airport in Westhampton. The WashEx chauffeur waited for the two executives in the company's idling six-door stretch limousine crafted by Eagle/Federal at Felix Highland's request. As WashEx's Chief Financial Officer, Highland decided when and if such purchases could be made. Grieg leaned against the limo, arms folded across his chest, studying the Washburn logo on the jet as it disappeared into the hangar, remembering Pops drawing it on a napkin at a restaurant in Kuala Lumpur twenty-years ago: a gold nugget at the base of an oil rig that formed the center of a W.

Grieg hung around until the pilot ordered the jet fueled and detailed inside and out. When he was satisfied, he joined Doug in the waiting limo. They looked like hell, unshaven, rumpled, red-eyed, and drained. The flight into Westhampton had taken the best part of twenty-four hours. Grieg's stomach roared in rebellion at the lack of food, his Heathrow sandwich long absorbed by stomach acid.

The driver slammed the car door the moment both men were seated. The smell of rank, sweaty men swarmed the back seat. Doug smelled an armpit. Grieg hadn't bathed since the drive to Nairobi, Doug since the explosion. Doug looked particularly seedy, his beige hair in greasy spikes and a half-inch of stubble on his chin emphasized the tired bags under his sorrowing eyes.

Grieg stared out the limo window, imagining a world without Pops. Among those who toiled to unlock the earth's secrets, it was a commonly held belief that the Washburn DNA included a chromosome that divined oil or any valuable mineral contained within the earth's crust. Spies from Big Oil followed Ray and Grieg Washburn from location to location, hoping to outmaneuver them before their signatures had dried on new contracts. Grieg willed himself to focus on the possible rhodium find in Turkey and the promise of yttrium held in a mud-puddle in Samoa, rather than the box on the seat. The tips of Grieg's shoulders rolled forward under the weight of what was to come. Doug coughed. Grieg removed his hand from the box before Doug slapped it away.

The driver dropped Doug off at his home near Westhampton. Doug patted Ray's box and exited the limo. Doug's wife rushed out the front door of their expansive faux-barn house, her arms ready. A moment later, hands held, the couple disappeared into the house. The barn-like door slid shut before the limousine driver carrying Doug's valise reached it. He knocked. When no one responded, he deposited the hard-sided suitcase and leather valise on the porch then returned to the limo.

"Meremer, sir?" the driver asked.

Grieg nodded. The driver angled onto the parkway towards Delia Washburn's neo-Georgian estate within the village limit of Water Mill, further out Long Island. Ray Washburn bought the 12,000 square foot home on twenty acres with stables and paddock as a surprise for Delia when Grieg was accepted to Yale. The first time Delia saw the vast lawn tumbling down to the ocean, she swept one hand dramatically across the vista, laughed and gurgled, "Mere mer," in a mix of English and French. Ray signed a quitclaim that same day. The deed read Delia Astrid Tveit Washburn. It hung in a gold frame by the glass and brass front doors. Without fail, Delia kissed two fingers then pressed them on the quitclaim upon entering the house.

The estate house was brick with matching angled wings. The wings sheltered a formal garden and lawn that swooped down to the Atlantic Ocean. Currently, clouds with purple underbellies scudded toward the Grand Banks and the roiling, indigo ocean skated up to the tall reeds at the seashore. A small wall of granite blocks kept the sawgrass from invading and the cold sea from browning the golf-course perfect lawn.

When he was a boy, Grieg's parents moved so often in search of the next bonanza that they packed his room as though it were an archeological specimen. His boxes and furniture were the first objects unloaded at any stop; his rock collection last. His room was reassembled using the numbers taped to each piece of furniture, each book, each picture on the wall. Moms uncrated his boyhood room one last time at Meremer. His twin bed, dresser, and desk sat under windows overlooking the ocean. One of those lamps with a screen balanced on a pin that moves from the heat of the bulb occupied part of his bunged-up boyhood nightstand. When the bulb was on a seashore with seashells, fish, crabs, and waves bobbed around the room. Glow in the dark stars on the ceiling formed his favorite constellations, Orion, the Southern Cross, and Cassiopeia, the vain queen. When he received his doctorate, his mother urged him to buy a co-op in New York City or a small place in Montauk at the tip of Long Island. Instead, he paid his mother room and board. Given everything, it made sense.

The limousine driver turned up a tree-lined drive, lowered the driver side window, stuck out his left arm, and fingered in the entry code. As the gates swung in, Moms' voice danced over the intercom. "Griegs? Griegs, is that you?"

Before Grieg could respond, the driver accelerated up the slight hill to the house. The right side of the double doors sprang open. Delia Washburn reached the end of the brick walk as the car rolled to a stop. A jaw clip held her blonde hair jammed in a twist. She wore skinny jeans, spike heels, and a tunic top that did nothing to hide her graceful frame. She wore no makeup, as evidenced by the freckles showing at the tip of her nose.

She opened the limousine's second door before the driver could reach it. "Oh, Griegs!"

Grieg climbed out of the car, reached back for the box, and handed it to his mother. Delia sat on the lawn, Ray's remains in her lap and fumbled with the hasp to reach her husband. Grieg had been wrong about her makeup, mascara laid black tracks down her cheeks. She rocked on her hips, moaning. Grieg reached down for the box. She struggled to keep it. Taking the box was the only way he could think to get his mother to her feet. He walked up the sidewalk to the front entrance, his father's remains tucked between his left arm and hip.

The limousine driver helped Delia off the grass. She watched her tall, broad-shouldered son walk his loose, comfortable stride. At the top of the steps, Grieg turned, his dark hair hanging uncut across his brow, his cobalt blue eyes following her progress, the strong Washburn cleft announcing his chin, and said, "Who told you, Moms? Who?"

"Sally Purdy." Delia fingered her son's shirt.

He covered her hand. "I'm sorry you didn't hear it from me. I told Doug not to tell you. I wanted to be standing in front of you when I did."

"Why Pops, Griegs? Why would he agree to meet anyone at an off-limits restaurant in Damascus? He knew it was dangerous." She held out her hand. When he didn't produce Pops' wedding ring, she tweaked Grieg's shirt.

"Pops was meeting Doug, not a client if that's what you were led to believe." Delia stroked her son's bristly cheek. He ducked his head. She raised his chin until she could see his eyes. "I've asked the U.S. Embassy for access to the police report, Moms. Doug claims it was a simple roll and run, that Pops feet were on the ground when the car blew."

"I begged Pops not to go to Damascus. It isn't the place we knew when we were young. Because of the sanctions, he had to jump through flaming hoops to get permission to enter. I asked what could be so important. He said he had Doug to keep him out of trouble. I believed him because they always came back. Always."

"Not this time."

"Oh, Griegs, what are we going to do without Pops?"

Grieg ran his right hand over the quitclaim at the door. "Get on as best we can."

"How can that be all of him, Griegs? How can that man fit into an eight-inch box? He was so full of life, such a force." Delia's hands flew to her mouth. Tears welled, then slid down her nose to her lips. She reached for the box and marched to a marble table beneath a window in her front parlor. She set it there, the silver in high contrast to the black-streaked white marble. "Are you okay, Griegs? Are you?"

Grieg sat on a straight-backed armchair styled to match the house. The seat was hard and so short, his legs were unsupported from mid-thigh to knees.

"You look ridiculous in that chair! Move."

"Moms, what possible difference can it make?"

"Move!"

Grieg stood, keeping his left hand on the cool surface of the marble table. "Have you made any arrangements?"

"We'll take him home. All the Washburns are buried in the family cemetery in Yellow Sky. Pops would want to be next to his dad. Oh, Grieg, I miss him. I miss him."

Delia ran from the room.

Grieg dragged himself up the stairs to his room. The beach light bobbled on its pins from the gust of his entry. He flung himself across the blue corded bedspread on his twin bed. After a sharp knock on his door, Jones, Moms' manservant of many years, entered with a tray of food. In his mid-fifties, Jones was of middle height, middle weight, and mid-English ancestry. An everyman, reliable, trustworthy, and able, he adored Delia Washburn. Five years ago, when things were at their blackest, Jones whispered his willingness to do whatever Delia needed to heal her family. At the time, she'd purred thinking it a romantic gesture. She hadn't peered into his steely eyes.

"Your mother has taken to her boudoir," Jones said, "She asked me to bring your luggage and dinner." And, warm milk in a cozy, two aspirin on a silver tray beside it. As hints went, it wasn't subtle. Jones placed the tray on a small table in Grieg's bay window. As Grieg lifted silver lids checking on his meal, Jones unpacked Grieg's suitcase. Done, he set Grieg's briefcase next to Grieg's boyhood desk.

Jones closed the door with care as he exited. Grieg half-expected to hear the key turn in the lock. When it didn't, he stared out the window into the empty, black sea. A comber crashed onto the floodlight spangled beach. He ate with the sea thundering and Cassiopeia shining overhead.

Grieg flicked the seashore lamp on and off. Shells flew by. His bedside clock ticked through the hours. He rolled to his right side and stared out the window at the lawn tumbling down to the sea. A jumble of memories begged for precedence, all ended at the same destination, why when he needed her had his mother taken to her boudoir like a Regency widow.

When the sun cusped the horizon, Grieg changed into riding breeches, a polo shirt, a light jacket, and an old pair of riding boots. His crop hung on the wall, his riding helmet sat on a shelf next to the last trophy his polo team had won at the Southampton Hunt and Polo Grounds, five years, two months and seventeen days ago. He trotted down the stairs to the garage, spun up Moms' golf cart, and drove to the stables.

GinnyGee, once rated the top polo pony in the country, nickered as he parked. By the time he reached the gelding's stall, GG's head was resting on the half-door. Two stalls down,

Delia's current stableman jabbed a pitchfork full of hay and gave Grieg a nod.

"Give me a hand," Grieg called.

The stableman dropped the pitchfork and sauntered toward Grieg, smacking his lips together as he came. Muzzle after muzzle appeared. The lanky, lean man grinned, offering a kind word to each animal. "You're Mrs. Washburn's boy, right? Polo player. Game saddle or hacking?"

"Hacking."

"They're in the tack room. Horse's name above them. Bridles, too."

"Saddle GG for me, if you don't mind. I want to say hey to the rest of the line."

"All but three of them is gone."

Grieg's dark eyebrows formed into a vee.

"You ain't been riding them. Only person comes around anymore is Sally Purdy. She's got a good seat. I don't think Mrs. Washburn was fond of her riding your line. One of your mares, BetsySue, went lame under Sally's hand, had to put her down. So, GG, GeeWhiz, and Geenius are all that are left. Course, Calypso Swale's Fructose is still stabled here. He's a goer. And, Sally's mare, Dimwitty."

"BetsySue went down? What about Elmira?"

"Mrs. Washburn sold her to the neighbors for their daughter. Good choice. Sweet-tempered girl."

Remembering the neighbor's hoity-toity ten-year-old daughter, Grieg assumed the stableman meant the horse. He couldn't imagine what the girl was like at fifteen. "And SueGee?"

"Sold to one of your old rivals, Christian Gilft. He said he couldn't live without her. Lost one of his line in a nasty accident on the field."

The stableman disappeared into the tack room as Grieg tried to place the sandy-haired man with a shambling gate. Unable to come up with a name, Grieg wandered down the row of stalls. GeeWhiz butted Grieg's hand with his dark nose. A white star blazing between his eager eyes. Grieg brought the soft nose to his cheek and nuzzled it. GeeWhiz nickered. Geenius, hearing the fun, butted his head against the stall door until Grieg whispered his name. Two dark eyes glinted out of the shadows. Geenius butted again. Grieg moved down the line, lingering his fingers on GeeWhiz's nose until he heard the clip-clop of GG's hooves. The stableman led the gray to mounting stairs. Grieg swung up, positioned his legs while the stableman set the length of the stirrups.

"Where are you riding in case you fall off and bust your head?"

Grieg laughed, "It *has* been a while."

"Used to watch you play. I 'spect muscles don't forget how to ride like that. Might be sore, though."

Grieg waved with the crop. "The paddock still up?"

The stableman nodded and pointed.

"Does anyone ever take Fructose over the jumps?" Grieg asked in passing.

"Sally used to, but not anymore. He refused a fence, dumped her on her noggin. He never refused a fence in his whole horse life, but he did that time. Big deal, too. Big show. Wham, down she went. Hurt her ego, nothing much else. But now the two of them just give each other the stink eye. You know all the hype about that horse, well, he was never the same. Not after Calypso disappeared. Not after that, he just didn't go for anyone else like he went for that girl. The two of them were a winged beast."

Grieg turned in his saddle. "I didn't get your name."

"Fred, Fred Post. Been stable manager for Mrs. Washburn for about four years now. Before that, I worked at the Club." He meant the Southampton Hunt and Polo Club. "You and that slip of a girl, the two best horsemen I ever seen. Too bad what happened to the pair of you."

Grieg clicked his tongue. GG trotted toward the paddock. Grieg posted the trot. The muscles in his legs and the flanks of his favorite mount melded. He steered GG around the perimeter fence until they were one again then roared out into the bright, spring day.

Fred stopped work to watch. With a shake of his head, he returned to mucking the stalls, happy at his dream job. With Mr. Washburn senior dead, Fred expected to be let go. He understood his position was contingent on keeping young Mr. Washburn's horses and Calypso Swale's flying Fructose in top condition. Five years, two months and seventeen, or was it eighteen days since the accident.

Grieg drove the golf cart back to Meremer. Catering trucks lined the drive. Tables pockmarked the lawn. Delia strolled between the tables. Her fingers danced over the silverware, straightened glassware, and adjusted flowers. She glanced up at her son and smiled, Grieg auto-smiled in response.

"You've been to the stables. Fred texted me. Are you pleased with how he has kept your line, I need to know? He's worried about his job."

"GG strode out like days of yore."

Delia fingered Grieg's blue polo shirt. Looking up into his intense blue eyes, she apologized, "Sorry about last night. I wasn't fit to be with man nor beast."

"My room with my stars felt light years away from you and Pops." He cocked his head, "You went out about eleven."

"I walked. Around. The surf pounded the shore. Clouds drifted over the moon. I held Pops' hand."

"Party time tonight?" Grieg spouted, breaking into the downbeat.

"Wake. It is amazing how quickly bad news travels. The telephone has been ringing since seven this morning. My smartphone beeps, grunts, whimpers, and chimes. I gave up. Or, gave in, not sure which."

"The A-list."

Delia nodded. "All of them, up and down the Hamptons. Hors d'oeuvre at 6:00 p.m., dinner at 7:00, remembrances from 8:00 until the booze runs out."

Grieg ran the back of his right hand down his mother's left arm. She produced one of her showgirl smiles. He kissed her left ear.

"Smile at me. Smile your father's smile," she begged. He did his best. Moms fingered back a hank of dark hair fallen over his brow. "Tom Swale is waiting for you, us, by the fireplace in the corner I call my office. Not that I need an office. I'm like some character from Jane Austen expected to decorate a room with her presence, do crewel work, dance, entertain, and be genteel. I suffer to do so."

Grieg chuckled. "Poor Moms."

She curled one well-manicured finger for him to follow. He obeyed. Her stride swung like the dancer she was. Long legs teased with the drape of her palazzo pants. Her blond hair achieved heights he knew were unnatural. She reached back for his right hand. They trooped, as one, into a room filled with light, furnished in rattan, and glowing with watercolors. A half-finished letter rustled on a secretary desk, a $300.00 gold pen keeping it from fluttering to the floor in the breeze from their entrance.

Tom Swale, Washburn Exploration's corporate lawyer, occupied a seat in front of a twelve-paned bay window. Tom's suit coat hung on the back of a chair. Sweat stained the underarms of his designer shirt. It was unclear whether the sun on his back or the chore ahead made him uncomfortably warm. Tom stood, straightening the pleat in his pants, struggling to keep his red-rimmed hazel eyes focused on Grieg.

Grieg crossed the room, his right hand extended. Swale stepped into the shake. "Sorry, sorry about your father." Grieg nodded and motioned Tom to sit. "It's hard at first," Tom continued, "Losing my father was tough. Losing my half-sister. Well, my family, so suddenly. One minute they're dressed to the nines laughing, the next pfft. It's tough."

Delia swished him quiet. "You brought Ray's will?"

"I did, but I'm not the executor, Judge Burridge is. He'll join us in a minute."

Burridge stepped through the open door of Delia's morning room. Crisp steps, tailored gray suit, clipped graying hair, and wire-rim glasses, efficiency radiated in Burridge's every stride. Grieg stood, as did Tom Swale. Burridge nodded, shook Tom's hand, kissed Delia's cheek, and looked up his long nose at Grieg. "Young man."

Grieg extended his right hand. Burridge scooted past him to the seat Tom had occupied. Grieg lowered his arm.

"We have a great deal to cover before the wake," Burridge popped open his briefcase and removed a mound of documents. "There will be a second reading of the will before the Board of Washburn Exploration to cover matters pertaining to that organization. Today's reading is for the family. Are all members here?"

Tom Swale left the room.

Burridge set a thick document held together by a brass brad on the desk. He reviewed the cover sheet, harrumphing a few times as he read. Grieg stared out the windows watching the preparations on the lawn. Delia fingered the hem of her silk blouse, the pearls around her neck, and occasionally, the woven rattan on the arm of her chair.

"Forgive me. This must be excruciating. I reviewed these last night, but I want to make certain everything is still in order. I drew up the will for Ray. He insisted. It was finalized the day we reached agreement on your sentencing." Burridge's steady brown eyes peered over the top of his glasses into Grieg's baby-blues until Grieg's dropped. "It wasn't a small thing you did, boy."

Grieg tweaked the pleat of his slacks.

Burridge squinted then poked his glasses up his nose. "Destroying a family. Killing a police officer's son. Drunk. Chasing a girl." Grieg served four months in jail before his trial and sentencing, Judge Burridge presiding. After which, the judge sentenced him to five years in prison for second-degree vehicular manslaughter. Since it was the first offense, Ray Washburn cut a deal permitting Grieg to serve his time as probation under his father's supervision.

Delia sucked in her breath and twirled her pearls. The string popped. Pearls pinged onto the floor and rolled. She shook her head to stop Grieg from pearl diving.

"Let's get this done," Burridge snapped, thumping the edge of the papers on the desk. "Ray Washburn willed his assets equally among his heirs, with the provision that in the event of an heir's death, the remaining assets would accumulate to the survivor. Which means, Mrs. Washburn and son, are equal partners in Washburn Exploration and are majority owners, with the concomitant voting rights.

"It was Mr. Washburn's expressed wish that Mrs. Washburn receive a pension based on four-percent of the value of the organization each year as payment for her participation on the Board of Directors. It was also his expressed wish that should his death occur while Mr. Grieg V. Washburn remained on probation that Mr. Douglas Purdy act, if you will, as regent Chief Executive Officer of Washburn Exploration until Grieg V. Washburn met the requirements of his probation. At such time, Mr. Washburn will succeed Mr. Purdy as Chief Executive Officer of WashEx until either by request or death he is, in turn, succeeded.

"The will requires the Board's compliance. However, the Board may define the period of Mr. Purdy's regency with little regard for the remaining length of Mr. Washburn's probation." Burridge stared at Grieg until Grieg squirmed. "I assure you that your father anticipated that you would be older, the scandal forgiven by the weight of your actions, and your records expunged at the time of his death. Not the case, of course."

"Sorry," Grieg muttered.

Burridge harrumphed, then asked, "According to Mr. Purdy, you were unsupervised in Kenya? That is a direct violation of your parole."

"It was my understanding that my father had permission from you and the parole supervisors stateside. With so little time left on my probation, it was an opportunity to see if I could behave in a civilized manner."

Burridge tapped the table with Delia's letter opener. "As it happens, the request arrived after you were in Africa."

"Perhaps, my father thought it better to ask forgiveness than…"

"The advisors approved it on my say so."

"Thank you, sir." Grieg concentrated on a pearl at the foot of his chair, willing himself not to pick it up.

"Your father reached out to me last week. What I'm about to say stays within this room. In consideration of the four months you were incarcerated before the trial, the Parole Board agrees that you will have met the letter of your sentence in three days. However, you are ordered into custody for the final two days of that sentence."

Burridge cleared his throat. When Grieg's eyes met his, Burridge continued, "You will turn yourself in at the Suffolk County Police Station tomorrow night. That gives you today and tomorrow to see to your affairs. Two days in the County facility, then release, with this stipulation, break parole before the final two days are served, and you're in jail for two years. If you jump this hoop, the governor has agreed to review your record in four months for a possible pardon. I spoke to your father the day he died. At his request, Doug Purdy is acting CEO until the governor's review comes down, or the Board votes a change."

"Why jail? Why now?" Delia asked, plucking at the two-carat diamond on her ring finger. "It will only serve as a reminder, freshen the rumors, make the papers. People have begun to forget."

"A final act of contrition hurts no one. There is one more item to discuss. Are you familiar with the purpose of Yellow Sky Holdings?" The Judge pointed his pen at Grieg.

Grieg stuttered, "Pops—Ray spoke of it to me only once. I admit I didn't understand his explanation. I was ten, maybe twelve. We were in Kuala Lumpur."

"Yellow Sky Holdings exists outside of Washburn Exploration, but is, in effect, Washburn Exploration."

Grieg shrugged. "What did I tell you, Moms. Pops wouldn't leave us unprotected."

Burridge quirked his mouth, the first chink in his armor of righteousness. "All of the land, patents, and rights from which Washburn Exploration derives its wealth are held by Yellow Sky Holdings. The Board of Directors of Washburn Exploration, the partners, if you will, profit from the wealth inherent in Yellow Sky. Yellow Sky Holdings is the sole property of the direct descendant or descendants of Rance Washburn."

Color shot into Grieg's cheeks. His father, Pops, had grown WashEx into the dominant company in its sector. WashEx was privately held by the families of the four original investors. Grieg's great-great-grandfather, Rance Washburn, a Montana boy, begged the rancher next door for help digging a hole. That's how the Culhane's got into the business. The hole filled with black gold. The Washburns and Culhanes were the first in their neighborhood to drill into the Bakken oil field.

Then, Rance went East to school and found pyrite. He asked his Harvard roommate for money. The Highlands came on board with the loan. After he graduated, Rance took a swing up to Canada with his boyhood friend, Tom Purdy. Rance dipped down to wash his hands in a streambed and found not gold, well, gold, but a diamond.

By the time, Rance Washburn got his degree, he had three partners, five oil fields, two diamond mines, one played out pyrite digging, and a gold mine. He just kept acquiring minerals, elements, and oil, dragging his buddies Culhane, Highland, and Purdy with him on the ride to the top. A little more than a hundred years later, all four families were listed in the Social Registers on both coasts and had married into the British peerage.

No kidding, they were rolling in dough. After all the principals and employees, investments, and bribes were paid, the Washburn Exploration Trust (or WET), overseen by Felix Highland's son, Hugh, retained huge swag in specified percentages for each founding family. Said swag was distributed as monthly stipends to the unsalaried family members. Grieg's newly widowed mother would benefit from the same to the tune of four percent per annum.

"That's a lot of power, son," Burridge noted, slapping a manila envelope with his open hand before sliding it across the desk to Grieg. The letters YSH were embedded in red wax across the closed flap.

"Any directives for Yellow Sky should there be no further direct descendants?" Grieg fingered the envelope, a folio nested inside, he ran his hand over the edges. A square lock defined the mid-point of the unbound side. "And, the key?"

"The assets of Yellow Sky Holdings would be auctioned, forcing the sale of Washburn Exploration's contracts and facilities. The capital from the sale would be distributed to the WashEx partnership. Yellow Sky is a memory, and WashEx disbands, leaving the partners and their families exceedingly wealthy for generations to come."

"The key?"

"Is in the envelope."

"The seal?"

"New. Last week after the final entry."

"What, in your judgment, Judge, is the most explosive information contained in these documents."

"I beg your pardon, Mrs. Washburn, I keep hearing the thumps and grunts of workers setting up your venue, now would be a fine time to attend to those arrangements."

Delia cocked her head, as though considering asserting her dumb blonde, something at which she excelled. Instead, she leaned on Grieg's arm to gain her feet, smoothed the silk of her palazzos, and pivoted on her strappy five-inch heeled Louboutin's. "Pick up the pearls, Grieg, won't you," she said with a flip of her diamond as she swayed out of the room, leaving the aroma of her signature perfume in her wake.

Burridge waited until the click of Delia's heels faded. Grieg relocked the door and returned to his previous seat. "First, Judge Burridge, I want to thank you for your fairness in the administration of my parole. I am aware of your kindness. My father spoke highly of you and of your consideration and concern."

"I miss him."

"I haven't had time. I'm frankly blindsided. When we parted, Pops was on his way to Turkey. I had located a mineral deposit that changed the game for us. I wanted his blessing and confirmation. Will the Yellow Sky entry explain why he was in Syria despite U.S. sanctions?"

"The last entry is *rhodium and yttrium*. Of course, I looked up both. Both are conductors and extremely rare. I completed the contracts for these at your father's request. Neither are signed, but once executed, will be held by Yellow Sky. Two days ago, your father suggested that if anything should happen to him while in Syria that you contact a Dr. Khalil at your earliest convenience to ask about Calypso's patent." Burridge slid a piece of folded notepaper across the desk. "You know the only Culhane Swale you didn't kill outright."

"The girl I was chasing, as you so crudely put it."

"Be at the police station tomorrow night at nine p.m. I'm going home to change into proper attire for the evening."

"You're enjoying this too much."

"Grieg V. Washburn, you are as big a speculator as your father was. I pray you are more prudent."

"Which means?"

Burridge straightened papers. "Think. Think before you trust." Burridge stood.

Grieg remained seated, staring at the space Burridge had occupied. Two nights ago, Pops had moaned to his son that he was having an issue of trust with someone within the WashEx family. Now, Pops was dead. Grieg shook his head and kneeled to gather his mother's pearls.

Grieg set the pearls on the desk then trotted up the stairs to his room and spinning light. His Henry Poole tuxedo hung in an armoire that dominated one wall of what had been an adjoining bedroom. Re-designated and rehabbed by Moms, half of the former bedroom was now a dressing room, the other a closet repository for her non-resident son's finery, polo gear, and work clothes, dress suits to jeans. Spit-shined black shoes lined the bottom of the armoire, next to worn boots. Grieg ran a hand down one sleeve of the buttery tuxedo fabric.

He dressed, didn't shave his stubble, but swept his wavy hair off his face and over his ears. He glanced in the full-length mirror Moms nailed to the wall in a misguided attempt to make him neaten his appearance. The shadow of his father gazed back at him. Grieg hunched his shoulders against the wraith. Feeling his father so present reminded him to contact Dr. Khalil. He typed Dr. Khalil onto the screen of his WashEx smartphone.

There were many Khalils in the U.S., but only one with the number he'd been given. When his search turned up Khalil's first name, Benjamin, Grieg tried LinkedIn.

Dr. Khalil headed a small mechanical engineering research group at the Massachusetts Institute of Technology. A quick check of his Movado wristwatch assured Grieg it was too late to call the Institute, so he sent a cryptic message via the online site.

Concerned Khalil might not check his LinkedIn account, Grieg texted Khalil's mobile phone and entered a note on his own calendar to call in the morning. He tucked the phone in a wooden box with a lock where he kept his first piece of quartz and a raw diamond found in an African stream. He hid the box under a stack of unread Geological Magazines in the middle drawer of his childhood desk and didn't ask himself why. Maybe hearing Calypso's name, maybe that. He shot his cuffs and walked out the door.

II

Grieg wended his way through inquisitive guests to the back patio nestled within Meremer's wings. The choppy sea dominated the horizon, tall grasses blew in a wind that ruffled tablecloths held down by clips at each leg of the tables scattered across the expansive green of the freshly clipped lawn.

Delia opened Meremer's grounds each year for a garden tour, her grounds a riot of color. The spring, summer, and fall tours drew crowds from as far away as New York City. Tickets to each tour were limited and awarded by lottery, proceeds went to various charities. The gardeners had spent the day scurrying from bed to bed, planting flowers for Ray Washburn's wake.

Grieg plastered a smile on his face. Felix Highland, Chief Financial Officer, of WashEx, came at him, gray-haired in a gray suit, his hand extended as though Grieg were the only earthly person Felix wanted to see. Felix planted a hand on Grieg's shoulder and stepped into the handshake.

"Sorry, son, sorry about your father. Good to see you in one piece. Doug indicated getting the jet and Ray out of Syria took some greasing and fast talk."

"We need to talk about WashEx."

"Burridge?"

"I'm sure you know Judge Burridge went over my father's will. Sorry to say, in four months, I'm your new CEO."

"Begging a vote and meeting the letter of your parole. You have considerable opposition given--well--everything."

"Such as?"

"The felony conviction, your youth, and penchant for showing off. For instance, haring off into the African bush. Did you even bother getting shots, it is positively amok with things that kill, starting with malaria?" Felix shook his head. "To the good, Doug reports that you have forged excellent agreements. However, discovery and negotiation aren't preparation for operating WashEx. Doug's settled and a good man."

"No Washburn, no WashEx," Grieg snapped, then heard Pops say *don't do that, don't let them know how you feel, ever. Hear me, Griegs?* Felix looked down his narrow nose at Grieg, not easy for a shorter man. Grieg sucked it up. He needed Felix' and Doug's support for the next four months to sustain Ray's momentum. The most immediate need being big bucks for a bubbling Samoan enterprise, bucks being what Felix controlled. "Sorry, Felix. I'm tired."

Attendees studied Grieg as he gained the lawn. This was the first time he'd been in the United States since his father whisked him away after the accident that took the lives of Larchmont Swale, his wife, Virginia Culhane Swale, and JT Willard, the driver of the truck that Larch Swale initially hit. The Swales had reigned supreme over the Hamptons until Grieg rounded the corner and brought it all to an end in a massive tangle of box truck, Cadillac sedan, and SUV. Because of his son, Ray Washburn exiled himself from his country for five years and often his wife. Now, he was gone. Grieg added Pops' death to his loaded platter of heads.

Delia Washburn floated across the garden to Grieg, her arms outstretched as though she hadn't seen her baby boy in years rather than six months ago during a month-long family, sun-soaked splash in the Aegean. For five years, Delia had watched her son finger the blades of knives, risk his life wrenching new acquisitions from warlords in Afghanistan and headhunters in New Guinea, sail too far out to sea, and jump from planes. He wandered his life uneasy in his skin, an amalgam of loss, hurt, and grief. No one approached him from the gathered crowd, but he was on everyone's lips. Which both angered and hurt Delia, she didn't know how to shelter him other than in her arms.

Sally Purdy, Doug's daughter, wrapped in a brightly colored bespoke dress, strode across the lawn toward Grieg, a neighbor's daughter, angled in from the right, and Annie Swale MacKenzie, Tom Swale's sister, aimed for Grieg from the left. Delia quick-stepped to join her son, barring all three women from reaching him. "Please. My son flew in last night. He's barely had time to rest and clearly hasn't had time to shave. Ladies."

Moms swirled away, expecting the other women to fall in line like ducklings. The neighbor's daughter touched a sleeve of Grieg's suit coat and whispered condolences. Sally smushed the air out of his lungs. Annie, swinging her right hand from well below her waist, slapped him as hard as she could. He put a hand to his left cheek.

"Of all the nerve, showing up here!" Annie screeched. Annie Swale MacKenzie lived life on high octane, men weren't pigs, they were swine, accidents were murders, people adored but didn't love.

"You bitch," Sally snarled.

"He'll be in prison by tomorrow night. Look," Annie swept the lawn with a hand, "He's still on a short leash, not supposed to be in public without a watchdog. Do you see one, do you?"

"I see three hundred at a guess," Sally responded.

"Three hundred guests couldn't stop him from getting drunk and destroying my family," Annie snapped in return.

Sally pushed. Grieg caught Annie before her heels mired her in the lawn. Annie twisted out of his arms, swirled, growled, and stormed off punching holes in the turf as she went.

"She's something, isn't she? You should have heard the trash Annie laid down about Virginia Culhane, though she *was* fond of her step-mother's money." Sally fingered the slap mark on Grieg's cheek. "Well, if a right-handed killer ever murders you, Annie is the first suspect."

"Funny, Sal."

"It must seem strange--being here, I mean. Five years is a long time to be away from home. Of course, this never really was your home, except while you were at university."

"Fred, the stableman, tells me Fructose refused a jump with you aboard."

"He did. Damn horse. My sister, Rebecca, couldn't handle him either. He was Calypso's horse. Period. No one rides him now. He runs with what is left of your string."

"Like a mob of Brumby. I took GG out today. Tomorrow, I'll give Fructose a ride, maybe he'll respond to me."

"Doubtful. Fructose is used to a woman's hand." Sally checked out the latest people to arrive at the top of the stone stairs. Finding no one of interest, she said, "You miss your Pops, I can tell by your chill, my boy. I hope you find your way, given that you never… It's nice to have you back amongst us."

"Dealt with the other deaths?" Grieg checked the assembling multitude. The crowd bedecked in their finery gathered like ghouls around the small table of remembrances that Moms had assembled during the day. They pointed at photos, toyed with Pops' favorite rocks, and gabbled. The line for the bar extended thirty people deep, all chatting, touching, and laughing. The freshly clipped grass, aerated by hundreds of women's heels, lay trampled under hundreds of feet. Pops hadn't known one in ten of the people gathered. The Hamptons weren't his thing, dirt, wind, rocks, sun, and stars were his alcohol of choice. Yet, tonight Meremer was the place to be. "What did your dad say happened to Pops, Sal?"

Sally leaned against him. "That it went down so fast he had no time to react. Ray climbed from the car and waved to get Dad's attention. A moment later, Dad was flat on his back. The front of the restaurant was blown out. People were screaming. Dad scrambled up and tried to pull your Pops from the fire."

Grieg pictured Doug's unburned hands on the stainless-steel box that held Ray. Doug's clothes, unchanged since the bombing, smelled of smoke but showed no fire damage. Doug hadn't scrambled to standing. Instead, he must have lain stunned as his oldest friend died. Though Doug couldn't have helped, he created a lie to cover his failure, something Grieg knew all about.

Grieg wrapped Sally's left hand over his right forearm and led her to the round table reserved for family. WashEx Board members were milling around, deciding the proper seating order. Grieg rubbed his scruffy jaw and gave Felix Highlander a lopsided smile. Felix was standing next to his son, Hugh, reminding Grieg of all the obsequious petty officials in petty countries that loftily tried to stop progress. He could almost smell the bear grease Felix and son used to force themselves into tight places. He reminded himself, the monthly stipend that would allow Delia to maintain her lavish lifestyle was issued under the Washburn Exploration Trust (WET) logo, complete with Hugh Highland's scrawl endorsing it.

Delia took Grieg's free hand in hers. The heels of her shoes launched her five extra inches into the air, enhanced her dancer's legs, and brought the top of her coiffured blond head to the underside of her son's bristly chin. Delia ran her free hand down her son's stubble. Her eyes lit, and her mouth bowed as she turned a smooth cheek for her son's kiss. A sly smile tipped Felix's lips. Felix was an eligible gray-back, his gorgeous, hedonistic, society wife one year overdosed on a cocktail of prescription opioids. Now, Delia, the dazzling Delia, was a widow. Grieg was uncomfortable with the possibilities.

"A lady on each arm, lucky man," Tom Swale kidded. "I hope your meeting with Judge Burridge went well. Are you going to share with us?" Tom held a seat out for his sister. Annie gathered her long skirt and sat next to her husband, Mark MacKenzie.

"Judge Burridge emphasized that the reading was private."

Hugh Highland strangled on a slurp of martini. The glass with its olives enhanced the whole James Bond of his attire, black tuxedo, white shirt, blanched face. Next to Hugh, Doug Purdy, still droopy-eyed from the flight, bore the insouciance of a man who wished he was anywhere but at a wake for his lifelong running mate.

Doug motioned Grieg to a bar set up near the patio stairs. Grieg requested soda water with a twist then raised it in a salute to the group. As they returned to the table, Delia raised her gin tonic to her lips, whispering, "Every one of them, but Doug is scared blind."

"And?"

"Why isn't he?"

"He knows he has four months to sell himself to the Board."

"Not just handsome, but smart. Be careful. Doug's a man, he's got an ego. Loyalty is earned and best nurtured."

"Really, what have you been reading?"

"I have a new Kindle Paperwhite, so almost anything I can download. I'm a total Kindle Select junky. I just devour books."

"Oh, Moms." Grieg gave his mother a squeeze as the Board of WashEx ringed the family table, having determined by hand signals the proper pecking order now that Ray Washburn was dead. Doug Purdy sat at the head of the table. "To Ray," Doug shouted, glass raised.

"To Ray," echoed across the lawn as three Suffolk County police officers rounded the corner of Meremer. Delia grabbed Grieg's right hand hard enough to pin his fingers together.

III

Assistant Suffolk County Police Chief John Willard checked the merrymaking on the lawn; people were hobnobbing, gossiping, or staring gape-jawed at the uniformed cops. "Sorry to disturb you at this time." Turning to the WashEx table, he ordered, "We need the Board inside now, no wives or children."

Felix and Hugh Highland, Doug and Sally Purdy, Delia Washburn, Tom Swale, and Grieg stood. The men adjusted their tuxedo jackets and shot their cuffs in near unison then fell in behind Willard in twos. Delia's houseman, Jones, stood at attention, holding the righthand beveled-glass French door into Meremer's drawing-room open with his back. The Board members flowed past him. Last in, Chief Willard nodded. Jones closed and locked the door. The two accompanying police officers stationed themselves one at each exit.

An easel provided the focal point for the room awash in the soft yellows and blues of French Provençal textiles. A two-by-three foot photo of Calypso Swale leaned on the easel, set up at an angle to the hearth of the gray Florentine marble fireplace. In the picture, the eighteen-year-old Calypso's luxuriant chestnut mane was ratcheted back into one of those buns required when horseback riding. She wore a red riding jacket, fawn jodhpurs, brown riding boots, and carried a crop. A silver and gold silk cravat set off the determined hazel eyes in her satisfied little face. She clutched a blue ribbon in her off-crop hand. Calypso and her horse Fructose were destined for the U.S. Olympic Equestrian Team training site. Her bags and Fructose's tack packed for transport that day five years, two months and days ago.

Grieg glanced at Moms. He couldn't breathe, half exhaustion, half stress, half Calypso Swale. Oops, that was 150 percent of something or fifty-percent of nothing. He gulped air, put his hands on his knees, and lost the battle to his memories. He was struggling to climb out the driver's side door, the front-end of the Lexus LX SUV he'd stolen embedded in a black Cadillac XTS sedan, his windshield smashed, glass everywhere including embedded in his hands.

Calypso's seven-thousand-dollar party dress was torn from her knee to her Manolo Blahniks. Blood ran from a gash in her head, in her leg, on her arm. She screamed for her mother. Virginia Swale was dead, her eyes lifeless. Calypso swung on Grieg, punched him in the gut, yelled, cursed, and yanked her dead mother from the wreck with enough force to break Virginia's neck had it not already been snapped.

Calypso and her father, Larchmont Swale, were taken to the hospital, Virginia Swale and the burned remains of the truck driver, DT Willard, were transported to the morgue. Lieutenant John Willard, DT's father, dragged Grieg away; his wrists cuffed behind his back. Larch died two days later. At the time of his death, Larch Swale was Chief Operating Officer of WashEx and a good one. The night he died, Callie's half-siblings accused her of injecting an air-bubble in Larch's catheter. Callie disappeared before Grieg came to trial.

"She was a pretty thing," Doug Purdy said over Grieg's left shoulder, appraising the photo.

"With an attitude that said I'm rich, don't tarnish me," Grieg squared his shoulders. Why were they spending their time on Calypso Swale? The Board needed to approve Doug's regency so Purdy and he could be in Australia in three days to meet with Aborigines over an ilmenite deposit. And, someone needed to follow up with the Turks, Kenyans, and Samoans. There was enough competitive pressure on the Arabic Peninsula alone for two Washburns and eight Dougs. Eight Dougs, did he have that little respect for Doug Purdy? Doug had for sure balked at several acquisitions lately. Grieg had filled in for him to the detriment of his prospecting.

"Still jealous?" Doug asked. Doug ticked his head toward his daughter, Sally, head cocked, attentive to Hugh Highland. "Sally's been a damn fine General Secretary. The best."

"You know, Doug, if I ever marry, it might be to ol' Sal. And jealous of what?"

"You're too late for Sally now that she has her bigtime job. As for jealous, Calypso grew up in a mansion in Quogue all high and mighty, swanky parties at the Dunes, and horses worth more than our salaries put together. Everything Larch Swale could give her." Doug leaned on the mantle.

"Your point?"

"You got your ass hauled around the world by Ray Washburn from dusty oilfield to desert oilfield to mineral deposit, to every goddamn outpost where a hole in the ground might erupt into a stream of black gold or give up some mineral."

"Exactly. Calypso got Long Island, and I got the world. Wouldn't trade."

"Besides, you'd look pretty goddamn silly in a red hunting jacket on a horse named Fructose." Doug lit a cigar and tossed the match casually behind the fire screen into the crackling gas flames.

"Stupid name," Grieg said.

"Great horse, I bought him for my youngest. They made it to the Olympic trials. But the damn horse wouldn't go for her, not like he did for Calypso. They would have won gold, the two of them."

"Still a stupid name for a horse."

"Don't let the picture get you all stirred up, boy. Especially now, with Ray gone and all." Doug opted for the self-serve bar on a brass trolley rather than the tended bar set up at the end of the room. Rolling it near Calypso's photo, he poured himself whiskey neat. Grieg used the silver tongs to fill a lowball glass with ice and soda water adding a slice of lime.

Drink in hand, Grieg approached Tom Swale. "Big picture of your little sister."

Tom tipped his drink toward his missing half-sister's picture. "You ever think about that night?"

Every night as dark settles. Every morning at waking. "Sure. I wish I had been sober, that I had been going the speed limit when I made the corner. I wish Virginia had lived." Grieg hesitated, adding, "Like everyone, I thought Larch would survive his injuries. I was sorry to miss Virginia's funeral, but they wouldn't let me out of my cell. I think they were worried I'd skip."

"Father *was* surviving until Callie went for coffee."

"That's beneath you, Tom. You profited from your father's death more than anyone. You gained one of the plum legal positions in the country and one hell of a future. And, by the way, you're good at it. With Larch alive, Callie had his money and every pretty little thing. She was hotly pursued by the Social Register boys. She had her big gelding and the Olympics. She didn't need to kill your father to get what she wanted, all she had to do was bat her eyelashes and ask daddy."

"My father's been a hard act to follow."

"I understand. My father spent his life preparing me to run WashEx. I plan to live up to his standards, as soon as I get the chance."

"The Board is leaning toward retaining Doug because he knows the oil business backward and forwards. You're a mess, been a mess for a long time, hanging on to your mother's apron and toadying behind your father. Look at you, unshaven, a drink in your hand. What's changed?"

Grieg ignored the dig. "Do either you or your sister, Annie, ever wonder why Calypso went on the lam?"

"I was too busy trying to take care of Dad's legal affairs and find my way. Doug Purdy stepped right into my Dad's position as Chief Operating Officer and galloped off with Ray Washburn to parts unknown. Now Doug's acting CEO. A guy could get used to being at the top, not want to give it up."

Grieg raised his eyebrows.

Tom furrowed his. "Any idea why Doug and your father were in Syria? WashEx has all the concessions it needs for the next hundred years. Our kids, when we have them, will be living off the swill in the WashEx trough as will their children."

"Things change, Tom. With the emphasis on climate change, Pops was betting on oil going out of fashion. He knew what he was doing, and I take umbrage at you questioning his reasoning. It's not about swill or legacy, not for the Washburns."

"Nice one. Maybe you're the reason Callie ran, Grieg, maybe you. You tore after her in a stolen goddamn car. At the trial, you admitted you were chasing her. How do you think that made her feel?"

Grieg sipped his soda. "Superior. That night she wrinkled her nose at me like I wasn't worth the perfumed oil she put on her ass. Made me want to slap her supercilious little face."

"How'd that turn out for you?"

"Killed two and ruined two lives. Calypso ran, and I spent four months in a jail cell, stood trial in front of my family and peers, and ended up a felon on a short leash."

"Your father threw his weight around and got your sentence reduced from seven years in a cell to five years' probation with him as your parole officer. They let you ride on money and Social Register standing alone. Since then you've been playing step-and-fetch-it for Ray Washburn and Doug Purdy, while my father and stepmother moldered in the grave."

Grieg sipped his soda. "Virginia was dead before I T-boned the car, Tom."

Her head lolled against the seatback, her eyes open. It hadn't mattered to the police, or Grieg's lawyer, or the jury, not with the truck driver's death added to the toll. Grieg had failed the breathalyzer test the police administered at the crash site. The truth was, he drank too much in social settings. Grieg blamed his father. Being raised around the world, he hadn't been to cotillion or pre-training for the Season, but he was on the Register, and certain graces were expected of him. As Calypso had so generously pointed out the night of the accident, he was a crude, swaggering junior wildcatter with a gift.

Hugh Highland, his right hand on one hip, his tuxedo laying in casual folds behind it, cleared his throat and tapped an index finger on the satin stripe of his slacks.

Delia snuggled up to Grieg's side. He slung his free arm around his mother's shoulders and eyed a wet stain down one shiny lapel of Hugh Highland's Armani tuxedo. Hugh straightened his stained lapel then the diamond-encrusted H cufflink on each of his embroidered cuffs before clapping his hands. "Please find a seat."

Grieg and Delia sat side-by-side on two folding chairs facing the poster. Delia held Grieg's left hand as though he were fourteen and sandwiched between his parents to keep him from fidgeting. The crackling flames in the fireplace lighting Calypso's face brought it alive. It was unnerving to have her so present.

Assistant Chief Willard ushered in a nicely built man in a dark worsted suit with a tie that belonged in the Metropolitan Museum. "I'd like to introduce you to Special Agent Kyle Dempsey of the U.S. Forest Service."

Nervous, Dempsey tapped the poster, it rocked on the easel. Tom Swale readied to rescue his half-sister's photo. Dempsey steadied it. "Mr. Highland assures me that you are all either members of the WashEx Board or family of Board members."

Willard stepped to the front. "As you know, Calypso walked out of Stony Brook Hospital the day of her father's death. She drove to her father's home, ransacked his safe, taking approximately three-quarters of a million dollars in cash, drove off in his BMW, subsequently found at Kennedy International Airport, and disappeared. Calypso left her horse and a promising Olympic career. The Suffolk County police attempted to locate her, as did WashEx. The circumstances of her disappearance were publicized, ads were taken out, rewards offered, and tips followed for well over a year and subsequent anniversaries of her disappearance. Her many friends in the horse world were contacted to no avail."

Willard cleared his throat. "Calypso's siblings, Tom and Annie, filed charges, certain Calypso was the agent of their father's death. According to Larchmont Swale's nurse, he was doing well. After her release from treatment, Calypso came to her father's hospital room to attend to him. Later, Calypso went for coffee upon her return, she offered her father a sip. He choked then gestured her down to his lips, whispering his last words. Whatever Larchmont Swale gasped upset Calypso. She threw the remains of her coffee in the wastebasket and ran."

"She walked, all stiff-backed and self-righteous, as though on a mission. We know her mission, grab Dad's money and run!" Annie MacKenzie snarled.

Willard gulped then continued, "Her mother, Virginia Culhane Swale, Larchmont Swale's second wife, died at the scene of the same auto accident as did my son who was pinned between the delivery truck he drove and the Swale's auto. It was considered a miracle that Calypso walked away with contusions."

"And a torn party dress," Annie threw back her drink. Her husband stopped her march to the bar.

"I believe I have the circumstances correct, Mr. Washburn?" Willard asked.

"Virginia Culhane Swale was dead before I hit their car." Grieg crossed to the bar, considering a touch of gin in the soda he'd ordered. A glossy magazine open on Delia's desk caught his eye. He fingered it closed. The cover was a photograph of the ranch house in Yellow Sky, Montana. WashEx IPO, Prospectus, and Gilft, Dummer, and Toff in gold letters filled the big sky over the ranch. Grieg tapped the cover, making a show of opening the prospectus to the page on which he'd found it. Several sets of eyes met Grieg's, Hugh Highland's cheeks colored, Felix shook his head, and Tom Purdy glanced rapidly back at Willard.

"Wasn't there a rumor at the time that Calypso colluded with Grieg Washburn to kill her parents for their money?" Hugh asked.

"No go. Larchmont Swale was broke. The Larchmont Swales lived on Virginia Culhane's WashEx checks." Willard answered. "Calypso was better off with them alive."

"The goddamn bitch killed Dad, with or without help from Washburn, ran off with Dad's money, and left us with nothing, except that godforsaken rambling house in Quogue. You try keeping it clean!" Annie roared.

The bartender raised his eyebrows, adding a cherry and slices of orange and lemon to Grieg's soda. Grieg leaned in, whispering, "I didn't collude, but listening to Annie makes me wish I had."

The bartender gave a snort and added a chunk of pineapple.

The moment Grieg returned to Moms' side, Moms took a stiff drink of her gin tonic, and stage whispered, "And away we go!"

Willard motioned to Dempsey, "SA Dempsey will take it from here."

Stepping to the front of Calypso's photo, Dempsey stared at the tuxedoed men. Clearing his throat, he began, "I've never done one of these black tie so I'll get to it. Two hikers found a silver Lexus sedan, nose down a cliff off a logging road in a rarely hiked area of the Sierra National Forest. The plates were registered to Amyna Jessup. Amyna disappeared about four years ago from a house leased in the Castro District of San Francisco. Two men rented rooms from her. Lucky for us, they took over the lease."

Willard placed an aerial photograph with an arrow pointing to the crash site on the easel over Calypso's photo. With a nod from Willard, Dempsey adjusted the sleeves on his ill-fitting, off the rack, navy blue suit coat and continued, "The night of her disappearance, Amyna drove off, leaving everything behind including fingerprints on a jewelry box. Her roommates kept the jewelry box and its contents for her assuming she had gone as planned to a friend's wedding in Las Vegas. When she didn't return, they stored her things in the garage.

"The police matched the fingerprints on the box to Calypso Jessamyn Swale. One of her roommates said Calypso thought a man was stalking her. We asked the roommate for a description." Dempsey stared at Grieg until Grieg hung his head. The mystery man must have been tall, dark-headed, nicely built, and Anglo-Saxon. Grieg checked the other men gathered, including Dempsey. Except for the fair-haired Doug Purdy, any one of them could have been her stalker, including the late Ray Washburn. Grieg glanced out the windows to the garden, the party roared on, flowers and cards had accumulated next to the spray of roses and spring flowers camouflaging Pops' stainless-steel box of ashes set on a linen-covered table.

"The night Calypso disappeared, there was a blizzard in the Sierra. Her car was totaled. Given the blood on the steering wheel and seat cover, and the weather, her chances of survival were slim to none. However, unless someone stumbles over Calypso's remains, there is no proof she died," Dempsey hesitated, "Since Calypso's disappearance, four other women have vanished in the same general area. None of them have been found either, not a bone."

"What are our next steps?" Felix Highland prompted.

"Unless circumstances change, you have few choices. You can petition the court for a death certificate based on the blood and condition of her automobile. I understand from Mr. Hugh Highland that Miss Swale's absence has been continuous and without contact since she disappeared. The WashEx Trust kept the search alive, responding to tips, placing ads, and continuously offering a reward. So, though, most states require a person to be missing seven years before declared legally dead, an experienced lawyer could get you an early judgment."

"Let's find her," Grieg shouted. Annie MacKenzie cut him a look that froze his eyebrows. Grieg added to no one in particular, prompted by riotous laughter from the rose garden. "Let's get this done. From the noise outside, the guests need sobering up even by wake standards."

Doug squeezed Grieg's shoulders, leaving a steadying hand on one. "Grieg's right. Go ahead, advertise in a few choice newspapers, enough to cover the U.S. and, say, one each in France, England, and Spain. If we do a bit more trolling, it will ease the declaration of death."

"It is a reasonable request, Doug." Hugh Highland responded. "I'll ask a media house to identify the appropriate organizations, perhaps, television as well. Maybe one of those *48 Hours* pieces or something to highlight the mystery."

Grieg swiveled until he could see Tom. "We have two PR firms on the books. Use the one that keeps WashEx out of the news. They'll know where and how to best spend WashEx's money for results."

"Calypso is one of the WashEx family and the last of the Culhanes, we need to spend the money to find her. If she can be found." Doug Purdy checked the bottom of his empty whiskey glass, then self-edited, "I mean found and if not found, then declared dead."

"We place the ads. Spend the money, Hugh. We owe her that." Grieg retorted, angry that the others were responding to Doug and not to him.

"You owe her that, you mean," Annie snarled.

"That's settled," Hugh said. The others stood to return to the wake.

"Before we adjourn," Grieg said, "Tell me about the IPO proposal and the purpose of entertaining it."

Hugh twitted his left pant leg. "It's a gimmick from a company seeking our business. After an unsolicited review of WashEx's holdings and strength, the company in question recommended an IPO. I followed up with our tax folks. They agreed with the recommendations made."

"Captain Willard, Special Agent Dempsey, though unexpected, the news about Calypso sounds hopeful. I'll contact you tomorrow about next steps. Now, if you'll excuse us, the IPO is WashEx Board business."

The two men made parade turns in response to Grieg's hint. Raucous voices and clinking glasses flowed into the drawing-room as Willard and Dempsey exited through the glass doors onto the patio. Waitpersons lit votive candles cosseted in glass bowls surrounded by flowers at each of the tables. Others placed salads at each place seating. Music from a local string quartet sifted over the lawn. Waves crashed. Trees shushed. The pages of the IPO fluttered in the breeze.

"Who the hell do you think you are?" Hugh Highland snarled at Grieg.

"I'm not going to let you sons-of-bitches walk all over me. If you were hoping to go public—not on my watch." Grieg responded.

Doug added, "The founding Washburn made it clear that Washburn Exploration was to remain a privately held corporation as long as there was a living Washburn." Grieg didn't like the sound of that. Doug Purdy must have thought better of it as well, adding, "Over my dead body and Grieg's, too."

"No IPO. No dead bodies," Moms said, squaring herself to her full spike-heeled height.

"Sally and me, vote no," Doug blurted, put a hand to his mouth, shot a look at Grieg, another at Sally. Grieg mulled over the General Secretary having a vote and wondered when the Board had voted the change to the Bylaws and why he hadn't been told.

"You're right, Doug. Sally, the summary of this Board meeting is as follows." Grieg ordered, "WashEx will use the services of Public Relations Company Two, I think that's its designation, to locate Calypso Swale. Money is no issue. We either find her or go to court to have her proclaimed dead. We will not hire a private detective but will rely on Special Agent Dempsey for onsite support when required. As for Hugh's little foray into an IPO, it stops here. Any questions?"

"No questions," Hugh responded. "I told the firm any discussion of an IPO was on hold until the Board settled on a CEO. I will ensure the recommended ads are placed. With that, the business of the night is concluded. Doug?"

"No. Not Doug." Grieg countermanded, "The night's business is concluded and to be clear, if there is any indication or information that Calypso survived, I go for her."

"Aren't you the last person..." Annie started. Sally stopped her with a sharp elbow to the ribs.

"I am the first person." Grieg stood, offering his mother an arm.

"You didn't leave the Board much room to maneuver, boy. You might want to work on that," Doug offered in passing.

"You might want to work on your presumption. This is my company, Doug, make no mistake about that, not in four months, now. You may be regent, but I'm the owner. Don't forget it!"

"Clear enough." Doug offered an arm to Sally, who rested a hand on his forearm.

Grieg escorted Moms to their seats at the family table. Captain Willard seated five tables distant held up first one finger, then two. One day, then two days in a cell, two days to figure out how to fit into his father's massive shoes with a hostile Board. Dempsey to Willard's right looked on bemused.

Delia poured Grieg a glass of champagne then raised hers. Everyone stood, their glasses filled. "To Ray Washburn, my hero."

Grieg raised his glass for the toast, then set it on the table beside his plate. Doug Purdy nodded his approval as though it was his to accede. It hit Grieg then that Purdy was sporting a swagger like a boa constrictor with a goat of its own. Grieg studied Doug as he ate. Doug reigned over the Board table. When the conversation turned to memories of Ray Washburn, new grandchildren, business successes, and fashion. Grieg wiped his mouth with his linen, folded his napkin, tenting it over his half-full plate. Standing, he bowed his head to the others and excused himself, strolling across the lawn toward the stables contemplating a moonlit ride on Fructose. It was more civilized than punching Doug Purdy in the nose.

Special Agent Dempsey excused himself from his table to join Grieg as he walked. "Were you in San Francisco four years ago?"

Grieg shook his head. "If need be, I can get confirmation from Judge Burridge, he's been handling my sentence as a favor to my father. As for Calypso, I haven't seen her since the accident. My probation clearly forbids me from being within a small country of her. I wasn't surprised to hear she was alive. I've always assumed she was somewhere warm, drinking Cuba Libras and Puissance jumping a rangy gelding over a seven-foot wall. She was too feisty to be dead."

Dempsey nodded his understanding, "Your description makes me wish I'd met her. I was taken aback by the reception of the news that her car had been found. People normally react differently to news like that, maybe it was the lack of body or bones. You do get though that everyone in that room was prepped to throw you to the wolves, except the overripe blond and Purdy."

"The overripe blond is my mother. And, Purdy, I suspect, thinks he has."

Dempsey chuckled. "Sorry. You handled them well. I got the bones for this job like the folks at my table say you have for yours. Watch your step." Dempsey reached into a smartphone pocket sewn inside his ill-fitting suit and produced a business card. U.S. Forest Service Law Enforcement & Investigations, Special Agent Kyle Dempsey. "Take it, Washburn. Just in case. Chief Willard tells me you're due in jail tomorrow night. Interesting timing."

"Maybe what I need is two days in jail with nothing to do but sort out what's happened. Of course, the local papers will spend the same two days reminding everyone that I'm a convicted felon." Grieg flicked the business card.

"Someone will mess with someone's wife, daughter, or hunting hound within the week, and you'll be old news. Keep in mind, bad happens to the good just like it happens to those who deserve it. If we find anything more out about Ms. Swale, I'll let you know. You do the same." Dempsey shook Grieg's hand before rejoining the party.

Grieg returned to the house, the romance of an evening ride on Fructose overtaken by his need to deal with Doug, the prospectus, and Calypso Swale. He grabbed the IPO brochure from his mother's escritoire, tucked it inside his tuxedo, and scurried up to the replication of his childhood room.

IV

Grieg's seashore lamp twirled. Cassiopeia glittered down from his ceiling. Grieg slept on his side, hands under his pillow like he had as a small boy. His mother's voice calling him to breakfast woke him. It was as though he was in a time warp, except Pops was gone.

Grieg dressed casually, jeans, a window-pane checked long-sleeve cotton shirt, tucked-in, of course, and loafers with socks. In his mother's honor, he shaved. God forbid he appear on the cover of the local newspaper handcuffed and scruffy though, by the time he turned himself in, he would have a five-o'clock shadow. Dark hair, dark beard.

It was nearly ten. The breakfast buffet was still fresh or had been refreshed in his honor. Moms, looking as though she belonged on the cover, was reading the latest copy of *Vanity Fair* magazine. She smiled at him over the pages of the magazine. "Lazy boy, about time you joined me."

Grieg stretched then kissed Moms on the cheek. "Sorry. It's been a stressful few days. Yesterday was no exception. Any gossip gleaned last night that you'd care to share?"

"Everyone is dying to know what you've got planned for today. After last night's little internecine battle, the Board is worried you'll grab the jet and take off for Calypso's last known. Our female neighbors are all hoping you'll take another hack on GG like yesterday. Sally hopes you'll drop by the City. She says she has the little desk next to the big desk all polished.

I think that was a joke about last night's game, set, match between you and Doug. Doug is sitting at the big desk, I presume. And, here you are letting everyone get the jump on you."

"Well, I guess I've been chastised."

Moms arched one carefully darkened blond eyebrow.

"I'm taking today and doing as Judge Burridge suggested, getting my frayed ends lined up. First, I'm going to thrill the neighbor ladies, then I'm going to go to my junior desk upstairs in my designated bedroom and make a few phone calls."

"You are welcome to use Pops' study." Moms turned a page of the society section of *Vanity Fair*. "It's yours now. Even his personal phone, if you'd rather use a landline. I'm meeting Felix for lunch." Which explained the designer pantsuit, the Jimmy Choo shoes, and the frivolously tussled hairdo. "It's my bridge night. I didn't cancel it. I hope you are okay turning yourself in by your lonesome. I'm not sure I could bear seeing you in handcuffs again." There was a hint, handcuffs were involved and, no doubt, paparazzi snapping photos for the morning papers.

Moms had adopted the very British custom of serving breakfast in chaffing dishes filled to brimming with eggs, bacon, ham, and muffins, though in all their travels, Great Britain was the one place they had never lived. India was another story. Grieg was born in Mumbai during a torrential downpour.

The buffet was set, plates to one end of the glass-fronted walnut sideboard, chaffing dishes to the immediate right, silverware, jams and jellies at the end after the muffins. Coffee was on the table in a silver pot, kept piping hot by a lit Sterno.

Grieg worked his way down the banquet table, slopping food on his plate. It was nice to be hungry. He hadn't been since the call came in about Pops. He set the plate on an unoccupied placemat then poured a cup of coffee.

"So, Griegs, whatever you do today, try not to do anything stupid." Moms turned a page.

"Which includes?" He asked, settling into the seat and spreading a linen napkin on his lap.

"Drinking, killing anyone, including yourself, or stalking. Striking anyone, specifically Doug, Felix, or Chief Willard. Checking up on Hugh. Let him be responsible for the advertisements. Don't go calling around about the IPO. They'll find out. And, of course, be at the police station spot on at 9:00 pm."

"Quite the list. May I ask they, as in?"

"Them. You know who I mean."

"I'll do my best. I'll be sure to tuck in my shirt, too."

"A tad flip, that scares me." Moms pointed at two sweating silver-rimmed pitchers mid-table. "Orange or grapefruit juice?"

"Grapefruit." Delia pointed to the leftmost pitcher. Grieg filled his glass and sipped, waiting for Moms' next salvo. She shuffled the ceramic jelly server his way. He peeked in--orange marmalade, of course. She imported King Kelly marmalade from California until the company went out of business, now she haunted Amazon and eBay cornering the remaining jars. He slathered a muffin.

Moms glanced up. "I thought about Calypso all night."

He shrugged, "I thought about the IPO."

Moms thumped her magazine to the table. "Leave it alone, please?"

Grieg ate, folded his napkin as he had been taught, scooted his chair back, replaced it, stood, and kissed his mother on the cheek. "Two days in a cell. Then, it's all over but the infighting, hate, weaseling, IPO, and Calypso. Right now, I'm off to the horses!"

With a wave, he walked out the French doors onto the back patio. It was a beautiful spring morning, why then was he obsessing over Doug Purdy sitting at Pops' desk in New York City and Sally's little and big desk crack. Sally and he were buddies since childhood, hurtling from country to country until Sally turned twelve and Doug moved his family back to Long Island.

Grieg walked to the stables enjoying the fresh breeze, the feel of the sun on his face, and his momentary freedom. He stopped, well away from the house, to call Donny Craig. The two had gone through Yale together, well, raised hell, played polo, drank and chased socialites for four years. Moms remained convinced that Donny had egged Grieg into haring after Calypso the night of the accident. He hadn't.

In the interim, Donny had made a name on Wall Street. Donny suggested meeting for dinner at seven at his favorite restaurant in Montauk. Grieg asked Donny if he would have the time to study the viability of an IPO for WashEx before they met. Donny said no, but he would give the prospectus a glance and Grieg an opinion. It would have to do. Grieg needed an outside perspective.

In the tack room at the stables, Grieg pulled on his riding boots, grabbed a ball and mallet, then took GG out. When they were both winded, Grieg posted GG's trot back to the stable.

"Drew quite a crowd," Fred, the stableman, said, taking GG's reins. Fred ticked his head toward the practice paddock built for Grieg and Calypso. Calypso's sidelined jumps still lined the fencing. The female neighbor from each side of Moms' property, a teenage girl, and someone who looked remarkably like Sally Purdy leaned against the fence rails chatting.

Grieg waved at his admirers. As she approached, the Sally Purdy doppelgänger turned into Sally. "Guess you didn't have the nerve to ride Fructose."

"Fructose is pastured. GG butted me as I went by his stall, no contest. Besides, I wanted to pound around with a mallet for a few. What brings you out this way?"

"Dad forgot some papers for a meeting today. Your mother had them. I saw you practicing. Couldn't help myself; I had to stop. I better git, though."

"Any idea who the meeting is with or about?"

"Felix and a new Human Resources firm, we are trying out to handle the hiring, firing, and benefits paperwork."

"Is that a threat?" Grieg jibed.

Sally sputtered. "Jeez, Grieg."

"Sorry, I felt a little embattled last night."

"You're not really going to hunt down Calypso, are you?"

"Pops would expect me to look out for her."

"I suppose. I miss your Pops, my boy. And you. You be careful tonight." Sally flicked his right hand and strode to her waiting car. She had a nice walk, a bit manly, but it became her as did her position at WashEx. She wore the authority well. Grieg handed GG over to Fred, who led the gelding to a stanchion, drew the reins through a ring, removed the saddle and blanket, and got out the curry brush. Soon, the two were communing over the serenity of currying and being curried.

Meanwhile, Grieg calculated the odds of receiving two warnings from two women in less than two hours.

Pops' study featured floor to ceiling windows overlooking the sweeping back lawn. Built-in walnut bookshelves crammed with a few books and more rocks dominated one wall. An index card under each rock identified where, how, and with whom it had been found. Grieg pulled a yellowed card from under a chunk of bland knobby basalt. The note, written in Ray Washburn's hand, returned Grieg to Alice Springs, Australia, and Pops balancing him on his new bicycle, training wheels screwed on for confidence. Pops pushed him down a wide, windswept street. Moms watched her hands on her hips, the wind wrapping her in the yellow cotton shirtwaist dress she wore. Grieg slipped the card back under the rock.

A Montblanc pen, a whistle, and, what else, a rock, creamy white nephrite from China, littered the green blotter on Pops' desk. Pops' daily flip calendar was turned to October 21 of the prior year. The page was blank. Pops didn't come to Meremer to work, he came to be with Moms. October last, Grieg had been in a jeep in New Guinea, Doug Purdy by his side. New Guinea hadn't panned out but did add another hair-raising adventure to Grieg's repertoire, maybe Felix was right to call him reckless.

Grieg settled into Pops leather desk chair and read the IPO prospectus. Stocks, IPOs, hedge funds, pyramid schemes, anything beyond financial reports were not in Grieg's toolkit. Rocks, geography, geology, weather patterns, habitation, migration, physical features, even the smell of a handful of earth were. Luckily, he knew men who were all about greed.

He brought up the contact list on his smartphone, wondering why Moms had suggested he use Pops' landline. He popped the back off Pops' phone, no bugs, not that he'd know one if he saw it. Satisfied, he slid the back cover on, tapped his smartphone on the edge of the desk then with a chagrined laugh at his ineptness, punched in the first number.

Executives at ExxonMobil, Saudi Aramco, Glencore, and Rio Tinto were happy to hear from him, voiced their sympathy at Ray's death, followed by concern about WashEx's new corporate direction. After the formalities, Grieg asked each person if he or she would buy WashEx stock if it were offered on the Stock Exchange. They all responded the same; as many shares as possible up to and including controlling interest. Then they asked him if WashEx was in trouble. He replied in the negative, asking as disingenuously as he could, why they asked. They responded that they counted on WashEx's existence, claiming that no other organization could compete with WashEx's legendary and desirable ability to get into countries under the radar, negotiate, and open-up resources. Big Oil was never under the radar.

Grieg noodled questions for Donny. Erased a few, wrote in a few others. Moms stopped by with a tray of sandwiches and a thermos of tea. She peered, reading the list upside down like any top-flight mother. She tapped one note with a long, polished fingernail.

"Why would you ask that? And, for that matter, who are you asking?"

"I'm meeting a friend for dinner tonight before the big *Grieg turns himself in* affair. Can I borrow your car?"

"Your Betsy is tagged and ready to rumble. Jones keeps her billeted in the old garage. He has the keys." Betsy was the Subaru Pops bought Grieg for transportation to and from various schools of higher education. She'd been stabled like his horses since the accident. "Is your driver's license current?"

Grieg flipped open his wallet to his international driver's license. "Thanks, Moms, thanks for keeping her."

"I hope you're not meeting Donny Craig. Really, Grieg, not tonight. Please."

"Why?"

"You've been gone a long time; he's got a reputation. People talk, you know. That's why." Moms waved and swayed out the door. Her comments couldn't have been more nebulous. He chose to ignore her warning if that was what it was.

He considered following her to ask a reputation for what. Instead, he poured a cup of tea, dark and dense like the teas they had enjoyed in Morocco before Moms had given up wandering and escorted her son to the U.S. for college. After the Swale accident, Moms stayed to keep an eye on the home office for Pops. Grieg bit into a sandwich, reread his notes, doodled then dialed a few of Calypso Swale's horsey friends. As advertised, the horse crowd hadn't heard from Calypso in five years. On a lark, Grieg dialed 411 and asked for a phone number for Calypso Swale, Callie Swale, Jessamyn anyone, then Googled Swale. Stumped, he grabbed his notes and went in search of Betsy, the Subaru.

Grieg climbed into Betsy, his twelve-year-old green Subaru Outback. An old polo jersey lay crumpled in the back seat, a discarded riding crop, an unopened bottle of beer, and a pair of paddock boots littered the floor. The car smelled like post polo match, half armpit and half horse manure. He checked the headlights, and the brakes then drove out the circular drive of Meremer unescorted. He should have called Doug, but he wanted to talk to Donny away from Purdy's prying ears. Instead, he called Judge Burridge for permission. Burridge grumbled but gave his blessing providing Grieg made his other date on time and sober.

Donny Craig's favorite restaurant hadn't existed five years before. Using the direction app on his cellphone, Grieg located it handily. Early, he strolled around Fort Pond, enjoying the evening. Male green-winged Teals with their chestnut heads, dark teal eyepatches, and grayish bodies dotted the quiet, reed-edged waters. One took flight showing off the white-edged green of his secondary wing feathers in the last rays of the sun. As the light played with the dark, Grieg stumbled to his knees in the rocky pathway at pond's edge, his head swimming. He picked up a shiny black oblong rock and pocketed it to cover his awkwardness. So many rocks, so little time.

Upon entering the restaurant, the host directed him to the bar. Grieg plunked down on a brown leather barstool and ordered a soda with lime. The restaurant's entrance was soon packed with couples waiting to be seated. In the bar, suited businessmen discussed the day's travails and quaffed large quantities of booze.

Grieg listened to the quack of the drinkers and enjoyed the mallards and teals cruising the quiet water of the pond outside. A teal came in for a perfect two-point landing then joined a conga line, paddling toward a stand of reeds. The occasional fish jumped, probably crappie. A couple cuddled, at a bench under a burgeoning willow tree, shivered a bit in the cooling air. Grieg sipped his soda and guarded the empty seat next to him.

At the stroke of seven, Donny Craig sidled through the crowded bar. He was in shirtsleeves minus a tie, the collar of his bleached white shirt open. Donny was tawny-haired, broad-shouldered, and a bit thickened by too many lunches at his desk. Rather than get straight down to business, the two caught up on the intervening years. When the waitperson came, Donny ordered two craft beers and steamed mussels as a starter, which migrated, with the addition of garlic fries, into dinner.

"So, old buddy, tell me the gory truth," Grieg asked, running a finger down the dewy mug of beer the bartender set in front of him.

Donny slurped his brew, wiping the foam from his lips with a greasy napkin. It left a sheen on his chin. "Well, IPOs are perfect for mature companies that need financing in a hurry."

The comment resonated with Grieg for two reasons; he had never considered WashEx mature or matured out of its market, nor, to his knowledge, had their competitors. "Why might a mature company need financing in a hurry?"

"Drop in sales, finance a new product, insufficient cash on hand, change in direction."

Hugh Highland claimed the IPO was a come-on, but what if a WashEx principal had requested it? Grieg's head buzzed with the possibilities. Pops seeking short-term capital to fund the change in direction? Doug to cut losses on the same directional change and return to the known? Or, Hugh to prop up WET?

Grieg asked, "Did you have a chance to look at the publicly released WashEx financials?"

"I did. You okay, you look guilty as hell, checking the room every few. I suppose ordering you that beer wasn't the smartest thing I've ever done." Donny surveyed the bar scene. "I hear tonight's the night."

"From whom?" When Donny raised his hand to order another beer, Grieg slipped his untouched beer in front of Donny. Donny lifted the mug and slurped.

"Sally."

"Didn't know you knew her?" Grieg raised his hand and ordered another soda with a twist.

"From the Hunt and Polo Club. Rode with her a few times. She took your sentencing hard enough that I wondered if you two were a thing."

"Sal and I were always buddies, nothing more."

"She said the same, so we started dating casually. Then she got serious about being uptown. I'm not an uptown guy despite my job. We broke up. Stayed friends. With her promotion to General Secretary, she moved onto real society, the kind that gets you noticed. Now, she's engaged, and the date is set."

Grieg rubbed the black rock in his pocket and stared out the window. The Teals paddled into the reeds unconcerned about Calypso Swale's current status and whether it had any bearing on an IPO prospectus or vice versa. A wise man would take the duck's advice and boogie to safety. "How does WashEx look to you?"

"Solid on paper. So much so, that those I consulted said an IPO would be taken as a scream for help. In fact, they thought investors would stay away in droves, enough to bring the company to its knees. Big Oil, Exxon, Aramco, etc., would swallow up the offering, absorb the company, give Grieg Washburn a big payday and show his ass the door." Donny's take verified Grieg's calls.

"What level of capitalization could WashEx expect from an IPO?"

"Well, unless the yearly reports are crap, there is no shortage of capital. Which begs the question."

Grieg wrote a note under the restaurant name on the drink coaster to remind himself to request the latest internal fiscal report, the pre-scrubbed one and slipped the coaster into the pocket of his jacket. And, though it was a strange thing to do, he didn't question his action, something was off with the night, with him, with Donny. "Still, how much might the Highlands expect to raise?"

Donny took a swallow of beer. "Well, the average number of shares offered in an IPO is around 17 percent, diluting the private holders by around a fifth or in the case of WashEx by about twenty votes. The capitalization on a 3.5-billion-dollar company averages just short of 400 million or ten percent, around 70 million in WashEx's case."

Grieg had negotiated WashEx into three new acquisitions in the last five months. ExxonMobil, Saudi Aramco, and Glencore were already bidding on the lease of one off-shore of Madagascar. If the Samoan deal popped, WashEx would be fixed for, at his estimate, 700 years. Pops' vision had gotten and kept WashEx at the top of the pyramid. "All things considered, issuing an IPO right now doesn't make sense."

"Unless somebody needs money. I heard Sally grumbling that no one on the WET dole got a cost of living increase this year. But then neither did anyone on Social Security. The WashEx Trust uses the same index." Donny shrugged and slurped.

If alive, Calypso was owed five years' worth of monthly checks from WET. If she were dead, Calypso's accumulated wealth would be split between her half-siblings. Once Calypso's estate was resolved, either she or her siblings were owed millions, assuming the money had been invested as required by the Bylaws with an average growth of six percent per year. A lot of hay. Annie MacKenzie must be wringing her hands and praying for one of Calypso's leg bones to be sifted out of the river.

Donny swiveled on his barstool. Grieg rolled his shiny black rock, waiting for Donny to speak. The smooth surface of the river rock calmed Grieg's discomfort at being in a room full of witnesses with a beer at his elbow. The bar lights quavered, radiating shafts a bit like a dandelion. Grieg closed his eyes, hoping the tension would wash away. Instead, he felt clammy, and his stomach roiled.

Donny cleared his throat. "There has been a lot of talk about you on Wall Street since your father's death. Questions raised about a convicted felon with a reputation for being rash running WashEx. Those concerns might be driving an IPO."

Grieg raised his eyebrows. "That all?"

"Well, that you're risking the family business fumbling after minerals that are on no one's radars. Some say the dash for whatever you found in Turkey got your father killed."

Grieg's stomach churned. Too damn much gossiping. Swaying on his stool, he checked the crowd for familiar faces. Eyes shifted his way, he steadied himself both hands clasping the bar. "It doesn't matter that I met the letter of my parole. That I'm paid up starting tonight."

Donny shrugged. "I'm just saying. Not the smartest move to meet me here."

Grieg rolled the rock between his fingers, his stomach lurched. "You chose the spot. You had the bartender line the beers up in front of me. Why?"

Donny slammed his current beer onto an old water ring on the wooden bar. "When you called, I admit I was curious about the IPO prospectus. But even more curious about what the years had done to you. The answer's not much, you still got the swagger, and your judgment hasn't improved, or you wouldn't have come. You better get going. You don't want to be late for fate."

Grieg checked his watch. He had time to drop by Hugh Highland's to demand Hugh burn all copies of the IPO prospectus then watch it consumed by flames. He wanted the information out of circulation before he was. Grieg bought Donny another drink and another order of clam strips, then disentangled himself from the barstool. "I'll wave to the crowd just before I'm cuffed," Grieg quipped, hearing his own bluster, he wished he hadn't. It just fed into Donny's beliefs.

On his way to the parking lot, Grieg stooped to pick up a piece of red skarn sparkling at his feet. He turned the glittery rock over in his left palm as he strode down the lighted walkway to the Subaru. He set the rocks on the passenger seat, started the car, and wound his way to the parkway, aiming for Hugh Highland's home on Dune Road in Quogue.

He never made it.

A bright light blazed in the driver's side window. Grieg blinked; pain roared through his head. He was surrounded by spongy gray matter. It weighed on his chest, his shoulder. Someone or something was rapping, tapping. He tried to cover his ears. His arms didn't work. The driver's side door opened. Grieg fell sideways.

A man stopped his fall. "You okay?"

Grieg opened his eyes, one eye, thinking yes, but why was the man asking? It didn't appear to be a bad crash, more an off-road excursion into a shallow ditch.

"Hon," the man called over his shoulder, "You better call 911. He's hurt. Can't tell how bad, but he's not talking to me, and I know enough to know that's not good." The man placed a firm hand on Grieg's left shoulder and squeezed. "My name's Germaine Hervey. My wife and I saw it all, we'll be glad to talk to your insurance company and, of course, the cops when they get here."

"What?" Grieg managed, attempting to push himself through the deployed airbags and out of the seat.

"Hey, take it easy. You telling me you didn't even see the guy? Big black sedan nipped your back left fender clear as day. He was driving maybe eighty or ninety. You were in your lane, he hit you, lost control, got it back and drove off like nothing happened. You're damn lucky your car took flight then nosed down. You look kinda green."

Mussels and garlic fries spewed from Grieg's mouth onto the deflated airbag and down his window-pane checked shirt onto his jeans. Mr. Hervey comforted Grieg as best he could, one hand on Grieg's left shoulder. "You're okay, sir," Hervey said. Hervey was black. One can never be too careful. Even if you drive a Tesla, are in a thousand-dollar bespoke suit and have a diamond ring the size of a marble, even then.

"Not, sir. Just Grieg," Grieg managed.

The grim line of Hervey's lips tipped up. Hervey turned as the police approached. "Officers, my wife Eileen and I witnessed the accident. The driver's name is Grieg, like the guy who composed the Peer Gynt Suite. Don't know if it is his first or last name, do know he's hurt."

"Greg?"

"Grieg," Hervey corrected. "He needs help."

Moms loved the Peer Gynt Suite, adored it. Pops thought she was crazy to like anything with the Hall of the Mountain King in it. Pops would laugh and say it was so Mickey Mouse, which made Moms giggle and their son, named for the composer, squint his small boy eyes at them. That was until they took Grieg to see a digitally restored version of *Fantasia*. He got the joke but no answer when he asked why they hadn't named him Edvard. For the same reason the Swales had called their daughter Calypso, he supposed.

The cop pulled out a form and asked, "Did you get a license plate number?"

"No. Eileen, license?" Hervey called to his wife, who waited in their car.

"I tried, but it was blacked out, or the license holder lights were out," Eileen responded.

"Make, model?"

Hervey closed his eyes, "An SUV. The finish was dark, could have been black, dark blue or red. It would have a new green dent on the right front fender."

Eileen leaned out the car window. "It was a Hyundai Santa Fe. I want one. I know the shape. And, it was the dark cherry red I want, too."

"Help, but not much," the officer said. Leaning in the Subaru's door, he asked Grieg, "You didn't see him?"

"What?" Grieg asked.

"The car that hit you, you didn't see the car or the driver."

"I need help."

"An ambulance just pulled up." The patrolman patted Grieg's left shoulder, "You're going to be fine, believe me, I've seen some stuff. You'll be fine."

Grieg doubted it. He was having trouble understanding the spoken word, his heart was pile driving, and he couldn't catch a breath. An EMT opened the door then called for a stretcher. Two EMTs eased him out of the car. On the gurney, Grieg noticed the ambulance, back doors opened, blocked the coroner's wagon from exiting.

Someone said, "He's seizing."

V

Delia Washburn ran through the sliding doors into Emergency as frightened as she had ever been in her life. She identified herself at reception, a nurse directed her to the waiting room. Doug and Sally Purdy were there, pacing. Delia didn't know what Doug or Sally was thinking, or how they beat her. She wrung her hands, saw her wedding ring, and burst into tears at the loss of her confidant and lover…now her son! Doug wrapped an arm over her shoulders. She shrugged out from under it.

Chief Willard burst into the room. "The onsite patrolman called me. Judge Burridge and I have been waiting at the station for Washburn. The eyewitnesses swear Grieg was forced off the road by a driver in a cherry red Hyundai Santé Fe. Grieg was too far gone to get anything out of him. All we know is he had supped on clams and garlic. We're trying to find out where he had been. Doug, you weren't with him?"

Doug shook his head.

"Jeez, what a mess. Delia, any idea?"

"Where's Judge Burridge?"

"Handling the paperwork, trying to keep your son from a two-year rap for no show at the station. There is stupid and stupider. Risking a no show is about as stupid as it comes."

"If witnesses say Grieg was forced off the road, he was, why aren't you out chasing down that lead?" Delia demanded.

"We have a patrol car out looking for a red SUV with a green dent in the right front fender. No one got a license plate number. Well, not true, they got one number: five. It was a New York plate. That should be easy to find!"

A nurse in scrubs stuck her head in the waiting room door. "Mrs. Washburn?"

Delia started for the door. Sally one step behind. The nurse shook her head. Doug shrugged, signaling Sally back. As Delia strode through the door, Doug, Sally, and Chief Willard circled, words flowing rapidly between them. Delia stared in the waiting room window. The circle broke.

The nurse motioned Delia to wait in the hall in front of a window with drawn Venetian blinds. Leaving Delia, the nurse entered the treatment room and opened the blinds. Delia's eyes locked on her bloodied son, hooked up to beeping monitors, lying deathly still. She slipped out of her shoes. Her bare feet hit the cold linoleum and snapped her back from wherever she had been. An intense, dark-skinned, dark-eyed doctor worked his fingers above Grieg's left ear. The nurse nodded toward the window. The doctor glanced up, finished his inspection, then joined Delia in the hall.

"I am Dr. Chaudhary. You are Mrs. Washburn?"

Delia nodded and reeled. Dr. Chaudhary took her by the elbow and directed her away from the window, as the coordinated Trauma team scuttled about, drew blood, prodded, poked. No matter what indignity they performed, Grieg didn't respond. Chaudhary led Delia to a short stretch of wall the color of sawgrass. Green to hide blood. They passed a uniformed cop stationed outside the buzz of the treatment room. Delia wrung her hands.

Dr. Chaudhary covered them with one of his own. "We've just begun treating your son. The airbags deployed, there are minimal internal injuries. It appears that his head was thrown against the doorframe. That and his temperature worries me." Chaudhary bobbled his head as he checked the admission papers on the lapboard he carried. "Has your son been out of the country recently?"

"He just returned from Kenya. His father was killed in Syria in an IED explosion three days ago. My son brought his body home. Tonight, he was on his way to turn himself in as planned to the Suffolk County Police. He called me to tell me he was stopping to see someone in Quogue. He sounded upbeat." She lied; something had been wrong. His speech was slurred, the cadence was too precise. It crossed her mind that Grieg had been drinking. She knew she was prattling, but she couldn't stop. "If for a moment…"

"Ah, that Washburn. You don't look old enough to be his mother." Dr. Chaudhary quirked his mouth and nodded toward the armed patrolman watching the Trauma team at work. The doctor cleared his throat, "I'll be blunt, your son has a fever of 104 degrees and a severe concussion, he's still unconscious, and we're struggling to stop the internal bleeding from the head injury. I need to know of any blood disorders in your family?"

Delia shook her head.

"Does he take any medication?"

Grieg was an overworked adult male who lived everywhere but in the United States. His father refuted the need for doctors. Delia reasoned his son did as well. "No."

"Heroine, pot, a handful of aspirin, anything? Anything missing from the medicine cabinet?"

She shook her head. "Aspirin. But I sent it to his room."

"How many?"

"Just two, each night that he's been home."

"Is your son a heavy drinker?"

Delia went on the defensive. "No, no blood disorders, no alcohol, no pharmaceuticals. My son's blood should be like distilled water."

Dr. Chaudhary gave Delia a quick hug. "What does your son call you?"

"Moms, but I think you should call me Delia." She blasted him with a toothy smile.

Chaudhary kept one arm over her shoulders. "Our first order of business is to stop the hemorrhaging. We've started a course of plasma and Vitamin K until we get his blood work back. It's a standard treatment. And, we need to find out what is causing the fever then bring it down as quickly as possible."

"Will he...what does it mean?"

A harried-looking nurse peered out of the ECU. Dr. Chaudhary patted Delia's arm. He swung through the door to the trauma room with a wave of the lapboard.

Delia returned to the waiting room. Doug and Sally Purdy were gone. Chief Willard wasn't.

The moment the door closed, Willard said, "Grieg was seen with Donny Craig in Montauk, drinking."

"Grieg may have been with Donny, but he wasn't drinking. He didn't even sip the champagne when we toasted Ray."

"We have witnesses."

"You have ghouls. Go find the damn car that did this to my son!"

Willard spoke to the cop outside the treatment room then swaggered down the long, linoleum floor and out the sliding doors of Emergency to an illegally parked patrol car. Delia waited, alternately chewing her lips and pacing, trying to forget that it was Willard's testimony that convinced the jury her son was a felon.

Dr. Chaudhary swung back through the door. "Lovely lady, your son's blood work is back. We did well to administer Vitamin K and plasma. The bleeding has stopped. But he has Dengue fever. Has he had it before?"

"What?" Delia blurted. "No. This was his first trip to Kenya."

"Dengue symptoms appear commonly within five days, dizziness, achy joints, fever, difficulty keeping a thought. It's too bad he didn't take non-NSAID instead of aspirin, but he couldn't have known. He is quite ill, I project it will take him the full seven days or possibly more to recover, and he may have short-term memory problems from the fever and head injury. For now, we need to administer fluids, keep him isolated and comfortable."

"I sent him the aspirin with warm milk to help him sleep. And…" Delia batted back tears.

Doctor Chaudhary squeezed Delia's right hand. "Sons, a mother's blessing and her curse. Is he your only child?"

Delia sniffed a yes. Dr. Chaudhary kissed her on the cheek then led her to the elevator and into a private room in the second floor ICU. Dawn blushed the horizon before Grieg was wheeled into the room. Nurses and Dr. Chaudhary arranged Grieg in his bed, placed a buzzer by his unresponsive right hand, checked the IV lines, hooked up a heart monitor then left Delia with the infernal beeping. His heartbeat was steady, his temperature was obscene according to the red numbers on the monitor. His head was bandaged, his left cheek and eye like pudding. Delia sank to her knees by his bed and twitted the blanket that covered him.

Grieg opened his right eye; the left didn't respond. A monitor next to the bed beeped like they expected him to die. Wherever he was, the lights were bright and kaleidoscopic. He shut his right eye; pain coursed to his left temple. Moms touched his right cheek, just a brush of the back of her hand, the same hand slid from his right shoulder down his arm to the soft cuff that chained his wrist to the bed. She interlocked his fingers in hers. He couldn't move his left arm. An IV, something clipped to a finger, straps…

"Moms," he managed.

"Oh, I'm so sorry, Betsy is totaled."

"Did I know her?"

Moms' free hand flew to her mouth. "Your car. Your Subaru. The whole front-end was smashed. The back-left corner and the frame are like a giant tried to make a taco roll out of her. Poor Betsy, I'm going to miss her, she was so you. I have this permanent mom picture of you waving as you left for school. I thought Pops would die at the thought of not having you with him, the two of you were so inseparable. More than anything, he wanted you safe and now look at you."

"Where is Pops?"

She smiled. "You're at Stony Brook. The EMTs brought you here. It was the closest hospital." Moms stared into his open right eye. "The Emergency Room doctor saved your very life. You have a bad concussion and a subdural hematoma though the bleeding has stopped. They took all sorts of blood tests. You have Dengue fever. Damn mosquitos. Dr. Chaudhary swears you'll be fine and feel like your old self in a few weeks, if not sooner." Seeing the confusion in her son's eyes, she added, "You were in a car accident. You were driving to the police station to serve your last two days. Remember?"

He didn't. Honestly.

"At least three people called Chief Willard ratting that you'd been drinking before you ended up in the ditch. That you stumbled out to your car."

Who had he met? Donny. He left the restaurant, fumbled for his keys, he wasn't drunk, but something had been wrong. He got in the car, rested his head against the headrest. Someone knocked on the Subaru's window. Grieg squeezed his eyes shut as pain pounded his left temple. Not a thought could be found. He twitted at the fabric of the blanket with his right hand. The coroner's wagon behind an ambulance, a black man with kind eyes. Grieg shut his. "I don't remember."

"Griegs, baby, you're going to be fine."

He couldn't grasp what she was telling him. She could see it in the blank hurt of his cobalt blue eyes. Delia patted Grieg's legs under the thin hospital blanket. They were hot. "Where am I?" Grieg muttered.

A nurse arrived in response to the buzzer. Moms said something to her that caused the nurse to hit the buzzer twice. A handsome man rushed into the room. Moms glowed at the sight of him.

"I'm Dr. Chaudhary," the man said. "And you are?"

"Grieg." Something. It started with a W, maybe not.

"Good start," Chaudhary said, sounding pleased for him.

"I…can't…" what couldn't he do. He couldn't remember what he couldn't remember, but if he remembered that then he remembered something. His mother's least favorite word slipped his lips.

"Griegs," Moms said aghast, embarrassed in front of her latest conquest. She could do that, lay waste to a man with her smile.

"Sorry. I'm having…I can't quite…"

"You need to relax and let the treatment do its work." Dr. Chaudhary touched the intravenous line dangling over Grieg's head. "Initially, we concentrated on the head injury, the Dengue fever aggravated it. The confusion should pass. The timeline varies. We'll take another CT scan tomorrow. I expect the scan to be normal. Hang on, young man." The guy, whoever he was, wasn't much older than…Washburn. WashEx.

Something, something urgent…Grieg tried to push up from the bed. The doctor put a hand on Grieg's chest and restrained him. "Nothing is that important. You're in a delicate time with the fever."

Moms stroked Grieg's cheek, her summer blond hair in spiky points, her blood-red sweater over leggings, her lipstick perfect, and her blue eyes as bright as if sunshine poured into the room. She looked away. She wore her care on her lovely face. The tight line of her mouth, the web of lines around her eyes, and small bags under them said it all. He'd scared her again.

"Sssh," She crooned, "We need to talk. Just us, first, you sleep. Do it, please. Your Moms is here until you're released. I got nowhere else to be other than by your side. Remember that." She stroked his arm, he shut his eyes and let her love wash over him. Moms put a hand gently on each side of Grieg's face and kissed him.

"Oh, Moms, I'm not eight."

Dr. Chaudhary squeezed Grieg's foot. "You will feel like an achy eight-year-old until the fever passes. Thinking will get easier. Your short-term memory will grab hold. Take this time, be patient, and recover. It's important."

Grieg wished he knew what the doctor was saying, he seemed so sincere. Moms plucked a tissue from a box next to the hospital bed and wiped her lipstick off his lips.

Chaudhary checked a lapboard at the end of the bed. "I'll be by before I go off duty. But, Delia, he's going to be fine. I'll collect on the dinner you owe me when you feel comfortable leaving this room. No rush."

Chaudhary opened the swinging door, a cop sat in a chair outside.

Grieg wondered who he had killed this time.

The minute Grieg's left foot jerked, Moms' eyes rose to his from the Kindle propped against his left thigh. A huge handknit sweater hung over her skinny jeans, the expensive kind that hug but don't cling.

She expected something, what, what, where was he? "Where am I?"

"Still at Stony Brook. You were in Betsy on your way to the police station to turn yourself in. You ended up in a ditch. Witnesses claim you were forced. Chief Willard is everywhere looking for the SUV. No luck."

"What could he manage in one day?"

"Three days." Moms shook her head and smiled her *oh my god, I love this boy* smile. She must have blazed like a Fresnel lens over the footlights in her Rockette days. Moms was a

Norwegian beauty with her straight nose, high cheekbones, expressive blue eyes, perfectly shaped eyebrows, and flirty, engaging mouth. How could he know that and not that he had been in an accident?

A thought flitted by; here was one. "Doug back at work?"

"Everyone's still here. You've had lots of visitors. Chief Willard has come each day to get a statement. Felix visited, so did Sally, Doug, everybody, I shooed them all away. Doug left a photo of you and Pops to help you remember. Sally brought this little bear." She held up a small gray stuffed Koala bear clutching eucalyptus leaves. "And read to you from a children's book you once told her you liked. I want the bear. Viper will enjoy using it for a chew toy." Viper, Moms' watch chihuahua, was yippy, nasty, and faithful.

"He isn't...?" Moms glanced at a large, soft leather bag lumped on the floor. On cue, her bag snarled. Moms had set up camp in the corner of the room where windows with Venetian blinds looked out over trees and into the sky. An armchair was angled into the corner. A deeply piled white blanket draped it. Her purse and Viper's soft carrying case rested against the side of the chair facing Grieg's bed. A small valise showered a nightgown onto the floor.

Moms pushed a button on a long cord. Grieg's bed rose slowly to a comfortable angle. "People were getting worried, words like coma kept coming up, but I assured them that you have been sleeping off injuries since you fell off your first oil rig. I even bragged about how you bounced before you hit the concrete."

"Moms," he tried to smile. Something was wrong with his face.

"I know. I have no shame. After all, what was I doing sending my six-year-old up the scaffolding after his brainless Pops?"

"Fearless."

"Fearless and brainless."

"Where's Pops?"

Moms held his right hand, "He's dead."

An explosion. A party. Calypso Swale. Fragments, fragments of thought.

Moms patted his leg. "Can't bring Pops back. Doug blames himself, not you. Griegs, you were in Africa contracting Dengue fever, anyway."

"Pops was…" Where was he?

"Chasing rainbows." Moms put her fingers to his lips and shushed him.

"No," he managed. No, what? No something, Doug, Pops, Syria. Grieg turned his face toward the door, unable to hold onto the thought.

"Thing is, Griegs, Pops expected you to take over where he left off. But you've got to fight for it. I know you can, no matter what obstacles the Board puts up. You were such a feisty kid, a protector of the underdog, fierce, and prideful. I loved to watch you play football, polo, anything you ever did. I know the accident, the parole, Pops' death, knocked the stuffing out of you. But now is the time to get your back up and fight."

For what? Pops. Judge Burridge. Meremer. Something. "Pops had a vision, Moms. We, Pops and I, were changing the tack of the rusting boat. Together. WashEx was Pops company—my legacy. No turning back. Are you worried the Board won't approve me as CEO over Doug, is that it?"

"You look so much like Pops when you smile, even with half of your face black like the Phantom of the Opera. You're fading into greens and yellows now, healthier for sure but not as dramatic." Delia shook her head. "The Board can't override Pops will."

"If I'm alive." Two whole thoughts carried forward. Grieg checked the IV lines. Maybe. This stuff was ingrained in him, it wasn't short-term memory; it was in the meat of him.

Delia huffed.

"Six months ago, during a telephone call, an Exxon executive told me he'd heard I was a felon on probation, even gave the details, two counts of vehicular manslaughter. Someone at WashEx purposefully sabotaged me with our competitors. The world is changing, unclaimed gas, oil, minerals are getting harder to find. Moms, I'm the only man for Pops' job. The Board needs to acknowledge my expertise, not deride me and fink me out."

"Griegs, because you haven't gotten over the accident, no one's forgotten. And, now there's Pops and this." She swept her hand the length of his hospital bed. "Did Pops know someone ratted you out?"

"Of course."

Delia took a deep breath, put one hand over her heart and wiped under her nose with the other. Grieg reached for her with a hot hand. His fever was back. She sat up and said, "Damn them all."

VI

Ponderosa and Jack Pine trees swayed in a harsh wind blowing up from the San Joaquin Valley floor. The roaring upslope didn't happen often, but when it did, fire was a concern no matter the time of year. A buckeye bush banged its branches against a hand-hewn log cabin, chinked with a mix of grasses, and daubed with muddy clay that had dried rock hard. Each carefully notched log rested on its brother, the wood grayed with age.

In spring, bears scratched their backs on the porch supports. A snake lived in the porch rafters. Raccoons waddled in for the nightly offering from the human who inhabited it. And, a skunk black as night with two white stripes down its back that merged at a glorious fan of a tail lived under the porch boards.

A ring of monster Sequoia trees loomed at the edge of the surrounding timber, dancing their crowns, impervious to the onslaught of the wind. They clung to each other's roots, effectively holding hands. The trees encircled the shattered trunk of the giant that had scattered its one-inch cones in a circle around its base.

Hundreds of years ago, winds like the current roar had fanned an ember into a fire. Released from the cones by the heat, the seeds of these new giants sank a fledging root followed by a feathered seedling that wormed its way through the deep duff on the forest floor into the dappled sun.

Jessie Woods perched on the porch of her cabin in a chair made from grapevines and twine, listening to the twisting and cracking of the wind in the forest canopy. She pedaled a generator converting her energy to electricity via a deep cell battery used for backup power on wind-free days. The creaking windmill near an outbuilding rotated, stoking electricity into a bank of batteries and pumping water underground into a 2,500-gallon holding tank made of linked water barrels.

Jessie reveled in the sound of the windmill blades whacking round and round. When she first arrived, the windmill's sole purpose was to pump water into a small cement cistern. It took most of her first summer to convert the windmill so that it could be switched from pumping water to generating electricity and vice versa. The water barrels came from a refuse dump near the year-round stream. She cleansed, linked, and repurposed them.

Today's wind introduced a profound restlessness. No amount of pedaling lessened it. Jessie hated the malaise. Memories invaded, threatening her as though the past crept out of the tall trees to stalk her. As it often did, the ennui drove her to the side of a hospital bed. Her father, weak from the automobile accident that had claimed her mother, his hand like a talon on hers, whispered for her to run. As the light faded from his dark eyes, he studied her, praying she understood his gasped words. Jessie had. She ran, changed her name, ran again, then again. She pedaled faster.

When the charge light on the battery popped to green, Jessie intended to go to the small ice shed dug into a hump behind her cabin and cut off a slab of bacon from the boar a fellow expatriate had killed, dressed, and salted for her. She paid the fellow with as many chickens and eggs as he could steal from her coop. He never took more than his share, often leaving an in-kind offering of a squirrel, wild sorrel, mint, or a gift meant to reassure Jessie that he was the thief and not some other man newly inhabiting her claim.

Jessie's world, once filled with soirees, mixed drinks, and rich white boys, was now the 2400-acres on which she squatted, the cabin, and its wild inhabitants, two of them male homo sapiens. The men came with the land, one to the north corner of the property, the other from the east near the dusty, nearly impassable track through the barbed wire onto her land.

Boomer Bognavich had been on the property since he was a boy, maybe twenty years. The other, Rafe Bolt, returned from various wars, had taken one look at his horrified family, unforgiving girlfriend, and walked out the door with two mud green duffel bags. He set up life in the north corner of the acreage not long before Jessie arrived.

It was Rafe, if that was his name, who hunted boar with bow and arrow. Rafe was tall, broad-shouldered and powerful from living off the grid or perhaps from his years in the U.S. Army. He had a generous nose, engaging mouth, sweet blue eyes, and a square chin. He wore his dusty blond hair in a thick braid, uncut since he had hiked into the mountains.

Jessie adjusted the reading glasses Boomer had stolen from a campsite in the vicinity, as he had the book whose pages she turned and continued pedaling. Boomer was thin and wiry and so gaunt that he caved at the waist. His hair was in long, greasy uncombed knots. His haunted brown eyes were deeply recessed slits. His nose was thick and made bumpy by at least one break and one scar. The scar across his nose was from the same era as the welted scar down his right arm.

Boomer worked the campgrounds both in the Sierra National Forest and Yosemite National Park. He was the bear no one ever saw. He stole food, books, clothes, whatever he needed to survive. If someone woke and found him near their campsite, he walked off with his hands in his pockets. If they didn't, he slipped away with whatever was easily accessible. He roved far and wide and was invisible to the Forest Rangers like a bear too wily to be caught.

If Boomer had plenty, he shared it. Sometimes, he disappeared for days returning with a present for Jessie like the tortoiseshell comb she jammed into her twisted and tucked hair.

The three of them were a generally congenial group. Rafe was possessive and worried about Jessie's welfare and well-being. Boomer clucked over her whenever she made some small change in her living arrangements. If Boomer voiced his concerns, Rafe jumped to her defense. The two men would circle and growl. She'd hand them a bowl of whatever food providence provided, and they would sit down like family to eat. Other than an admiring glance from one of her men, her reflection in the glass of the cabin windows, or the shiny bottom of a pan, she hadn't seen herself during the four years the three outcasts had cohabited.

A branch high on one of the Jack Pines cracked, rocketing to the forest floor. The red light popped to green on the battery, whanging Jessie back to the present. She quit pedaling. The windmill kept whirling, the generator she'd found, repaired, and attached would produce enough electricity to light the cabin for another night if she chose. Most nights, she relied on her oil lanterns, fueled by fat saved from frying.

A redwood, a hundred and fifty feet of emotion, tossed its head. A hawk flew. A rabbit beat-feet across the pasture toward the newly turned dirt for this year's vegetable garden. A shadow cruised at the edge of the timber then cut across the open field. Rafe Bolt slapped a brace of rabbits on the porch boards at Jessie's feet. She put her hands behind her head and sighed at life's perfection.

VII

Jones brought Moms a change of clothes, chic black slacks, a hand-knit sweater in blues and greens that set off her eyes and a pair of black ballet flats. Jones, by way of Moms' personal assistant, also produced a navy-blue designer bathrobe with light blue piping and a pair of royal-blue silk men's pajamas for Grieg. He donned the robe, handed back the pajamas with a thank you, and begged Jones to take Viper. Jones refused. Viper snarled from Moms' makeshift abode, which now included a thick quilt, a footrest, and her favorite goose down pillow.

As soon as Grieg woke, Moms set his cellphone on the nightstand beside his bed. "Chief Willard returned it this morning. They found it in poor old Betsy."

"When?" he asked, reaching for the phone, surprised he could.

"While you were sleeping. Chief Willard uncuffed you, too, and removed the guard. You still need to turn yourself in when you can stand. That's what the Chief said. You should check with the Judge first." Viper snarled. Moms tucked the beast in her purse. "I better take Viper out to the park across the street before he pees in my purse."

The door swung shut. Grieg waited until his mother's footsteps were out of hearing, then propped his smartphone on his food tray and punched at it with the fingers of his right hand swollen from days cuffed to the bed. The police, by the greasy fingerprints on the screen, had reviewed his contacts and calendar and, from the number of taps, had played a few games, such as who has rights to all the uranium in North Dakota.

Delia returned, stuffed Viper back in his carrier, and commented, "I had the nicest lunch with Patty Gilbert today, we were Rockettes together, way back when. She married well, not as well as I did, but well enough to live in Southampton. Anyway, she was all rumors about Annie MacKenzie. I shrugged. No one, not even Annie, could be as outré as Patty purported. Well, maybe. Anyway, Patty heard that Annie was going to dump Mark. Imagine, after all these years. She said Mark wanted children, and Annie was like not only no, but hell no. Well, that's what she heard."

"Should I know Patty?"

Moms shook her head. "No. Pops did. He always said Patty had the best shoulders he'd ever seen on a woman. I told him if I ever caught his lips on one of them, I'd use my cherished Waterford vase on his head. Patty's fun. It's nice to have her near."

"A friend you don't have to wonder about?"

Moms patted his right thigh, adjusted the angle of the bed, and generally spoiled him rotten. He was having a good day and night. His thoughts were clicking, he remembered most of what he'd just said. The one thing he couldn't do was integrate ideas. "What difference can it make if Annie dumps Mark. He's a bit of nothing?

"Annie needs money, of course." Moms pulled the sheet and blanket up to his chest, tucking it in like bunting, then turned the end of the sheet back over the blanket and smoothed it down. "As we know, WET shelters the Board members and their families from destitution and makes WashEx look like kindly old uncles to a variety of non-profits. I just love it when I'm watching a Public Broadcasting Station program, and it starts with *Made possible by the Washburn Exploration Trust*. Gives me goosebumps." Moms clutched his right hand to her chest. "The rumors imply that Annie plans to dump Mark then snag Hugh for his salary and stipend."

A snippet of his conversation with Donny wandered through, something to do with filling the coffers from an IPO. "I don't understand."

"Nor do I? Besides, who cares. But there is something I need to show you. After all, we are Pops' trained and two-thirds of the team of three, right?"

Grieg nodded, remembering Pops teaching them trigonometry so they'd never get lost, geometry so they'd never be out of square, and statistics so they'd always be wary.

Moms set an unsigned sympathy card on his metal tray. "It's postmarked Fresno, California. Calypso sent it. I know it. Pops thought Calypso was a gas. He loved the way she'd flip her hair, put her hands on her hips and all but scream *you don't own me.* He said she was savvier and smarter than anyone gave her credit for and that he wouldn't have been all that surprised if she did whack Larch and rob his safe. Don't you see? Who else would have sent an unsigned card from Fresno?"

"A geology colleague, a rockhound."

"But it is a clue."

"To something."

"Sally left this." Moms handed him a copy of the book *A Wrinkle in Time*.

"To let me know Pops is working on the Tesseract Project. We used to joke about it, how our dads were scientists lost in search of the timeless."

Delia grabbed Grieg's ears and planted a huge, wet kiss on his forehead. "Pops is gone, Griegs." Moms stared at him, memorizing his pulpy face. "Ever wonder what Pops sees…saw in me."

"Never, never wondered for a day. He adored you, Moms. He wanted to be with you until you were both too old to do anything but sit on the front porch of the old ranch house in Yellow Sky and rock. He told me that lots of times." The thought dislodged a dim memory of Ray Washburn and Doug Purdy leaning on a drill rig in Malaysia, enjoying a smoke and chat. "Moms, has Doug ever talked about owning a cabin in the Sierra?"

"Ask Doug." When Grieg's eyebrows descended into a vee, Delia added, "Okay, I'll ask Doug. I'll be seeing him tonight at my function."

"He isn't in Australia? Tell me someone went, Moms."

"Tom Swale. Doug was worried about you, so he gave Tom the lowdown and made him promise not to give away the farm."

"The headmen won't trust Tom."

Moms patted his leg.

Ilmenite. A new site Grieg had identified deep in the aboriginal lands of Western Australia. It was on Grieg's list. One more checkmark, not one of the rare minerals, but one of the most useful. Now, Tom Swale at Doug's bidding was in an Aborigine village, culturally ignorant, trying to talk the well-versed aboriginal headmen into ceding mineral rights to an area equal to two hundred square miles. Grieg sighed.

As soon as Moms left for the evening, Grieg entered the GPS coordinates for Calypso's wreck into Google maps. The car was nose down in a river off a dirt road in the Sierra National Forest somewhere between the southern entrance to Yosemite National Park and the mountain terminus of Highway 168, east-northeast of Fresno, California. The small town of Fish Camp, northeast of Oakhurst, was the closest settlement to the wreck's location though over eight miles distant via rugged terrain.

The unsigned sympathy card was postmarked Fresno and could have been sent by an admirer of Ray Washburn or by Calypso Swale. Grieg called the Fish Camp Post Office to ask if they had their own frank. They did. So, if Calypso sent the card, she either lived in Fresno, or she trekked out of the mountains to mail it. To do so, she would need a vehicle which she obviously didn't have, or Dempsey would have popped her registration. Of course, she could be calling herself Snake Plissken for all Dempsey knew.

Grieg wrote a note to call the California DMV. He queried Google maps for Post Offices in Fresno. The closest was on Minarets off Blackstone, the first exit off Highway 41 going south. No matter Calypso's current name, the real mystery was how she heard of Pops' death? If she had, if it was her, if she was alive.

Ray Washburn was a national figure, a larger than life explorer when all believed earth's exploration over. His obituary could have appeared in any number of newspapers. Grieg started with the *Sacramento Bee* then skipped through obituaries in the *Fresno Bee*, the *San Francisco Chronicle,* and the *Bakersfield Californian,* hoping each time to find his father's tribute. The *Californian* had run one, which made sense, given Bakersfield's ties to the oil business. He checked circulation. The *Californian*'s circulation area didn't include Fresno or the small towns up Highway 41.

Stumped, Grieg searched the internet for his father's name. The answer popped on the second page of sites. Ray Washburn's life and death had been covered on National Public Radio during *Morning Edition* the day after Pops was killed. Grieg found and listened to the broadcast, unable to stifle a grin. Pops had been something. He telephoned Valley Public Radio in Fresno. Pretending to be a graduate student in media, he asked for their broadcast area. The individual he spoke to emailed it to him.

He needed a map. Grieg swung his legs off the side of the bed for the first time in four days. Cuffed to the bed, he had been forced to ring for a nurse and a bedpan. Whenever the nurse entered, Moms drifted out, claiming changing his diapers had been enough for a lifetime. Now, dizzy, weak, and off-balance, he thudded his butt on the edge of the bed and rang his buzzer. The night nurse arrived in a flash. He asked her as winningly as a man with thirty stitches and a green and yellow face could if she might print the map for him then forwarded it to her email account.

The nurse helped him back into bed, pulled up his covers, adjusted his pillow, checked his temperature and tsked, all before leaving with a smile. She returned a few minutes later with a print-out of the KVPR radio broadcast area. He gave her a lopsided grin in thanks. She gave him his cup with the bendy straw. He slurped happily as she left with a flick of the monitor. Beep. Blood pressure 110/50, pulse 45, temperature 103.5.

Grieg adjusted the thin hospital blanket then swung the metal meal tray over his lap. With a hospital provided pencil, he drew an X on the map where Calypso's car had been found and a second on the Post Office on Minarets in Fresno. He checked the bus lines, knowing the Calypso Swale of old had never ridden one. The Yosemite Area Rapid Transit, YARTS, connected Yosemite National Park to Fresno with a stop each in Fish Camp, Oakhurst, and Coarsegold. So, she could have taken a bus then walked a few blocks. Going so far off the reservation to mail a card seemed crazy to him and a great deal of exposure for her, given she was still on the lam. It also assumed she had a radio and reception.

Grieg drew the hypotenuse between Highway 41 and Highway 168 along the crest of the Sierra, shading in the triangle between them as they formed a vee to Fresno. The Valley Public Radio station reception area was within the triangle. If alive and in the mountains and mailing cards, Calypso lived within those coordinates. The door to Grieg's room crept open, he knew by the speed it wasn't his mother. Moms dashed everywhere she went. He folded his right arm over his notes like a sixth-grader caught cheating.

"Well, don't you just look like you saw one of the undead," Doug Purdy said, stepping into the room. "Delia sent me to keep you occupied while she chats with your doctor, said you had questions about the Purdy cabin. Not much to tell you, I sold it fifteen years ago. Some great-grand Purdy uncle of mine built it during the gold rush, no gold though, just the land, about five acres of it up Virginia City, Nevada, way. I never saw the damn place, just paid taxes on it until I got tired pissing good money after bad on something I never used."

Grieg grabbed his pencil and scrawled property taxes on a note, had to, his short-term memory was like a sieve, some chunks stayed while the small stuff slipped on through. "Two questions, Doug, why the hell aren't you in Australia and have you given the IPO any more thought?"

"Talked to Felix. He told me the company in question was annoying the crap out of Hugh, so to get them off his back, Hugh said go ahead. When they delivered it, Hugh refused to pay, claiming they'd burned out their candle. It made sense to me, so I dropped it."

"But why would a company curry Hugh, Felix is Chief Financial Officer?"

"Didn't think about that, but you're right. My Sally hadn't heard anything about it, and she generally knows what's cooking being WashEx's General Secretary."

Grieg tried to raise his eyebrows. One still didn't work. "I don't like Hugh thinking, Doug. Have our books been independently audited in, like, the last century?"

"Keepin' the damn company healthy and making sure WET keeps the stipends and contributions flowing is the only work the Highlands got, Grieg. Says so right in the company Bylaws. They have absolute authority over the financial side of the house, used to be called favored status. Means whoever the hell the CEO of the company is, me right now, can't question them. That's the way it reads, boy. And the way it has always been."

"I don't like it." Grieg moved his right arm, exposing the corner of the map. But then if he couldn't trust Doug Purdy, who could he trust? For that matter, when had it become a matter of trust? When Betsy landed in a ditch and the coroner was the first responder. That's when. Doug tapped Grieg's uncuffed hand and cocked his head. Grieg shrugged, snapping, "And why the hell are you still here?"

Doug snorted. "I sent Tom, filled him in, told him to tell the chief to set up a new meeting in about a month when Mr. Purdy and Dr. Washburn could attend and not to take any shit off the headmen. Tom was raring for an adventure. By the time those crafty bastards are through with him, he'll quit asking to come along. I wish I could be there."

"You're pretty casual with my business."

"You know that meeting can wait. First, we need to sort out what's next with Ray gone and all. Besides, it's nice to be with my girls for a change. Good to be home. Sorry about the wreck, though, you still don't look too good." Doug gave him a peculiar look. "What's eating you?"

"Honestly, that we're one death from no Washburns."

"True enough. But that's cause you Washburns, like the rest of us wildcatters, eventually gotta pay for all the hell you do. That's all, boy. That's all there is to it. Sometimes I look over my shoulder expecting the same hand that grabbed Ray to grab me. You remember that when you're flying or driving or climbing a rig or sitting in some tent with a sheik."

"Got a warning notice, three days in a kraal, and I end up with Dengue fever."

"Explains the temperature reading on the monitor. You know that stuff can lead to hemorrhagic fever, bleeding from the gums, eyes, kidneys, whatnot. Better take it easy. Don't go traipsing off looking for what's gone." Doug patted Grieg's shoulder and exited with the warning.

Grieg nestled into the pillows stuffed behind his back. He thought of calling Sally Purdy, checked the time, and didn't. Instead, he mulled over Doug's comment about what came next. He didn't like the implication, and he didn't care for Doug's presumption.

When Moms didn't arrive, Grieg dialed her telephone number. It rang in her everything bag slumped at the foot of his hospital bed. Viper woke with a snarl.

Bored, he tapped the message icon on his telephone, wondering what else the police had uncovered. Two distinct prints indicated that at least two men had read the text sent by Dr. Khalil received while Grieg was in Emergency. Cryptic and interrupted it read: *See yellow sky cloud.* Grieg googled Dr. Khalil. The first link was his obituary. He had been found at his desk at MIT, dead from a massive stroke sometime after texting Grieg.

It made Grieg's brain hurt.

M oms slammed through the hospital room door. She tapped Grieg's right hand and raised the hospital bed until he was sitting.

Grieg opened his sleepy eyes, pretty sure the night nurse had drugged him. Moms handed him his cup with the bendy straw. He narrowed his eyes and sipped, waiting for some explanation. The clock on the wall displayed a time well after midnight. Moms wore a stunning gold lamé designer gown her stylist must have selected to emphasize her trim figure. Her purse matched.

"What good does it do for you to have a smartphone if you leave it in that thing!" Grieg pointed to the hump of leather sitting in the corner. Viper snarled at the sound of his voice.

"My, aren't we in a mood! The MacKenzie's gave another one of their Society benefits. Annie's a bitch. Patsy's right. Annie's sunk her fangs into Hugh and is sucking him dry. But I think he likes it. It's a no-hoper, Grieg, like they say in Australia. Remember Australia? I loved it there. Just us and the dust. Remember when Pops would say that?" Moms pulled up a chair and draped her slinky frame in it, making it hard to envision her in a cotton shirtwaist dress, black skimmers, her hair controlled by a scarf tied babushka-style against the pervasive wind. A metal triangle hung on the front porch of their house in Alice Springs. She rang it to call Grieg for lunch and dinner or when he needed to come home. He'd had an Australian sheepdog named Yipes. The dog went everywhere with him. Yes, he remembered Australia.

"Wow, Moms, that's just plain nasty." Grieg waved the map. She didn't notice. Moms was on a toot. So, he went for it, "Doug said you came with him and stopped to flirt with Dr. Chaudhary." Grieg looked pointedly at the clock, wondering if he should bring up Dr. Khalil.

"No, he didn't. I did talk to Hari then ran into one of the Boswells. It doesn't matter which one, there are seemingly thousands, all on Long Island. Anyway, I think it was Marcetta. She was all whack-a-doodle over the article in the New York Times about how Calypso Swale was la and dah and so and on. I grabbed a copy of the newspaper on my way up." Delia threw it on the blanket at Grieg's waist. A photo of Miss Swale occupied much of the paper above the fold. He had to admit they chose a good one. Though, he was still reeling from Moms casually flinging out Dr. Chaudhary's first name, Hari.

"Wow."

"Wow, again? I think it is a bit tacky, too big, too melodramatic. Heiress missing five years sought by family. As though every loony in the United States won't try to kidnap and ransom her for her fortune. Of course, there is no fortune, just the stipends. Read the paper!" Moms waited.

"This reads more like an APB than a sympathetic article about someone whose family fears dead."

"It reads like a manifesto for a kidnapping. Sweet young socialite missing, family will pay twenty thousand for any information that leads to her discovery. Left under mysterious circumstances after the tragic death of her parents in an automobile accident. Everyone worried. Unable to move forward. Ya-da-ya-da-ya."

"The article couldn't very well read: we hope she's dead, she was a bitch, and we want to vote on an IPO but can't do it until she's either dead and doesn't matter, or she's alive to cast a vote, could they?

Moms cocked her lovely head and squinted. After taking a deep breath, she said, "Twenty-four hours have passed since this article appeared. Sally Purdy is getting phone calls from all over the United States with information about our dear missing Calypso."

Grieg rotated the map so that Moms could see it. She held it up to the bedside light for a better view.

"If Calypso is alive and sent the card, a big if, bets are she's living somewhere within that triangle. I need one more point of reference. I'm that close to pinpointing her possible location."

Returning the map to the table, Moms tapped one of her manicured gold polished fingernails on it.

"Tell me that isn't real gold," Grieg said, "Then cough up what else you haven't told me."

"Hari says you can be released under my recognizance as soon as your fever goes down if you promise not to use your head for anything other than pillow batting."

"But Calypso…"

"She's managed to stay hidden all these years, she can wait a few more days." Moms nestled down in her chair, pulled up her footrest, and covered her legs with a hand-knitted afghan. Blocks of color in varying shapes of red and gray were outlined in black to create a striking and intricate design. She pulled out her Kindle, flipped off her shoes, stretched her polished toes, and settled in for the night. Her eyes bobbed up to her son's.

"Did Pops ever mention a Dr. Khalil?" Grieg asked.

Her Kindle hit the floor, she leaned over and picked it up. "Dr. Khalil sounds like a character out of some spy movie. Dr. Khalil and Sasha were last seen getting into a 24-karat gold Mercedes, driven by their faithful servant Blovnik.

He ignored her teasing. "Do the words yellow sky cloud mean anything to you."

She laughed, "Same movie, he played the noble savage."

"Damn it!"

"I'm sorry, I shouldn't tease. Not when you are so out of sorts. Go to sleep, Griegs, tomorrow, huh?"

"Dr. Khalil's funeral is then, too."

"Griegs!"

"Moms, where is Pops wedding ring?"

"I didn't have the heart to sift through the ashes and bone fragments."

Grieg shut his eyes. Every muscle in his body ached, maybe even his bones. He tossed off the blanket. Moms flipped it back over his legs and rang for the night nurse. She brought three pills, he dutifully swallowed them. Fifteen minutes later, the pain eased.

Next morning, the fever had broken, when it hadn't returned by late afternoon Moms sprang him. The ever-present Jones liveried them to Meremer. Exhausted by the short drive and flight of stairs to his room, Grieg stretched out on his twin bed in a sea blue jogging suit with a nifty gray stripe down each pant leg. He wished it had a matching watch cap to cover his stitches and missing hair. His body still ached, leading Grieg to conclude that he should have been dead. Tired from all the thinking, he napped, to be jolted awake by the piercing decibels of his own screams. Virginia Culhane Swale her eyes wide. Chief Willard waving as Betsy tore over the verge. Hervey thumping on the car window. The coroner's wagon.

After a quick knock, Moms threw open his bedroom door. "Griegs?"

"Sorry."

"Your scream echoed." Delia went to Grieg's closet and selected the more casual of two dress suits and a white shirt with trendy embroidered collar and cuffs. She held them up for him, then helped him dress.

When he was clothed, Moms motioned for him to neaten up as in shave and brush his spiky hair. Grieg went into the en suite bathroom chocked with his toiletries and outfitted with a razor and did his best given the bruises, cuts, and stitches. Done primping, he descended the stairs like an old man, stepping twice on each stair, wondering who the evening's entertainment would be. It was a small party. Felix Highland, Moms, Annie Swale, and Mark MacKenzie English country lord dashing in butter wool slacks and a seven-hundred-dollar hand-knit designer sweater.

"Thank God you're okay," Annie said, rushing him. Grieg took a step back. "Sorry, I forgot you aren't touchy-feely."

"I'm still a little off balance is all." He wasted a perfectly good gesture to his bunged-up head.

Delia sipped her drink. Felix placed a manicured hand around her waist.

"So soon," Grieg muttered.

"How childish. Child-like, really." Felix removed his hand, shot his cuffs, and checked the effect in the mirror over the mantle. "Keep in mind that Doug is CEO for the next four months and possibly forever depending on how the Board votes."

"Trust me, I get that. I'm letting you have your little moment because the Board has no discretionary control over what is, essentially, a hereditary position."

"Oh, my boy, we do have discretion over your position, it was voted into the Bylaws the moment your father so inconveniently died."

Grieg cut a look at his mother. She wiped her lips with the tip of her little finger. Angered, Grieg responded to Felix like a jealous teen. "I am offended by your casual acceptance of my father's death. I find your attention to my mother obsequious and disquieting. Don't smirk at me. It disgraces the work done by your plastic surgeon."

"Understand, if it weren't for your father's will and Doug Purdy, you would be history. Doug claims some misguided affection for you, and despite our advice and that of our advisors, he has asked that you be allowed to continue on as Chief Exploration Officer."

"Really? If WashEx needs an IPO, it's because of you and your wimp-ass, woman groping son."

Felix pitched his drink at Grieg, who side-stepped it and turned his back. By the hush, Grieg knew he'd made his point. Delia placed a hand on Felix's forearm to stop him from making a move on Grieg then shot Grieg a warning look. Grieg got the message, offended she had taken Felix's side.

"You're nothing but a messed-up boy," Felix sniped. Moms guided Felix away from Grieg. "You should know it is a delicate time for organizations like ours, international trade agreements aren't always beneficial, mineral rights can be elastic. We're getting considerable backlash for our latest acquisitions from companies and countries who rely on us to produce. Doug can get us back on track. Let me be blunt, you need to get on board.

"Those were some newspaper articles," Grieg snarled. Acting like an ass and seemingly unable to check himself.

"But necessary," Felix responded, "Without a death certificate, needed changes can't be made within WashEx. Good news is Hugh tells me that in a scant 24-hours of the article appearing, we have five solid leads."

"Five?"

Felix mixed another drink, considering whether to answer, but finally replied, "Two in Mustique, bones found near the wreckage, and two from Quogue. Schoolmates of Calypso's claiming to have received a phone call from her. When pushed, they said it was about five years ago. She supposedly called from Santa Fe, New Mexico. We know she was in San Francisco at the time. That leaves Mustique and a dead body."

"Mustique and Dad's money," Annie harped.

Annoyed at Felix's tone and Annie's avarice, Grieg sniped, "So, Annie, what do you and Hugh have planned for Calypso's money?"

Annie slapped Grieg. Her husband stopped the second swing. Grieg excused himself with a wave of his right hand, his left covering his already bruised cheek. "Sorry, I'm not feeling well."

Which was true.

Delia sipped her drink, one hand on Felix, her eyes on her son. Her voice trailed him out the door, "Be careful going up the stairs, you're weaving."

Moms stalked into Ray Washburn's study, her skirt swirling around her legs. "You were a beast. If you were twelve, I'd have insisted that you make your apologies before leaving the room."

"Sorry, I can't stand the sight of you anywhere near Felix." Grieg sat at a cherrywood reading desk. An atlas lay open on the desk's slanted surface, his smartphone propped against the base of a Tiffany lamp. He scrolled through the Mariposa County property tax records to no avail. Wherever Calypso was hiding, it wasn't in the Mariposa County portion of his triangle. He shaded in the county boundaries lightly with a red pencil as his mother strode over to the desk.

"Your behavior wasn't adult, manly, civil, or any other word I can conjure. As for Felix, your father suggested that if anything happened to him, I grab onto Felix and not let go. I'm following orders. And, you…you didn't help your cause tonight. I was embarrassed."

"Oh, poor Moms!"

"What's the matter with you?"

"I'm tired of the Swales and the Highlands and their goddamn pettiness. No wonder Calypso hightailed it. I hope she has made a wonderful life for herself scaffolded by Larch Swale's paltry seven-hundred-fifty thousand."

Moms pulled a chain. A bronze bell jangled near the paneled walnut door, another rang in the hallway. When Jones arrived, Moms ordered scotch and soda for two then proceeded to pace. Grieg enjoyed watching Moms move, she had the lines of a ballerina and the elegance of a ballroom dancer.

"Don't stare at me like that, it makes me feel...I don't know, like..." Grieg lowered his eyes to his map.

Jones arrived, dressed as ever in dark slacks, a bleached starched shirt, and a black tie, pushing a walnut trolley. The tray on top held two lowball glasses, a bottle of Laphroaig Islay Scotch old enough to vote two times over, soda and a bucket of ice. He positioned the moveable upstairs bar near the overstuffed divan. Moms poured two fingers and delicately dropped two ice cubes in a glass, she taste-tested, smiled, then poured Grieg four fingers of soda from an unopened bottle, adding a slice of lime. They clinked glasses.

"Any progress on your map?"

"There are two counties in the triangle, Mariposa and Merced. The Mariposa County tax records are a no go, no Swales, no Culhanes, no Jessym. Of course, Calypso, if she is alive, could be calling herself Princess Leia. I pulled up the Merced tax records and have figured out how to narrow my search to the triangle in the Sierras, but that is as far as I've gotten. If it hadn't been for Doug, I wouldn't be that far."

"Doug?"

"He said he got rid of his property in Nevada because he was tired of paying property taxes. I wrote it down. After you brought me home from the hospital, I found a note in a pocket of my jogging pants that read taxes in capital letters, and Moms, I didn't remember writing it. Another note said, California Department of Motor Vehicles."

She grabbed his face and covered it with kisses. "Poor Griegs. You feel a little warm." She jammed a thermometer in his mouth, "If the fever spikes again, I'm supposed to run all stoplights and get you to the hospital." The moment the thermometer beeped, Moms removed it and read it: 99.8 degrees.

"Well?"

"I was instructed to bring you back if it reached 100.1." She wiggled a hand, "Awfully close. You better take it every fifteen minutes or so. And, no aspirin." She brushed his hair off his forehead. "Naproxen sodium, only, you've bled enough." Moms held out a pill with a glass of water. "Tongue. Drink. Swallow."

He did as ordered, then asked, "Did Larch and Virginia love Calypso as much as you and Pops loved me?"

"Impossible!"

"No, really, did she grow up surrounded by people who loved her?"

"Yes. But she also had horses and every lavish thing. You, my poor little puppy, had your bedroom furniture."

"I had it all, Moms."

"Your Pops promised you that WashEx was yours, that you would explore the world together. He shouldn't have done that."

"If he'd lived, it would have been as he promised."

"But he didn't, Griegs. And that's the problem. You were flying from Kenya to Syria when the Board voted. The vote on the floor was to oust you…period. Out of everything. Off the Board. Pay him off, and he won't care. In the end, we reached an agreement that, as Pops specified, Doug was regent until you proved you weren't irresponsible and determined to go off half-cocked on wild goose chases. Tom was very forceful in your favor. Kept saying what possible difference can it make if we give him a chance, after all, the Board took a chance with me."

Grieg wasn't sure he believed her version, not after the scene with Felix. "So, Moms, what's next?"

Moms stroked the hair on the undamaged side of his head, checked her watch then swirled out of the room to rejoin the dinner party. He heard laughter, raised voices, music, doors opening, closing, cars coming and going. He crawled through the tax records on his phone. Around two in the morning, the house silenced. The central air furnace shushed, and the trees rested in hushed silence. With warm air from a wall vent brushing his ankles, Grieg flipped to the next sequence of records. The letters swam. His head hurt, and he couldn't focus. He stuck the thermometer in his mouth, still under 100 degrees, 99.9 to be exact. He rested his head in the wedge of his bent right arm. When the dizziness subsided, and his stomach quit roiling, he turned back to the small screen of his phone, enlarging the font to accommodate his wavering vision.

He scrolled down the page. There it was. Notification of taxes due and paid by Yellow Sky Holding on a 2400-acre parcel of land. A search on the property records provided the coordinates and essential information, such as a deeded easement and the value of three extant improvements. He slid his rudimentary map mid-desk.

Stymied, he worked his way through the Merced County files until he found the plot lines of the property. Armed with the coordinates and the plotlines, he called up Google maps. He entered the coordinates then zoomed in on the satellite picture, or biggered it up as Moms would say, until the roof of a small house with a meadow in front appeared. He enlarged the photo again, an old sawmill or stamp mill, it was hard to tell which, a workshop or chicken coop, and possibly a windmill shared the property.

In the image captured by a passing satellite less than six months ago, a white haze drifted over the cabin's chimney. A section of land near a meandering streambed appeared plowed. The property was occupied. Held by Yellow Sky Holdings, it seemed unlikely Felix would have any knowledge of the property or who might live on it. Grieg suspected that the claim was so buried by age that no member of the current Board knew of its existence. Just as Calypso Swale, hiding in plain sight, was unaware of the hell coming her way.

The furnace belched to life, fluttering the pages of the open IPO prospectus. The night of the accident, Calypso took her father's money, her patent, and disappeared. If her roommates in San Francisco were square with Special Agent Dempsey, someone had followed her and forced her to flee. The person who scared her into the mountains might rightfully believe she had disappeared for good, that her share of the WET distribution was his or hers to use. Which meant, if she was alive, it was likely someone needed her dead.

Grieg balanced down the hall to his bedroom, determined to dress in the morning, walk down to breakfast, and remember what he had just deduced. Which was that if he was able to follow the clues to this cabin in his half-delusional state, any other Board member could have done the same. Though, unless Moms had shared the sympathy card with the others, she and Grieg were the only people who expected to find Calypso alive. That had to be an advantage, didn't it?

Live people hide, fight back, think, dead ones not so much.

VIII

Jessie stroked the soft nose of Rex, one of her two rescue horses. Rex was a tall, gangly buckskin with a dark mane and tail who was game for anything. Her other horse, Frisco, was standoffish, and who wouldn't be? When Boomer found Frisco wandering in Nelder Grove, his ribs were etched in his side, his left, back hock was injured, and he had scars on his withers from a beating.

Boomer had thrown a rope around the brown and white pinto's neck and led him to Jessie. Jessie hadn't been sure she could heal the small horse, but Frisco tolerated her. More détente than anything. A sharp noise, blowing dust, an animal scurrying from his pounding hoofs set the tobiano pinto off. She never lifted a hand against the shy gelding, she cooed, curried, and feed her shattered boy. Now, Frisco butted Jessie in the small of the back. She reached back and stroked his head. He nickered softly. She stayed sandwiched between the two horses for a few moments relishing their warmth.

At a whopping sound, Frisco shot his muzzle skyward, his eyes rolled back until the whites showed. He reared, pivoted, and ran undercover of the slender woven-roofed shelter Jessie had made for them with Rafe's help. Jessie, one hand shading her eyes, searched the sky. A pinprick to the west morphed into a helicopter. She clutched Rex's mane and led him under the shelter. A red helicopter roared over and kept going, checking further up the mountain for marijuana plantings, squatters, and illegal logging. She had nothing to fear from this flyover, not like the first time a helicopter appeared four years ago.

April 15 that year, the morning light glowed with the promise of a warm day, so she left the fire unlit and bounced out the door to pick miner's lettuce growing near a vernal pool at the edge of the timber. Pawprints lined the banks, raccoon, skunk, fox, maybe even coyote. She often heard the echo of their bayed messages in the still of the night. Deer tracks, possibly boar tracks, and she swore the cloven hooves of a goat wandered in for water. Busy place. Jessie filled a small handmade basket with the grass-green lettuce, identified the lighter green leaves of sorrel, and picked that as well. Hearing a helicopter, she hid on the rim of the small pond in the scraggy shadows of a manzanita bush. As she watched, a small dot on the western horizon grew into a chopper swooping in and out over the property.

The pilot checked each structure, each pasture, each road then roared off in a tumult of wind and dirt. When she was sure the helicopter had left, Jessie hiked to each place where it had hovered. She drew a sketch of each spot in a spiral notebook, a gift from Boomer, including any trees, bushes, or other identifying characteristics that would be noticeable if changed. From then on, she referred to the drawings, managing any improvements in increments.

Boomer and Rafe both claimed that this was the first non-Forest Service chopper to check out the property. So, on the 15th day of each month for six months, she rose early, left the fire unbuilt, and hid in the woods, advising Boomer and Rafe to make themselves scarce as well. As a result, those days were holidays, no pedaling the generator, no washing of clothes, bodies, horses, or anything else, no hunting. Instead, the three friends gathered in the cabin without a fire, making up silly songs, and eating the previous day's leftovers. When night fell, they lit a fire and danced wild, cavorting, whooping, nonsense dances in celebration of one more month undiscovered. October 15, the helicopter swooped back over the property.

Precedence set, each April 15 and October 15, the dark-green chopper with an oil rig stencil swooped in like a finely wound Swiss clock tracking the passage of time. Jessie began to long for its return, marking it as a highlight of the year, acknowledging it as fleeting contact with the outside world. She fantasized that the WashEx pilot searched for her, hoping to find her alive and ready to come home, that her father's last words had been a lie, in fact, that his death had been a charade.

Rafe often reminded her that someone had tracked her to San Francisco and forced her to disappear into an El Niño rain, and now surveilled the mine property via chopper. So, she missed her horse, Fructose, her friends and her plans, and kept her life on hold, perhaps forever.

The helicopter pilots sought signs of habitation such as smoke from the chimney, a cistern where none had been, changes in the stamp mill, new digging along the riverbank, and new structures or fencing. For fire safety, Jessie grazed the horses on the long grass in the meadow, reasoning that munching deer would cause the same sort of damage.

She built the horse corral on the timber side of the stamp mill from fallen branches. She converted the mill into a stable without changing the outward appearance. When her cabin roof developed a nasty leak, she searched days for aged-redwood to hatchet into shingles so that the bright red gleam of new wood wouldn't give her away.

At first, she was overwhelmed by the work needed on the sparsely furnished log cabin with window glass so old it rippled. She reminded herself that though she was a city girl, she was an Olympic level athlete. Of all the things she missed, she missed her gelding, Fructose, and the possibilities of greatness he had afforded her most. An astounding horse, a goer, brave of heart, fearless against the jumps and hedges, they made a great team.

The week of her father's death, she was readying her gear and Fructose's tack for the trip to the Olympic Team training site. Now, she lived off the grid in a cabin furnished with items stolen, bartered for by Rafe or Boomer, or made by her own hands. Her continued anonymity, if Rafe's conspiracy theories were true, her very life depended on their community of three.

She banked on the men's need to remain as hidden as she from the world that rumbled around them, the small towns, the tourists, the National Park Service, and the nightcrawlers that swooped in stole and burned. Unlike Jessie, Rafe and Boomer trekked off the property to civilization. She envied them.

Her men brought her gifts, small things, old books, lawn chairs discarded because a strap had broken, the odd bottle of liquor stolen from a picnic table, playing cards and games left behind by campers. She had no telephone, smartphone, or computer. She hauled her water, pooped in the woods, and hoarded each piece of paper found. Rafe, bless his heart, occasionally brought toilet paper, but each sheet used became refuse. Another problem.

Jessie buried her garbage in a midden of her own design, an acre from the house and an acre from the nearest stream. Near it, she devised a rudimentary outhouse that blended into two leggy manzanita bushes. Often, she wasn't the only occupant. Beady-eyed possums stared, waiting for her business to be done. If they got nourishment from her excrement, good for them. Occasionally, she did her job in a bucket on the enclosed back porch and used it for fertilizer in her garden, digging it deep into the soil, then left the ground fallow for a month or so hoping to enrich it without endangering her life. So far, so good.

Most of Jessie's first spring was spent, using a stick to set the rows for a garden beneath the towering trees and near the year-round stream. Her first garden was ragtag, short of water when the plants needed it, short of sunlight to ripen, short of good quality seed. She managed to produce enough root crops to see her through the winter. Otherwise, her lack of experience meant near starvation, well, except for the meat the guys provided. She lusted for greens that whole winter.

The next spring, she used a rusty shovel from the mine to dig irrigation ditches from the stream to the garden. She devised a sluice to manage the flow. The first time she let the water run, it went nowhere. So, she graded the trenches in small increments until when she raised the dam board, water flowed down the sluice out to the furrows then past each plant.

Rafe brought seeds, stolen she suspected from the hardware store located in the nearest decent sized mountain community. One day, Boomer dropped a swath of camouflage netting on the front porch, claiming he found it discarded on the forest floor. Jessie assumed Boomer stole it from the marijuana farmers further up the mountain whose plants Rafe used as his personal pharmaceutical outlet.

After a week, when no armed men appeared to retrieve it, Jessie strung the net between four trees and prepared the newly sheltered land for planting. Each year she let the best-looking plants go to seed then gathered and stored the seeds for the next spring. Now, she had fresh vegetables from June to October, harvesting her last crops on October 10. With the harvest in, she rolled up the netting and covered the garden in pine needles, so when the helicopter made its October swing only sunburned grass and dirt showed.

She canned what she could in glass jars gifted by Rafe, which she religiously sterilized and reused each year. There was no greater sin than breaking or chipping the glass or losing a brass ring or metal lid.

She kept the root crops deep in the cellar dug into the side of a hillock by some hopeful prior resident. She fashioned a door from milled wood found by a rusting sawmill and rope made from strips peeled from a willowy bush that grew near the water. Her potatoes, carrots, turnips, rutabagas, cabbage, and Brussels sprouts kept well through most of the winter.

When she asked Rafe how to make sauerkraut, he produced a pamphlet copied on the five-cent a page copier at the small library in the small town. Now, she kept a crock of sauerkraut fermenting year-round. The sauerkraut sweetened and tenderized the gamey meat the men brought as offerings.

Grapevines, a gnarled fig tree, and several ancient apple trees dating back to 1849 peppered the property. She picked fruit from the trees, preserved what she could, and served the rest as a sugarless sweet dessert. When sugar was available, she used a pinch of her yeast and experimented with fig wine.

Jessie made a point of sitting on her porch each day before and after the hard work of survival, even if only for fifteen minutes. Her life here was tenuous, dependent on her continued strength and good health, and on the goodwill of Rafe and Boomer, though she wanted to believe otherwise.

As she sat, a disturbance at treeline grabbed her attention, she shaded her eyes to see against the sun. Rafe covered the distance from the timber in his long, smooth stride. Something about the way he moved reminded her of a soiree in the Hamptons during her debut year. It had been a spring night; the stars bored holes in the sky. Her elegant, chestnut-haired, hazel-eyed mother in a black dress covered in bugle beads hand-sewn at some house of Haute Couture had an odd gleam in her eye as though she were keeping one of the world's best-kept secrets.

A tall young man in a blue blazer and khaki pants stood beside Virginia Swale. His hair was brown, a little ragged and on the unkempt side as though he'd been to a cheap barber. His eyes were an intense blue shaded by long dark lashes, his nose straight and without character, and, to make it worse, he had a cleft chin below a sullen, masculine mouth. She looked at her mother puzzled and said, "Really? Isn't he a little scruffy?"

Her mother tittered as she sometimes did. "You should give him one dance. I think he is quite handsome." The young man blushed disarmingly as though unaccustomed to compliments. Jessie found that hard to believe. He had that cocky kind of insouciance that she found annoying in overly confident men. And, an athlete's body.

"I'd rather dance with a hippopotamus than be seen with him, there are people here who know me, really, Mother."

Virginia Swale raised her finely shaped eyebrows and broke into very unladylike laughter. "I promised his father that I would introduce you."

"I don't care who you promised, I'm not dancing with anyone with scuffs on his shoes." And, he had them. His shoes below khaki Dockers were brown and unpolished.

Another more appropriate suitor joined them, Jessie accepted his offer of a dance, but she was left with the memory of hurt eyes, a sardonic mouth, and a snort that made her feel small. Whoever the stranger was, whoever her mother had promised the introduction, he wasn't the man for her.

Halfway across the meadow, Rafe called out, "What's so funny?"

"Memory," Jessie responded, striding out to join him.

"We need to talk." The tone of Rafe's voice grabbed Jessie's attention. "About Boomer."

"Boomer's okay, isn't he? I mean, he didn't get hurt, or arrested, or run over while on his rounds?" Jessie worried about both men. Rafe could manage in the world for short periods, even hold a job, but not Boomer. Boomer lived in a lean-to of brush chinked with mud. Humans other than Rafe and Jessie were anathema to him.

"He's okay, I guess. It's just…I…followed him last night. Don't know why, sometimes he talks crazy, well crazier. Look, Jess, he spent the night watching this female camper like she was a deer or something. He waited near her campsite and hung on every shadow she made on the canvas of her tent. He…he jacked off while he was doing it. You know what the means, right?"

Jessie raised an eyebrow.

"Okay, so when he…he didn't just walk into the woods. He waited until her lantern died down, then went to her car and took something. One thing. He put it in a pocket of his ratty old fishing vest and headed off. But, Jess, it was…"

"Disturbing? Sometimes I masturbate."

"Don't tell me that," Rafe said with a lopsided smile.

"It doesn't mean I'm crazy or a rapist. It gets lonely up here. Don't you ever wonder what it would be like to walk into a room full of women and have them ogle you? You're good looking and move like a cat, any woman would notice you."

"Do you notice me?" Rafe asked.

Jessie smiled, enjoying the view, including his supple muscles and strong hands. He even managed to remain clean-shaven and clean clothed, his blue jeans and shirts faded from bleaching.

"Some nights, I think someone peeps through my bedroom window. I always chalked it up to worry that I'd be found and forced to run. You don't suppose it's Boomer?"

"That's why I told you…has he ever…"

"No. Never, oh, the odd accidental brush up." Jessie sat on the porch. She patted the chair next to her. Rafe sat. The sun blazed gold, orange, tinting the clouds maroon as it set. Her fifteen minutes were up. She had chores to do and a fire to build. She planned to make bread and leave it to rise on the warm hearth overnight, which meant mixing and kneading it before bed. She sighed. Rafe offered her a hand, she took it.

"Don't worry about Boomer."

"There's a story there," Jessie said.

"Boomer told me he ran away from home when he was thirteen. His parents picked fruit in the San Joaquin Valley for a living. He claims his dad beat him regularly. I feel sorry for him; then, he does something like he did last night."

"Did you see the chopper?" she asked, squeezing Rafe's left hand.

"I did. Realtors. Can't stand the thought." Rafe helped her to her feet and followed her into the cabin.

Dinner was a stew of leftover rabbit and root vegetables. It was the time of year when the stores in the root cellar were sparse but not the rabbit population, thank goodness. Outside of Jessie's few chickens, rabbit was the easiest meat to acquire. As if to prove it, Rafe always seemed able to nab one.

Rafe plunked his lanky frame into one of the armchairs made from twigs and homemade rope woven from hemp found at the fringes of the property. The dense stand was a boon given Jessie's first rope making disasters using wild mallow from the banks of the stream. If nothing else, her rope making expertise assured her she wasn't cut out to be an Ahwahnechee Indian.

The chair creaked from Rafe's weight. He lifted his bottom and adjusted the horsehair cushion fashioned by Jessie from a beige blanket with wide orange stripes near the edges. The blanket, provided by Boomer, was sewn into a pocket then stuffed with hair from Frisco and Rex, carefully saved after each grooming. Jessie stitched the raw end closed with hair from Rex's long tail. As cushions went, it wasn't plush, but it was better than sitting on the pointed ends of woven twigs. There wasn't enough weight on any of the cabin's inhabitants for that.

Rafe whittled a piece of pine. Jessie tossed chopped vegetables into an iron pot hanging by its handle from a tripod over the fire in the open hearth. She braised the rabbit over the single burner propane camp stove she'd packed in all those years ago. Rafe kept her in propane. If she fussed when he brought it, he asked for a cup of coffee which Jessie interpreted as quid pro quo.

When the broth was aromatic, she added the rabbit, tender vegetables, and potatoes. Rafe watched her work, his lips curved into a sweet smile. They were partners in this rugged life, not committed to each other, but an abiding, respectful friendship existed between them.

He didn't ask her questions, not after that first morning when he found Boomer tending her. She didn't ask him about his past, either, just listened. She knew little about him, but she knew this, Rafe had gone to war and come home at war. Nights when he stayed over, he checked the shutters on the windows two, three, sometimes seven times. Rafe doused the fire, no matter how cold the night. He shut the bedroom door once Jessie was under the covers and then slept on the drafty, hard, plank floor with a blanket wrapped under and over him. Any noise, a mouse, a rustle in the roof, a whistle through the door brought him to alarming instant wakefulness, his eyes seeing everything, his body tensed, and his hands searching for a weapon.

Rafe lived frugally in a rough-hewn cabin at the edge of the property furthest from the road. When he was strapped for money, which wasn't often, he would go into town, get a job at the hardware store, and bunk in a tent at a homeless encampment nearby. Sometimes he would be gone for a month, generally less. When he returned, he thoughtfully brought Jessie something to make her hard life more comfortable.

Once it had been a toothbrush and tube after tube of toothpaste, another time a bright, flowery cushion for the double-seated couch she'd fashioned from grapevines and rope, another time bedsheets and a fresh pillow, and, of course, the small bottles of propane for her stove and coffee. Jessie suspected he went down the mountain for work when the coffee supply was getting low. But no matter his reason, upon his return, he would tell her of men in town looking for a missing woman with chestnut hair.

At a thud on the porch, Rafe stood, grabbed his shotgun and pointed it at the door. The door swung open. Rafe's finger twitched on the trigger. Boomer stepped into the room, his right arm shining in the half-dark. Blood dripped from his wrist pooling before slipping through the plank floorboards to the dirt beneath the cabin. Rafe grabbed a rag hanging on a stem of wood by the door and wrapped Boomer's wrist, his response to the wound so automatic that Jessie added it to her internal ledger titled Rafe.

"What happened?" she asked, pulling the Dutch oven of stewing vegetables from the fire and replacing it with a pot of water.

"Bear," Boomer managed.

"Bear, my ass," Rafe responded but said nothing more. Jessie motioned Boomer to the chair Rafe had vacated and went for her first-aid kit. Boomer's wrist looked like it needed stitches, but she knew better than to suggest the men trek into town for medical care. Questions would be asked that neither of them would be comfortable answering.

Jessie treated and bound Boomer's wounds then hung the stew back on the fire. Behind her, the men spoke in hushed, heated tones. Like Rafe, she recognized the scratches for what they were: fierce, deep rents made by four desperate fingers and a puncture wound caused by anything from a knife to a fingernail file.

"The woman camper?" Rafe growled. Boomer held his injured arm across his chest. Rafe paced then loomed over Boomer.

Boomer stared at the bloody stain on the floor.

"Look at me!" Rafe grabbed Boomer's chin. "The Park Rangers will call the police. If the woman describes you, they'll put up posters. How long do you think it will be before they come here? How long? You better not have lured the cops or anyone else up this mountain!"

Boomer closed his eyes, tired and oddly at ease. Jessie stirred the stew. There seemed always to be someone new in Oakhurst, or Fish Camp, or at the Park asking about her. She quailed at each report. Rafe soothed her, cajoled, promised to protect her. But he couldn't, not really, not from them all. Sooner or later, someone would come, and…she should destroy the damn thing. She should go into the mine and set the timer and blow the prototype of her patent to hell. What had she been thinking when she built it? That her theories were legitimate, that it was viable, that it would change the world. All those things. All of them. And, pride, pure pride, well, and arrogance, and...

"It's not just you!" Rafe pointed at each of them in turn. "It is all of us. We are squatting on this land. It's our home." He slapped Boomer on the shoulder.

Boomer snarled at Rafe, "I didn't touch the lady. I didn't."

"Oh, right, she's not your type! Get out of my sight," Rafe shoved Boomer toward the door.

Jessie rushed between them. "Rafe, you can't send him out. He needs food and shelter."

Rafe glanced between Boomer and Jessie, his hands in fists. "This stew better be damn good. Damn good."

Boomer cowered in the chair closest to the fire and stared wordlessly into the hearth.

Boomer's tiptoeing woke Rafe. The cabin door creaked heavily. Both men were gone when Jessie rose. The smell of the yeasty risen dough signified its readiness to be baked. Each Monday, Jessie tended her yeast family. She loved the chemistry of it, noting that her bread tasted distinctly different from Rafe's, signifying that she had developed a unique line of single-celled fungi. Three loaves of bread, two wheat, one rye, would get her through a week, even with male visitations.

In her first year, she constructed a kiln in an open space out the backdoor of the cabin using cinderblocks found at the stamp mill. Her first attempt had been a miserable failure. Then one night, watching the fire in the hearth, she realized her mistake. Three broken fingernails and one black thumbnail later, she had a functioning oven for baking. She found a wide flat board at the mine and fashioned it into a paddle to shovel dough onto the warped metal grill of her kiln. Boomer provided the grill liberated from a campsite fire-circle.

As she checked her bread loaves, she heard the soft plop of horse hooves on dirt at the front of the cabin. The riders stopped, dismounted, and called. Jessie dropped to her belly and crawled under the cabin's raised foundation. The door screeched overhead. Footsteps thudded on the floor above. The aged floorboards flexed. Only Rafe or Boomer had ever dared trespass into the cabin. This was neither man.

"Hey," the man called from the near middle of the main room. "I know someone is here, no one up here is fool enough to leave an open fire untended."

Jessie refused the bait.

The man thumped to the front door. "Someone is squatting here. Looks like our culprit is hiding in the woods. There's dried blood on the arm of one of the chairs, recent enough to smell coppery. Of course, it could mean nothing, these folks get beat the hell up all the time."

"I'm feeling a bit compromised here, huge No Trespassing signs, Private Property Keep Out, Trespassers will be prosecuted," an older sounding male responded.

"I guess anything we found would be inadmissible since we weren't escorted onto the property."

"I keep expecting to take a shot to the head. We're being watched by someone who knows how to stalk. I feel it if you don't."

"Let's mount up and get out of Dodge. I want to go out the way we came in. I saw a phone number posted to call in case of trespass. I'll call it. Let the property owners know they got squatters."

"They may have a caretaker, lots of places up here employ one."

Jessie heard the shuffling of feet in dust and hooves as what she assumed were two Forest Rangers mounted their horses.

"Hey, look!" the younger of the two shouted.

"Put that gun away. I'm unarmed," Rafe called on the run. "This is private property, all sorts of signs posted. I got permission to shoot first and ask questions later."

"You live here?" the older Ranger asked.

"I caretake it."

"You know the owners?"

"I know the name on the check. My employer told me this property is what started it all, some old prospector in 1849 staked out the place, pulled gold out of here 'til the 1890s. They keep it for sentimental reasons, there's no gold left. I run delirious gold panners out of the stream two, three times a year."

Jessie believed Rafe, though, as far as she knew most of what he was saying was gleaned from her, the signage, or lies. Especially the bit about being the caretaker. She rode the fence line, restringing the barbed wire when it broke and weaving the spiky branches through the fence to further deter visitors. With Boomer's help, Jessie maintained the cabin and the land so that her presence wouldn't be noticed. Her footprint on the property was that small. To be fair, Rafe did keep her safe and her whereabouts secret.

"You know your stuff, that's for sure. But, fella, don't be leaving an open fire in the hearth, not with the drought around here. Hey, do I smell bread baking?"

"Just left it for a minute."

"Before we mosey on out, a female camper says she was attacked last night, some guy peeping at her. She claims she felt his eyes through the canvas of her tent. She tore out of the tent with a rat-tailed comb, practically knocked him off his feet, then ripped at him with her fingernails and stabbed him with the pointy end of her comb. Seen anyone that looks like he tangled with a wild cat?"

"Nope," Rafe answered, "The camper's okay?"

"Yep," the younger man said, "She loves the attention, that's for sure. So much so we're all kind of wondering about her story. Plus, no one we've run into has seen anyone all tore up like she described. But keep an eye out. Here's our number."

"My partner thought he smelled blood inside," the older voice commented.

"Rabbit, sir. Got back late, dressed it in front of the fire, then turned it into hasenpfeffer. I'd offer you some, but I scarfed it down."

"Better get your bread, smells like it's burning. And, watch those fires."

"Ask him," the young Ranger urged the older.

"I forgot. Last night, a girl went missing from a campsite at Texas Flats. We expect her back, but just in case you see someone looking way lost, let us know."

"Sir," Rafe said.

The clop of horse hooves underscored Rafe's quickstep around the cabin to the kiln. Jessie stayed hidden until Rafe whistled. She rolled out, coughing, covered in a layer of fine dust. Rafe hummed as he worked the paddle under the loaves of bread.

"If they'd hung around another five minutes, your bread would have caught fire." He said without turning to her. "They're looking for Boomer."

"I heard."

Rafe poked the bread with a forefinger. It sprang back. "I should have turned Boomer in, led the two Rangers on their fine horses over to Boomer's place, and said here you go, boys."

"But you didn't."

"Crazy bastard." Jessie couldn't tell if Rafe was chastising himself or vilifying Boomer. "How's your flour holding up?"

Jessie pursed her lips. Rafe grinned and shook his head. "I'll head into town, see what I can find out. Anything else I can get us while I'm down there?"

"No, just don't be gone too long."

"Boomer?"

"It's just—my first night, I felt someone's hands between my legs. He could have been trying to warm me up, but it felt more like strokes than bracing rubs." She felt the hands now. A fire crackling dangerously in the fireplace, embers ready to hop out to the rug, the shadow of a man, like one of Snow White's dwarfs dancing on the cabin wall. She shuddered. Rafe threw an arm over her shoulders and pulled her in for the world's most platonic hug. She rested her head on his chest.

Kissing the crown of her head, he soothed, "I'll be back by sunset with flour and maybe some special treat. How long has it been since you had something pretty?"

"Years."

Rafe patted her butt, grabbed his rifle, and strode away. Jessie took the loaves of bread into what passed for the kitchen, a short wooden counter covered in pounded tin, a few shelves, one cabinet, and an enameled metal sink. By screwing an RV hose, a gift from Boomer, onto the windmill pump, the pump deposited a week's worth of water into a 53-gallon whiskey barrel that gravity fed to the backdoor of the cabin.

To accomplish this, she dug the blue RV hose into the earth eighteen inches deep at the barrel, deepening it to thirty-six inches at the cabin. At the flip of a switch, a small electric pump powered by one of the deep cell batteries she pedal-charged brought the water up to the sink. With a twist of the tap, ice-cold or lukewarm water, depending on the time of the year, flowed into the basin. Before the advent of the hose, Jessie filled buckets each sunrise from the cistern beneath the windmill.

Jessie set the loaves of bread on the trestle table to cool on three sections of freshly laundered cheesecloth. Later, she would wrap the cooled bread in the cheesecloth for storage in a wooden bread box. The box had a chicken painted on the front. The chicken, a Leghorn by its paint job, was more than a little worse for wear. Like the dishes she used, the bread box came with the cabin.

As she stepped onto the porch, chickens chuckled in the distance. A soft whinny drifted on the light breeze. Bugs floated past in the golden light of midday. The still overcame her; it rarely bothered her to be alone, today it did. She crossed to her bedroom and wrestled out a leather suit bag hidden behind her few clothes in her small closet. Kneeling, she unzipped the bag. A slip of silk drifted out. She removed a Stella McCarthy dress, purchased for the wedding reception in Las Vegas. Holding the dress to her much-slimmed frame, she brushed the fabric against her cheek, wished for a mirror, wondering what her life might have been.

Rafe was quick to remind her that if found, she would be hauled home, possibly in handcuffs, to face more humiliation. When he raged like that, she assumed he meant she would be arrested for her father's death and humiliated by the subsequent trial as her sibling swore her guilt. Tom would testify that he had been seeking buyers for Fructose at her father's request, hoping to sell the horse to keep the family afloat. Larch Swale had been that broke. Her parents had been arguing about Fructose when...it was all the motive anyone would need to send her to prison for her father's death.

Jessie held the dress to her shoulders and danced around the room, imagining swaying on the arm of one of the West Coast social elite. A tall boy, dark-haired with eyes that mocked her, flooded her thoughts. She stopped. The dress wrapped around her legs. This was silly and wasteful of time. The horses needed to be fed, the shallow irrigation ditches cleared of winter's detritus before planting.

She sat on her bed and wept instead.

IX

Grieg Washburn woke from a fairy tale sleep, a dreamless death with rebirth in the morning, expecting to find the slate clean, the sun out, flowers blooming, and birds chirping. His right hand, wrist bruised, grazed the stitches on his forehead. He was still him, and the slate was still covered with eraser dust.

He opened his night goop rimmed eyes. The five stars of Cassiopeia stuck to his bedroom ceiling zigzagged overhead forming the distinctive W for Washburn. When he was little, he was convinced the constellation belonged to him. Moms may have been involved in the misapprehension, as in, look Griegs, look at the W, Pops says it's yours, all yours.

Grieg managed to dress and wobble down to breakfast, dreaming of a hack on GG. That was all before he sidled up to the buffet and couldn't figure out how to hold a plate, spoon food, and not tip over. Moms jumped to the rescue, whisked him through the line, set his plate at the head of the table, and poured him a cup of coffee. This loosey-goosey daftness was getting dreary and more than a little worrisome. Dr. Chaudhary promised him his brain would jell. Grieg reckoned the doctor left off the O and fingered the notes in his pocket, trying not to look bewildered by Felix Highland seated next to Moms.

Highland read the newspaper, ignoring Moms in her black leggings, black spikes, and a multi-colored tunic top with a boatneck defined by her clavicles. A single diamond, the size of a child's fingernail, sat in the dip between the two bones. Her hair was in wild disarray, carefully planned by her stylist. Felix wore gray slacks, a long-grained polished cotton shirt of the palest blue, his initials in navy blue over the pocket. Grieg was resplendent in sweatpants, an untucked white man-tailor shirt, walkalongs, and two days' worth of beard.

Grieg sipped his coffee, unable to generate one thing to say or, for that matter, two consecutive thoughts. His eyes lingered over a photograph of a middle-aged man printed above the fold in the New York Times. "Who is that?"

Felix flipped the paper. "Dr. Ben Khalil. Too young to die. But aren't we all?"

"You knew him?" Grieg asked.

"Judge Burridge introduced us. He had some interesting ideas about the future."

"The future in general, or WashEx in particular?"

"In general, he was one of those who felt that gasoline-powered vehicles would be obsolete in ten years. Your father teased him, said something like not until Grieg's Subaru dies. You should talk to Judge Burridge. We were in Burridge's office on a video call with both Khalil and your father. Doug, too, he walked in on your father's end though he contributed nothing."

"When?"

Felix shrugged, folded the paper, tapped the handle on his coffee cup, and adjusted himself in his seat. "A month or two ago."

"Hmm."

"Which means?"

"Just hmm." Grieg fingered the newspaper. Felix handed it to him.

"By the way, we've had some disappointing news. Special Agent Dempsey telephoned. The bones found near the wreckage of Calypso's car weren't hers, but they are female, and we do have a name. Amy Dunstable, a college student, disappeared four years ago while camping over Spring Break. Her family is devastated. It seems that they held out hope she might walk in their door. Poor, poor family."

"How refreshing." Grieg gibed. All the deaths were piling up. Larch and Virginia Swale, Pops, Khalil, this girl, throw in Calypso's patent, and the only apparent connection was Calypso Swale.

"And what is that supposed to mean?" Felix tossed his folded serviette onto his empty plate for emphasis. Grieg slid the newspaper off the table then into his lap.

Moms refolded Felix's napkin and placed it under Highland's fork. "I do see his point, Felix. You seemed disappointed that the bones weren't Calypso's."

"I'm disappointed because WashEx needs to restructure, my dear. We can't unless we find Calypso or her bones."

"How many missing women can there be in that section of the Sierra Nevada, not to mention the odds of two of them dying so near each other? I bet the girl's bones were planted. Without DNA testing, anyone finding the wreck would assume the bones belonged with the car. Maybe Calypso killed Ms. Dunstable for that reason." Grieg downed a forkful of eggs and ham. His stomach rebelled. He slurped some water. It helped.

"That's disgusting!"

"It may be, but..."

"Amy Dunstable was camping in the Sierra National Forest at the Rock Creek Campground with a group of friends." Felix cut in. "She disappeared from their campsite. Her friends searched but never found her. Nor did the Forest Rangers or the police, according to Special Agent Dempsey. The coroner is attempting to identify the cause of death, but given the limited number of bones, he isn't holding out much hope."

"I'd like to talk to Amy's family. Do you have their contact information?"

"Why, why would you?"

"To sympathize." Grieg scooted his eggs around his plate, grabbing for a strand of thought that had flitted past. Failing, he added, "Perhaps there is something I could do to help them."

"I doubt it. Further, there is nothing to be gained by disturbing Amy's parents, if you think that you of all people can ferret something…look at you!"

"Cut me some slack, five nights ago someone drove me off the road. I'm doing okay considering."

Highland scoffed, "Really. I think the Dengue has you hallucinating."

"Am I?" Grieg slapped the newspaper against his legs. Dr. Khalil.

"Are you what?" Sally Purdy walked behind Grieg's chair and squeezed his right shoulder. "Sorry I missed you at the hospital, my boy." She bent and kissed his ear.

"Hey, Sal. Do you think someone murdered Pops and happily tried to do the same to me?"

She kissed his ear again. "Why, when they could get you drunk, put you in a car, and call the cops. You'd be back in a cell so fast your keister wouldn't miss the seat of your vehicle."

Grieg craned his neck. Ol' Sal looked terrific. He wondered if some pod person had stolen into her thin, plain frame while she slept. She had gone from mouse-brown hair to a rich bay streaked with golden light. Her eating-disorder wracked frame was no more. She even had hips. Her pale blotchy skin was a golden tan. Only, those eyes of hers, whose humor and honesty Grieg had relied on, were still hers. Clear as a cloudless day and filled with light.

"My, my, Miss Sal," he said, "What have you done with yourself?"

Sally laughed, "Spent lots and lots of money on me. That's what. Went to one of those gonna end your eating disorder clinics. Did. Went to one of those gonna fix your crappy skin clinics. Did. And, went to one of those if you're going to be a big shot General Secretary for the best goddamn mineral exploration company in the world learn how to dress clinics. Learned." She waved a hand up and down her filled-out frame, flowing by her exotically patterned tunic, down her skin-tight black slacks to the tip of her pointy-toed high-heeled boots.

"It worked, my girl."

She kissed Grieg's ear again. "At each turn, I kept asking myself, what would my boy think if I did this or that. Well, what does my boy think?"

"He thinks you're still Ol' Sal the best gal he never married."

She flashed an engagement ring roughly the size and shape of Saturn. "Had your chance. I found a wealthy, un-disgraced, non-felon, and fell head over heels. If your murderers don't succeed, I'll introduce you to him one of these days."

Moms piped up, "She's going to marry a lawyer, with political ambitions, who will likely be president within the next ten years."

"Hey, my girl, did you lasso Calypso's Kennedy?"

"Better."

Grieg raised his eyebrows over a bright grin. Damn, he loved this girl, her sauce, her self-deprecation, and her fearlessness. Sally Purdy had stood by him, believed him, and steadied him when everyone else turned away.

"Tell me about your fiancée, Sal. I'd like to know who I am losing you to?" Grieg asked. "Family name?"

"Guilt...Gilft," Sally stumbled.

"As in Gilft, Dummer, and Toff?" The name stenciled all over the IPO prospectus.

Sally nodded. "Christian Gilft. The Gilft of Gilft, Dummer, and Toff is his father. You played polo with Christian."

"Against him. And, even though he bought one of my ponies, he's a bully, my girl."

"I like him."

Grieg pursed his lips and nodded. "Good. That's the way it should be. When is the big day?"

"Christian is working on a huge project. We're waiting until it's completed so we can take our magnificent honeymoon."

"The big project isn't a hostile take-over of WashEx, is it?"

"Grieg!"

"Sorry, my girl. Got a burr under my saddle about the IPO. Sorry, it wasn't us." He kissed Sally's ear.

With a wrinkle of her nose, she said, "We wouldn't have been good, not in the long run. You're too impulsive, and I'm too…well, nothing."

The message from Sally was the same as the others, too impulsive. Even he, impulsive risktaker that he supposedly was could take a hint. The Board wanted him out and badly. "Back to the subject at hand. Anything come across Pops' desk at headquarters that I should know about?"

"Work. At breakfast? Horror of horrors, taking business out of the office is absolutely forbidden, my boy. Ray Washburn's rules. I live and die by them."

"I hope not the latter."

"I suppose Felix has already told you about the bones. That's why I rushed over before hopping the train into the office."

"I forbid you to go to the office dressed as you are. Good gad, Sal, you won't make it off the platform in one piece."

"Oh, my, oh, my, now that's the compliment I've been waiting to hear."

Grieg lifted Sally's left hand from his shoulder and kissed each of her knuckles. "We need to talk."

"That sounded like the once and future CEO to the GS."

"Sorry. I'm new at this."

"Ray used to call and start with goddamn it, Sal, what the… So, we need to talk scares me, especially since we can't. My Dad's CEO for at least the next four months, remember?" She recovered her hand from his. "Look, you look beat. Don't come into the City or even try. I'll drop by tonight, and we'll have that talk. Love you, my boy." She filled his water glass from a small crystal pitcher. "Drink your coffee and your water, like a good lad." He put the glass to his lips. Sally signaled thumbs up, spun and left her scent, something soft and earthy like freshly mown grass.

Felix cleared his throat. "She's going into the office to prepare the agenda for a review of the IPO. We do need to look to the future."

"No IPO. And as for the meeting, if I'm not there, and Moms isn't there, and Tom's not and the Culhanes are all still dead or missing, that leaves you, Doug, and Hugh at the meeting."

"And Sally."

"Good old, Sal," Grieg stuffed a forkful of hash browns in his mouth and was instantly sorry. When he'd swallowed, he said, "Remember, while you're discussing, the IPO that we Washburns hold 52% of the company and still have the veto. Tell Sally to compose a letter that officially turns Gilft, Dummer, and Toff down and warns them away. Sal can bring it by for my signature tonight. And, Felix, tell the GS to bring me WET's financial reports for the last two years as soon as."

Felix stood and stomped out of the dining room. Grieg squinched his eyes as much from the sharp pain coursing his skull as from the desire to drive Highland into the ground with one fist. Instead, he turned on his mother, whining, "Whatever you think you're doing, don't betray Pops to keep me CEO. Don't do it, Moms."

"Doug and I *will* be at Felix's meeting. The IPO goes nowhere, now or in the future. You need to get well, and you need to shave. You could have shaved."

He sighed, he could have, but he'd forgotten. "Do you know how I might contact Amy Dunstable's family?"

Moms pulled a folded slip of paper out of a side pocket of her tunic and fingered it over to Grieg. "I slipped it off the nightstand when Felix wasn't looking."

"Gads, Moms!"

She shook her head and gave him a gentle smile. Still, what was Felix doing in Moms' bedroom?

"It wasn't my bedroom, Griegs." She answered his thought. "He stayed in the guest room despite some petitioning. The number was by the nightstand in that room. Why am I explaining this? Shame on you! Call her family, Griegs. Oh, I think it's brilliant to ask Sally for the WET financials. I'll remind her."

He watched Moms walk from the dining room, another thought flew past something to do with Khalil. It was gone before she swayed through the arch into the hall. It wouldn't be long before his lack of short-term memory became not only a disability to him but an asset to whoever had run him off the road. Convinced a walk might help his recovery, he rolled the newspaper and stepped through the French doors out onto the patio.

The wind tore at his shirt. He considered returning for his jacket, but it was upstairs in his room. It was as though the physical grace he had counted on since he was a teen was ebbing away with his mind. He walked toward the stables, slapping the newspaper on a thigh. Winded, he sat on a bench under a weeping willow tree, crossed his legs, and watched the sea thunder. When he could breathe again, he unfolded the newspaper.

Dr. Khalil, a renowned futurist, had preached climate change, the need for non-combustion engines, predicted that within a few years, a self-sustaining engine would be developed and practical for everyday use. From the tenor of the text, most in his circle thought Khalil was whimsically mad. He was fifty-two, ran five miles a day, and a vegetarian. But, then, Grieg ran five miles a day, didn't drink, didn't smoke, and felt like crap. In India, a friend's father had died while eating dinner. He too was young. Death by natural causes came in many incarnations. Still. Grieg folded the paper, searched for his smartphone, realized he'd left it in his bedroom, and prayed he would remember to call the reporter named in the byline.

Reaching the stable, Grieg made a smacking noise with his lips to call GinnyGee half-thinking of a ride but settled for a lean against the gelding's warm flanks. The horse hung his head over Grieg's right shoulder, whickering until Grieg rubbed his nose. Fred, the stableman, stopped by to say hey.

Grieg stroked GG's nose. Fred rubbed the gelding's chest and commented, "Beautiful animal. He's got all the moves."

"You worked at the Club. Any memories of Calypso Swale, you'd share?" Grieg leaned harder, the horse and he sighed in unison. They'd had a polo love affair. He wondered if GG's sigh signaled his hope that Grieg would mount and ride him into action. GG stamped his left front hoof three times, indicating he was anxious to enter the fray. "No, boy," Grieg said, stroking the gelding, "Maybe never again."

"Now, that would be a damn shame," Fred responded. "Memories. Both Fructose and little Miss Calypso didn't like to lose. If some comer took a higher rail, Fructose would narrow his eyes and calculate the height. The minute he got the knee from Calypso, bam, they'd be over the course. That slip of a girl was no pampered petunia. She took falls so hard they jarred my teeth. She'd get up, dust off, stroke the horse, mount, and win. Like I said the first time I saw you, I wouldn't know who to bet on in a side-by-side."

Fred ran a hand down GG's chest, thinking. "Another thing about Ms. Swale. In the month or so before the accident, she started sneaking into your polo matches. I caught her giving Geenius a carrot and whispering sweet nothings in his ear. She blushed when she saw me. The same day, she was leaning on the running rail watching the game. You did that Comanche thing, you know, hanging sideways in the saddle so no one could see you from the right, and walloped the ball between the goalposts. She turned to me with a grin wide as the whole world. The reason I mention it, it was the happiest I ever saw her."

"And Sally Purdy?"

"She was there that day, too. Looked at Calypso like she wanted to serve her under glass." Fred cocked his head, "Anyway, Mr. Washburn, sir, if you don't mind me saying so, you don't look well. I'd be happy to drive you up to the house in the golf cart Ms. Delia bought me. Would you let me?"

Fred was right, Grieg wasn't feeling well. Fred pushed GG back into his stable, shut the door, then pointed to a bright yellow golf cart with a green striped awning or Bikini top or whatever it was called. Fred helped him aboard when it was clear Grieg's doddering wouldn't get the job done.

They chatted like old buddies for the few minutes it took to reach the kitchen entrance to Meremer. Fred insisted on helping Grieg up the stairs to the door. Grieg didn't protest, he was wobblier than ever. He made it through the kitchen and up the stairs to the second floor by keeping his right hand planted firmly on a wall and his left on the stair rail.

In his father's study, he spread his map and notes out on the desk and gathered himself. A deep breath later, he dialed Amy Dunstable's family. It was an unpleasant conversation. Amy's mother sobbed between choked words while her father gulped. Between sobs and gulps, they recounted Amy's disappearance. On a lark, she had gone camping with her boyfriend and two other young couples over Spring Break. All six were students at California State University Fresno, known as Fresno State. On the first day, Amy hunted for sugar-pine cones near the campground. She returned with three perfect ten-inch cones, accusing her boyfriend of lurking in the trees to tease her.

Two nights later at two a.m., Amy left for the bathroom in pajamas and sneakers and was never seen again. Her family suspected her boyfriend, but the police never had. The other couples and the family tenting in the next site swore that when her boyfriend woke and found Amy gone, he searched the campground for her. He called the Forest Rangers then organized all the campers he could to help search the campground and immediate area. They fanned out checking behind trees, in gullies, buildings, under logs, in parked cars all to no avail. A larger search followed.

Grieg located the campground on his map and marked it with a blue X. It was south and over rough terrain from where Calypso's car was found but within the triangle between Highways 41 and 168.

He scribbled a note to call the Madera County Coroner regarding the cause of Amy's death. One thing he knew, a woman nervous about being followed wouldn't wander five miles in pajamas to Calypso's crash site. Someone had taken her, killed her then buried her remains at the site to protect Calypso. It was the only assumption that made sense. The only problem with that line of reasoning was that it meant Amy's killer knew the driver of the wrecked car was female, implicating Calypso.

Grieg shoved the note in his pocket and found another. It read: California Department of Motor Vehicles. He stared at it. He called 411 for the number. Connected, he asked the DMV clerk if a Jessamyn Amyna had a currently registered vehicle. The clerk snarled no. So, Grieg asked about a Callie Swale, Calypso Swale, Callie Culhane, or Swale anybody. He wrote each name down so he wouldn't forget he'd asked it. The clerk's response sounded straight out of Viper's foul little Chihuahua mouth. When Grieg tried for one more name, the clerk slammed the receiver into the cradle.

Grieg slapped the folded newspaper on the desk, trying to remember why he had it. Dr. Khalil's photo stared back at him. The reporter. He placed a call to the New York Times and was forwarded until the husky-voiced reporter answered. There was no big reveal. Khalil lived like a holy man because he had, as they said in Australia, a wonky heart. Everyone the reporter had interviewed claimed it was only a matter of time. Time, timing, Khalil survived Ray Washburn by three days. Ray, Khalil, and

Felix had talked via video call, Doug in the background. The two deaths days apart felt too coincidental.

Grieg folded the map and put it in the pocket of his sweatpants, then gathered the rest of his materials and crumpled them into a metal trash can. He opened a window, lit the papers, and stirred while they burned. He dumped the cooled ashes out the window. When all the ashes had drifted to the ground, Grieg balanced himself to his bedroom and pulled the map from his pocket.

A note to call the Madera County Coroner floated to the floor. He sprawled on his bed, stuck the thermometer in his mouth, and stared at the ceiling. The stars spun. His legs and fingers ached. The walk to the stables had worn him out. The thermometer beeped: 100 degrees. He considered calling Moms, decided against it. But did take another anti-inflammatory from the bottle on the nightstand by his bed.

He plumped a pillow behind his back and punched in the Madera County coroner's number. The case had been sent to the Fresno County Coroner. He called that office and identified himself as the CEO of WashEx. The woman who answered asked him why he was calling back. Had he called? He thought not and said as much. His call was forwarded with a sigh to the coroner of record. He, too, wondered why Grieg was calling but answered his questions with the patience born of explaining unnatural death to those sorrowing. The coroner was unable to identify the cause of death, but by the bits of evidence at hand and without specific knowledge of the case, the coroner set the time of death within the last three years.

Grieg wrote three years or less under the coroner's telephone number, then asked about the bits of evidence. The bones of one leg and a jawbone with a full set of teeth and a hank of black cloth. Grieg commiserated, thanking the coroner for his patience. Then thought to ask the coroner if his voice sounded different than it had during his prior call.

The coroner chuckled and suggested Grieg talk to his secretary. Annie, Delia, or Sally? The modus of Amy's death had value to one of them. Each had a reason to wonder. He suspected his mother was attempting to cover all the bases for him. Then he suspected Sally.

Out of curiosity, Grieg called Amy's family to ask what color pajamas Amy had been wearing when last seen. According to her hiccupping mother, the pajamas were white flannel with blue clouds and rainbows. Amy had gotten them for Christmas. Nothing black.

Grieg wrote three years by the coroner's telephone number then doodled subtracting it from four. Amy Dunstable had been held captive for over a year before she was killed. But why? And where? And by whom? Grieg entered the crash site coordinates on Google maps one more time. When the area came up as a satellite photo, the only structures within ten miles were on the Yellow Sky Holdings acreage.

X

Rafe whistled once then opened the cabin door. Jessie was no longer amazed at his ability to get to town and back so quickly if six hours was quick. She deduced he used a motorcycle or bicycle for transportation. Jessie sliced parsnips and carrots, and diced ham. Happily creating a new recipe, she dumped chunks of one of the nearly burned loaves of bread at the bottom of the Dutch oven then added a layer of diced ham and vegetables, followed by a layer of crumbs mixed with onion and chopped sorrel hoping to create a sort of crust.

Rafe plunked his knapsack and a ten-pound bag of flour on a chair. He fished in the front pocket of the pack, finding what he sought, he offered it to Jessie. Jessie wiped her hands on her jeans and took the small jewelry box from his hands. Rafe nodded for her to open it. She lifted the lid, then a pad of cotton. Rafe furrowed his brows, worried. She plucked the packing from the small gift exposing silver earrings, one of a horse at full gallop, the other of a horse grazing. She laughed at the perfection of the present.

"You like them?"

"Oh, Rafe, they're…" She pecked his cheek. "I love them."

Relief washed over his face. "Good. I saw them last trip and worried they'd be gone. I should have gotten them then and saved them for a special occasion."

"Like tonight?" Jessie asked, confused.

"What better way to say if Boomer ever touches you again, I'll kill him than a mismatched set of earrings?"

"I won't let him, and I won't let you waste your life avenging me if he does. I love my earrings. I'm putting them on right now." Jessie slipped the earrings into her ears, remembering the day she'd had them pierced, her best girlfriend by her side. Her friend cried when the needle passed through her ears. Jessie laughed, imagining her mother's reaction when she walked into the house with garnet studs in each lobe.

Rafe cocked his head, his eyes asking her to share her thoughts. She shook her head. He ran a hand down her arms. It felt too proprietary. She worried about what it might mean for Boomer if the two men ever came to blows. She needed to lighten up. She swung her head from side to side and crowed, "Does it look like the horses are trotting?"

Rafe's belly laugh echoed around the room. When silence returned, he finished unloading a small bag of tangerines and a head of celery. Jessie grabbed the celery, removed two stalks, and chopped them into her pie-ish thing. As she did, Rafe unwrapped six bulbs from a sheet of newspaper and placed them in an empty reed basket. He crumpled the paper and threw it on the logs by the fireplace. Jessie reached for the paper; he grabbed her wrist.

"They're narcissus bulbs." He explained, knowing any paper that made it to the cabin was used to wrap food for the root cellar or jump-start the fire. Particularly juicy articles were read aloud for entertainment, often with alternate outrageous endings. But eating narcissus caused convulsions, though dizziness or severe abdominal gas was more likely. None of the symptoms seemed pleasant. "I got the idea when I saw the shafts of some wild daffodils by the grapevines two days ago. I wanted to sneak the bulbs into the ground as a surprise."

"That's even better than the earrings! No, wait, it's not. But it is more perennial and thoughtful. I promise not to peep out the window while you plant."

Rafe blushed. Jessie adored his blushes. They started on his broad nose and spread down his arms to his strong hands. He studied her either unable or unwilling to move. There was little for him to admire just worn jeans, a T-shirt, under a tattered red and blue plaid flannel shirt dusted in breadcrumbs.

Five years ago, Jessie wouldn't have been caught dead mucking out Fructose's stall in the clothes she currently wore, sadly they were among her best. She was in better physical condition than at eighteen and an athlete due to the daily grind of living off the grid. The occasional *US Magazine* liberated from a store or from campers that came her way highlighted women who paid people to give them a body like hers. She liked her old one better, a little rounder, nice legs, and a high tight bottom from riding.

Rafe placed a hand lightly on her left shoulder. "Hikers found your car. It's all over town. The cops and the Forest Service dragged it out of the creek and towed it to the police impound station on Highway 49."

"You're sure it's mine?"

"Silver Lexus sedan, plates expired the year you showed up. I checked the creek on my way back, the wreckage is gone."

"What else…what else have you heard?"

"A Special Agent Dempsey from the Forest Service checked out the site according to Joe Ramirez at the CHiP substation. Joe said he was a tall guy, looked like he wasn't afraid of mountains and dirt." Rafe wrapped a comforting arm around her. "I didn't know the Forest Service had investigators. Did you?"

Jessie shook her head, seeing a tall, dark-haired man waiting for her in her garage. Fear tensed her stomach driving any rational thought aside. Another tall, dark man, then another…then… "Anything else?"

"Bones. Under the car, around the crash site, not that there were many to collect, a leg bone, a jaw maybe."

Jessie wiped her hands on the thighs of her jeans. The police would check the DNA. Her car, someone else's bones. They'd come. She had to think like them now, like a Washburn, like men who could smell tiny flakes of chemicals in the earth's crust. A shiver ran up the length of her body. Rafe held her tighter and kissed the top of her head. She leaned into him. "I'll keep you safe, girl."

Boomer knocked once then opened the door, eyeing Jessie in Rafe's arms. "What's happened?"

"Rangers came by."

"Here?"

"Here. Don't be bringing your shit down on us, Boomer. Stalk deer, not women. Okay?"

Ignoring the ice in Rafe's voice, Boomer answered, "I didn't hurt her. For Christ's sake, she hurt me. That woman just sat in that tent with the light on like nobody could see her playing with herself like a porn film on canvas."

"You think she was performing for you?" Rafe asked in a furry voice. Jessie ducked out from under Rafe's arm. Checked the kettle, the potpie was golden brown. Food might redirect the energy in the room...or not.

"She damn well knew or hoped someone was watching." Boomer edged into the room. Jessie filled their plates. Rafe put out the silverware. Boomer smoothed the crumpled newspaper on the bench seat of the table, concentrating on a story on the flip page. When Rafe's back was turned, Boomer tore a corner from the page, jammed it into the back pocket of his jeans, then crumpled and threw the remnants of the paper into the fire.

Jessie called the men to dinner. Boomer kept his eyes on Rafe as he sat at the table, and, incidentally, on the article in his pocket.

Boomer had been in the money jar. The lid was cross-threaded, and money was missing. It wasn't the first time he'd taken a dip. Jessie kept the jar on the kitchen shelf. It was a diversion. The last thing she wanted was either of the men to search the flour bin, dig in her closet, or start rummaging in the mine. Now, like the money, Boomer was gone.

Jessie shook Rafe awake. He'd stayed the night on a pallet in front of the fire. "What was in that newspaper? There was something in it you didn't want me to see. What?"

"You. A photograph of you in a slinky dress. An article all about you, Calypso Swale, heiress of Virginia Culhane. Culhane as on the Board of privately-held Washburn Exploration." Rafe stared at her. "Washburn Exploration is offering a reward for your return."

"How much?"

"Too much. Hard to resist."

"Are you implying that Boomer is going to cash in on me?"

"Boomer is an opportunist; this is an opportunity. He'll try for the money. I know he will. I'm not sure I can protect you from whatever WashEx can rain down, not like from the others."

"Others?"

"Others. Like those Forest Rangers yesterday. Like the men who periodically show up flashing their privileged selves around town. Why here?"

"I ran, Rafe. I ran from WashEx and my family. My half-brother and sister claimed I murdered my father. I took all the cash I could find and walked out of my life. Some part of each day, I relive the car crash that killed my parents, my siblings' anger, everything. My mother's neck snapped. The other car roaring around the corner out of control." She put her hand to her mouth. "In San Francisco, I saw articles followed by ads asking me to return. I didn't. I was too scared."

"Maybe the death of your parents gave you an excuse to run from a meaningless life. Look at you, look at what you've accomplished here. You're glowing right now."

"How could you possibly know what my life was like? My father told me to run. I did. That's all you need to know."

Rafe hugged her, "I read the article, remember?"

"My life may have been entitled, but it wasn't meaningless," Jessie muttered, grabbing a fistful of Rafe's T-shirt. "What am I going to do? I've been working with my seeds, getting ready to plant the spring crops. I have plans."

Stroking her hair, Rafe asked, "What is this about, Calypso Swale?"

"I swear I don't know!" she lied, quelling her desire to run to the mine. Of course, she knew what it was about. She'd be lucky to make it out alive.

"Let's start with your name."

"My parents were vacationing in Mustique. They were listening to a Taj Mahal song when my mother went into labor. My father named me after the song. My name is awful, I know it. I was teased about it all the time."

"Only the über rich would name a girl Calypso. You'd either have to grow up to be a lah-dee-dah or a hooker/pole dancer."

"My friends all called me Callie."

"But you were all lah-dee-dah. Social Register. According to the article, you're not some little rich girl who grew out of her desire for a pony, you were considered for the Olympic Equestrian Team."

"I was orphaned, instead."

"I love to watch you work Rex. You don't move, and he does exactly what you ask of him."

"You watch me?" She cocked her head. He smiled in response.

"Sometimes." Rafe fingered the ends of her hair.

"It's called dressage. Rex isn't very good at it, and I'm not either. Not anymore. Rex moves well over jumps. But he isn't my mount Fructose. I think the Olympic Committee wanted my horse more than me."

She backed out of Rafe's arms. He gripped her upper arm to keep her near. Why hadn't Rafe shown her the article? Why hadn't Boomer?

Outside, frost laced the ground in white. Clouds heaped up in the west, promising rain, snow, wind, or all three. The inside temperature was in the low forties. Rafe fairly leaped into his jeans and flannel shirt. She stoked the fire and started grits, ground with a pestle on a flat rock like the Ahwahnechee had. Her first attempt hadn't gone well, as so many of her experiments hadn't, but Jessie did get cornmeal out of the deal. She used the cornmeal to extend the sacred flour Rafe provided and to make cornbread that kept well like hardtack.

But she wanted hot breakfast cereal, not cornbread, and not the oatmeal Rafe carted up the mountain from time to time. Rafe suggested the corn needed to be nixtamalized and produced a how-to article from the library, which was good because she didn't know the definition of the word much less the science of it. Following the directions on the wrinkled photocopy, she layered her dried corn in a stone pot with ash from her kiln, poured water around the edges then soaked it before washing and drying it. The output was hominy. What surprised her was that the hominy ground with ease. The resulting grits were yummy served with fruit. Plus, whenever a hock of wild boar appeared on her porch, she had hominy for pozole.

"Talk to me," Rafe said, his elbow on the hewn trestle table, the sleeves of his plaid flannel shirt rolled up two turns, his hands interlaced. Jessie started to talk, and the whole inglorious truth tumbled out. Her parents, who lived on Long Island, took a co-op in New York City for her debutante season. She was an A-lister, so the nights of dancing and being wooed lined up in a parade through the winter months. Beau after beau tracked her down to the apartment on Central Park. A few of the young men were interesting, but most were self-absorbed and indolent.

Her father, Larch Swale, kept a limousine driver to livery Calypso to Fructose, stabled at Meremer on Long Island, allowing Callie to train whenever she had a free moment during her dazzling season. There wasn't a week she wasn't in the *New York Times* or a month she didn't make the pages of *Vanity Fair*. It could all go to a girl's head. She glanced at Rafe. He offered a hand to hold one of hers. She busied herself with breakfast, her mind racing over the months.

Her beaus began to meld like a box of crayons melted in the sun. She lumped them into categories ranging from dull but exceedingly rich to wild and desperately in need of a rich wife. Whenever she had a free moment after working Fructose, she hung out at the Southampton Hunt and Polo Club, often bumping into Sally Purdy leaning on the whitewashed fence or dancing divots back into the ground between chukkers. Sally was a boyish, skinny, old thing, but fun.

It was clear to anyone with eyes that Sally couldn't keep hers off the heir apparent, Grieg Washburn, who though a hell of a polo player was the very definition of a bumpkin. He hadn't a clue how to handle himself in society, he was a rude, cocky, and consummate nerd. They met twice. Her mother introduced them at a debutante party, and he spied on her at his doctoral award party thrown by the ever-opulent ex-Rockette, Delia Washburn.

The night of Washburn's graduation party, Calypso's father handed her an envelope. She's ripped it open in her excitement, unfolded it, and let out a whoop. She shouldn't have. Washburn junior's eyes slid over her father's shoulders and locked on the schematic. She folded her patent, knowing it was too late. Grieg Washburn shadowed her the rest of the night, drinking until he could barely stand. When the Swale's left the party, he roared after them--her.

Her father survived the accident, her mother hadn't, nor had the driver of the truck they'd struck. Callie knew her Olympic career was DOA, just like her mother. She blamed

Grieg Washburn, and, when she was honest, she blamed herself. If she hadn't been so damn cruel to him when they first met, maybe he wouldn't have stalked her that night. Too drunk to understand what he'd done; he destroyed her life, and any chance she had to be something more than a headline.

The minute the news of the accident hit the airwaves, Larch Swale's two older children circled his hospital bed like sharks in chummed water. Callie tried to keep them from her father, but they bullied their way in or finned or something. Her father clung to her, his fingers pinching and twisting the bloody skirt of her ballgown.

The gown had been a beautiful thing, rusty like the color of her eyes, tightly fitted to her form with a long swirl of beaded skirt. Beads bounced on the linoleum floor. Strands of thread hung where beads had been. One shimmering sleeve was torn, her skin bruised beneath. Her shoes were missing in action. She needed more sensible clothes. She began to obsess on bathing and changing into something practical so that she could sit with and protect her father, she opted for a cup of coffee.

When she returned, Larchmont Swale pulled her down to his lips, his chest heaving, and spoke his last words, shooing her away from his bedside. She walked out of the hospital, her patent jammed in her purse, taxied home, opened the safe, and grabbed what her father told her to take, a thick 8x11" envelope and a tin box.

She filled her super-sized suitcase with as many clothes as would fit, took her father's BMW and drove to Kennedy International Airport. She bought her way onto the first flight leaving for anywhere. Luckily, she had her passport, the jet landed in Miami. She took the next departure to Trinidad, then a hop to Mustique, having been born there, she had dual citizenship.

When she learned that her siblings clamored for her arrest, she changed her name, bought a new passport with what she discovered was a wad of cash in addition to yellowed ledger pages in the thick manila envelope. Newly minted as Amyna Jessym, she flew to San Francisco and melded into the Castro district, rebuilt her life, developed friends, worked her first actual job, and enjoyed what the City had to offer until the lean, dark-haired men came for her.

"Your father's last words?" Rafe's question startled her out of her reverie.

"His last word *was* run." She wiped her hands on an old linen towel, more interested in what Rafe gleaned from the article.

"From whom?" He refolded the cuffs on his shirt, they hadn't needed it. He was curious, and he was uncomfortable.

"Washburn."

Rafe furrowed his brows.

"The moment Dad died, my half-sister blocked the door, the hate in her eyes invaded me. I threw my coffee cup in the garbage, elbowed her aside, and walked out of the hospital. I kept going for the same reason Ray Washburn got his son out of town. I didn't want to spend my days in prison for a crime I didn't commit. Grieg's father bought him five years' supervisory probation despite his guilt. I didn't have a father or a mother. Just two siblings who hated me. What were my odds?"

"You changed your name, moved to San Francisco." He urged, pulling the worn cuffs of his thermal shirt down so that they showed below the rolled cuffs of his flannels.

Callie shook her head. He'd shot his cuffs like he wore a tuxedo. She blushed at the memory of Grieg Washburn giving her the finger as she swung away from him on the arm of a more suitable beau. "Sounds preposterously simpleminded, doesn't it? Still, it took them six months to find me."

"Four years this time. Why here?"

"Off the grid, no phones, no credit cards, no lines of contact, off their radar as long as nothing on the property changed." His interest alone ensured she would never tell him this land was hers, the mine perfect for her needs, her two male guards an unexpected benefit.

He bobbled his head, unhappy with the response. "Can I call you Calypso, you've kept me hostage for four years?"

"I'm no Greek nymph," Callie spooned hot grits into two bowls and joined Rafe at the table. "Let's eat. I'm tired of all this talk."

Rafe poured a wavy stream of syrup over his grits. "One last question. How much do you hate this Grieg Washburn?"

"He destroyed my life and got away with it."

XI

Delia strolled toward the sunny conservatory on the south side of Meremer, lured by the conspiratorial hush of Felix Highland's voice. He held a cellphone to his ear with one hand and leaned on the buffet with the other, his eyes studying a painting by an old Dutch master who had mastered light. A golden aura lit the woman and the cats toying with the hem of her apron in the frame. Felix fingered the painter's name longingly. Ray gave the painting to Delia when she asked for a cat. He was allergic. His solution, cats by an old Dutch master.

Delia hid behind a vase of palm-size, fragrant pink peonies set on a green marble table. She pinched her nose to stop a sneeze as she repositioned herself to comfortably listen to Felix's end of the conversation without being seen.

Felix fiddled with something in the left pocket of his gray flannel slacks. "Yes, you do have her coloring correct. Yes, the photograph in the newspaper was black and white, as you point out, but you could have found a dozen color photos of her on the internet. You need to provide a photograph of Calypso as proof."

Felix was the consummate banker, never riled, able to negotiate any deal, smooth, sleek, and stylish. If Delia liked that sort of man, she might have been attracted to him. Instead, every moment she was forced to spend with Highland reminded her of her gentle, silly, adoring Ray.

Felix shifted, adding in his best financier tone, "Don't threaten me." A squawk came through the receiver. "You listen to me!" Felix snapped, "I frankly don't care whether she's dead or alive, I need proof either way. Do you understand."

Felix listened. "Good. If you want the reward, you must do two things. Provide a photograph of the heiress as you so indelicately put it. Second, meet with a WashEx representative at a location *we* specify. Do you understand?"

The voice on the line gabbled like a pigeon in high dudgeon.

"You're rather worried about the woman you are betraying, aren't you?"

Felix listened. When the squawking stopped, Felix snarled, "The body by her car. Did you place it there? Remember, WashEx can find you and squash you wherever you are. All we need is your cell phone's location. Do you get that?"

The pigeon roared.

"See here," Felix said, "If you can't trust me, how can I possibly trust you? You are right, you do know the area."

Felix wrote something on the notepad kept by the house phone, pulled the sheet from the pad, and slid it into his pocket. "Send the photograph to this telephone number. If the photograph is of Calypso, we will confirm the meet. You will be paid when Calypso is returned to her family, not before."

The high-pitched male voice prattled, nervously.

"Preferably alive," Felix snorted.

Felix hung up and dialed a new number. Delia drifted toward the conservatory door preparatory to making a breathless entrance the moment the call ended. She grinned at her reflection in a mirror opposite, uncertain whether she was playing the Merna Loy or Barbara Stanwyck role. She cleaned up her lipstick with the tip of her little finger while checking for Felix's reflection in the mirror. He was still out of view, which meant she was out of his line of sight.

"Hugh," Felix said. "Another lead. Rough customer. He said he was calling from Oakhurst, California. He knew Calypso has red to chestnut hair and hazel eyes. Hard to surmise from a black and white photo. I'll text you his number."

Felix listened.

"No, no. I gave nothing away. He either will or won't text a photo of Calypso within two days. We can ID her then. Have Chief Willard contact Dempsey to follow up on the caller. Boomer...no last name. It shouldn't be hard to locate a man named Boomer in a Podunk town like Oakhurst. By the way, he claims Calypso is in danger. I couldn't help feeling it was a threat."

Felix listened again.

"Good, good. I assume Willard knows what he is doing. I'll feel better once Dempsey is contacted."

As Felix hung up, Delia swung into the conservatory, peonies fluttering in her wake. "Oh—I hope I didn't disturb you."

"Not at all, my dear." Felix crossed the distance between them in two strides. He kissed Delia's cheek then backed away. "I have the best news. We have a solid lead on Calypso. Finally. The right area. A description that would be hard to derive from a newspaper. It's quite hopeful."

Delia drew a deep breath and let it work through her diaphragm. "Next steps?"

"I called Hugh. It is in his hands now." Highland kissed her again, a peck really. She handed his smartphone to him. The incoming call originated from area code 303. She escorted Felix to the front door, praying it was the direction he intended. She guessed correctly. His chauffeur held the door open for him.

Felix kissed her again, on the lips this time, then tapped her nose. She smiled, concerned that she had overplayed her hand. "We are good together. Gossips are already talking of marriage."

"It seems soon even for our gossip mongers. And, certainly, you understand I can't commit to anyone but Grieg until he's well."

With a disdainful shake of his head, Felix climbed into his limousine. As soon as the car crackled out of the drive, Delia bounced up the stairs to the second floor and into Grieg's room. She opened the curtains, a rush of afternoon light left streamers on the rug. She shook Grieg awake. "Sit up!"

"Why?" He yawned.

"Griegs!" Delia threw her hands in the air, "Listen to this, someone telephoned Felix claiming to know where Calypso is. Felix asked the man to send a corroborating photo. Felix called Hugh. Hugh called Willard. I gleaned that they hope Special Agent Dempsey will meet the man in Oakhurst, California, in three days. Is Oakhurst within your triangle? Is it?"

Grieg nodded. Oakhurst was mid-way on the left leg of the triangle. The mountain town's central district was formed by two shopping centers, one anchored by a Von's grocery store and the other by a Raley's. Oakhurst seemed to have everything one needed, even a Starbucks.

"The man called from a 303-area code. Colorado. The whole state. The area code for Oakhurst is 559. So, either the man is visiting Oakhurst, or he borrowed someone's phone, or his area code doesn't reflect where he lives."

"Slow down, Moms, before you pop a stroke, please. I'm still fuzzy."

She cocked her head then shook down the thermometer and jammed it between Grieg's lips. With her hands on her hips, she said, "He could have stolen it."

"What?" Grieg muttered around the thermometer.

"The smartphone, silly. Anymore, people leave them on their table next to their coffee cups when they go to the bathroom at Starbucks. Everyone has one. No one is careful unless it is some fancy-pants newfangled model."

"You go to Starbucks?" He asked, removing the thermometer, 98.6 degrees. The second Dengue spike was over. "But he didn't have a photo? What kind of man expects ransom without corroboration?"

"He didn't kidnap her."

"Excuse me. He knows where she is, and he won't tell us until he gets payment. It sounds like ransom to me."

"No. Well, I don't know. Felix left after the phone call. I think to meet Hugh. I'm not sure."

"About what?" Sally Purdy asked, her piled-high hair artfully drifted from colorful fabric wound through it. The fabric matched her Boho dress. The straps of a dark brown leather bag occupied her right shoulder. "Did you tell him?" she asked, slipping into the room.

Delia shook her head. "He hasn't a smidge of fever."

Crossing to Grieg, Sally placed the back of her left hand on his left cheek. "You asked for the latest WET ledgers a few nights ago, my boy. I brought them by that very night, but you were grumpy in the extreme. I didn't know what to do with them having slipped them out of the safe. As majority owner, you have that right. I checked the Bylaws." She set her bag on his boyhood desk and pulled out two journals and the Annual Report.

"Did you peek?" Grieg asked, slipping into a robe to cover his bare chest and flannel pajama bottoms.

Sally shook her head. Delia had no such qualms. She opened one journal and thumbed through it, then did the same with the second. She huffed, slammed them shut, and stared at Sally. Grieg cocked his head. Moms gave a wiggle of her fingers to keep him quiet.

"What?" Sally whirled; her mouth pinched into a hardline.

"These are WET records, but they aren't current." Delia stared Sally down.

Sally threw her hands in the air. "Check the bindings! Check them."

Delia did.

"What are they, if they aren't what the bindings claim?" Sally asked. "Why would someone…who?"

"Who indeed. You tell me. You're the General Secretary, Sally Purdy. Who, besides you, has access to the records room?"

"Ray and Felix."

"And Hugh?" Delia positioned herself behind Grieg, her right hand on his left shoulder.

Sally shrugged, her fingers rapping a tattoo on her purse. She kept her fingernails short, manicured and polished. The current color was a light salmon that matched the same color in her dress.

"Order a safe. Have it installed and ensure I'm the only one with access. Put all the WET records in it, freeze online access. That means not even you, my girl. I don't want you in the middle of whatever this is," Grieg ordered.

"But I'm General Secretary. And my father is regent."

"Do it, Sal, or find a new job."

Sally grabbed the journals and the Annual Report from Delia, jammed them back in her purse and stormed out the door, muttering, "Who the hell does he think he is?"

Grieg couldn't resist snarling, "Your paycheck, damn it!"

Delia spied down the hall until Sally disappeared then listened for her descent down the stairs. "What the hell?" Delia asked, turning into the room.

"She's lying." Grieg untied his robe and slung it over the headboard of his boyhood bed. Chilled without the extra layer, he dug around in a drawer slipping on a worn Yale-blue sweatshirt, Bulldogs stenciled on the chest in gray.

"Why? Why would she, where can she go after this, no one would hire her, a General Secretary who can't keep track of the company records." Delia tugged the sweatshirt down and smoothed it over her son's broad shoulders. He was still pale. She ticked the unshaven cleft in his chin.

"She's protecting Hugh and Gilft. I wasn't kidding Gilft's a charming, monied, swaggering bully."

"Sally waited for you for a long time, he's what's left. And, besides, leave out the bully, though you just gave a good imitation of one, and Gilft could be your twin," Moms responded.

"Thanks, I'll add it to the accumulating list: charming, monied, swaggering, offensive, risk-taking, impulsive, murdering bully. How am I doing?"

"You're a pisser, my boy!" Moms responded in her best imitation of Sally Purdy.

"Did you call the Fresno County coroner pretending to be my secretary?"

"No. If I had, I would have called myself Sally Purdy."

Grieg chuckled, appreciatively. "So, how do you interpret what you overheard between Felix and the man on the phone."

Delia responded to her son's grin with a sigh, knowing that the list of his evils was even longer. The Board believed that Grieg was destroying WashEx by driving it away from its traditional moorings in oil. She'd heard moron, idiot, dolt, and worse applied to a man who graduated top of his class, gotten his doctorate in record time, and was a future-facing genius, not unlike Khalil. A shiver overtook her. Grieg threw an arm around her shoulders. She snuggled into the cusp of his, missing her husband more than she thought possible.

With a sigh, she said, "The man's name is Boomer. Special Agent Dempsey will meet him, but only if he produces a picture of Calypso. One thing, though, this Boomer implied that Calypso was endangered."

"By what, whom?"

Delia shook her head. She ducked out of Grieg's arm to pull the notepad from her pocket. "I did the Nancy Drew thing with a lead pencil and shaded the impression in the notepad paper. The meet will be at a restaurant called Pete's Place on Thursday at 9:00 a.m."

"This Boomer?"

"You can't really call a man Boomer. It has to be a pseudonym. That's what! So picky."

"Three days?" Grieg cocked his head. Delia pursed her lips. "Number please, Moms." He knew that it had only taken a glance for her to get and retain the number, though it was a skill commonly applied to menus and objects with dollar signs.

He dialed the 303 number Delia rattled off. A woman answered with a chipper hello.

"I must have the wrong number," Grieg responded.

"Look, I'm getting tired of this. I'll tell you what I told the last two callers. No one used this phone. It is never out of my hands or sight."

"Where are you?" Grieg asked.

"Tenaya Lodge in Fish Camp, California."

"Did the others ask you that, too?"

"Yes. I'm still at the Lodge. Now quit bugging me!"

The others? A Highland, SA Dempsey, Doug Purdy? Someone else? Who besides WashEx had an interest in Calypso's reappearance? He returned to his desk, took out his map, and unfolded it. Grieg tapped Fish Camp with a pencil and grinned. Moms peered over his right shoulder. "What's making you happy? The thought of going out into the wilds weak as a kitten or facing down death?"

Still tapping, Grieg said, "I'm going for Calypso. I need someone back here I can trust."

Delia laughed. "My job is to make sure no one but you becomes CEO so I can keep Meremer. Your job is to figure out what is going on. Why the IPO? Why Calypso now? Why Pops?"

"Why Khalil? Why run me off the road."

"Exactly."

"Back a few. Why Calypso now? Do you think someone knew about the wreck and waited until Pops was dead? To make me squirm, go bats with guilt, do something rash, and end up in jail?"

"Exactly."

"Moms, you're infuriating me."

"Now you know how it's been to be your mother." She gave a beatific grin and swirled out of the room. Stage-turned at the door and added, "Clean up the mess you made in your father's study, will you."

"Why? Does he need it?"

She slammed the bedroom door behind her.

XII

Callie dreamed that she and Fructose were taking the final jump in a timed event at the Olympics. Fructose clipped the top post. Callie flew over his head, flailing toward the hoof-compacted earth. She woke. Rafe held her, one arm under her pillow the other stroking her right arm. A tattoo of a bullet piercing an eye blazed lurid against the muscle of his right bicep. She pulled away.

"Don't do that?" he soothed. "I'm all that's between you and losing everything."

"Maybe." Callie said, pulling her jeans from the hearth, "but right now, we need breakfast."

"Right now, we need to talk about next steps. They're coming for you, Callie. I've got a motorcycle with an old sidecar. We can get away in that."

"How can you be sure? What makes you think I won't welcome it? Sometimes I go into my closet and fondle the dresses I had in the car the night I crashed."

"I know." Rafe smoothed his hands over her shoulders and down her arms to her fingertips.

Her eyes stayed on the bullet tattoo. As the bicep rippled, the bullet moved. It was disconcertingly not Semper Fi or Mom. "You know?"

His caramel-brown eyes narrowed. A rumble then a roar swooped over the cabin. The embers glowed in the hearth, and reedy trails of smoke vaporized before reaching the chill morning air. The cabin was wrapped in the half-dim of early morning, the mountains blocking the eastern sun. Rex and Frisco were stabled in the shed under the trees. Nothing else stirred.

The helicopter made another low pass. Rafe placed his hand over Callie's mouth, pinning her to the mat in front of the fire with his legs. She shoved to get him off. He wrestled her under him.

"Sorry," he huffed, removing his hand from her mouth. "We don't know where Boomer is, or who he has sicced on you. One way or another hell comes today, I can feel it. I can feel things closing in on us."

"Me. They are after me!" Callie rolled and scrambled to standing, slipping on her jeans and a shirt. "This is about me!"

"I won't let them take you or harm you. Jessie, Callie, we're family, right? I'm committed to keeping you to myself, keeping you safe."

Rafe dressed. Callie turned away. He grabbed her chin and turned her face to his. He kissed her hard, as though it proved he could keep her hunters at bay. She buttoned her flannel shirt to avoid further contact though he ran his hands down the sleeves of her shirt.

The helicopter swooped back over the cabin. The logs shuddered as the massive blades whipped the trees into a frenzy. The chopper hovered overhead its updraft sucking air from under the cabin. Frisco screamed. The chickens gabbled in terror.

Rafe grabbed Callie's arm, dragged her into the bedroom, and slammed the door. Callie pounded on the door. He set the bar lock. She ran to the window.

The chopper landed in the pasture. A man in a blue windbreaker with Special Agent stenciled on the back, and a California Highway Patrolman dismounted, cocking shotguns as they came. Callie dropped the curtains into place. The SA knocked the butt end of his gun on the front door. "Special

Agent Dempsey and Patrolman Ramirez, open up, now," the SA barked.

"Just a second," Rafe responded. The cabin door squeaked open. Callie swung a crappy paint-by-number of El Capitan aside and peered through a knothole in the bedroom door. "Sir," Rafe said, stuffing his shirt into a faded, torn pair of button-fly jeans, as though they'd caught him dressing.

Ramirez barged in stomping his feet on the timbers loud enough to bring worms to the surface of the damp earth beneath. Callie dropped the painting into place and rolled under her narrow bed. She piled blankets, dirty clothes, rugs to the front of her, then jammed her back against the outside wall.

"Why's this door locked, Rafe?" Ramirez asked, rattling the bedroom door.

"Hell, if I know, Jaime," Rafe responded, signaling Callie that he knew Ramirez. "The bar drops. The damn drop lock won't keep anyone out."

"It could keep someone in." The door opened, Ramirez called, "Anybody in there?"

"There's a window in that room. Glass. And, a chair. A person could get out easy enough," Rafe noted, close on Ramirez's heels.

Ramirez crossed to the window and checked the sash. The sash lock was open. In fact, the window was propped open two-inches at the bottom with a stick as a carbon monoxide deterrent. With a humph, Ramirez strode to the closet. Metal hangars squealed on the wooden clothes rod. He knocked on the back wall and sides of the cabinet, hollow thumps indicating empty space beyond. He unzipped her suit bag, by the quiet Callie guessed he was fingering her Stella McCarthy or maybe the Valentino. Done with the closet, he opened the top drawer of the three-legged chest of drawers. He must have held up something feminine.

Rafe cleared his throat, huskily, and said, "You know I'm the caretaker. What you see was here when I started working.

Maybe the wife of the prior caretaker. I wouldn't know. I don't come in this room. The reason it's locked."

Ramirez huffed. He strode to the bed and bounced on the mattress. Callie flattened. Not enough.

"What's under here?" Ramirez asked, jamming the barrel of his rifle repeatedly into the blankets massed under the bed. Callie sucked in her stomach like that half-inch would matter. Done with the side, the cop jabbed the gun barrel into the bedding at the foot of the bed. Callie's legs scraped as she tucked them in. She held her breath, waiting to be discovered.

"Anything?" SA Dempsey asked from the doorframe.

"No, nothing here, sir. Well, women's clothes, but we're not looking for someone who'd have clothes. Plus, as expensive as they are, they're out of date."

Out of date, what were women wearing now? Those dresses were Callie's connection to who she was, if they were outdated, then she was. She grabbed an armful of blankets for comfort. The cop shuffled then dropped onto the bed. The old springs hung, squashing Callie to the floor.

"Beds made," Ramirez noted.

"Then, like the man said, he doesn't go in there," Dempsey responded.

"Damn it!" Rafe roared, sounding pissed and dangerous. Callie prayed he would contain himself long enough to deal with the cops and get her out from under the bed. She wasn't sure she could stand the heat and dust much longer. His next words were controlled, "I have a mind to call…"

Dempsey stepped through the doorframe. "No need. A girl disappeared from Summerdale campground. Her parents have stirred up a shitstorm. We're searching the known sites and encampments. And, there's the Swale woman, wouldn't hurt if we turned her up, too."

Callie mulled over being a woman and not a girl, when had that happened, was there some moment when you passed from joy into drudgery, a look, the length of a hem, deepened lines at the corner of your mouth. Her girlhood, her days of teasing, and being chased by the right sort of men had fled. She clung to the pillow.

"No women here," Rafe said, shifting his weight.

"You seem a mite nervous, what's up?" Dempsey asked.

"What makes you ask?"

"A lot of swanky women's clothes. And, as you say, no women. We found Swale's car, blood, but not her bones. The bones were Amy Dunstable's, missing four years and now these clothes, maybe four-five years past due."

"Like I said, stuff was here. I stay here 'til summer, no one's out trying to mine iron or shoot game when the snow is flying. Otherwise, I live up north on the property all the better to catch trespassers off guard."

"Seen anything unusual in the last few days?" Ramirez sat up, his feet on the floor. Callie took the opportunity to uncover her head and face.

"Just you guys and a couple of mounted Forest Rangers. I'm surprised they didn't tell you they'd been here."

Ramirez eased into the main room. Dempsey followed, leaving the bedroom door open and the impression that Ramirez and Dempsey had spoken to the Park Rangers. "We checked the lean-to down near the gate. That's Boomer's place, right?"

Rafe closed and barred the door, asking, "Hope you don't mind?"

"We need to get going, we have a couple of more sites to check. Your summer place and another higher up White Chief." Dempsey rattled the door. "Funny thing to keep it locked why not sleep in it?" He kicked the bedroll by the fire.

"Like I said, I don't go in there. The room gives me the creeps. I can save you some time, nothing at my place."

"We'll buzz it to see if any bears come out. Thanks for the info," Ramirez said, stepping onto the porch. Dempsey's footsteps landed next.

"Anytime, glad to help," Rafe called after them.

Ramirez clomped down the stairs. Callie waited for Dempsey then counted to sixty before rolling out from under the bed. She stayed on the floor until Rafe whistled all clear. She peeked out the window. Rafe waved as the two men mounted the chopper. The blades wound up, creating a dust devil that deposited a layer of fine silt on the bedroom floor.

Rafe slammed through the cabin door and unbarred the bedroom door. Callie ran into his arms. He clutched her to him, holding her head to his chest until she gasped for air.

"The poor girl. Her parents." Callie said, every word jumping with nerves. "Do you suppose…"

"I suppose nothing, except that Dempsey is Federal and he's got a bee under his bonnet. I'm going into town to create a diversion. Anyone comes near this place, use your hidey-hole. Don't come out until you hear my whistle. I'll be back by tomorrow night at the latest. Think about what you need, gather some stuff up. I'm taking you out of here tomorrow night. Idaho isn't that far, maybe Montana, we can stay lost there."

Callie backed out of Rafe's arms, WashEx and Montana were synonyms, let him believe there was somewhere safe he could take her. He kissed the top of her head.

"Be careful. Please!"

Rafe grabbed his rifle and strode out the door. Callie watched until he was out of sight. Worried he might circle back to check on her, she bundled a can of spam, some beans, and a half-loaf of bread in a kitchen towel then added her tin cup and a flashlight. Once she had the possibles-pack Rafe demanded ready, she set about her day confident she couldn't be caught by surprise. She had enough food hidden in the mine to keep her for weeks, if necessary.

XIII

Highland's rounded vowels didn't fool Boomer, the man was mean. Boomer had warned Highland not to upset Calypso's tenuous living arrangement. Highland misinterpreted the warning, convincing Boomer that some suave gunman would be sent to deal with him. Which was all to the good, since it would take a hired gun to get Calypso out alive.

Boomer studied the woman whose phone he had hijacked. She was slender, toned, and currently hot under the collar, her blond ponytail bobbing with her ire. Highland redialed Blondie's number as Boomer knew he would. The woman answered. The second caller surprised him, the third one confounded him.

Borrowing her phone had been stunningly simple. Blondie set it on an end table in the lobby. Preoccupied, she left it when she went for a cup of coffee at a small wheeled cart like a tea cart, as though Boomer knew what the heck a tea cart was. As she doctored the mix, Boomer slipped the woman's phone into one of the many pockets of his fishing vest, drifted onto the stone patio, and made his call. Blondie sat down, put down her coffee, picked up a magazine, and read. Call finished; Boomer cruised past, setting her phone on the corner of the table behind her right elbow. When the first call came, she reached for her phone and answered it, blabbing her location to all three callers.

Returning the phone to the mouthy broad was a regrettable mistake! WashEx would send a man to stakeout Tenaya Lodge.

They had that kind of money. Boomer's stomach churned. He was in this mess to save Jessie, not for the reward, he had plenty. She wouldn't see it that way. Rafe wouldn't let her, he'd whisper lies, lies with just enough truth to make them beguilingly believable, for instance, the current one about the lady in the tent. Boomer ran a finger over the crusty wounds.

Now, he needed to heist another phone to capture Calypso Swale's image. Boomer eyed the crowded lobby. If he chose carefully, he'd have Calypso's photo taken and sent before the cellphone was missed. Then, all he had to do was arrive at Pete's Place on Thursday for the meet. If the guy they sent smelled right, Boomer would take him to Calypso. Damn, it was hard to think of Jessie by the name of the swanky dame in the newspaper article. If the guy smelled, Boomer would still get the money so that Jessie could escape and start over.

He could tell by Highland's upper-crust voice that the man thought women were arm wear. Boomer figured Highland didn't know Ms. Swale. She'd tie his dick in a knot and yank. As for Rafe, the son-of-a-bitch was getting way too big for his britches. Threatening him, telling him what to do, following him.

Rafe thought Calypso was all hot for him, that he was her big protector. But nothing was going on there, nothing meaningful. Boomer knew what a woman looked like when she was ripe. Jessie wasn't ripe, not for Rafe and not for him, no matter how much Rafe wanted it, and he wanted it bad. Right from the start. The snowy night Jessie arrived as soon as Boomer turned his back, Rafe ran his hands down her icy body.

Goddamn Rafe!

Jessie was beautiful. All muscle like a finely tuned Ferrari, he bet she did 150 miles an hour in bed. Whenever he could, Boomer sneaked his nose into the thick mane of her chestnut hair and reeled from the scent of her homemade shampoo. She needed to smile more like she did when she rode one of her horses. He knew her schedule and spied when she worked

Frisco. When she took Rex out, Boomer paralleled them in the trees hoping to be on hand if the horse balked a fence or threw her. It was a small offering. Jessie was only the second person in his life who cared whether he lived or died.

His father had run him off when he was fourteen. And, for what? The girl next door? Sure, he peeped, but he never touched her. Never. Same as the beauty in the tent. He trailed her as she strolled the trails, dressed in hiking pants, the kind you can zip off to make shorts. She had. She didn't shave her legs. She didn't make a phone call in the three days he observed. She ignored nearby campers. She sang to herself in a soft alto voice, read, and played with herself crooning.

Boomer shook his head to get back on task. He needed a phone with a high-resolution camera, like an iPhone or Samsung. Maybe an older iPhone so the owner wouldn't go ballistic.

An older couple sauntered into the lounge holding hands. The man's hair was salt and pepper, his wife's a soft brown with blond streaks. They were nicely dressed, but not in designer wear. She had a lovely, gentle smile, her husband adored her. Her diamonds were impressive, he wore an onyx ring with a diamond center. They found a seat in front of the open-hearth fireplace. She began to crochet. Her husband pulled a flip phone from a hip holster and dialed. No go.

A man in a corduroy suit coat and blue jeans strolled past. His clothes put him in the sixty-year-old range. The phone case at his waist was oblong, a smartphone of some sort. He sat. The phone stayed at his waist under a fold of soon to be fat. No go.

Boomer leaned against the gray river stone wall near the lobby's entrance watching tourists come and go. An older woman, soft around her edges, her hair laced with gray was at the gift shop counter paying for pricy geegaws. She emptied her purse to find her wallet, setting a bejeweled iPhone case to one side.

Boomer stepped into the store, grabbed a bottle of water, joining her at the checkout counter. He covered her phone with his forearm, trying to look friendly. The woman sniffed then stepped to her right, shoveling her belongings into her purse. It was clear she wanted to be anywhere but next to Boomer Bognavich.

The moment she trotted out of the store, Boomer bought the bottled water and a San Francisco Chronicle for the day's article on Calypso Swale. This one railed poetically about her horsemanship and her plans to become an Olympian before tragedy struck. The smarmy article made Boomer gag.

He tapped the stolen phone with his index finger, hoping he didn't need a password for access. The screen and apps lit up. His good luck. The owner hadn't used it in four days, unlike the kids now who couldn't carry a thought without checking their phones first. Perfect. She wouldn't miss it for a few hours or days. He took a picture of the faux-rustic lodge. The camera was excellent.

He jammed the phone in a pocket of his fishing vest and trotted down a hiking trail that led to a path that wound its way to Jessie's cabin. As he walked, he wondered if Jessie had ever wondered whose food was on the shelves, whose life she interrupted when she arrived that snowy night.

The deep-cell battery was drained, so Callie pedaled and knitted, enjoying a day without men. Rafe regularly took Callie's chicken eggs to a couple who lived higher up off the grid. They had goats. The woman spun wool from their shearing. It was hand-carded and soft to touch. Callie loved working with it. The yarn was always natural in color, which meant black, brown, or white. Everything here was so dear; cloth, thread, rope, seeds, coffee…everything. Her latest creation was a thick double-knit afghan to replace the worn one occupying her bed.

She loved the soft light of morning when chill hung in the air. It was the perfect time to pedal and reflect. She noodled over her family's story, wondering how it had all gone so horribly wrong.

Her father, Larch Swale, fell in love with the myth of the Washburn dynasty. Articles rhapsodized Ray Washburn, descended from Montana cowboys, to whom minerals and oil attached themselves as though he and they were magnetized. And, if Ray Washburn was a superconductor, his son was destined to be a supercollider until, of course, he embedded a stolen SUV into a Cadillac.

The Washburns made dollars out of the periodic table. Larch Swale did what he could; it turns out he was a master organizer. He kept WashEx tuned like his Lamborghini. Ray gave him a few of the family shares in a vote of confidence then pointed his hapless, drunken son Larch's way. It had all been over so fast.

Sometimes, not often, Callie wondered what would have happened if she had stayed, taken the heat under oath then popped her patent on them. Disaster. That's what.

Branches rustled, she looked up distractedly from her knitting, squinting into the dense timber on her left in time to see a bright flash of light. She dropped her knitting, but not her needles. Leaving a trail of yarn, she ran for the tree line, the knitting needles jammed between her fingers, the points at the ready.

Boomer slunk out of the trees. Callie thought nothing of it. Boomer slunk everywhere he went. He was like a coyote that way. She lowered the needles to her side.

"I saw a light flash," she sniped.

"Nope. Maybe this, I brought you this." He held up a keychain with a shiny bauble at the tip and a key on the ring.

"Either you're giving me a free car, or you've been breaking and entering again?"

"Nope. I found it. Thought you'd like the bobble, it's pretty." Boomer stuffed his hands in his pockets. "Rafe here?"

"No," Callie said.

"Just wondering if I could take a dip in the rainwater."

She gestured toward the pond. Boomer whistled happily as he walked through the knee-high grass towards a small basin of diverted water. She left him to it, the last thing she wanted to see was a naked, scrawny, bug-infested Boomer.

Pedaling and knitting, Callie wondered why Boomer wanted to bathe, given his belief that soap stole your karma. She considered sneaking to the pool for a peek. The thought made her cringe. Still, she was tempted to go through the pockets of his clothes while he scrubbed in hopes of finding the camera or smartphone that he'd used to snap her picture. He wore a rasty fishing vest day in and day out, in or out of season, each pocket filled with hidden treasures, searching it would be too much of a violation. She shook her head and pedaled.

Boomer felt clean by his swagger as he waved and walked into the timber. Clean, Boomer looked no different than dirty. No matter how many times you bathe, if you put on the same clothes, it results in the same smell. Like his clothes, his head hadn't been touched by water or soap, leaving the encampment of vermin that lived in his greasy locks to live well and multiply.

The green battery light lit. Callie brought out her jars of seed, plain white paper, and a straight cardboard piece from the back of a cereal box saved as a ruler. Singing a song popular five years before, she laid out her garden. She designated Rafe's narcissus bulbs for the edges hoping that with one bite gophers might seek nourishment elsewhere. She drew, her left-handed right-sloping printing carefully delineating each plot.

The distinctive whap-whap of a helicopter broke her concentration. She gathered her materials and dodged into the cabin. A fire smoldered in the fireplace. She closed the damper and opened a window. Helicopters rotored by from time to time, hosting people scouting property or the U.S. Forest Service keeping an eye out for fires. What they didn't do was hover over private property. This one did.

It swooped so low over the pasture she feared it would land then roared off down the mountain toward Fresno, the message clear, they were coming, Boomer or no.

Callie jogged to the mine. She inventoried the food stored on shelves in a hidey-hole. When she was sure no one followed, she ducked down a long tunnel. Electric lights flashed on as she neared a bolted door. She used her pocket-knife with the screwdriver to unscrew the bolts and dodged through the opening. Lights strung around the perimeter lit the large dugout.

Her engine grumbled along. She stopped it, counted to sixty, then pushed a button. It cranked back up. Maybe she had found the solution. But how many starts and stops would the chemicals sustain? She patted the repurposed John Deere tractor engine then left, bolting the door after her. Reassured her secret was safe, she took the time to straighten the skull and crossbones that warned of cave collapse.

XIV

Grieg slipped into jeans, an olive drab T-shirt and a canvas overshirt straight from the L.L. Bean catalog, feeling at once like his rock hound self. The self he had planned on being, a wildcatting mineral monger like his father. Doug was an oilman, uncomfortable with anything that didn't gush black. Which was why Doug wanted to return WashEx to its roots. Moms claimed Doug had flown to America Samoa, Grieg prayed he hadn't. Doug would make some small mistake, as in telling the locals that the ground was full of yttrium and europium and possibly other rare elements essential for smartphones, lenses, even hybrid vehicles, and blow the deal. Or perhaps that was what Doug intended, planning to claim that the enterprise had been a misguided risk-taking, sneaky, con game Grieg dreamed up to drive WashEx to ruin.

If so, Doug would have a hard time selling it. The Japanese had located a similar deposit on one of their islands. Like Japan, the U.S. needed the chemicals for production, and WashEx needed it to build out Callie's patent. The island would be underwater by the end of the century unless its protective reefs were enhanced. WashEx could do that, but their price was mining and mineral rights that would continue long after the island was subsumed.

With a deep sigh, Grieg made reservations to FAT, the acronym for the Fresno Air Terminal, and the butt-end of pilot jokes everywhere. He called Judge Burridge, promising to turn himself in five days to the day. Burridge took three deep breaths and consented.

Grieg considered his situation, WashEx was one death from the votes needed to release an IPO. And, Big Oil, two graves from ensuring Calypso Swale's patent never saw the light of day. Somehow, he needed to keep both he and Calypso alive, and if not both, Calypso.

Moms drove him to Kennedy International Airport. Grieg gave her a peck on the cheek, squeezed her left shoulder, then hefted his knapsack on his right, ready for adventure. The weight almost brought him to his knees. Moms called, "Griegs. If your temperature tops 100.01, go to the nearest Emergency Room. Promise."

"If you promise to identify Yellow Sky Cloud."

She laughed, "I was told he looks like a young Anthony Quinn." He snickered and waved, wishing later he had kissed her goodbye.

The wheels of his flight bumping to a stop on a runway at Fresno-Yosemite International Airport waked him in his first-class seat. Grieg pulled his knapsack from the overhead, shrugged into the straps, readjusted his load, and proceeded down the jetway into the terminal.

During the long walk from the gate, he studied anyone who glanced his way. He knew he wasn't the only one hunting Calypso. Dempsey, with Willard, would scout the property before they met Boomer, and there would be others, some to save, some to destroy what Calypso had built. As for him, if he rescued her, he hoped she would forgive him for killing her family and her future. In this fairy tale world, he'd get a big sloppy kiss then wave goodbye with a *what might have been* smile, leaving her happy on her mountain.

If she didn't shoot him on sight.

The terminal was tidy and easily navigated, as was the onsite rental car lot. A bright red Jeep awaited him. He returned to the desk for something less Magnum P.I. The Jeep was the only 4-wheel drive they had.

He exited the lot in all his red splendor, eventually merging onto Highway 41 north. Roughly ten miles later, the road narrowed to two-lanes then wandered through rolling green hills spiced by chunks of granite jarred into place with a heave of the earth's crust. Valley oak trees shaded verdant pastures of grazing cattle. Streams trickled then eddied around rocks, pooling deliciously for herons, horses, and wildlife.

After an Indian gambling casino, looking more like a Tibetan monastery than a den of iniquity, Coarsegold, the one-stoplight Gold Rush town of strip malls and gas stations, appeared. The road continued through the village following a bounding stream. The remains of a roadhouse now frequented by the ghosts of two-steppers, drunks, and steak-eaters dominated one sweeping corner, shortly after which the highway began to climb. After Deadwood summit, the road descended into Oakhurst twelve-hundred feet below. There were no guardrails along the curvy drive, just a freefall ricocheting between rocks and trees before a plunge into someone's home.

In town, Pete's Place was on the right at a stoplight. A little further up the road, Grieg checked out the chain motel holding his reservations. It occupied the side of a hill, a steep road wound from the lobby and restaurant level to the rooms. He pulled off to check the restaurant's hours.

He had until 8:00 pm to check-in and get a meal. Grieg continued up Highway 41 toward Tenaya Lodge, planning to locate the owner of the phone Boomer had used to call Felix, hoping to be the first to interview her, worried his competition, whoever he, she, or it was, had beat him there. Tall, dark, lean, and male, he guessed.

The drive up the mountain was twisty. Pines, ravaged by bark beetle blight, dotted the hillsides, the bark of their trunks a distinctive cinnamon color, their branches empty of pine needles. Where trees had died, others clung to life, making it difficult to tell if the forest was dying or remerging. Grieg chose the latter.

Seeing a sign announcing the town of Fish Camp, he passed the entrance to Tenaya Lodge. Fish Camp turned out to be a redwood-sided general store, a post office, and a closed gas station. He pulled into the store parking lot. Neon signs advertising beer hung on the faux log cabin exterior. Draped Tyvek signs proclaimed the quality of live bait sold within.

A bell jangled as Grieg opened the door. A young man with a happy grin popped up from behind the counter, wiping his hands on a paper towel.

"Sorry, I was cleaning. Can't stand the feel of the cleaning agent." He waggled his fingers. "Can I help you?"

"Not sure," Grieg answered while checking out the shelves and a glass display case. The store was stocked with crackers and cheese, nuts, sandwich meat, a few oranges and apples, and basic personal needs. It sold everything a resort gift shop might only grittier and more to the point, including a shelf of bandages beside stacked cases of beer. Grieg picked out an apple and took it to the counter.

"You live up here," Grieg asked the kid who was, according to his name tag, Dennis from Sugar Pine.

Dennis from Sugar Pine nodded his head.

"Then, you know everybody who lives in the vicinity?"

"Know the ones that come in here to shop. Which is mostly everyone. Sooner or later, they need something between trips to Oakhurst. Of course, we get lots of tourists."

"Do you know a man named Boomer?"

"Sure, he's kind of a character around here. He lives off White Chief Mountain somewhere. I guess. Hard to know, but I've seen him walk up that way."

"Anything you can pass on about this Boomer?" Grieg bit into his apple, it was mealy from being in storage. Still, the flavor was decent.

"Lots of talk, no proof. I heard he raids tents in the park."

"No job?" Grieg took another bite of the apple.

Dennis shook his head, adding, "He worked for Roads two summers ago. The way he lives, that money could last him another year."

"Which is?"

"Off the grid on the mountain."

"Ever see him with a woman?" Grieg asked, his eyes on the apple to mask his curiosity.

"No, but I've heard rumors that he can't keep his eyes off them. A peeper. I'm not sure I buy that. Ya know. He doesn't shoplift. That sounds stupid, but someone low on morals wouldn't hesitate to shoplift. At least in my book. And, he carries himself like something bad happened to him, you know?"

Grieg nodded. If Dennis was right, Grieg had his common ground for a conversation with Boomer. The kid cocked his head. Grieg realized he hadn't paid for the apple. He dug in the pocket of his jeans for coins. Dennis said, "They're by the pound."

Grieg went back to the bin and picked the roundest apple he could find and made a show of placing it on the scale. He didn't want to be known as a shoplifter either, something else he and Boomer had in common.

"That'll be $1.20."

"This Boomer never lifts anything?" Grieg asked, counting change onto the counter.

Dennis shook his head.

"I passed Tenaya Lodge on my way here. Is the Lodge open to the public or only to people with reservations?"

"Public. They've got a gift shop, liquor store, spa, and restaurant you could check them out. Lots of folks go in there that aren't staying the night. Popular place."

Grieg waved his half-eaten apple, the bell jingled him out the door.

Grieg pulled his police-repellant red Jeep onto Highway 41 toward Oakhurst, a quarter-mile later multi-colored ledgestone pillars announced Tenaya Lodge. According to a sign on one post, the lodge was hiring. Business must be good. He turned in and drove up a long drive to a parking lot.

He nosed the Jeep in under a madrone at the far edge of the lot then checked out White Chief Mountain on Google maps. Roads wound up and around the mountain deep into the Sierra National Forest and eventually into Yosemite National Park.

He finished his apple while using the note feature on his phone to capture his thoughts. What Grieg didn't want was to run into more than he could handle and as tired as he was from the flight, drive, and the two stairs into the Fish Camp general store, anything was too much.

On a lark, he typed in Yellow Sky Cloud, there seemed a certain symmetry with White Chief. Nothing in the area. Google did suggest Yellow Sky, Montana. He clicked on the reference for chuckles. A photograph of the clapboard general store popped up, the population was 253, and the main occupation was ranching.

The section in Wikipedia that describes founding and naming chronicled Obadiah Washburn homesteading in 1856. Old Obadiah named his ranch Yellow Sky poetically enough because of the morning sky. Once a railhead was established for Washburn cattle, people settled there. Native American troubles brewed in the 1870s, not too surprising since Yellow Sky was in the southeastern part of Montana. Interesting, but another Yellow Sky Cloud dead-end.

Grieg climbed out of the car, reeled a bit, steadied himself on the front fender, wondered if Moms had packed a thermometer, then, after a deep breath of piney air, crossed the parking lot. Tenaya Lodge was built to mimic the WPA lodges at the National Parks. Pillars of stone and walls of redwood were shot through with wood-framed windows. The entry was under a large portico with tall double doors of yellow Douglas Fir that had brass handles the size of a man's femur.

Grieg entered the foyer, a beamed ceiling soared over tiled floors. Rugs in stylized Native American patterns covered sections of the tile, creating conversation and quiet reading areas with groups of rustic furniture. Grieg studied the people chatting, reading, and sipping drinks throughout the lobby, deciding to begin his quest in the gift shop.

The store, at the back-left corner of a stone-faced lobby, carried Yosemite National Park themed gifts, such as bear carvings, magnets, and Christmas ornaments of familiar landmarks. Sweatshirts, T-shirts and a variety of women's blouses hung from hangars. Newspapers from as far away as New York City were racked in one corner. Calypso's photo highlighted the front page of the three papers with the largest circulation. In contrast, the headline on the Fresno Bee blared that a teenage girl had disappeared while hiking in Yosemite.

Glass-doored coolers offered sandwiches, ice cream bars, cheese assortments, and beer. Racks held chips of every sort and bags of popped corn. A wine rack ran half the length of one wall, shelves next to it displayed alcohol and mixers. Grieg fingered a swivel rack of keychains. He found one with a pewter fob of El Capitan that he liked and joined the line at the counter.

While the cashier rang up the people ahead of him, Grieg thumbed through a stack of matted photographs. A picture of a mountain meadow laced with purple lupine reminded him of Yellow Sky. He added it and a copy of the Fresno Bee newspaper to his purchases. When he reached the counter, he handed his picks to the young woman at the register. Lacy, according to her nametag, took the three items and scanned each.

"Any excitement around here?" Grieg asked, handing her cash. She held the two twenty-dollar bills up to the light and snapped them. He shrugged, wondering if he should apologize for having paper money. Lacy ducked her head shyly as she slid his purchases into a plastic bag bearing the Tenaya Lodge logo. "I take that as a yes?"

"Depends on what you think exciting is. An older gentleman dropped dead in the lobby this morning." She narrowed her eyes, checking to see if that met his requirement, adding, "Apparently, trophy wives don't keep you young, they kill you. Let that be a lesson to you, and me, and all of us. Marry someone your own age."

"Wow! I was thinking more like phones being lifted, that sort of thing."

"Oh," she sighed, "Well, this lovely lady. Oh, that's her sipping caffeine at the coffee shop. Gray-haired, cute gramma." Grieg pointed. "That's her. Her phone was stolen. It happened here. I wasn't behind the counter, so I don't know any of the details."

"Must be some gossip, though." Grieg cocked his head, it wasn't easy to pour on charm unshaven in a watch cap, rumpled sweater, and a healing black eye. He suspected he was a tad on the pasty side, as well. Maybe not, he felt flushed.

She tilted her head the opposite direction and tapped the counter with fingernails, each polished a different tint of blue. "My friend, John, was cashiering at the time. He thought it might have been a dirty, kinda troll looking guy, his words, not mine, hanging around that day. It was kind of weird because earlier that day, another guest got a series of calls from back East from men she didn't know. Then, Mrs. Townsend, that's her name. Her phone was stolen. She didn't care much except for losing her photos."

"Did you see the guy?"

"He comes in now and then. He told me he helped build this place. I believed him. As icky as he is, he has sad eyes." She stared meaningfully at Grieg. Was he icky or sad-eyed? He neatened up his sweater the best he could, pulling it down and smoothing it. "Not that I want to be anywhere near him, but I've seen men dripping with money creepier than he is."

A man, newly in line, cleared his throat and pushed Grieg aside.

"See what I mean," Lacy said, plastering on a smile as she addressed the other man, "How can I help you, sir?"

Grieg considered rubbing the man's nose on the glass counter. Imagining the sound of a cell door clanking shut, he crossed the lobby to Mrs. Townsend perched on a high stool at the coffee shop. She was small, round, and busy. She folded a napkin under her coffee with one hand while stirring cream into her cup with the other. Her right foot tapped. Her left foot was the only thing at rest on her person.

"Mrs. Townsend?" Grieg asked, wondering why Moms hadn't stuffed one tailored Egyptian cotton shirt, his onyx cufflinks, and a cashmere sweater in his backpack. Moms came from the dress for dinner crowd and clung to the tradition. He felt betrayed. She should have known better than to pack only what he'd requested. He checked for a menswear shop. According to a sign overhead, there was one around the next corner.

Mrs. Townsend glanced up, batting long darkened lashes behind the thick lenses in her pink and gray glasses' frames. She fingered her glasses up her nose. "Yes?"

"Lacy in the gift shop told me that your phone was stolen."

Mr. Townsend reached over and brushed a leaf off his left shoulder. "Are you resort security?"

She straightened the hem of her asymmetrically cut tunic. The cotton fabric bore a Mondrian-like print, in grays and pinks, separated by red bars. It reminded Grieg of the afghan Moms had in her corner at the hospital. Townsend had paired the tunic with leggings and wedged heeled shoes. It all went very nicely with the rock on her finger and the diamond tennis bracelet wrapping her wrist. Some grandma!

"Yes," Grieg lied, "When did you first miss your phone?"

Like Lacy, Mrs. Townsend tapped her fingernails on the table. Unlike Lacy, her nails were lacquered pink and crystal-studded. The rhinestones went nicely with the half-carat in each of her ears. "It happened while I was purchasing gifts for my grandchildren. I couldn't find my wallet."

She showed him a brown hand-tooled leather purse large enough to hold Viper. "So, I shoveled things out onto the counter. When I found my wallet, I scooped everything back into the maw willy-nilly. A man was leaning on the counter next to me. His hair was—oh—what do they call it—dreadlocks? He smelled like compost. One arm was bandaged with little nibs of blood showing. He just made me all jumpy. I left the store as fast as I could. I didn't miss my phone until last night when I wanted to show photos of my granddaughter to some nice people that my husband and I met in the bar."

"Did you notice anyone else nearby?"

"No. Well, not then. A little later, I saw the man leave. As he did, a man followed him out the front doors. I wouldn't have noticed except the man following him was such a contrast. Tall, clean, bleached jeans. Shouldn't you be taking notes?"

"I'm recording on my phone," Grieg lied again. "You do know your phone likely walked out the door."

"My husband told me the same. I'm gradually coming to terms with it. I had so many pictures of the grandbabies on it. Lawrence bugged me to save them on the computer. Now, I wish I had."

"And the taller man?"

"Dark-haired, walked with a swagger, you know, the ex-big man on campus strut. I took an immediate disliking to him. He was probably a cop."

"As opposed to me?"

She touched the sleeve of his sweater. "Our boy is about your age, he's a father, has two children, works for a big software company."

"I guess you wouldn't buy that I'm the CEO of a world-famous exploration company seeking someone named Yellow Sky Cloud," he teased her.

"My son works in the cloud. Well, not actually in a cloud, but, you know, back and forth, forth and back, info in, info out. Reminds me of that little movie robot that kept saying input, input. My son had the nerve to tell me that if I'd saved my pictures in the cloud, I'd still have them. Phooey! I like the earth."

Grieg blushed at his own naiveté, she assumed it was her charm. "Me, too. I'm sorry about your pictures, maybe your son is right about the cloud."

"It's bad enough I can't hold a Kodak in my hand anymore. Nope, no cloud."

"Thank you, thank you for your time."

"I hope you find the little weasel."

Grieg grinned, she patted his left shoulder. When she beckoned to a tall, beefy man with gray temples and fists the size of basketballs, Grieg headed back to the gift shop to follow up with Lacy.

"Back so soon," Lacy asked with a welcoming smile.

"Do you sell trail maps for this area and for Yosemite?"

Lacy turned to the rack behind her and selected three. She fanned them on the counter. "I backpack. This is my favorite." She tapped the middle map with a teal blue fingernail.

"Then that's the one I'll buy. Have you heard tales of a woman living alone and off the grid, maybe in the White Chief Mountain area?"

"No. I know there are a few old mining claims up there. Iron, zinc, and uranium. The old uranium claim is all fenced off. Ca-chink, like a prison cell, not that the iron claim is much better with all its trespassers will be shot signs."

"Mines can be risky," he answered, following her fingers until she indicated the iron mine on the map.

"Shotguns can be riskier," Lacy quipped. "I used to feel safe up there, but with girls disappearing from time to time, well, I just stay away from anywhere that gives me the creepy crawlies."

"And the uranium and iron claims do?"

"Yes."

"I saw the front page of the Fresno paper. Haven't read the article, when did the girl disappear?"

"Four days ago. Her family is staying here while the Park Rangers and police search for her. She was camping with friends at Summerdale campground, went to the john and that was that. Everyone is hoping she got disoriented. So far, the search parties have come back empty-handed. And, frankly, she isn't the first to disappear. They just found the bones of one of the missing girls, her name was Amy."

"Where did they find her body?" Grieg asked, despite knowing.

"Just southwest of the iron claim."

"How many girls have gone missing?" he asked, suddenly hungry. The smell of seared beef floated in the air; the restaurant must be serving dinner.

"None, at all, until Amy. None at any rate that didn't come out under their own steam, lost, sprained ankle, angry with a boyfriend. Now, six, if you count the car wreck, and except for Amy, none of them have been found."

"You be careful out hiking, Lacy. I don't like the odds."

"Check the bulletin board, you'll see why I'm not too worried about hiking alone." Lacy pointed to the wall behind the gift shop door. "Our version of a milk carton."

Grieg couldn't resist. Four brunettes with light eyes stared back at him all between sixteen and twenty-two, two empty frames. All over five feet six and athletic. Amy's picture was at the top. It could have been a black and white of Calypso Swale. Grieg swung his eyes back to Lacy. She glanced up and trotted over to join him.

"They're all brunettes, and you, Miss Lacy, are blond."

"Also, I'm shorter and chestier. I guess I'm just not the killer's type."

"Still, stay out of the tall timber and specifically stay away from the iron claim. That's my advice if you want to make twenty-two."

"You're cute," Lacy said. Grieg grinned. "Really, cute. Though I'd lose the watch cap and maybe shave the stubble."

He fingered the bristly cleft in his chin. "Is there some way I could drive back to the iron claim. I have a Jeep."

"Not unless you want your picture on this wall. It's a maze of trails, roads, cliffs, streams, and rocks. People make big money around here guiding folks that want to go off-road."

"How far a hike is it?"

"Hours. And, cute as you are, you don't look up to it." She pointed at the tip of his healing scar. "Though I bet with that bod, all things even, the hike would be a song for you."

"All things being even." He leaned over and pecked Lacy on the cheek. She put a hand to the spot and looked guiltily around the store. "A thanks for all the help."

He drove down the winding road to Oakhurst. A breeze blew shadows into strange shapes, pterodactyls flew through the limbs, he slowed for each curve until the woman passenger in the car behind leaned out her window and shouted, "For the love of God, pull over!"

He did as she asked at the next pullout. She honked as did the six cars behind her. His fingers clutched the steering wheel, his head hurt. He unlocked his fingers, took a deep breath, and pulled onto the road.

Grieg checked into his hotel then drove uphill, parking outside his room. He grabbed his knapsack and purchases, flung them on the bed, and headed to the restaurant for dinner. He asked the wait staff if anyone knew a Boomer, they looked at him with blank eyes. He guessed not.

Back in his room, he turned the television to CNN for the latest come-to-Jesus talking headlines, showered, and crawled between the covers of the king bed in his skivvies. Family searches for missing daughter through rugged terrain just south of Yosemite National Park made the headlines.

The girl, Bobbi Munro, was eighteen, the same age Amy had been. She was five-feet-seven, had reddish-brown hair, weighed 120 pounds, and spoke Spanish. She had been with friends, as Lacy reported, left for the campground bathroom and was never seen again. Her friends raised the alarm within twenty minutes of her disappearance. They spread out with flashlights, but she was gone. One young man claimed he was struck from behind. He had the knot to prove it.

A CNN reporter interviewed a woman, dark-haired in her early thirties who claimed to have been stalked the night Bobbi Munro disappeared. The woman had injured her small, hairy attacker. Mrs. Townsend claimed Boomer had a bandage on one arm. Which meant absolutely nothing living in the high timber as Boomer did, scratches and bumps would be a daily occurrence. The young man at the General Store found Boomer harmless, making it hard to imagine the scrawny man described having attacked the outraged, feisty woman interviewed.

Grieg's smartphone vibrated on the nightstand. He considered not answering but did.

"Hey, Griegs," Moms said. "Are you listening, this is important. Felix got a photo via a text message. He showed it to me. It's her, Griegs. It's Calypso. She's pedaling some contraption on the porch of a log cabin. She's in ratty jeans and a baseball hat. Griegs, a baseball hat! Her hair is looped out the back strap like some girlie softball player. She's so…"

"Alive, Moms. And given the high incidence of missing brunettes out here, that's a miracle. Brunettes who look like Calypso. Maybe Boomer's warning wasn't so off base."

"Unrequited crazy. You see it on TV shows all the time. You be careful. It would be too ironic if someone besides Calypso shot you."

"Cute. So, Moms, what does it mean when a man gives a woman the creeps?"

"First, I love that you need to ask. I suppose it means he makes her skin crawl, like bugs. Some men have that effect on women. It doesn't mean they're evil, or that they would ever act, just that they raise hackles. A lecherous look legs up, breasts down. Eyes that see your history in one glance. I've had men stare at me as I passed them that made me feel like their whore. And, they've been someone's loving husband. The most dangerous men hide behind faked concern. A woman can feel safe with them. It's a lie. If you understand…which I hope you don't because I'd scream if I raised a boy like that."

"You didn't. I've been assured that I'm cute. Not cut out for a five-mile hike, but cute. Though apparently, I need to shave."

Moms laughed. "It must be hell being so darling. It's your cleft, you shouldn't hide it. It makes you unique."

"Yet, Moms, may I remind you that I too am a killer."

The silence at Moms' end lasted a bit too long. "Don't ever say those words to me in that tone of voice. Besides, you are more correctly a manslaughterer. One more thing. According to Sally, Hugh didn't come into the office today. According to Judge Burridge, Chief Willard is missing in action."

"You didn't mention Doug? And what about Sally."

"You can't be serious."

"I wish I weren't. Three people called that woman at Tenaya Lodge, right? Felix, me, and who else?""

"Who cares?"

"You should, the third man might be chasing down your darling son. So, if you see old Felix, ask him for the address and password for the Yellow Sky site in the cloud? Could you do that? Then use the password to access it and text me what you find. I'm sure that's where Pops and Khalil communicated."

"I'll see what I can do. Find Calypso and fix this mess, okay? Griegs?"

"Goodnight, Moms."

"Before you go, I've been thinking about us, you, me, Pops, I was wondering if you remember the cat we had in Indonesia, the one that would literally climb the wall if you yelled buggy, buggy, buggy. Do you remember her?"

"Bye, Moms!" He didn't, they'd never had a cat because of his father's allergy. But he got the message. People were listening.

Grieg stared at the TV, trying to remember what he'd said, what he'd asked. Too much was the answer. Done with worrying for the night, he took his temperature with the thermometer Moms packed. Not great, but good to go.

Delia set the receiver on the cradle. The telephone was bugged, had been since she returned from taking Grieg to the airport. Someone had been very busy in her absence, maybe they expected Ray to call her from the great beyond with an astral message or Grieg to babble his next find.

Jones swept the house dutifully, reporting every two hours on the health of the various bugs. The one in the phone, the one under the buffet in the dining room, the one at her writing desk in the drawing-room, well, the one in every room. If the interested parties knew her at all, they would expect her to remove them, so she left them in place, relying on Jones to take any action needed.

She tightened the belt on her favorite lounging robe, a soft silk kimono in iridescent colors. Gliding to the traveling bar, she wondered how long it would take Felix to pop in for a drink. She mixed a gin tonic and sat on the ottoman, slipping her bare feet in and out of her favorite fuzzy red mules. She suspected Felix or Sally shared the transcript of her telephone conversations, chuckled a bit, and worried more. She hid nothing. Patty Gilbert aided her with her fun, calling twice under the pretext of keeping Delia's poor widowed spirits up.

They gossiped unmercifully about everyone and everything. Patty missed nothing, including Sally Purdy skulking around the stables asking leading questions of Fred, the stableman.

There was no question about Fred's loyalty. Fred's salary topped the stableman's listing, he belonged to Delia, lock, stock, and pocketbook. He earned it, and Grieg confirmed it. Further, Fred believed Grieg Washburn to be one of the top horsemen, if not the foremost, anywhere. How could she doubt a man who bowed at the foot of her son? Besides, Fred was darling in a horsey, bucktoothed, slightly unkempt way…and reedy strong. She'd bet on Fred against everyone she knew, except her husband and her son.

The jingle bell on the front door jangled. The scurry of Jones's footfall echoed down the hall, followed by a crisp, "Sir, we were wondering when we might expect you."

Delia slipped into her mules, tightened her belt and readied herself. She didn't need to hear Jones' emphasis on *you* to know it was Highland. She checked her watch. Though after midnight, he appeared at her door ten minutes after her call with Grieg ended.

"Delia, my dear," Felix, ever dapper in a tailored suit, crossed holding his arms out. "I'm sorry I'm so late, I was afraid I'd find you in bed."

"I assumed you'd skipped me tonight."

"With Ray and Grieg gone, I feel the need to provide some level of protection."

"I have Jones and Fred, two perfectly capable men, I don't need extra protection. I'm a threat to no one. I have nothing of my own except this house and a position on the WashEx Board."

"Oh, Delia, don't attempt to disarm me with your poor little Rockette persona. You're as formidable as Ray."

"I just spoke to Grieg, he asked for the location and password for Yellow Sky, a site he claims exists in the cloud, by which means Ray and Dr. Khalil communicated." Felix started to speak, she held a finger to his mouth and continued, "Grieg ordered Sally to buy a new safe for the WET records and to freeze online access to WET accounts. Has she done it?"

Felix ran his hands down Delia's arms ending hand in hand. She shook herself free, spun, and strode across the room to the door. "If you aren't willing to answer, I want you out of here!" She pointed at the open door for effect. She could see Felix balancing being caught on tape against losing access to Delia. She attempted to keep her delight out of her eyes.

He crossed to her desk, where he fiddled with her lamp. "Beautiful flowers," he said, dropping a hearing aid battery sized disk in a vase designed by Picasso. Had Jones told Felix about the bug, or...? Or seemed to fit the occasion.

"Well?" Delia demanded, slapping the heel of one of her crimson silk mules, the fur vamp fluffing with each tap.

Felix pursed his lips. "Ray insisted we had a mole inside the organization, someone being paid by Big Oil. I'd wondered for some time about the information that was on the street, Wall Street, that is, and amongst our competitors, so I took him seriously. His vote was Doug, mine was Hugh, tough for both of us. We agreed that anything to do with what we called CaMP, short for Callie's Machine Project, would be done via a cloud site dubbed Yellow Sky."

"Who has access?"

"Me, Ray, Judge Burridge, a Dr. Khalil. Ray's last CaMP message was for me to take care of you if anything should happen to him." He wrote the site and password on a slip of paper and slid it to Delia.

"Why doesn't Grieg have access?"

"Our competitors claim Grieg lost his temper with a bigwig at Aramco. Big Oil descended on us like the legendary hounds barking and snarling. They drove us out of a rare-earth find Ray needed. Grieg found an alternate at Cizre and managed to keep his mouth shut. Still, Ray's dead. Since then, I've had second thoughts about who the mole might be."

"What did Ray need to tell Doug that couldn't be shared at their hotel?"

"Ray was tired of Doug fighting him every inch of the way. Doug couldn't or wouldn't change how he worked. He'd become a roadblock. Ray intended to give Doug an ultimatum to either get on board or sail away with his stipend."

"And now Doug's in control of the company? Is keeping Sally on as General Secretary wise?"

"Doug is our only choice for the moment. As for Sally, there is no doubt she gave Gilft, Dummer, and Toff the information they needed for the IPO prospectus."

"And my Griegs *is* the liability?"

"Hear yourself, Delia. Grieg Washburn is a grown man, engineered by his own mistakes, who keeps running blindly into burning buildings. He's not your little Griegs anymore."

She steadied herself one hip against her writing desk. Grieg Washburn wouldn't risk WashEx unless he was attempting to prove something to or protect someone he idolized, and only one person on the face of the earth met that standard, Ray Washburn. Fathers and sons, she thought in a mirror of Dr. Chaudhary's comment to her. "Who do you see as CEO, if not Doug or Grieg?"

"Maybe Callie if she survives being saved by your son. The girl's clarity of vision is what we need."

"You hope. And Grieg?"

"No other person on this earth shares your son's capabilities."

"Yet he is a liability?"

Felix humphed.

"What about Hugh?"

Felix sighed. "Sons. You know, Delia, I miss Ray daily. He was, to be crude, a hell-bent genius."

"You're all wrong about my Griegs. All of you. And you can take your bugs away. I'll not betray my son, or Calypso, or

WashEx. Sally Purdy's office must be a veritable sieve of information. Put the damn bugs there."

"They're not all mine. And, Delia, you just referred to your thirty-one-year-old, felon, fire breathing son as *my Griegs*. Look, we know you've abetted Grieg in every way. Including sending him off knight errant to save that girl."

"Calypso's no girl, Felix. That little eighteen-year-old on the poster is a twenty-four-year-old woman who has been living off the grid for four years. Apparently, with at least one, rasty, filthy, mentally wounded mountain man."

Felix humphed. His humphs were quite expressive. Delia bit her lip. Felix wrapped his arms around her and set his chin on the top of her head. Ray would have thrown her to the top of her desk and made her giggle.

XV

Thursday morning, Grieg Washburn turned heads as he entered Pete's Place, a small diner boasting a gray mansard roof overhead and newspaper stands on the sidewalk outside the double entrance door. Glass windows encased the road-side of the restaurant located where historic Highway 49 tees into Highway 41.

Grieg wore jeans, a navy blue long-sleeve thermal Henley under a forest green hoody to meet the small, sleazy Boomer. He pulled the hood over a black watch cap hoping to hide the scar on his left temple. Though he'd shaved the night before, he hadn't that morning, so his disreputable stubble darkened his jaw. He worried his jeans were too clean and his hoody too much.

Grieg scanned the tables as he entered. Seeing no one who could pass for Boomer, he joined the line at the elbow-high counter that fronted the kitchen and stretched across a quarter of the restaurant. Orders were delivered by wait staff to the customer's choice of table. Grieg wasn't sure how the staff knew whose food went to whom, but the process seemed to work.

He ordered coffee then breakfast from a selection of specials written in blue marker on a whiteboard. Order placed; he found a booth with a view of the parking lot. When no one served him coffee, he divined that you poured your own from a coffee mess at the end of the main counter.

Pete's Place was packed with locals. Working people with working people worries and friendships, there was considerable laughter and slapping of backs, pecking of cheeks, and hugging. Grieg imagined either of the Highlands walking into this place and snorted. Pops would have made five life-long friends by the end of his first breakfast. In Pops honor, Grieg smiled at a couple in the opposite booth. The woman grinned, and her husband nodded.

A careworn woman in her thirties slid a plate of eggs and French toast onto the Formica tabletop in front of him. She refilled his coffee cup, asking with a hand on one hip, "Anything else, hon?"

Grieg read the name tag pinned above her ample breasts, Eleni. Eleni grinned a big wide, toothy grin and laughed, "You're a bad boy then, heh? I think I'll let you keep your own coffee cup filled."

"Got a question for you, Eleni, before we go all self-serve and such. You know a man named Boomer?"

"Sure. He hangs out with the homeless up off 124B. There's an encampment there. But he's rarely around."

"I'm supposed to meet him. I wouldn't know him if he walked in naked with a B tattooed on his chest. Can you point him my direction when he arrives?"

"I'll do you one better. He's short, maybe five foot six. Hasn't washed his hair since he was two years old. Shaves, though. Lots of nicks. His nose goes one way and his mouth the other. Wears the same darn clothes, no matter the season, grungy Dickie work pants, and six layers of stinky shirts topped by a fishing vest. You'll smell him as soon as he opens the door."

"Does he come in often?"

"Tries. The manager threw him out last time. He kept staring at a table of ladies. He's off. You know how some people are? You can't pin it down, but it just sorta makes you go all goosebumpy. Though I hear it from women, he might not strike you that way at all."

"But he pays?"

"Always. He may not take a bath, but he scrounges money somewhere." Eleni filled his cup to the brim. "Come to think of it, money is better than clean. He's a good tipper. If I see him, I'll give you a nod. Tell you one thing though, if you want to look tough, shed the hoody. It makes me want to take you home and feed you soup."

"Thanks for the tip."

Eleni walked off, whistling a song from the early sixties. *I Want to be Bobbie's Girl*, he thought. Grieg considered calling his name out to Eleni but settled for a chuckle and a time check. He expected Dempsey and some WashEx emissary any moment. He needed to waylay Boomer before they showed. Grieg ruffled the wad of cash he'd stuffed in his backpack, not the $20,000 offered but plenty for a start.

He ate with one eye on the door. The eggs tasted buttery and rich, the French toast sweet and satisfying, the sausage greasy and filling. His heart fluttered in horror. He stuffed food in his face, chowing down, glad of the oversized portions of comfort food. He felt his 99.3-degree temperature dropping and was considering buying one of the Greek omelets touted on the board when a man smelling like the back end of a burro wafted in the restaurant. Grieg motioned him over. Eleni confirmed his instincts with a nod. The man checked out the door then approached Grieg.

Boomer stared at Grieg until Grieg got the point. The moocher wanted food. Grieg pulled out his wallet and fanned fifteen dollars Boomer's way. Boomer snatched the bills then sidled up to the counter. A couple mid-order mumbled something, paid, and stepped away. Grieg wished he had a personal air purifier hanging from a lanyard inside his zipped-up hoodie. Mostly, he was glad he had already eaten.

Food ordered; Boomer joined Grieg in the booth. He rested his elbows on the table, his hands clenched, his fingernails deeply impregnated with grime. He was small, almost delicate, his eyes were an unsettling color of washed-out brown without the green and blue flecks of hazel. They flitted from a picture of a Greek fishing village to the two young women in the booth across from them, to Grieg then back to the painting. The teenage girls were dressed in bulky sweaters and tight black slacks that ended in booted feet. They were happily animated, hands gesturing between, during, and after bites.

"You Boomer?" Grieg asked, trying to get Boomer's attention.

"Same."

"You got proof?"

Boomer pulled an iPhone with a red spangled cover from a vest pocket. He set it on the table and spun it with a finger. "Show me the money." Boomer kept his grubby right hand on the phone. This man wasn't afraid of germs, he was one.

Grieg slid a white business envelope to mid-table, keeping his hand on the flap, praying Boomer wasn't the counting type.

Boomer pushed the phone Grieg's way, then eased the envelope to the edge of the table and counted. "You promised $20,000."

That answered one question. Grieg improvised, "Not for the photo, for the girl and the photo. For all I know, she's hundreds of miles away. Two-thousand bucks now, the rest four days from now when we're sure it's her and she hasn't been harmed."

Boomer's food arrived. He didn't chew. His mouth emptied with a bob of his Adam's apple. Grieg checked the photos on the stolen phone. Calypso's photo popped first, followed by several of a young woman making breakfast in a campground. One picture of Calypso, fifteen shots of the dark-haired woman. The remaining images were of Mr. Townsend, Mrs. Townsend's cats, her grandchildren, sunsets, and Half

Dome from an angle that showed more of the humped side of the mountain than the oft-photographed sheer wall.

"Want your phone back?"

Boomer, mouth stuffed with food, nodded. Grieg deleted Calypso's photo with the swipe of his thumb as he handed the smartphone back. No picture, no money. Not from Grieg, not from WashEx.

"Okay. Where is she?"

"First, you got to tell me who *she* is. How do I know you're not planning to dump me in the woods and claim the reward? You got to show me some trust." Boomer said, spewing hash browns to mid-table.

Grieg studied Boomer's face. It was a mess. He'd been beaten, more than once, by someone who enjoyed it. And, he'd been young by the age of the scars and breaks. If Ray Washburn had known Boomer's father, they'd be looking for the man's body.

"You provide directions. I check your Calypso Swale out. Alone."

"When you shortchanged me, you guaranteed me as your guide. You're not out of my sight until I get the rest of my money. You haven't told me who *she* is, not yet."

Grieg fidgeted, amazed Special Agent Dempsey and whoever WashEx sent hadn't strutted in the double doors. "Calypso Swale," Grieg said, adding, "She was a fine horsewoman. She and her horse, Fructose, jumped obstacles well over six feet tall. She's maybe five-foot-six, slender, and has hazel eyes spangled with gold."

Grieg expected Boomer to ask for some detail not mentioned in the newspapers. Instead, Boomer cocked his head, a smile curved his lips followed by a soft chuckle. About the time Grieg was ready to grab the weasel by the throat, lift him to his feet, and shove him out the door, Boomer stood. "Let's go. The road is rough. You up to hiking. You don't look like one of them tony back East boys, you know all smooth-handed and smelling of green, but you don't look too fit neither."

Grieg shoveled dollars on the table for Eleni, wishing he could give her a big sloppy kiss on the cheek and followed Boomer into the parking lot. Boomer headed for a large SUV. Grieg pulled his hoodie over his eyes, grabbed Boomer by the elbow, redirecting him to the Jeep.

Special Agent Dempsey emerged from the SUV, followed by Chief Willard, his nascent stomach leading. A Highway Patrol Officer joined them from a nearby patrol car. As Grieg herded Boomer to the passenger side of the Jeep, a man about Grieg's size approached Dempsey, his hand outstretched. Dempsey acknowledged him, leaving Grieg with the impression the two men had met before.

Grieg shoved Boomer into the car. "Try not to look so damn obvious, and whatever you do, don't roll down the window and yell, *hey*!"

When Willard entered the restaurant, Grieg pulled out of the parking lot onto Highway 41. Clearly, neither Dempsey nor Willard had gone to the get there first, get what you need, get your ass out of town school of management that defined Grieg's career. But someone from Big Oil may have.

Grieg rolled down the window, to disperse the stench from the passenger seat. Boomer cut him a look. "Who was the tall guy?" Grieg asked.

"Rafe Bolt. He's…" Boomer watched the turn to Bass Lake glide by seemingly unable to structure a complete sentence.

"Bolt is?"

"He knows where Callie is the same as me."

"Does he know you ratted her out for the money?"

"'Course, that's why he was there!"

"You afraid of Rafe?"

"Sometimes. We gotta get to Jessie first."

"Jessie?"

"Jessie Woods, that's her name. Has been since she turned up on the claim. I never told nobody anything else."

Grieg mulled the comment over. "Who was the camper on your phone?"

"I take pictures sometimes, it isn't against the law," Boomer snapped, convincing Grieg that it was. He couldn't get Eleni's estimation of Boomer off his mind.

"You ever take pictures of Calypso besides the one on the phone?" Grieg asked.

"How? How could I? I stole the phone."

After a while, Boomer pointed right. Grieg turned. "You notice anyone in the diner that looked out of place, someone you've never seen before, someone that doesn't fit the town?"

"One guy. He was sitting to the left of the door. Brown hair, flannel shirt, shiny shoes. Had a brand-new canvas jacket on the seat."

"What--no gun holstered in his armpit?'

"Nope. Maybe it was in his car. He drove up in a rented RAV4, hope he doesn't think it is four-wheel drive."

"Did you see me pull up?"

"From the dumpsters."

The road turned from gravel to dirt. Boomer pointed left. Grieg turned left. Boomer grabbed the dashboard and yelled, stop. Grieg stopped.

Boomer jumped out, leaned in the window, and ordered, "Follow this road for five more miles to a red post. Don't worry, it's the only red post. Hike in a mile and a half northwest until you see a stamp mill. Make a left, follow the path 'til you see a cabin. But if I were you, I'd head back."

"Why?"

"Rafe. He's like an Anubis where Jessie's concerned." Grieg didn't ask but got the answer anyway. "I read. Books. All kinds. Ever hear of Amelia Peabody?"

Grieg never would have guessed that, not Egyptology. "Tell me about Rafe. He looked pretty hardened."

"Thinks he is. Like I said, you ought to head back. Ain't no place up here for somebody like you. He'll smell you, eat you for dinner like a mountain lion. He doesn't like competition. You're competition. But that's not all, you're…"

"Then why did you bring me this far?" Grieg interrupted, not wanting to hear what he was, he'd had quite enough of that.

"I can't protect Jessie, not from Rafe. Sometimes he hides, waiting for me, I hear a shotgun cock behind my back. Or a voice yell bang. And I can tell things like you're as bruised as she is. Rafe's a bruiser. That's why I'd go back if I were you."

As appealing as that thought was, Grieg knew he'd be found shrunken and starving before he could wend his way down the mountain to Oakhurst.

"If you want your money, take me to Calypso, like you said you would."

"You killed her parents." Boomer challenged.

"Her mother was dead. But, the truck driver, yeah. I killed him. Put her Dad in the hospital, he died there," Grieg responded, grappling with the fact that Boomer had recognized Grieg before Grieg motioned him to his booth.

"So, you know. She doesn't talk about it. Not to me. I read the paper, that's how I know who you killed. She isn't over it. I see her sometimes with her fancy clothes. It's sort of life interruptus, like me, can't go forward, can't go back, can't stay put. That's your doing." Boomer turned downhill.

"Come on, Boomer." It sounded plaintive enough that Boomer returned to the open window. It had finally happened, Grieg's mind was fully operable, he was reading his opposition as though prepping to negotiate. Maybe not, why had Boomer chosen to meet with him. He must have seen the patrol car drive up before he entered the diner, he may even have recognized Willard and Dempsey?

"I can't. Rafe'll be back gunning for me. He finds me. I'm dead. You're dead the minute you step foot in that cabin. All he wants is Jessie, get it!"

"Get me to Calypso, I'll help you. I promise." Boomer's right hand slid to the door handle. Possessed by the odd angles and furtiveness of the other photos on the stolen phone, Grieg challenged, "Did you take the missing girl? Have you got her stashed away?"

Boomer's head spun around, his eyes wide, the only thing missing was pea soup spewing from his mouth.

XVI

Grieg followed two tire grooves worn through grass so tall it rubbed the underside of the Jeep. In the summer, when the grass was dry, the Jeep's catalytic converter would ignite a firestorm. The jarring, rudimentary road ended at a barbed-wire fence decorated with gutshot *No Trespassing* signs attached to every fourth fencepost for as far as the eye could see. The warning was explicit. Violators, who survived, would be fined to the extent of the law.

"Pull over and park. It's the end of the road. Now, we hike. You got that in you, Mr. Washburn?"

Grieg tried to look hardened. He got the definite impression it hadn't worked when Boomer broke out laughing. "If I was a girl, that look would make me want to lay you. Just so you know."

Grieg grabbed his backpack from the Jeep. He strode through the young grass to the fence. After ducking under the barbed wire, he held the last strand up, Boomer oozed under it. "How'd you know who I was?"

"One of the articles, great picture of you in handcuffs. Thing is one of the men standing by the SUV was in the newspaper picture, too, only in a cop uniform. The article said you'd skipped parole."

Grieg gestured Boomer ahead, struggled into his knapsack then fell in behind. Boomer struck a good pace, a little too good. Grieg gasped for air, his heart pounding from the diminished oxygen at five-thousand feet. Big trees waved overhead. The shush and a rattle of a freshening breeze trailed them up a steep hill, then down into a swale with a stream wandering through it. The grasses swirled as the blow reached the ground. Boomer pointed at the sky. Cumulus clouds, their bellies heavy with rain, swelled down from the north according to the mossy side of the pine trees. Grieg zipped his hoodie wishing for the parka Moms had packed. The one flung across the bed in his hotel room.

Cold air slid down the trees. The clouds lowered and spit the occasional raindrop, hard rain, the kind thinking seriously of being hail. Boomer trudged on, his pantlegs wicking water from the grass until he was damp to the knee. Grieg tucked his pant legs into his boots. Chilled at first by the wet cuffs, his ankles warmed with each stride. Still, the wind-whipped air ate into him.

His jaw ached, then his head. He stumbled. Boomer reached back and grabbed him before he fell. For a small man, Boomer was reedy strong, enough to overpower a woman or pull a man to standing, as he just had. Grieg lurched in Boomer's footsteps.

By the time the log cabin appeared, the rain had flattened the grasses in wavy windswept patterns. Boomer jogged. Grieg continued his slog. Leaping onto the cabin porch, Boomer pounded on the door. When no one answered, he entered. A moment later, he emerged, shaking his head and grumbling under his breath. Grieg stopped ten feet from the porch, his clothes plastered to his skin.

"Jessie's gone."

"Gone as in packed up and left?" Grieg called.

"No. Worse. Her stuff's here."

A handmade bench, carefully woven from lengths of slender branches, invited Grieg onto the porch. He'd made one like it as a teen in Malaysia from reedy willows that grew during the wet. He clambered up the porch stairs out of the rain then sat, his hands hanging between his legs, and gulped air. "Why worse?" he rasped, expecting the answer he got.

"Means Rafe got to her. Let's look around."

"You go. I'm wiped out."

"You're with me, or you're on the ground like an arrowed deer."

Grieg stood.

Boomer bounded off the porch into the pounding rain, across an open field toward a stand of thick undergrowth. Two horses nickered at their approach. Boomer held a flat palm out. A big buckskin with dark mane and tail nosed his flat palm. Boomer opened the gate and led the horse into a shed that looked more like a rickety stamp mill than an all-purpose barn. A brown and white pinto plodded behind.

The roof of the redwood-framed building was composed of hand-hewn shingles. On close inspection, some looked new. Recently pitch-forked straw covered the bare dirt floor. Grieg leaned over for a handful. It wasn't store-bought hay, nor had it been baled. The grass had been scythed from the angle of the cut, gathered, and spread onto the earthen floor. A handmade ladder of stout sticks tied with stripped reeds provided access to a storage loft jury-rigged of spare boards over trestle-like rafters. Hay wisped over the edge.

A western saddle and two hackamore bridles hung over a poorly made gate meant to keep the horses at the far end of the small building. Framed windows on three sides were shuttered. The shutters were held closed by one-by-four boards lowered into brackets. The brackets, like most things Grieg observed, were made from whatever was available, in this case, castoff metal bars.

Boomer rubbed the buckskin gelding down with a worn gunnysack. The horse nuzzled him. The curly-maned pinto stared at the back wall. Rain pounded on the roof, dripping onto a tin bucket turned upside down near the feed.

Grieg propped himself on the gate, glad to be out of the weather. The pinto worked his way over to Grieg. Grieg played his right hand down the horse's withers to the scar on his stock. The tendon was sound, as was the bone. The horse nickered.

"Wow," Boomer said, "Frisco doesn't like men. Jessie claims it was a man who hurt him. But he sure likes you."

"Where did he come from?"

"I found Frisco all beat up wandering down by Nelder Grove. I figured he'd either escaped from a backcountry pack-in camp or his owner cut him loose to die. Frisco let me get a rope around him, so I brought him to Jessie. She fixed him up. Named him. After that, she had to keep him. Shouldn't ever name a thing, even parents, that way when their kid goes bad, who cares. Easier for everybody."

From Boomer's tone, he was speaking from experience. The small man's shoulders were undeveloped and his legs a bit rickety, giving the impression he'd been tossed out before he matured. Boomer handed Grieg the gunny sack then leaned against one of the two weight-bearing posts idly cleaning mud off his boots with a stick. The stamp mill was old, the framing was pegged. The nails tenpenny and square.

Showing the sack to Frisco, Grieg asked, "Does Calypso ride him?"

"Sure. He bolted on her once. Rafe ran after them. When he got close, Frisco reared. Jessie took a heck of a spill. Rafe came back carrying Jessie. She was pounding and screaming for him to let her down, Frisco right behind. Rafe didn't, not until he got her in the cabin and checked her out real good." Boomer stroked the soft spot on the buckskin's nose. Rex bumped in for more. "Horses prove she's around. She'd never leave them in the weather."

Boomer opened the door motioning Grieg to follow. Hail. An inch of it covered the ground. Grieg huddled into his wet hoodie. Boomer glanced at him then trotted back into the stable, returning with a canvas field coat lined in plaid flannel. Grieg didn't ask; he just shrugged into it. It fit. It wasn't Boomer's, and it wasn't Calypso's unless she'd grown six-inches, that left Rafe.

"Where to?" Grieg asked, buttoning Rafe Bolt's coat.

"The mine. Jessie's got a hidey-hole about twenty-feet in. Pretty good set-up. Tins of food. Bottled water. Bedding. She's been on the run so long that she doesn't feel safe without a place to hide."

Grieg started to ask if there was another hidey-hole, one large enough to hold an engine prototype, then thought better of it. The less Boomer knew or thought Grieg knew, the better.

Boomer trudged into the timber, through a stream swollen with mountain run-off, straight for a rocky outcropping perhaps a quarter-mile distant. Snow drifted stark against the dark of the trees. Hail crunched into slick footprints of ice, garnished by a thin layer of snow.

A crudely made door blocked the entrance to the inactive mine. A warning sign bearing the periodic weight of uranium telegraphed that uranium had been hauled out of this mountain. "It's safe in there," Boomer said. "Miners just tacked that up to scare claim jumpers away. Mined iron here." He spat then laughed.

"And, you know this because?"

"I got a Geiger counter."

Grieg figured *got* was the operative word. Boomer cocked his head listening. After which, he yelled at the top of his lungs, "Jessie, it's Boomer. Get out here."

Grieg dusted snow off a shoulder of Rafe's field coat. Boomer hopped from one foot to the other, slapping what passed for his biceps with ungloved hands.

"Don't move," a woman growled at Grieg's back. Boomer smiled until the click-cluck of a rifle being cocked stopped him. "You son-of-a-bitch!" the woman screamed. "God damn it, Boomer, what have you done? What? We promised each other!"

"Trying to get you safe, that's all Jessie. That's all!"

"Last time I saw those shoulders, the owner stumbled drunk out of the car he used to kill my mother?" she snarled. "Turn and face me, Washburn. Just do it!"

Grieg's feet were frozen to the cold ground. Snow drifted onto the shoulders she remembered and onto his sopping hood.

"Put your hands out to your side. Now!" Grieg held his arms out as though being arrested, a position he knew too well. "Turn around, keep your hands out. If you don't, I'll shoot you, and I'm a good shot."

A bemused look flitted across Boomer's face, followed by arched eyebrows. Grieg got it. Jessie Woods couldn't hit a barn with the gun barrel against the wood. Grieg turned.

"Wipe that grin…Oh, crud, oh hell, sweet mother, crap." A roar split the air.

The bullet chipped granite at the mine entrance, ricocheted against an old mining car, took a nip out of the right sleeve of the field coat, then bored into a tree three feet to Grieg's right. Grieg grabbed the rifle from the reedy woman and tossed it to Boomer.

"Great, great, give it to him!" She landed a punch on Grieg's jaw that rattled him to the core.

He grabbed her right fist and rotated her arm behind her back. Calypso kicked Grieg's right shin then stomped on his instep. Pain shot up his right ankle as he threw her to the ground and placed a boot in the small of her back. "Stop it."

She spat. It dribbled off her chin. Ray Washburn had been right about Calypso Swale. She was what no one expected.

"Get off her," Boomer ordered, cocking the rifle. Grieg showed his palms and removed his foot from Calypso's back. "Step away from her."

Grieg did. Calypso ratcheted herself to standing using the ore car. Mud caked her canvas coat. Her hair was wet and curly with so many rats' nests in it, she'd be working a comb through it for days. Grieg doubted washing it would help. Her hazel eyes bored into him. He smiled at her, unable to help himself, contrasting Calypso Swale in her beaded rust dress, her hair upswept, hate pouring from her eyes with the wildcat in front of him.

She ducked into the mine emerging with a hank of woven rope, more hemp than sisal. "Put your hands behind your back," she ordered, slapping Grieg on the right shoulder.

Boomer waved the gun to promote Grieg's compliance.

"Damn it. Put your hands behind your back," Callie roared. Grieg complied. She may not know how to shoot, but she knew how to tie. He wasn't getting his hands free without a knife. She shoved him against the ore car and frisked him. "Nothing."

"You expected?"

She slapped the back of Grieg's head, urging him up the path to the stamp mill. He stumbled, she yanked him up. When they reached the mill, the horses nickered welcome. She threw the loose end of the rope binding Grieg's hands over a fence board and cinched it.

"What the hell do you think I'm going to do to you?" Grieg grumbled.

She slid the bar lock back. The barn door squealed as the rusted rollers bumped along the rail. Boomer tracked Calypso's every move, his scrawny frame bent, the rifle at his side. Grieg mouthed: *help me*. Boomer whispered something to Calypso, his hand molded to the slope of her back. She batted at her ear then slapped his hand away.

Boomer propped the gun against the fence and followed Calypso into the stable. Grieg fingered the rifle. The problem was, he needed Calypso's trust, and he needed it before Rafe waltzed in with Dempsey and Chief Willard to haul them both away. Grieg stepped away from the gun. It fell into the deepening sludge.

Calypso stalked out of the stamp mill. Grabbing Grieg's right arm, she turned him, glanced down at the rifle in the mud, and elbowed him against the fence. He let out more of a whimper than a cry.

"Oh, don't give me that crap. I've seen you take a harder hit than that playing polo." She yanked him up and uncinched the rope from the fence. "Get in there."

Boomer blocked the door.

"Get out of my way!"

"No, Jessie. Even with the horses, it will be near freezing. Look, he's bleeding. You shot him. What's that matter with you?"

Grieg checked. He shouldn't have peeked, the pain hit then.

"Get out of my way. Don't let him fool you. I know how tough he is. I know. I've seen it!"

Grieg leaned on the fence. He was sweating inside Rafe's field coat. His right arm, wrists, and head ached, while patterns danced at the edges of his vision leaving sparks of light behind. His hands were numbing. The cold ate at his fingers. He flexed them to keep blood flowing. He leaned his head against the fence, his life in the hands of a weaselly, sad little man as dependent on Calypso Swale as Grieg was at this moment.

"Jessie. He'll die out here. You don't want that on your conscience. Whatever he did to you, whatever you think he wants to do, you're wrong."

She braced Boomer. "You, sleaze, you watch me. You think I don't feel your eyes climbing all over me, that I don't know what you do in your spare time?"

"I admire you, that's for sure. And I like to watch you taking care of your world. I do. It's not a crime. A crime is tying a wounded man in a stable and letting him freeze to death."

"You led him here! You took his goddamn money! You sold me out!"

"No…no…no, Jess, I did it for you. The money is for you." Boomer reached into his sack and pulled out the bills Grieg had given him. "For you, the horses. Us."

"There is no us. Never will be an us."

Calypso wrenched Grieg to standing, picked up the rifle, and stomped off, dragging him behind her. She shouted back for Boomer to close and latch the door.

When Boomer caught up, Calypso handed Grieg off then disappeared into a wall of falling snow. Grieg relied on Boomer's wiry strength to keep him upright until the cabin materialized like heaven's gates out of a swirl of snow. Boomer balanced Grieg up the steps under the shed roof of the wide porch. Grieg stood in the doorframe bleeding, his hands cinched, the rope snaking between his legs onto the deck.

Inside the chinked log cabin, Calypso lit a fire in a large grate, a Dutch oven, suspended on a wrought iron tripod, dangled above the growing flames. Boomer put a match to each of four oil lanterns. Their yellow light flooded the room and leaked out the windows laying streamers of light on the porch decking.

Boomer stripped off his wet clothes, revealing a thin body that could have stood in for jerky. Under a grungy T-shirt, scars raced across his back, the kind you get from being beaten with a belt. Boomer eyed Grieg while setting a pair of top-rated, muddy, hiking boots on a mat by the door.

"Shut the door!" Calypso ordered, without turning. "Can't heat the great outdoors."

"Do you want him in or out?"

"Out." Callie slammed the lid back on the Dutch oven. "Forever. That's what I want!"

"But…"

Grieg thumped his cold butt onto the porch bench. He couldn't feel his hands. The icy wind on his wet jeans chilled him to the point of hypothermia. He leaned against the bench's woven back, his hands between his thighs for warmth. His crotch froze instead. A draft of wind blew around the northwest corner flooding behind the bench. He needed inside, or Boomer's predictions would come true. Grieg tried charm. "What if I take off my boots before I come in like Boomer did?"

"Screw you!" Calypso snapped, slamming the front door.

A small blanket was folded at one end of the bench. Grieg skootched until he could bury his hands within the soft knit. Velvety drifts of snow gathered on the stairs. A persistent drip from the roof froze into a nascent icicle. He checked to the left of the door for anything that might provide warmth. The pedal generator from Boomer's photograph sat battery-less next to an armchair rocker.

His hands warmed, which helped control the body-wracking shivers but didn't stop the bleeding in his right bicep. Grieg tried to balance the brittle, angry debutante he had known with the comfort of the chair, the care of the horses, the flickering soft light, the smell of yeasty bread floating under the closed door, and the gentle, happy smile on Calypso's face in Boomer's photo.

One of the horses whinnied. A rabbit scurried from under the cabin's porch into the night. Grieg fell asleep to the muted echo of voices within the cabin, the soughing of the wind in the pine boughs, and the silence of the falling snow. He woke when his body thumped to the bench. His hands were free. He sat up and rubbed each bloodied wrist until his blanched hands pinked.

The cabin door stood open. Light angled across the porch.

"Can I come in?" he called.

No answer.

Grieg fumbled to untie his boots, then placed them next to Boomer's by the door. Calypso's wet chestnut hair was wound and tied into a bun, wisps of it strayed down her back. Her flannel shirt sleeves were rolled up, as were the cuffs of her jeans. A pair of well-used, pointy-toed, slant-heeled cowboy boots shown beneath the cuffs of her pants. The fire popped in the fireplace, its warmth nibbling at the chill. He cleared his throat. No response, so he entered in stockinged feet and shut the door on the glacial night.

"About damn time," Callie snapped. She set the table, then returned to a small counter and hacked at vegetables on a cutting board as though each was part of Grieg's anatomy. "I chop each block of wood burned. It isn't delivered. Tomorrow, you chop."

Directing her wrath at Boomer, she ordered, "Go out to the icehouse and fetch a pound of butter and a loaf of rye bread. Bring the pie, too, it should be more than cooled by now."

"But I got my boots off," Boomer whined.

"Get them on and get." Boomer swiveled worried eyes from Calypso to Grieg and back. "Get!" she yelled, swatting at Boomer with a towel. He all but ran to the door for his boots, jammed his feet in them, and tumbled into the blizzard outside.

Calypso stormed across the room to Grieg. She picked up a lantern and checked him over in the light of it. "You need to get out of those wet clothes." She shook her chopping knife at him, then disappeared into the only other room in the cabin.

Grieg checked overhead for a loft. There was none. The great room was functional and fitted with sturdy homemade furniture. The seats had cushions, some stuffed with horsehair, some fashioned from old blanket fabric. The trestle table was so solidly built an army could have bivouacked on it. The windows, with shutters exterior to the wavy glass, had slide curtains made from mismatched fabrics. Bright yellow flowers with orange centers hung over the window nearest the kitchen, printed tomatoes and lettuce decorated the next, then a green leaf and strawberry print followed by white clouds on a blue sky.

Braided rugs covered the planked floor beneath the table, the front of the hearth, the entry, and beneath the chair where Grieg sat. The oval rug under the chair was lopsided, not the next. The rugmaker improved with each attempt. Nothing in the room matched, but everything did.

"You're still dressed," Calypso said, tossing a pile of clothes at Grieg from the bedroom door. The clothes landed in a heap at his feet. Before he bent to pick them up, she was back chopping vegetables.

Grieg wobbled as he stood. She cocked her head. He tried to get his right arm out of the field coat, got lost in the fabric, and thumped into the chair. Calypso crossed to him, signaling for him to stand. He ratcheted himself upright one hand on each arm of the chair. She unbuttoned the field coat, holding the left side up until he removed his arm then eased the right from the bloodied sleeve.

She hung the jacket by the door, returning she unzipped his sopping hoodie. She kept going until he was in his skivvies, his cold skin livid, blood trickling down his arm from a deep, jagged tear. She lifted his chin and clicked her tongue. Cool, soft fingers ran over the bruise she'd left on his jaw. She danced her fingertips over the welts left by rope and cuffs at each of his wrists.

She offered him a chair nearer the fire then disappeared into the back room, returning with a red bag with a white cross on it. She dug in it. Cotton balls, antiseptic, gauze, and white tape. Her tongue showing between her lips, she dipped the cotton balls in the antiseptic. "I'd say this is going to hurt, but…"

He bucked the minute the astringent hit the graze on his bicep.

"Stop that," she ordered. Grieg did by biting his lower lip. "It's still oozing, not good. You're not a bleeder, are you?"

"Right now, apparently," he muttered, worried the Dengue had moved into hemorrhagic territory. He'd been warned. "Can you hurry up, everything is shrinking."

She slapped an industrial size bandage across the crease. Blood showed immediately. She clucked. "Sorry."

"That an apology for shooting me?"

Callie scooped water into a tin cup from a covered barrel and handed it to Grieg. She had made a home here, it showed in the carefully wrought furniture, the mobiles of bird feathers that swung and swirled overhead in the drafts from the fire, and in the yeasty smell emanating from a sanded board on the table.

She helped him into a pair of jeans from the pile on the floor, then covered his shoulders with a gray crocheted blanket from a lopsided collection near the fire. He sighed. She quirked her mouth. Grieg pulled the cover around his chest and wiggled his stockinged feet. Callie noticed and wrapped another blanket around his ankles.

"If we're going to eat, I need to keep chopping. Tell me what you're doing here?" Callie ordered, slicing three carrots with a finely-honed chef's knife.

"Hikers found your car. The Park Service contacted Hugh Highland. Highland called a Board meeting the night of Pops' wake. There was a lot of pressure to have you declared dead, your DNA was on the steering wheel, the seats. I convinced them to advertise."

She scraped the vegetables from her cutting board into the Dutch oven.

"Then they found bones. But the bones, a jaw, a femur had been a girl named Amy. She was kidnapped from her campsite four years ago. Thing is, Calypso, according to the coroner, she was alive for almost a year after she disappeared. She didn't die at your crash site, someone buried her there. Someone, like you, who hoped the bones would stop further searching."

She dismissed him with a shake of her head.

"I found you. Anyone else could do the same."

"Because of Boomer. Because he took my picture and sent it to whoever for the reward."

"No, I found you before that." Grieg took a deep breath, it hurt. "Somethings…"

She came at him with a cup. He clutched it between two shaky hands. She wrapped a second blanket around his shoulders. "Tea. We don't drink anything hard here. Oh, Rafe and Boomer pinch the occasional bottle, but I don't have any I can offer you."

Grieg closed his eyes. Callie wet a washcloth in a pan of hot water bubbling on the fire. He shrank from the heat of it on his raw jaw. She put it to her own face to test it, swished it in the air then tried it again. Calypso cleaned the disintegrating stitches on his left temple, then his cheek and around the color fading from his left eye. He took a chance. He reached for her hand. "I'm sorry. So, sorry. For everything, Calypso. I…"

The washcloth dripped onto the plank floor; the drops pooled in a low spot before dripping between the boards to the dirt beneath the cabin. A gust of wind shook the cabin. Cold air surged into the room from the crawlspace, guttering the flames under the kettle. Callie dropped his hand and turned to the fireplace, adding kindling until the fire blazed.

"For finding me! Then why did you? Why would you? Haven't you hurt me enough? What the hell were you doing that night! What?"

Grieg shook his head. "It made sense at the time."

"Drunk as you were, it likely did."

"You made this furniture, the blankets, everything by your own hand?" he changed the subject, trying to nudge the conversation to neutral ground.

"I'm not that girl, not some vacuous debutante. I had that torn out of me in one crushing, thunderous, ripping moment of horror. You have no idea!" Her anger resolved itself in persistent rhythmic chopping. This time it was a hapless small mammal she dispatched into minced squares of meat.

"You fled to Mustique. Changed your name, got a tan, then moved to San Francisco. I didn't tear the party girl out of you."

She glanced up, the gold in her hazel eyes flashed. "You're right, I had a life in San Francisco. I gravitated to the social scene, it was all I knew and where I was comfortable. I knew it couldn't last." Calypso raked her hair off her forehead with her fingers. "When I heard they'd held you for vehicular manslaughter I—I would have come back, I think, if you hadn't gotten off. I don't know. But you didn't get off, did you? It's on your record as a felony. Isn't it?"

Grieg huddled in the blankets, shivering. "Five years' probation under supervision. I wasn't anywhere by myself, until Pops' death. I was either with him or Doug Purdy, our hired guards, never unsupervised, those were the parameters of my parole. I had two more days to go; instead, I went AWOL to save you."

"That's rich!"

"It's also the truth, except the part where you need saving."

"Sometimes…sometimes I do. Sometimes memories of the accident squeeze me so hard I can't breathe. When they do, I'm climbing out of the car. You rocket around the corner. I hear the squeal of the brakes. I saw it all, Washburn."

He stood. The blankets fell around his ankles. He reached for the shirt on the floor, thinking he should leave. Boomer could walk him back to his Jeep through the snow then provide directions, worse case, he could sleep in the car.

She touched the bandage. "You can't go anywhere tonight. You're not well."

Calypso set the clothes on the end of the trestle table then helped him into a thermal undershirt and flannel outer shirt, all warm from the fire. When he was dressed, she lowered him into the rocker and coddled him in blankets. The cushion was hard. He recognized it as horsehair. "You made this cushion, didn't you?"

"Technically, Rex and Frisco did. Boomer supplied the worn blanket. I blanket stitched it together with hairs from the horses' tails."

She put a hand to Grieg's brow. "You've got a fever."

"I wanted to ask you out. I think I wanted to take you somewhere and embarrass you in front of the rest of the tight-ass little debutantes."

"I treated you like… You were trying to impress me. You whipped off the graduation gown like you were all new beneath it, but the pants of your tailored suit stuck to your socks from the static. I hear my words, I see you turn for the bar, and I just… Whose car did you steal that night?"

"Hugh Highland's, he was leaving early for a date, so it was prepped. I jumped in and drove. Every decision I made that night from the moment you cast your eyes on my socks was driven by embarrassment. It was like I took stupid pills."

She fingered his dark hair. "Can we forget how awful we were to each other, can we?"

"Depends on whether what's cooking in that pot is as good as it smells." Grieg rocked in the chair, the warm clothes and blankets worked the cold from his limbs, his eyes grew heavy with sleep. He couldn't sleep. He might wake up in a snowdrift or not at all.

Dempsey, Rafe, and Willard talking like old friends wormed its way to the fore. How did Rafe figure into it? For that matter, who was the guy that twanged Boomer's strings at Pete's? Too many players. Grieg lowered the blanket to his lap, admitting he was too weak to go anywhere tonight, knowing his plan to rescue Calypso was a fool's errand, odds were, she would end up saving him.

"I've gotten pretty good at rabbit stew. I have a hard time killing my chickens. I named them. Don't ever do that."

"Boomer told me something similar when we put the horses up, well, when he led the horses into their shelter. Tell me about your other man, Rafe, isn't it?"

"You were wearing his coat."

"Is that like walking in someone's shoes? Boomer handed it to me. Rafe must have left it in the stamp mill."

"First, let me tell you how sorry I was to hear about your father's death. He believed in me from the start."

The tumble of her words soothed Grieg to sleep, he batted his eyes to stay awake then nodded off. He dreamed that Doug

Purdy fought him for the reins of a stagecoach mired in ruts. Calypso was mid-sentence when his chin hit his chest and woke him. "He is the source of most of my meat, brings me rabbits, and the occasional nice thing."

"Rafe?"

She fingered an earring. "Tokens. He keeps strangers away. We're pretty settled."

"Romantically?"

"No. Well, maybe." She wiped the cutting board with a clean stroke of the knife then scrubbed it with salt. "He thinks so."

"Have you ever…"

"Sometimes, when the moon is right, our stomachs are full, and everything is aligned. Why?"

"I'm trying to get a handle on my competition, that's all."

"You should shave. I could do it for you."

Grieg shook his head.

"Tell me the dimple is still there?" She fingered through his scruff to his cleft chin. Her eyes danced for a split second, then went cold. She touched the stitches at his hairline. He peered up at her. She gave a quirky grin and smoothed the side of his face with the back of her right hand.

"Drove off the road about a week ago. The coroner was the first responder, the ambulance second," he answered the question in her eyes.

"Were you drunk, I mean, had you been drinking?"

"No, I was driving to the Suffolk County Courthouse to turn myself in for the last two days of my sentence. I never made it. Someone tagged me from behind and sent me into a ditch. My head got bounced around. My short-term memory was shot for days. To top it off, I'd been in Kenya and contracted Dengue. The fever comes and goes."

"And?" Callie clucked.

"While I was hospitalized and after, I followed the clues I was fed until I located you." He stopped. He hadn't connected the snippets of information he'd been provided until now, but what he'd blurted out to Callie was the truth. There was no doubt. "Rafe was in town when I met Boomer. Why?"

"A police helicopter landed in the pasture yesterday morning. Rafe claims he is the groundskeeper. No one questions it, he looks the part. He went into town to waylay you, he told me to hide until he came back."

"Me?"

"Whoever was sent?"

"Were the cops looking for you?"

"Maybe, but Special Agent Dempsey and Officer Ramirez were tracking a missing girl."

"She's the fifth or sixth, you know that, right?"

Callie shook her head. The door flew open. Rafe Bolt filled the frame, shotgun comfortably shouldered, leaving no doubt he knew how to use it.

Grieg jumped to his feet, the blanket over his shoulders fell onto the chair, the one over his legs to the floor.

"Dempsey and Ramirez landed their chopper right there." Rafe gestured with the tip of the shotgun to a point outside the back door. "Scared her. That's why I went into town, to intercept Boomer, little bastard."

"How long have you been listening?" Grieg asked. Rafe rested the gun on two wall pegs by the door. Crossing to Callie, he put a territorial hand on the small of her back. Grieg watched the hand slip south. "I asked you a question."

"Long enough to get the drift," Rafe answered

"The stew is done," Callie interjected into the boiling testosterone. "Rafe, have you seen Boomer. You know, he never misses a meal."

"Nope. Didn't see him."

"Then make yourself useful. Get some wood from the porch. We'll be four for dinner."

"From the rope burns, looks like you had rich boy tied. Why'd you let him go?"

"Boomer convinced me that I didn't want a dead man on my hands." Callie rested her right hand on the back of Grieg's chair. Rafe's dark eyebrows disappeared into his hairline. Grieg covered Callie's hand with his. Bolt didn't like it, not one bit.

"I met a Chief Willard in town, he claims Washburn broke parole. Says he's stepped in it this time. Willard had the paperwork on him to prove it. He's just itching to get Washburn in a chopper and haul his ass to prison." Rafe jerked his head Grieg's way. Rafe threw an arm over Callie's shoulders and edged her away from Grieg. Hugging her, he added, "Good news is the local cops are so busy chasing after Washburn, Boomer, the missing girl, *and* their own tails, we got time to pull up stakes and scramble out of here."

Boomer slammed through the door; snow swirled in behind him. He had a pie, butter, canned apples, and a loaf of frozen bread. He scanned Rafe. Bobbling his head, Boomer held the apples out to Callie. She accepted them, leaving Rafe's arm dangling in space.

"Smells good," Boomer said, setting the rest of his goods on the table before plunking his butt on the bench.

Callie assisted Grieg to the bench seat at the trestle table and wrapped the blanket over his shoulders. Rafe watched with hooded, unreadable eyes. Boomer, with a happy, goofy smile on his crooked face, straightened the blanket over Grieg's shoulders. Rafe sat next to Grieg. Grieg's early warning system that had kept him from being decapitated by a scimitar-wielding later day potentate twanged.

"Let's eat." Callie ladled rabbit in a thick broth into a blue willow bowl. The stew smelled wonderful. A taste test proved the accuracy of Grieg's nose, hasenpfeffer seasoned with bacon, onion, garlic, crushed peppercorn, bay rosemary, and juniper berries. A feast for the nose. The rabbit was a bit tough, but the aroma and stock made up for it. A glass of water appeared at his left elbow. "Warning. The latrine is through the woods."

"I'm male, what's the difference."

"I'm learning," Callie said. Grieg glanced over his shoulder to see if she was kidding. Her gesture said everything. "Tromping out there gets old. Not to mention the bears, cougars, and bobcats. So, I've determined that by the end of the year, I will be able to drop trou and take a whiz without hitting my socks."

Grieg started laughing and couldn't stop, quipping, between guffaws, "I'll still be able to beat you for distance."

Boomer giggled, spewing stew from his stuffed mouth. Rafe stood, planted a hand on Callie's right shoulder, kissed the top of her head before ladling more rabbit into his bowl. Grieg's eyes locked on the bowie-sized skinning knife hanging unsheathed from Rafe's belt.

"You?" Rafe asked. Grieg held up his bowl. Boomer curled over his and continued to eat, dredging a thick slab of bread in the spicy stock. A bowl in each hand, Rafe kneed Boomer in the back, nearly planting Boomer's face in his stew.

"Hey!" Grieg challenged.

"We had a good life here, Boomer messed it up. Went for the money. Told lies. Damn it, Boomer!" Rafe slammed his right palm on the table next to Boomer. Boomer jumped.

"Stop it!" Callie ordered. "Rafe, why didn't you tell me the police had identified the body found by my car?"

"I just heard in town today," Rafe responded. He settled on the seat next to Grieg. Boomer scooted his body and bowl to the far end of the table out of Rafe's reach.

"Grieg figured out where I was without photos flying back and forth. Leave Boomer alone."

"Grieg? Is it? What kind of a name is that for a grown man?" Grieg laughed. Rafe elbowed him hard enough to make him gasp. "Don't piss me off, Washburn. Chief Willard couldn't stop talking about you, said you were a worthless piece of murdering shit. Seems some man named Purdy went to the cops with quite the tale about how you set your old man up for the kill. They find you, you likely won't see daylight again."

Grieg stared at Rafe. Using a splinter from the edge of the table as a toothpick, Grieg dislodged a piece of rabbit meat from between two molars. Callie rolled her eyes.

Rafe snorted, "So, mighty white hunter, Purdy claims someone sounding like your old man called demanding a meeting on the wrong side of Damascus. Purdy went. Says the last thing your old man did was ask Purdy why here? Then blam! Purdy claims it was you on the phone."

"I got an alibi. I was in Kenya contracting the Dengue, no cellphone reception as my bodyguard can testify. Purdy wants WashEx."

"Ha!"

"Don't piss me off, Bolt," Grieg snapped. Rafe tried for a second rib shot, Grieg stomped on Rafe's right instep then scooted down to join Boomer at the end of the table.

Callie plunked Grieg's water glass in front of his new seat. "Drink. You need it. Food then bed." Rafe reached for her, she slapped his hand away. "I shot him. So, drop it, okay. You can continue playing junkyard dog in the morning. Both of you." Her eyes scolded Grieg.

Boomer grinned, dredged, and chewed. Grieg followed Boomer's lead, eating in silence while Callie traipsed in and out of the cabin, humming. When she was done with her housekeeping, she touched Grieg on the shoulder and motioned him to the corner farthest from the door and fire.

Two burlap feed bags served as a mattress. Callie had covered the resulting palette with a beige blanket striped blue and yellow at the edges and topped it with crocheted afghans of various neutral colored wools. Grieg didn't bother undressing. Boots already off, he lay on the bedding, pulled up the afghans and rolled to his left side to avoid his throbbing right bicep. His ribs hurt, his head hurt, he figured the pain would keep him awake.

Boomer slapped out the door with a parting snarl aimed at Rafe, startling Grieg awake. The grain in the bags shifted. He wiggled down until he found the correct support and resumed snoring.

Voices woke him a second time. Rafe and Calypso sat by the fireplace as communal as an old married couple. The fire flickered across their faces. She was relaxed. Rafe's eyes drifted Grieg's way. Their voices became whispers.

The white noise soothed Grieg back to sleep. A Russian oligarch snarled displeasure over WashEx opening a Turkish rhodium field. Ray sent Grieg to Kenya and took on the risk. Doug wasn't needed for the deal. Only a Washburn could sign the contract. Now, Pops was dead, and Doug was regent.

Grieg rolled to his back. The clock wound back five years. He was drunk, embarrassed, and pissed. The car keys were in the ignition, waiting for the driver. Someone knocked on the driver's side window. Grieg gunned the car. Two men were talking at the gated entrance, Doug Purdy waved as Grieg tore out the drive. Awakened by his own nightmare, Grieg nuzzled into his pillow, unable to find sleep.

By the stars framed in the doorway, it was near midnight when Rafe left. The blanket of snow on the cabin's roof insulated the interior against the descending cold. Callie sat by the warm hearth, knitting, humming, and wagging her stockinged feet.

When the fire had roasted down to embers, she rubbed her hands together, then checked Grieg's brow. He opened his eyes and smiled at her. She tucked the blankets in around his shoulders. He fell asleep making a guttural sound at the back of his throat, not a snore, something more akin to a purr.

Callie smoothed Grieg's hair from his eyes as he slept, disarmed by the contented rumble of his breathing, overcome by her own cruelty the first time they were introduced. That night, one of the Kennedy boys was paying homage to her. He was considered the catch of the season. She knew she was stunning in her Valentino with its plunging neckline and shimmering fabric in a color of garnet that managed to set off both the hazel of her eyes and the chestnut of her hair sculpted into an up-do that dared gravity. Her mother's diamond tiara, on loan for the night, provided structure for the sculpture. A gold necklace dangled in her cleavage, showing off a brilliant yellow topaz and diamond bobble. Her shoes matched the color of her dress. They had spiked heels with half-inch platforms and were held on her feet by skinny little straps. The dress was slit up the left side. When she walked, one long, lean athlete's leg dusted in gold powder flashed. She strutted, flipping her skirt, hoping her latest conquest was in pain undercover of his tuxedo's trousers.

Callie's mother floated toward them; her gloved hand appropriately placed on the offered arm of a young man with a bad haircut. Callie's conquest threw his head like her horse, Fructose, and made a similar sound as he checked over Virginia's escort. Maybe it was the way the guy on her mother's arm cocked his head or the amused curve of his lips, or his eyes daring her beneath dark lashes, or perhaps the effortless grace of his slim, broad-shouldered body that made her want to slap him. The self-assurance he radiated, as though he could take down anyone in the room, diminished her. Calypso opened her mouth and gave the stranger the full Darcy. The tone of her voice, the small chuckle of amusement from her beau, the anger in her mother's eyes, and the hurt in the stranger's flooded her anew.

As her Kennedy led her away with pride in her wit, she glanced arrogantly over her shoulder. The man she had disdained put two fingers to his lips then folded one. She threw her chin up as hot color rouged her cheeks. In her wake, three women approached him, then four, then five. His suit didn't fit.

The style was outdated. He blushed, excused himself to her mother, then danced with each of the women. And, he drank.

Callie beckoned her mother to her side. Virginia Swale glided to her daughter.

"Momma, who was that?"

"Ray Washburn's boy. He plans to join his father once he receives his doctorate from Yale. You wouldn't be in that dress, at this function, without Ray's ability to find a fortune asleep in the ground where everyone swore there was none. Grieg's his heir, Ray says his boy is a magnet for minerals. Ray asked me to introduce him to you."

"Oh, Mom, he is, I...I don't know."

"I do," Virginia said, slipping away to dance with her husband. Callie's parents glowed in the lights of the chandelier overhead, but not as bright as the scarlet blush that descended from Calypso's face to her chest. Across the room, Sally Purdy, arms folded across her flat chest, tapped a toe. When Grieg Washburn extended a hand to her, she incandesced.

Callie's Kennedy held out his arm, forearm bent for her hand. He led her into the table for dinner. Throughout the meal, Callie spied on Ray Washburn's boy regretting every word that had passed her jejune lips. The next Saturday, she drove her coupe to the Southampton Hunt and Polo grounds and watched Washburn play. He was a monster on the field as physical as his seat was beautiful. She'd rushed into the paddock to congratulate him, turning back when Sally Purdy put a daintily gloved hand on Washburn's mount.

And, so, it was she who set the trajectory for the tragedy to come.

XVII

Dr. Chaudhary straightened the shawl Delia wore to ward off the late spring chill as they strolled by the sea along Meremer's curves and inlets. The beach, besides its beauty, provided a bug-free environment, unless one counted the sand fleas, bees, and flies. Delia didn't, Hari might.

Hari swatted a fly from his eyes. "I hate flies, ever since I was a boy in Mumbai. Too many flies in the world for my taste." Delia birthed Grieg there while Ray fanned, keeping her cool and fly free. She should tell this lovely man that she had lived in his town of birth, that he shared it with her son. She didn't.

He swung Delia's picnic basket in his left hand so that he had a hand free to hold hers. Delia packed the basket with the most scrumptious Indian tea items she could imagine: Mirchi Bajji made of green chilis, tamarind, and coconut; Aloo Bonda potato-filled nummy drops with coriander chutney for dipping and Mawa cakes. Two small thermoses, one brimming with Masala Chai, created by adding elaichi, cinnamon, ginger, cloves, and herbs, malty, brewed Assam tea in the other. She needed Hari's help, and, yes, she hoped all the special treats would make it hard for him to refuse her request.

A bistro table topped by a mosaic of blue, green, and gray tiles with two matching chairs occupied a concrete platform surrounded by half-inch plexiglass designed to keep the wind at bay and the view astounding. Gulls swooped, terns ran hither and yon, under clouds that rushed across the slate water to the Outer Banks.

Delia motioned Hari to sit. He followed directions well. She poured the Assam tea into two China teacups so thin that the level of the liquid was revealed. She arranged the treats on a small tray brought for that purpose. Hari started to grab a Mawa cake then retracted his hand like a crab into a cave. He wore his delight on his face, a broad white-toothed smile lit his dark eyes.

"For me?"

"For you?"

"What do you want, fair lady?" he grinned, with a swoop of his right hand.

"A favor?"

"It is well known that I will do anything for a Mawa cake, it is untested what evil I might perpetrate for an Aloo Bonda. The day may not turn out as you planned."

Delia reached across the table, taking the hand Hari intended for the Mawa cake. "First, I want you to know that I know that all Indians living in the U.S. do not know each other."

"That's good, especially since many Pakistanis are mistaken for Indians. Also, I am Christian and an egg eater, all bad." He managed to stuff a Mawa in his mouth with his free hand.

"I had no idea. Still, is it possible you know a Dr. Khalil from MIT."

"You *do* know that Khalil is an Arabic name?"

Delia shook her head. The freshening breeze had blown strands of hair loose from the scarf she wore to keep it from doing just that. "But I'm sure he was from India. I'm sure."

"Are you speaking of Ben Khalil?"

"I am. He just died."

"He was from Mumbai. His father was a diplomat. But he was a Muslim and an Arab according to his obituary."

"You didn't know him?"

"No."

"Oh." Delia glanced out to sea, sipped her Chai tea, and wondered where she could possibly go from here. She had convinced herself that Hari Chaudhary could help her. She looked up his name online, it meant the one who removes evil. She needed his superpowers in a big way to save her husband's company and her son.

Hari squeezed the hand he held. "My brother, Ajay, a professor at MIT, does…did. They were not in the same department, but Ajay spoke of Ben Khalil. I would be happy to ask Ajay any question you would like asked, though I cannot guarantee an answer."

"You wouldn't mind?"

"For you, fair lady, no."

"I need to know if Dr. Khalil died of natural causes and what became of the items in his laboratory. He was working on a special project called CaMP, all caps except the a. I need to know what became of any CaMP items."

"Wow, this is like some thriller, like in books."

"No. It is about my son. Hari, you saved him. I've never asked you what you thought of Grieg as a man. Maybe you never thought of him as anything but a patient, but…"

Hari kissed each knuckle on her hand. "I liked him. I liked how he loved you. How you love him."

"Do you think he is…"

"I think he is a man who has been in the shadow of his father all his life who lost his young manhood to a tragedy of his making. When the person they strove to emulate is taken from them, the struggle becomes more difficult. Men like that do things, take risks they shouldn't." Delia sighed. Hari smiled, "I think he has a lovely mother. I will call my brother tonight. Should I call you if I learn anything?"

"No. Hari, my house is bugged, every room."

"My dear?" His hand tightened on hers, a surge of comfort swept through her.

"If you hear anything I should know, call me to the hospital. I'll drive right over."

"Have you checked your purse for these bugs—your car?"

"I'd like to chastise you for watching too many spy movies, but I have. Daily."

"But why?" He toyed with her fingers, his dark eyes intent on hers.

"Would you believe that I am at the center of a maelstrom surrounding the future of the world?"

A grin split Hari's handsome face from cheek to cheek. "Even as I believe you can dance your way out of it. Shall we enjoy our tea by the sea? I can't go without a Mirchi Bajji for a moment longer. And, more tea so that I may stare over my teacup at you while reminiscing over the luck I had to be on Trauma the night of your son's accident."

"Blessings," Delia said, pouring tea, and pushing the Mirchi Bajji Hari's way.

Jones arranged flowers from the early blooming beds in a Waterford vase on the hall table. He slipped a hand behind the frame of the Mary Cassatt painting of a vibrant vase of flowers and dropped the bug in the water. When the telephone rang, he answered, ringing the hall bell to let his mistress know the call was for her.

Delia answered it in the drawing-room, a small fire warming the evening chill away.

Hari Chaudhary said, "Mrs. Washburn, I had a little free time this afternoon and took the opportunity to review your son's scans. It is important that I see you. Are you available this evening?"

"I am, is there a time that is best for you?"

"The sooner we meet, the better. I need to discuss this new diagnosis with you." Hari was so convincing, Delia almost believed him. She was certain any listeners would.

"It will take a bit of time, Fred, the stableman, is currently buffing my car, he keeps the windows bug free. Be assured I'll be there as soon as possible."

"It would be best if we met in the cafeteria. Shall we say in an hour?"

"I'm on my way."

Delia called down to the stables, Fred pulled the swept car up to the front door then held the door open for her. Jones drove.

Dr. Chaudhary sat at a table in the center of the hospital cafeteria, an open patient folder covered the tabletop. Hari stood as Delia entered. She crossed to him, still in the tight-fitting jeans, flowered shirt, shawl, and babushka she'd worn on the beach. His smile made her feel fresh. He waved her to a chair, then sat and thrummed the patient folder.

"Your son requires additional surgery, as you can see from this scan. I don't know how I missed it. You may want a second opinion, please take the recommendation." He slid a page of notes from the folder. She folded them and stuffed them into her purse.

"Summarize?" she asked.

"Ajay recommends that I do not ask any more questions, that I am careful who I speak to and that I leave no tracks. That doesn't sound innocent to me. Apparently, persons tore up Khalil's garage and house. Neighbors reported it. Before the police arrived, an explosion destroyed the garage and set the kitchen on fire. Anything in or near the garage was a total loss. His computer was breached then wiped. Finally, one of Khalil's workmates claims though Khalil had a wonky heart (Khalil's word for it), he managed his health and was in no danger of dying anytime soon. In short, the nature of his death is being questioned."

"What was in the garage?"

"An engine. The incendiary device shredded it."

"But…"

"Ajay says the same friend noted that Khalil used an online dropbox. The police want in, but no one knows how to access it or even where it exists. What's this about?"

"The engine was a prototype. That's all I know," Delia lied.

Hari laughed, "I suppose he found a way to use water instead of gasoline."

"Imagine what that would do to the price of water!" Delia joked.

"Imagine what that would do to the price of oil and the economy of the oil-producing countries."

Delia covered Hari's right hand. "Thank you. Please be careful, tell your brother the same. What seemed a simple corporate takeover just made a left turn. This may not be about WashEx at all unless WashEx is to be collateral damage."

At Delia's request, Jones drove toward Meremer, his eyes sweeping the review mirror every thirty seconds. Seeing no one, he diverted to Felix Highland's home on Dune Road in Quogue. Meremer fit into the left wing of Felix's Castlelaine. Balconies burgeoned from the red with white trim faux Dutch barn exterior, all with views down to the Sound. With nine bedrooms and fourteen baths, the entirety of WashEx could have an overnighter. Jones drove to the front door. Felix' butler rushed out sweeping open the car door for Delia. Jones parked and remained with the car in the tarmac parking area by the garage.

Felix met Delia as she entered. "My dear, you look positively frazzled." Felix pecked her on the cheek. Delia put her hand up to stop the next pass.

"It's the babushka, it keeps frumping my hair." She surveyed the entry. It was spotless, not a tossed newspaper, not a note, not a mote, not a stray hair, no DNA floating in the wind, spotless. It made her want to gag. Houses were supposed to be a little rumpled around the edges by the detritus of the occupants. For all the beauty of the rooms, the furniture, the priceless paintings, the sterility of it jarred her nerves. Though she did lust after a Utrillo painting of the rooftops of Paris that hung over his entry table.

"Don't get me wrong, I'm honored that you stopped by. Will you join me in a gin tonic?"

"Two if you got' em," Delia said, mimicking Mae West though she hadn't the hips or the breasts or, well, anything in common with the vamp. Felix shook his head in mock horror. She followed him to his observatory with its wet bar.

One wall of the room was a sheet of glass that breathed ghoulishly during high winds. The view of the Sound dotted with sails and yachts was astonishing even by Delia's jaded standards. At the unmistakable clink of ice in a glass, Delia turned to Felix. He was dressed casually for him in gray gabardines and a polo shirt complete with the tiny embroidered polo pony over his left breast.

"You lied to me," Delia said, taking the proffered gin tonic. Felix used only Bombay sapphire and very little tonic. "Khalil left a damn sight more than a note about the engine at Yellow Sky. He uploaded everything he could before he was murdered."

"Oh, Delia, you are quickly turning into your son. I see now where he gets his charming lack of reality. His willingness to chase after a chimera. What makes you think Ben Khalil was murdered and had sufficient warning to post whatever to Yellow Sky."

"You are aware, aren't you that persons unknown blew the prototype sky high. That Ben Khalil was at his office at the university when his garage went up in flames. He knew. He knew they were coming for him."

"They?"

"The persons who bug people's houses."

"Oh, I see. We now have a conspiracy of *they*."

"Don't belittle me," Delia slapped Felix as hard as she could. Felix put a hand to his left cheek.

"You really are overwrought." His cool was disturbing.

"I'm not some stupid showgirl, Felix Highlander. I kept Ray's travel expenses and off-site books. Six years ago, Larch Swale was blackmailing your son. What has Hugh managed since? Ask yourself now, because when my son takes the reins of the company, the favored Highland status ends. Hear me? Do you hear me?"

Felix placed his hands on her upper arms and stepped into her frame. For a tiny second, she was afraid of what he intended, then his eyes softened. "I'm so sorry, Delia, so sorry for all this."

"Tell Sally I want those ledgers. I know they exist. If you've got them, give them to her and help her save face."

"I don't know what you're talking about."

"Ask your son then." Delia pulled out of his hands and stalked out the door. It wasn't until Jones pulled out of the drive that she fixed on Felix's parting words; Sorry for all this? What this?

XVIII

A pounding staccato woke Grieg. Scrambling to his knees, he grabbed the nearest weapon, a broomstick, and advanced on the cabin door. Callie beat him. She must have been standing watch by the fire.

"Let me in!" Rafe called, hammering, rattling it with each hit. "Wake up, dammit!"

Callie raised the drop bolt. Rafe fell in mid-pound, the stock of his shotgun serving as a doorknocker. Grieg stepped back, lowering the broom to his side like an ROTC cadet. It was around five in the morning from the haze of light on the horizon. Grieg checked his watch. Five-ten. Not bad.

Rafe put his hands on his knees as though breathless, despite the measured footsteps he'd left in the snow. Grieg stepped in front of Callie. She didn't like it, but she stayed behind him. Pops would have said two stallions and one mare, bad business.

"What is it?" Callie asked, over Grieg's shoulder.

"Boomer's got the missing girl tied up at his place. I wondered why he took so long getting the butter and pie, so I waited and followed him. I've been suspicious of him for a while, haven't I, Callie?"

"How do you know how long it took Boomer to bring the food?" Grieg asked.

"Something Callie said when he came in like you're here like he'd been gone a long time. What difference does it make?"

The difference was, it was a lie. Callie had taken the pies from Boomer without comment. Callie snuck a hand in a back pocket of Grieg's jeans as though acknowledging his thoughts.

"Grab your first aid kit and come with me. If we don't move now, the girl will be gone or dead by daylight. Come on, girl!" Rafe clapped his hands. "Get a move on."

Calypso took her hand from Grieg's pocket and pivoted toward the bedroom.

Grieg stopped her. Callie brushed Grieg's hand away. Rafe's lips quirked. Grieg snapped, "She's not going. I've seen pictures of the missing women. Damn it, they all look like Calypso, everyone."

"Oh...oh...no," slipped past Callie's lips. She plunked down onto a chair.

"Washburn, you're elected. Get a coat."

Grieg yanked Rafe's field coat from a hook by the door. Callie helped him maneuver his stiff right arm into the sleeve. Rafe watched Grieg's every move. Something Moms had told him grappled for the surface, something about men who hurt women. Grieg thought he should warn Callie but about what? Rafe grabbed Grieg and pivoted him toward the exit, pushed him onto the porch, slammed the door, and yelled, "Bolt the damn door!"

The bolt rasped into the bracket as Rafe set the pace and Grieg realized he'd been outmaneuvered. Bolt had come for him.

Rafe moved like silk in the wind through the rough, snowy terrain. Grieg struggled over every little hump in the duff. He thudded, harrumphed, and tumbled over downed branches trying to keep up. Rafe didn't seem worried about the racket despite sneaking up on a killer with a hostage. As they neared the gate onto the property, Rafe held his right hand up, made a fist then brought it down. Grieg knelt. Rafe ducked behind a tree trunk that could have hidden a small town and motioned Grieg to a tree five-feet to the fore of his. Grieg slid to the tree, melding behind the trunk, one hand on rough bark that smelled of vanilla.

Despite the lip of gray at the horizon, a bright moon bounced light off the snow. Rafe signaled Grieg to follow. Twenty steps farther, he disappeared. Grieg worked his way to Rafe's datum. Rafe pointed. Hidden by the vast girth of a redwood, Grieg studied a lean-to built in the understory.

The structure was roughly fifteen feet long, its walls formed by branches woven between four handily positioned tree trunks. Only the reedy trail of smoke sifting through the peaked branches of a shed roof indicated something other than a badger, fisher, or fox lived within.

Rafe flashed a signal. Grieg scooted to the base of the structure as instructed. He lay in the snow-covered duff. The cold of early morning ate through the borrowed field coat and into Grieg, reminiscent of a star-filled night in Afghanistan when he awakened covered in frost next to a warlord who possessed a valley full of gold and iron ore. Now, like then, he lay still. With the breath of dawn, the forest cracked, groaned, whispered, and soughed. A cap of snow fell from a pine branch with a plop.

The outer walls of Boomer's lean-to were remarkably weatherproof; in fact, cracks were chinked with a mixture made of mud and pine needles. Grieg held his hand next to the chinking. It was warm. He searched the ground for something to augur a peephole. He wheedled a stout pine twig through the mud until he had a clear view of the interior.

Boomer's digs were basic. Shelves of raw boards and tin cans kept a few goods off the earthen floor. A lumpy bearskin rug near the central flue of a metal fireplace served as his bed. The fireplace exited through the roof of blackened canvas topped by heavy, interlaced green boughs. Boomer, minus the ever-present fishing vest, stoked the fire with pinewood, his shadow dancing on the canvas tarp that lined the long interior wall. The smoke smelled green.

"Please," a husky voice whispered over the shushing wind. "Please."

"Water? Food?" Boomer stirred something warming over the fire in a Dutch oven. "Tea, soon."

Boomer tested the brew with a dirty finger. Satisfied, he warmed his hands against the mug as he crossed to the bearskin. He threw a layer of fur back, exposing a teen shivering in her pajama top and underpants, her brown hair limp and tangled with leaves. Her upper arms and thighs were bruised, displaying clear fingermarks. Her wrists were bloody, where rope had bitten into them. Boomer ran his hands down her arms. She whimpered. He put an arm behind her back and eased her to sitting, then held the mug to her lips, his eyes wandering her body as she drank small, thankful sips.

Rafe brushed the canvas door aside.

"Get out!" Boomer growled, gesturing him away.

Rafe pounced, shoving Boomer through the fire and knocking over the Dutch oven. Liquid hissed in the sparking wood. Boomer turned on Rafe. From a crouched position, he drove his head into Rafe's mid-section. The lean-to shook with thudding bodies. Grieg rounded the structure and ducked into the small space.

Rafe had Boomer pinned in the far corner, a burning branch held over his head. Grieg grabbed the limb on the backswing and wrestled the torch from Rafe's grip, dousing it in the spilled water. Rafe growled. Boomer cowered, clawing his way into the brush at his back. Rafe yanked a rope from around his waist and whipped the forearm Boomer used to cover his face. Boomer dropped his arm. Rafe lassoed Boomer's neck and yanked until Boomer crawled out. When Boomer reached mid-room, Rafe tied him hand and foot then kicked him in the lower back. Boomer's head thudded to the dirt floor.

Grieg swung Rafe around. "What the hell is the matter with you?"

"He's a monster!" Rafe shoved Grieg away, turning his attention to the contents of the lean-to. He swiped a forearm to empty one shelf, then his hands, throwing everything he found into the center of the small space.

Grieg knelt beside the bearskin, unsure how to comfort the girl. He hummed, showed her his right hand then stroked her hair from her forehead. She closed her eyes. He thought that was a good sign. He uncovered her inch by inch, soothing her as he went. Her blue eyes popped open. She shook her head. His beard hid his lips, he was covered in dirt, he was terrifying her.

"Are you hurt?"

"I'm hungry," she muttered, her voice void of emotion. Bruises blued her arms. Grieg wanted to check further, but decency stopped him. If he had been hurt as she had, the last thing he would want would be to be gawked at by a stranger.

Grieg checked the lean-to for clothes. There were none. Strips of cloth leaked out of the knocked over kettle. He gathered the clean, boiled lengths torn from a T-shirt. Returning to the girl, he stroked her right wrist until she relaxed, then with her fearful eyes watching, he bandaged her injuries. He checked her ankles; she'd been fettered. He bound the tears in the flesh of her ankles, then bundled her in the bearskin and tied it robe-like with a leftover hank of cloth.

She didn't move, not even to stretch. Trance-like, she stared at Rafe's shadow on the walls as he dumped food tins on the ground, rooted behind the shelves, and dug into the walls. Boomer lay still, unwilling to play into Rafe's wrath. Rafe rummaged under a pile of tarps. Turning to Grieg with a cry of triumph, Rafe flipped open the lid of a cardboard cigar box.

"Look, look at this!" Rafe held up a signet ring with the initials AP, a necklace of fake pearls, a deck of casino souvenir cards, a happy birthday card, and a hank of chestnut hair. "It's enough to hang him."

The girl quaked. Grieg squeezed her left arm, hoping to telegraph that he would protect her.

"For all we know, he buried his victims near here," Rafe stomped on the well-swept dirt floor. Boomer's meager belongings humped in a disorganized pile tilted then slid into the still glowing embers. Rafe grabbed the rope around Boomer and pulled.

"You son-of-a-bitch. You've brought hell down on us."

Boomer whimpered, raising his bound hands to Grieg, pleading, "I found her like that, in the snow, on the rock where the coyote hangs out. I brought her here to help her. Please."

"Liar!" Rafe bellowed. He jammed the cigar box in a knapsack, then yanked Boomer to his loosely bound feet and shoved him out the canvas into the melting snow. Returning, Rafe shouldered Grieg aside, picked up the girl and carried her into the growing day, the knapsack bouncing on his back.

Grieg untied Boomer's legs.

"Leave him!" Rafe yelled over his shoulder. Grieg helped Boomer up. Rafe stopped, shifted the girl in his arms and growled, "He's a blemish, a wart. You've seen the way he looks at Callie. You've seen it. Like he wants to lick her."

"How far to the cabin?" Grieg asked, trying not to visualize.

"Another half-mile. I can carry the girl, no problem," Rafe responded.

"My Jeep is closer. The keys are in my jeans. We can drive to town, turn Boomer in, hand the cigar box over to the cops, and take the girl to a hospital."

Rafe's long strides increased the distance between the men. Grieg struggled to keep up with Boomer staggering behind him. "You tossed Boomer's place like you knew what you were looking for," Grieg called.

Rafe pivoted. "You think I planted it, rich boy? I'm doing my best. Don't you think I checked your car? The battery is missing. That Jeep isn't going anywhere."

"You saying Boomer took it?" Grieg stopped. Boomer fell face first on the forest floor and rolled to his side.

"He was closest to it. He has the most to hide. Wants us stuck up here on this mountain. Sure, as heck, doesn't want the cops up here. He's got to kill the girl, us. I mean, what are his options. You don't get it, we're in a world of hurt."

"Bull. Look at him."

Rafe shifted the girl in his arms and strode out. "Callie is an expert with poultices and herb teas. If anyone can help this girl, she can."

"The girl needs more than that." Grieg skip-stepped. Feeling dizzy, he tied Boomer's rope to his belt and put his hands on his knees, hoping the altitude explained it.

"You go for help then. I'll stay to make sure the girl, Callie, and the bottom feeder are here when you arrive with the cavalry. Course, Chief Willard will nab you, sic the cops after Callie for killing her old man, can't kid me nobody cares about Callie."

Rafe strode off. Grieg yanked on Boomer's rope. Boomer fell to his knees, crying, "It wasn't me. Wasn't. Those aren't my things. Not mine. How can I have stuff, I don't have? How?"

Grieg helped Boomer to his feet. "Look, I saw the pictures you took with that phone. It was the woman from the campground, the one that attacked her stalker. Maybe not the same day, but the same woman." Grieg pushed Boomer's right sleeve up, exposing his forearm. The puncture wounds were bloody from Rafe's whipping, the edges raised and infected.

"It wasn't me."

"It was, Boomer, seven times you."

Boomer stared at the oozing blood on his arm then woefully up at Grieg. Grieg pointed to a branch across the path. Boomer stumbled over it. They arrived at the clearing as Rafe leaped onto the cabin porch and kicked the bottom of the door. Callie swung the door open in response to Rafe's thud.

"Take her into my bedroom," Callie ordered, peering out the door toward the timber. "Where's Grieg?"

Rafe turned sideways to ease the girl through the door. "He's bringing in Boomer. Boomer did this, Callie."

"And the others? Did he kill the others?"

Rafe left Callie on the porch. She stared into the trees before following him into the cabin. Grieg stayed in the shadows with Boomer at his side.

"Please, please keep Rafe from me. Please." Boomer nearly crawled into the field jacket with Grieg. A filthy hand oozed up between them. Boomer placed it at Grieg's throat. Grieg lurched back. "Fever, you've got a fever. A bad one," Boomer withdrew his hand. "You need to go to the hospital with the girl. I'm not kidding, I can feel the heat through your shirt."

Grieg put a hand over Boomer's mouth. Boomer's eyes danced wildly above it. Grieg shook his head. Boomer settled, turning his back into Grieg's coat. The little man was cool. It felt good. He prayed the Dengue hadn't morphed into hemorrhagic fever that what he felt was instead disgust, dismay, and too damn much tramping in the mountains in the snow.

Rafe carried the teen into Callie's bedroom, placed her gently on the bed then took a step back. The moment Callie touched the pelt, the girl's eyes flew open. A whimper escaped her chapped lips. Callie cooed, "You're fine. You're safe. We'll get word to the police. They'll let your parents know you've been found. You'll be with them by tomorrow night at the latest."

Callie untied the rope that held the bearskin closed. Seeing the girl's body, she overcame the desire to warm a tub of water and give the girl a good scrubbing, she knew better. As filthy, scratched, and bloody as it was, her body was her testimony.

Callie settled for stroking one of the girl's bony shoulders. "You go and do what you need to do, Rafe. I'll take care of her. She'll testify."

Rafe cleared his throat. The girl whimpered.

"Go. She's frightened, and a strange man leaning over my shoulder isn't helping. Go…go," Callie made a shooing motion with her right hand.

"She's okay then?"

"Physically, I guess. Get out of here."

Rafe left the door open a crack. Callie closed it as she passed on her way to a three-legged chest of drawers, the fourth leg a brick. She rooted for a flannel nightgown, a gift from Boomer, had he taken it from one of his victims? Callie glanced at the bearskin rug, the girl stared back at her through red-rimmed blue or gray eyes. It was difficult to tell in the slanting light that eked through the wavy glass of the window, but her hair was a match for Callie's.

Callie helped the girl into the nightgown then removed the bandages from the girl's wrists. Her comfrey poultice would soothe the wounds. She had been experimenting with distilling plantain leaves with the calendula and yarrow flowers in the mix. "My name's Callie," she said. "Yours?"

"Bobbi, short for Roberta--Munro." Callie ran a light finger over deep bruises at the front of the girl's throat. The impression on the left side was darker than that on the right. Mallow tea would ease the internal soreness of Bobbi's throat and the wheezing in her lungs. Callie had no magic for the bruises.

Callie felt the girl's forehead. "No fever. I'm going to leave you for a minute to make some tea. It's my own concoction. It will soothe your throat. And, I have some stew leftover from last night that I can heat up. Both would be good for you. When was the last time you ate?" Bobbi held up two fingers. "Do you think you can eat now?"

"Water?"

Callie offered Bobbi the glass of water she kept on the nightstand beside the bed. Bobbi two-handed the glass between filthy hands with chipped nails. She lipped the cup, barely drinking at all. Callie covered the girl's shaking hands with one of hers. "You're safe here. The man who brought you will go for help as soon as he eats. You're safe with me, tomorrow safer still. The doctors will know just what to do for you at the hospital. If there is… they'll take care of that, too."

"No…no…no," the girl's response built into a wail. Callie rocked Bobbi, humming a favorite lullaby until Bobbi slumped onto the pillow.

When Bobbi slept, Callie slipped out of the room. Rafe peered guiltily over a bowl of stew. Callie checked out the window. No one was there. She built up the fire. It didn't matter if it smoked, in fact, she wanted it to, hoping it would bring the cops. Callie's idyll was over, no matter the outcome for Bobbi. As soon as Rafe left for help, Callie planned to sneak deep into the mine shaft and prepare her exit.

"I thought you said Grieg was bringing Boomer in. Where are they?"

Rafe cocked his head, his jacket askew, his eyes remote. Washburn wrapped in her blankets, rocking and staring into the fire, unable to voice his emotions invaded her thoughts. Rafe stood, wiping his hands down the front of his jeans.

"The girl needs a doctor. I'll hike out to the Fish Camp, use the phone there, then stay until a unit comes to the gate. I'll advise them to bring reinforcements for Boomer and Washburn. You're sure she is Bobbi Munro?"

"Positive," Callie answered, adding wood to the briskly burning fire.

"If I go, the cops will bring Chief Willard."

"Willard was the first responder the night my mother died. Isn't Willard out of his jurisdiction. Isn't that what they say?"

Rafe shrugged. "No leniency for the rich boy this time."

"Take Rex if you want. I'll saddle him for you." Callie stepped out onto the porch. She was going to miss this place. The way the sun grazed the meadow, the song of the trees, the snake in the rafters. All of it. She walked with Rafe to the horse paddock.

Callie lifted the bar and pushed the barn door open. Rex nickered. Frisco whinnied. She scuffed through the straw. Rex hung his head over the gate in greeting. She scratched his nose. An image of Washburn hanging sideways in his saddle like a Comanche, polo mallet at the ready, made her grin.

"No horse. I'd be a sitting duck on it." Rafe slung his rifle over his shoulder and his packed knapsack on his back. He kissed her on the cheek and swung out the door, his long stride eating up the distance to the timber. She rubbed her cheek and shaded her eyes, scanning the understory for shadows, seeing none she crossed to the cabin.

Three fugitives, one victim and a murderer, well, two murderers. Well, one murder and one man convicted of vehicular manslaughter, hunted by a man who had made it a mission to jail him, all on this mountain. All she could do was ensure Bobbi's safety and hers and pray for the innocent.

Boomer plucked at Grieg's sleeve. When he had Grieg's attention, he whispered, "I have a hideout. If you can make it, I got some supplies. You can figure out what to do." Grieg studied Boomer's lopsided face and earnest eyes.

"We go in, worse case Rafe ties you up in the stamp mill until the police arrive. It's not a bad idea. I'll be here in case anything goes wrong."

At a sharp crack, Boomer dropped to his knees. "Rafe, shooting at shadows. We can crawl out of here. Maybe twenty-feet on there is a gully. We get into that, and we're home free."

"Boomer, you hunted and killed four women. Bobbi would have been five."

Boomer shook his head. Tears welled in his eyes. "If you let Rafe tie me up in the stamp mill, I'm dead. Rafe'll kill me, then you, then the girl, then grab Callie and run."

Grieg crouched behind a granite outcropping. He fingered the mica blinging in the rock, transported for a moment to the rhodium site in the Turkish hills, his father alive and standing beside him grinning.

Boomer popped his head up over the rock, checked the path behind them, satisfied, he joined Grieg. "You don't look good. Callie would know what to do. She's amazing, like a chemist. But we can't go in, not with Rafe around. You got money. I could get you to the Lodge. You could get one of those plush rooms and sleep."

"I'm not leaving Callie on this mountain. Alone."

"I knew that. I knew that the minute I saw you. One look and I knew who you were, who to trust. Highland messaged pictures of Willard and Dempsey to me. I erased the pictures from the phone before I handed it to you like you erased Jessie's when you handed it back."

"But not the photos of the woman at the campsite?"

"She was something, dancing herself across the canvas of her tent. She knew I was out there. She wasn't scared."

"Something scared her."

"Someone." Boomer answered but went no further. "You ready?"

Grieg stood and swayed. Boomer cocked his head then threw Grieg's right arm over his scrawny shoulders. Grieg untangled himself, embarrassed to be leaning on the bowed bones of the damaged man.

"I don't mind, you know," Boomer said. Grieg nodded, continuing to plod, then held his arm up for assistance. Boomer shrugged his shoulders under the arm, saying, "It's not much farther."

And it wasn't. Boomer signaled for Grieg to stay put. Not a problem, Grieg didn't have another step in him. The world was awash in misty gray. He used one of the ever-present granite outcroppings to lower himself to his hands and knees. Feeling fugitive and lost, he waited for Boomer to reappear.

He was lying on his side in the fetal position, his hands tucked between his legs, when Boomer returned. Boomer took one look then grabbed each shoulder of Grieg's borrowed field coat and dragged. Horrified, Grieg managed to clamber to his hands and knees.

Boomer put a hand on Grieg's back, guiding him through a bush into a crevice in the rock face. A roof woven of branches spanned the hole. Nature had dropped pine needles on the roof, weeds and grass grew in the rotting needles, their roots creating a solid weatherproof, insulated ceiling.

A pipe made of tin cans jammed together snaked through the sod roof to the outside. The clever flue exited a wood heater fashioned from the giant tin cans in which hominy, crushed tomatoes, even canned peaches came. Food stores occupied the cool reaches of the crevice.

Four cases of bottled water were stacked next to a two-person wrought iron table. The table sported a flowered tablecloth and a set of picnic salt and pepper shakers. A cot with an Army blanket folded at the foot of a sleeping bag lined with a sheet was opposite the table. Boomer helped Grieg onto the bed then covered him with the Army blanket. Grieg curled on his left side watching Boomer's misshapen shadow on the granite.

Why hadn't Boomer brought the girl here? Another picture wormed its way into his foggy brains, a window covered in blue flannel with white clouds. Amy's pajamas. He shivered, strobing the small cave for other mementos.

Boomer unscrewed the top from a bottle of water and offered it to Grieg. He sipped. Darkness invaded him. He was back at the corner, that corner, *the* corner, embedded in the side of a limousine, Virginia Swale's head bobbing with the impact,

Lieutenant Willard's son crushed then burned to death beneath the truck he drove.

XIX

Grieg opened one eye then pushed himself up onto his elbows. The minute he was at an angle, Boomer delivered a bottle of water to his lips. Grieg gulped. It ran down his chin. Boomer kept pouring liquid into him. Grieg tried to keep up. Boomer angled the bottle away, wiped Grieg's lips, then came at him again. Grieg was ready to confess to pretty much anything to stop the flow of liquid. One bottle of water remained from the top case. Empties stuffed a large plastic bag.

"Tea," Boomer asked.

Grieg groaned, "What time is it?"

Boomer cocked his head to read the watch on Grieg's wrist. "Says its 1330."

Grieg fell back on the cot. "I have to pee."

Boomer stepped back from the cot with a sly smile. "Good," he said, sweeping his hand like a valet toward the brush-covered exit. "How long has it been since you last went?"

Grieg stood. Major first step. "Can't remember," Grieg answered with a shake of his head following Boomer's directions out of the crevice into a radiant spring day. It had warmed into the 60s, the loam was damp, some spots marshy from melted snow.

The world smelled like vanilla, new leaves, mold, and life. Grieg stretched then ran for a bush, praying he'd make it before he peed his grimy, reeking jeans. A smile coursed his lips, remembering his challenge to Callie. As he relieved himself, he enjoyed the abandon of a good whiz in the woods. He stretched, palms up in praise of the sun, then headed back to Boomer's hideout.

Boomer, grungy as ever, was full of news. "We haven't got long."

"To do what?"

"Get Jessie and the girl to safety." Boomer jabbed at Grieg's sleeve like a mud hen pecking dirt.

"I'm not helping you…" Boomer put a hand over Grieg's mouth, Grieg swatted it away then spit onto the dirt floor. Boomer took two steps back. "What's on your hands?"

Boomer held his hands out and turned them over several times. "Maybe mushroom. I picked some turkey tail while you were out. Jessie dries them. Keeps them for special. Maybe that."

Grieg spit. It didn't help. Boomer handed him a half bottle of water. He drank, swished, and spit again. His teeth were furry, he needed a toothbrush. From Boomer's responding smile, Boomer hadn't used one since he hiked into the mountains. Boomer was bouncing on his toes, his mouth quirked, his eyes dancing.

"What?" Grieg prodded.

"I snuck down to the lean-to. Rafe was back sifting through the pile he made of my things. He found more stuff that wasn't there."

"That makes no sense, how could he find something that wasn't there?"

"Like the girl." Boomer plucked at the outer-most scruffy shirt of the six he wore.

"The girl was in the lean-to under the bear rug, Boomer. I saw her." Grieg took another swig of water, swished and spit. Earthen floors were handy.

Boomer shook his head so hard that his unintended dreadlocks bounced. Freed, a bug scrambled down his right cheek. Boomer scratched, leaving a red mark. "But she wasn't.

I...oh, not the first. She wasn't the first. Another girl. Four years ago, near the same place. Dead. She was dead."

Grieg moved toward the entrance, wanting out. Away from the vermin, all of it.

"I didn't know what to do. I used my parka. I wrapped her body. She was naked. I dragged her to Jessie's car." Boomer picked a new hole in his shirt. "I...took my windbreaker. I left her, partly in the river. I checked. The scavengers came. I shouldn't have done it. I know. I know. Can't go back."

"Her name was Amy."

"No names." Boomer's agitation grew exponentially. He hopped from foot to foot and twisted his hands. Grieg placed his right hand on Boomer, attempting to calm him. Boomer looked up.

"Was your windbreaker black?" Boomer's nod explained the black fabric found with Amy. "Did you give me anything, anything at all, to help me sleep?"

"Water and some tea Jessie made for me once when I had a fever. That's all. You were somewhere between dehydration, exhaustion, and hypothermia. I just put you to bed and made you down water and Jessie's tea. You're looking perkier now."

"Okay, I'll bite, what wasn't in your lean-to?"

"Stuff, stuff I didn't have like the cigar box."

Grieg plunked on the cot. "Start over."

Outside the cabin's bedroom window, the afternoon was warm, defying the snow of the day before. The leaves on the deciduous trees had opened and spread, reaching for the sun. Catkins hung on the Black Oaks rimming the edges of the front pasture each tree a genetic replica of the other. Yellow pretty-face flowers and orange poppies danced in the light breeze.

Bobbi slept, had been sleeping for hours. Callie rocked and knitted, keeping an eye on Bobbi through the bedroom door. The cabin had warmed. She stood and unbuttoned the flannel shirt she wore over a woman's thermal T-shirt, another Boomer gift given wrapped in a paper bag, as though she were a queen. The shirt hadn't been new, but it smelled of laundry soap. Boomer stroked it, saying he picked it for the color. It was a soft mustard yellow. Funny little man. The first time she wore it, Rafe kissed her on the cheek and whispered a compliment.

Callie tip-toed into her bedroom, tucked the covers around Bobbi, left a note on the nightstand, shut and locked the window then danced out into the spring day. She leaped down the front stairs twirling, her arms out to her sides.

Rafe cornered the cabin.

Callie shielded the sun from her eyes. "You're back?"

"I couldn't leave you alone, not now. I went to my cabin for a few things we might need. It's been searched, do you believe that! Came in by helicopter, skid marks, flattened grass. Emptied the place, left my furniture, everything else is gone. Not just my place, Boomer's, too. It's just us. We need to get out of here. Fast."

Callie bobbled her head, registering the rifle over Rafe's shoulder, the bow and quiver of arrows he carried, and the knife at his waist. Rafe led her onto the porch.

Grieg hunkered behind a rick of wood and spied. Thanks to Boomer, he was on his feet, and though he wasn't operating at one-hundred-percent, he was damn close. Which was good, because he didn't like what he was seeing.

Callie and Rafe sat side by side on the porch, Rafe with a possessive arm around her shoulders. Grieg stayed low, making his way to the stamp mill through minuscule white flowers that flowed across the surface of the meadow as though the snow had never melted. Tall yellow flowers bobbed their heads. The stumps and trunks of charred trees pockmarked the grassy plain. A marsh with incipient Tule grass covered a quarter of the field leading to a small pool. Reaching it, Grieg knelt rustling the grasses.

Rafe stood. "Washburn and his new best buddy are dangerous, Callie. Don't think they aren't."

"I'm not afraid of either man. Lord knows, Boomer's had ample opportunity to hurt me and Grieg's so weak I could take him down." Callie crowed with all the bravado she could muster to cover the lie. Washburn didn't lack guts, he never had, not on a polo field and not facing sentencing.

She clomped down the stairs and scuffed through the dirt toward the stable. When the horses calmed, she returned to the porch. Rafe greeted her tangling his hands in Callie's thick chestnut hair. Callie took his hand and lowered it to her side.

"I have a plan to get us through the night. One that will prevent Boomer from finishing what he started."

"Five women, Rafe. Five. Grieg described their photos. They all had dark hair, light eyes, and were tall and thin. Why not me? Or, were they *all* me?"

"How many times did I warn you about Boomer." Rafe smoothed his free hand down Callie's right arm. He shook their clasped hands. "And, you know as well as I do that Washburn will destroy your world unless Willard snares him first."

Callie slipped free of Rafe's arms, he grabbed for her. She tripped down the stairs, standing hands on her hips, staring toward the restless horses. Rafe stretched his legs and put his hands behind his head, every sort of comfortable. Grieg bobbed up from the grasses, out of sight of the porch but not of Callie. Callie flicked the fingers she rested on one hip, shook her head, and rejoined Rafe on the porch.

Grieg worked his way through the woods behind the stamp mill. Rex tossed his head. Frisco kicked, splintering boards. Grieg moved involuntarily. Rafe's head swung to Grieg's position, the hand that held Callie's right bicep clenched. She squirmed loose and ducked into the cabin. The bar lock dropped into place behind her. Rafe leaned on the door, "Let me in, girl. We got to stick together. It's you and me. Me and you."

Grieg edged through the shadows toward the back of the house, sprinting between granite boulders. In the summer, the groundwater would be laced with uranium leached from the rock. In addition to uranium, Callie's granite contained quartz crystals, mica, and feldspar given the pink grains. The cool of the rock belied the hot minerals it shielded and its beauty. Hard enough to resist abrasion, inert enough to resist weathering and glaciers, its glory shone in the sheered face of Half Dome. Grieg rested behind a rocky ledge.

Waiting for Callie to appear, Grieg considered the trust he had placed in Boomer. Boomer was on his way to the Lodge gift shop with a note to Lacy, Dempsey's business card, and Moms' phone number. If Grieg was wrong about Boomer and Rafe was right--Grieg shook his head to vacate the thought.

One of them had killed the missing girls if they hadn't done it together. This meant that Callie shared her life with a murderer or murderers, the kind of men Grieg had never been, men obsessed by the act of dominance and death. That kind of obsessed. Yet, she felt safe with them. He wondered if she fully comprehended her predicament trapped between her parents' killer and a predator.

Rafe roosted on the porch, his rifle next to him on the bench seat. He surveyed the edges of the farmyard every two minutes. As soon as Rafe's eyes swung to the far left, Grieg took off at a stooped run, taking cover in the backyard behind the kiln.

Seeing a shadow play across the kitchen curtains, Grieg threw a pebble at the window--then another. Callie stepped onto the back stoop, one hand on a hip, the other shading her eyes from the sun. Grieg popped up from behind the kiln. She pointed to the chicken coop and held up ten fingers. Grieg ducked as Rafe cornered the cabin and slid his left hand into Callie's right back pocket. Callie cocked her head.

"Thought I heard movement back here."

"Just me. If you really want to make yourself useful, man the pedal generator." She pointed toward the Aeromotor windmill lolling in the doldrums. "No generator. No electricity. No water."

Rafe slapped her butt. Callie swatted his hand away. His eyes alight, he rounded the cabin. Callie wiped her hands on her rear. When she heard the creak of the pedals, she reached inside the door for a basket with a blue kerchief lining. She walked to the chicken coop, whistling and swinging her basket. She opened the chicken wire door. Chickens tumbled out onto a patch of tall grass, squabbling, squawking, and strutting. Once Callie strewed chicken feed for them, happy clucks filled the afternoon hush.

Callie slipped into the chicken coop and pulled out the shallow drawer beneath the first nest box, one egg, the next the same. Elsa, the chicken, squatted in her box. Callie knew better than to take Elsa's eggs with Elsa present. She had scars as reminders of Elsa's sharp claws and pointy beak.

When the egg basket was full, Callie crossed to the cleaning station located on a counter beneath a chicken wire covered window. She popped the lid off a coffee can full of sand harvested from a small deposit on the banks of the year-round stream. Filling her hands with the abrasive, she rubbed the dirt and feces from each egg, placing cleaned eggs point down in a lined, cleaned carton. The cartons were in order oldest to newest to ensure she used the eggs within a week or two of gathering. Humming as she worked, she kept an eye on Rafe through the chicken wire door. Every few minutes, he scanned the front pasture from tree line to tree line.

Easter, three years ago, three tiny black chicks appeared on the door stoop in a cardboard box, a gift from Boomer. Callie knew nothing about chickens. Eggs came in cartons. Over the years, the three chicks became twelve layers, one rooster, and many dinners. The rooster was a beautiful thing, iridescent black, red comb, a strut that belonged at the front of a parade. She named him Willoughby, inspired by his good looks and pride.

"Willoughby," she called out the window. The rooster strutted to the fencepost nearest her, puffed his chest, and crowed. Rafe watched.

When Rafe lost interest, Washburn ducked through a half-door at the back of the coop in his green hoodie, dirt-covered jeans, and boots that knew work. "Willoughby?"

Callie placed her hands flat on his chest and flicked her head toward the window. Grieg bent to peer out. "We've got to get you out of here. Tonight. You and Bobbi. You're not safe."

"Rafe said the same thing. Who would you trust?"

He shrugged. "Hard to say. A rash manslaughterer or possible serial murderer. Tough spot you're in."

Callie lifted a large can with a tight-fitting lid from a rickety shelf nailed above her small egg cleaning station. An advertisement for marshmallows, red letters on white, covered the exterior of the can. Callie pulled off the lid and dumped chicken feed onto the shelf. She lifted a straightened coat hanger with a small hook at the end from a nail on the wall and shoved it down the inside wall of the can. A false bottom popped up as did the twice folded envelope. "These were in my father's safe."

Callie flattened the envelope using the edge of the egg station then handed it to Grieg. He slit the envelope open with a tarnished kitchen knife and withdrew the papers, smoothing the creases as Callie had. Four pages, front and back, dated January twelve years previous.

"Now's not the time. Rafe is…"

"I don't know who to trust. You ran off with Boomer. Rafe says Boomer's the killer. For all I know, the two of you have hatched some hare-brained plot to turn me in or kill me."

"That's ridiculous."

"Is it? Boomer gets Bobbi, you get me…Rafe…I don't know what he gets. Okay, he kills you and saves me."

"Where's the engine."

"Why possibly would I tell you? So, you can direct the WashEx chopper in and haul it out? The patent is worthless in two years." Callie tossed her burnished hair over her shoulder. Grieg lifted the strays.

"Boomer says it's in the mine. He heard it. And, Callie, it's a go. Pops and I have acquired the rights to all the minerals needed for your engine design. Pops always wanted to save the world. Maybe we can do it for him."

"No. My father's last words were for me to run from him—you."

"Specifically?"

Her father's grasp had been so tight that her skirt ripped further up her thigh. Callie put a hand down to stop the tear. He pulled her toward him, hand over hand up her skirt like he was climbing a rope. She leaned, he put a hand in the cleavage of her dress and drew her toward him. When her face was inches from his, when she could smell death on his lips, he whispered, "Washburn. Run. Only hope."

Callie's eyes locked on Grieg's, she cocked her head, one hand flew to her mouth. "He meant run to Washburn, not from Washburn, didn't he? Your father, not you. I hated you, obsessed about the accident. I was so afraid. I knew what I'd done, what the engine would do, who would kill to stop me. Instead, I ran when all l had to do was raid Dad's safe and take its contents to your father."

"Those men, the ones that kept looking for you. I suspect Pops sent them to keep up his end of the bargain with your Dad."

Rafe stopped pedaling. He stared at the chicken coop then stood. Grieg hunkered down while Callie pretended to clean eggs. Rafe stepped off the porch, the ubiquitous shotgun slung over his shoulder. Callie put a finger to her lips.

"Callie?" Rafe called. She slipped out of the coop with the eggs, crowing, "Eight!" Rafe took the basket from her. She flicked five fingers behind her back.

Grieg balanced his butt onto a poop dotted chicken perch well below the window. He flattened the ledger pages on his knees, wishing he had a ruler and better light. The ink was sketchy in places from age and poor treatment. He was still digesting the numbers when Callie returned. She ducked in, "Sorry, it took so long."

Grieg waggled the pages at her. "Time for straight talk. The Highlands were not pleased that your car was found and disappointed the bones weren't yours. And, there has been a lot of smoke within WashEx, even before Pops death."

"Signifying a change of popes?"

"That's a little close for comfort. All the smoke is black at present. The Board is more than uneasy. These ledger pages prove that Hugh Highland has been embezzling from WET for at least ten years. WET owes you five years of allowance plus interest. You die, no problem. Since you have no will, the Bylaws dictate that your money goes back into the non-existent pot. The minute you show up to collect your back dole, the chicken poop hits the fan. Hugh needs you dead or an IPO to produce cash."

"And?"

"As long as I'm alive, there's no IPO. Hugh only wins if we both lose. I've got as much to lose as you, Cal. I'm the good guy here, and you know it, known it since the minute I showed up."

Callie joined Grieg on the roost, which offered an unobstructed view through the chicken wire door of the front porch. Rafe skinned a rabbit trapped earlier. Knife in hand, he eyed the coop. Time was short. "I can't believe I Darcy-ed you."

Grieg nudged her. "I can't believe I flipped you off!"

"Tell me your version of your graduation party, skipping right past the part where I was a cruel, spoiled society girl."

"Albeit a beauty." Grieg squeezed Callie's right knee. "Okay, my side. I used my feet to lower my pant cuffs. Danced with some ladies, not nearly as saucy as you, and drank. You flitted around the room, showing yourself off, attracting drones to your hive. I wanted you like I'd never wanted anything before. And, that's saying something because there was this piece of black quartz I lusted after for Christmas one year. I dropped clues for my mother. I stationed cheap chunks of man-made quartz on my Dad's desk. I mooned in the rock shop window."

"How old were you?"

"Ten. We were living in Australia."

"Did you get it?"

"I did. But I didn't get you. You left with your parents before the party wound down. Drunk, I thought if I could be alone with you, you'd see I wasn't some worthless sock-hiking, drunk hick. I stole a car idling in the drive, the valet had gone for the owner. Ten minutes later, I rounded the corner, going eighty. Your limousine was across the road. Passenger side towards me. A truck at an odd angle on the driver's side. I braked. Someone screamed. The car shuddered to a stop. Your mother was dead. The truck driver was dead. You socked me. The cops came. I was cuffed. I did time. I got sober. I spent five years in the field with Pops. He was blown up. I'm here."

"Rafe says that you broke parole when you came for me." Callie bumped Grieg.

He shook his head. "Between the chickens and me, they'll have a hard time making that stick. Tell me how your car got in the river."

"I dabbed my blood all over it, started the car, and watched it bounce."

"What did your fellas say when the car was found?"

"My fellas?"

"Rafe and Boomer."

"Rafe told me as a cautionary tale about tramping out in the woods by myself."

"How'd Boomer react?"

"He wrung his hands. Poor Boomer, he's been living up here since he was a teen. I don't know his story, but there have been incidents. A few things missing. Scary noises, banging, footsteps outside my window that sort of thing. Still, I felt safe. Until now." She cocked her head. "Rafe claims he is the caretaker. He knows more about WashEx than I do."

"This property is held by Yellow Sky Holding, not WashEx. Anything he knows about WashEx, he read. He wants you for himself, Callie, trust me. I know the look."

"Is that the one?" she asked, smiling into Grieg's cobalt blue eyes. He blushed.

Rafe hung the rabbit from a hook on the porch, expertly removing the feet and tail before pulling the skin off with the dispassion of a winter jacket.

"I better tell you my story. It's short. My folks had a huge fight. Over money. We came around the corner, the truck was there, the car spun. Mom's neck snapped. You hit us. The truck driver was crushed between the two vehicles. Dad was murdered. I ran."

"Does Rafe know about the patent?"

"Absolutely not."

"He met Willard, Special Agent Dempsey, and a patrolman outside Pete's Place when I met Boomer. Rafe acted like he knew them."

"Dempsey and a Ramirez searched the cabin. Rafe knew Ramirez but not Dempsey. Why should I trust you more than either Rafe or Boomer, they've stood by me through it all?"

"Because you do."

"You think Rafe killed those girls, don't you?"

"Boomer was keeping Bobbi safe, I bet on it. Rafe set him up. He ransacked the place, found things that, according to Boomer, weren't there. I got Boomer out of harm's way. He's at Tenaya Lodge. Now, it's Bobbi's turn."

"I'll think of something to convince Rafe he needs to go for help. Get him out of the way."

"I'll hang around ready to assist."

"In your green hoodie?" Callie kissed Grieg on an ear. "Look, I rigged the lab so I could blow it if necessary. If you need to set the timer, the lab is to the left, deep in the mine. Skinny through what looks like a collapse then follow the tunnel. There's a door, you'll need a screwdriver to get in. Okay? There's one with the tack in the stable. Then just set the old windup clock. Maybe run. It's my first bomb."

She stood and threw open the coop door. Rafe jumped off the porch and met her halfway, he held Callie's right hand and made her laugh. Grieg wanted to tackle him.

XX

Boomer reached Tenaya Lodge in a record two hours. He felt it, too. His legs burned, and the stench of his body attained a level of intolerability that even he hated. He scratched a sweaty sideburn, and a flea jumped on his finger. He likely had lice. He preferred not to think about it.

He plopped on a bench under an incense cedar near the entry. He took a deep breath letting the tree's spicy camphor scent decongest his lungs. He checked reception on the stolen phone then dialed the number Washburn had given him. A woman answered. Her voice was lively and fresh. Boomer pictured her, bright, breezy, happy, and out of his league. Of course, he had no league, well, perhaps a league of his own.

"Mrs. Washburn, my name is Boomer Bognavich."

"Where is my son?" Delia enunciated each word presuming he had the IQ of a turnip. "He hasn't been exerting himself, has he? Dr. Chaudhary warned him."

"Right now, he is on the mountain with Jess…Calypso Swale. We got a problem or two, but nothing we can't handle. I'm at Tenaya Lodge. It's the closest cell phone reception."

We? Who was this man? He sounded as though he worked for her or her son or her husband. We? Delia smoothed the scarlet tunic she wore over pegged pants. Jones signaled an okay having swept for bugs earlier. When she discovered which member of her staff, the WashEx family, or whoever was culpable, she'd use her tweezers on their shorthairs then hand them over to Grieg.

"Grieg's fine. Your son doesn't need his mommy. He's a smart, capable man, ma'am."

"How dare you talk to me like that!" Delia snapped. Felix Highland walked up behind her. Delia shooed him away. He stalked into the drawing-room and slammed the door. The last thing she needed was to be overheard. This was her son, her only son!

"Two things. Grieg wants to know if you followed up on Yellow Sky cloud. And, second, he wants Judge Burridge to call off Chief Willard."

"Chief Willard?"

"He's hunting your son like a dog. Spreading rumors. Says he's going to shoot him on sight. I haven't told Washburn. Grieg's got a lot on his plate. He'll be lucky to get out of this mess in one piece, given all the folks looking for his head." Boomer was enjoying picturing the woman he spoke to as tall, slender, blond, and dripping in diamonds. She would be toned, her skin soft. He shook his head to clear it.

Delia adjusted the diamond stud in her right ear. "I did follow up on Yellow Sky Cloud. I'm not comfortable passing the information on to someone who would hold a girl hostage for money."

Boomer had been uncomfortable going for the reward, but it was either he or Rafe. By preempting Rafe, he had control. Or thought he did, after last night he wasn't sure. That son-of-a-bitch planted the cigar box, and who knew what else in the lean-to.

Delia fiddled with her earring. Boomer Bognavich waited for her to respond, he didn't interrupt, he didn't talk over her. She didn't like misjudging people, and she didn't enjoy being used. "Aren't you the weasel who demanded money in exchange for Callie's whereabouts?"

"I did, but…" How far should he go? He leaned against the trunk of the cedar. The flattened sprays with their scale-like leaves bobbed overhead. He turned his head toward the sun and drank in the heat.

"My point exactly." Delia tapped her fingernails on something hard like marble. He bet they were long, lacquered, and fake.

"Look, Mrs. Washburn, I met your husband in Bakersfield when I was a kid. I'd run away from my folk's place. My dad had beaten the crap out of me. Your husband told me about this property. Told me to take advantage of it, that he'd appreciate having someone living on it, keeping an eye out. I've been up here ever since. I lived in the cabin until Callie showed up, been living in a lean-to since then. Haven't spoken to Ray Washburn in twenty years. He sends me money about every four months, he knows I'm alive when I cash the check. I didn't know who Calypso was until the newspaper articles, honest. She was just another one of the refugees up here. Never said a word to nobody. This life suits me, I'm not good for much else."

Bognavich's story was so Ray that Delia wanted to believe him. "Go on."

"I've done my best to keep Jessie, I mean Calypso, out of harm's way. There's another man up on the mountain. His name is Rafe Bolt, he's dangerous. It would be helpful if you could find anything out about him."

"I can try?" Maybe Jones would know how to track a man down. Felix called Delia's name and rattled the knob of the drawing-room door. She yelled, "Go away!".

"Me?" Boomer asked.

"No, not you," gurgled over the line.

"Yellow Sky Cloud?"

"Dr. Khalil posted a note at Yellow Sky, a cloud repository, the night before Ray's death. Do you have a pencil?" Her fingers drubbed, someone knocking on a door provided background percussion. She took a long slow breath.

Boomer pulled a pen from a pocket of his jacket and a pad from another. "Yes."

"The post said. 'Today is the fourth anniversary. It has been running without fail averaging 16000 kWh of generation per period without recharging. It works.'"

The motor that thrummed behind the locked door in the mine. "Which means?"

"A self-perpetuating power source that can be used in factories or in autos. I don't know how long the turbine will run without the chemicals that create the power being replenished, Khalil suggested ten years, in a car 16,000 miles a year that turns the world upside down. In a factory, who knows?"

"Are Willard and Dempsey the only ones after Grieg and Callie, Mrs. Washburn?"

"You seem very in the know." She had almost said au courant.

"Ever hear of magazines, newspapers? I got a lot of spare time." Boomer sounded as defensive as she did when people underestimated her.

"Me, too. I'd send you a Paperwhite if you had any way to charge it."

"If you send it General Delivery to the Oakhurst Post Office, they'll hold it for me. Who?"

"Grieg shouldn't take his eyes off Exxon, Aramco, any of Big Oil, there is a mole in WashEx, so Big Oil knows of the engine. You can imagine they have a vested interest in it not seeing the light of day unless they hijack it and control it. And, even if they didn't know, any engineer with imagination can line up the list of chemicals and make an educated guess. Which is why Ray and Khalil are dead, murdered. Grieg will want to know Khalil was murdered."

"The engine is that big a deal?"

"Think oil, think no oil." The fingernails stopped tapping. Delia covered the speaker with her hand, someone had entered the room. "Felix, I'm on the phone! It's a private call."

"With whom," Highland asked. Boomer shuddered at his tone. Delia Washburn had her hands full.

"Get the hell out of my drawing-room, Felix. Now!" Highland closed the door, light eked through a crack. Delia stomped across the floor and slammed the door, hoping to catch Felix's ear in it. When there was no yelp, she said, "Talk fast, I haven't much hope he'll stay gone."

"Willard?"

"I'll talk to Burridge." Felix walked across the patio, pausing to look through the French doors into the drawing-room. Delia faced the fireplace. "Hurry this up."

"Next steps?"

"I don't care who you have to shoot, kill, or maim, help Grieg. I've got things at this end." She hoped.

"I'll do my best to get your son out alive," Boomer offered.

"How much will it cost me?"

"Nothing. If it weren't for your husband, I wouldn't have seen fifteen."

"Bless you. How do I contact you?"

"You don't. I'm returning this phone to its owner." Boomer hung up. He deleted the photos he'd snapped and pocketed the phone. He stretched his legs, put his hands behind his head, and considered how to use what he'd just learned to its best advantage.

Delia opened the French doors. Felix walked into the room. "Who?"

"Boomer Bognavich. He claims Ray pays him."

"The call demanding the money was the first I ever heard of a Boomer Bognavich. I assure you if Ray pays him, it isn't through the corporate accounts."

"Still, I believe this Boomer."

"I hope so, you told him everything."

She hadn't, quite purposefully. Khalil's message had ended: *It's ready if the driver never stops for a stoplight.*

Boomer read Dempsey's number off the business card Grieg had given him and dialed. The call went directly to messages. He left the message Grieg had dictated to him should Dempsey not answer.

Boomer oozed into Tenaya Lodge. A woman perched on a tall stool at the coffee shop. A gray sweater with buttons at the diagonal wadded at her waist. She was knitting a pink hat with ears. One of those, Boomer thought. She took off her reading glasses and squinted at him. He strolled over to her, waves of stink rising as he did, handed the cellphone to her, and grinned. She set it on the table and nudged it away with a fingertip.

When she didn't bother to thank him, Boomer wandered into the gift shop and bought a bottle of water, a convenience package of aspirin, and a San Francisco Chronicle. He settled into the lobby for the night as Washburn had asked him to do.

The job was simple if the man he'd seen at Pete's Place and/or Willard, or Dempsey appeared, he was to keep them occupied long enough for Grieg to bring the two women out. He read the paper he bought, sipped water, and pretended he belonged. When two out of three of the men showed up, Boomer folded the newspaper.

Ignoring Grieg's orders, Boomer headed back to help as he'd promised Grieg's mother he would do.

Fred handed Delia five envelopes and an Amazon box collected from the curbside mailbox. She set the Amazon Prime box on her entry table and shuffled through the letters. Three bills, one invitation, plus the envelope she held.

She studied the handwriting on the envelope, boxy letters designed to hide the sender's identity. It was franked two days earlier in New York City. Delia went into the drawing-room to her secretary desk. After a brief search, she turned up her letter opener, slit the envelope, and slid out the card with the tip of a lacquered fingernail.

She flipped the cover back with the letter opener, one couldn't be too careful. The same printing scrawled across the inside of the card. An address in Fisher, Indiana, and a telephone number. Nothing more. Patty's perfume wafted from the note, reminding her to thank Patty later for the lead.

Delia itched to dial the number, but, at Jones's insistence, she made all calls from burn phones, conducting her personal business on walks or during lunches out. She grabbed her latest burn phone, loving the whole spy thing of it, then went for her mid-day walk along the beach.

A gale flattened the grasses, she tied a scarf tightly under her chin and fought her way through the drifting sand to her favorite call spot. A splash of red behind a hillock warned her to keep walking. A flash of light signaled that her current watcher had taken a photo for the record. Damn it!

She trod back to the house, diverted to the garage, and drove to the nearest drug store where she purchased a new phone. Phone in hand, Delia drove to the local McDonald's, ordered a latte, and called the number from Patty's card.

No one was home. Delia waited for voice mail. A man's voice said: *You've reached the Wygart residence, neither Betty nor David are in, please leave a message.* She thought she had squared all the angles, but she hadn't even considered this one.

Delia logged onto the internet available at McDonald's and typed the name David John Wygart into the tiny screen on her latest phone. The name popped up twice, one an obituary from the 1800s, and on a social network for professionals. She entered Ray's social network sign-on. No go.

The other option was one of those companies that promised all the poop for $9.99, she bit. One PayPal deduction later, she had verification. She emailed the document to Judge Burridge then threw her phone and her latte in the McDonald's trash bin. She walked to her Mini-Cooper Countryman and drove to the courthouse.

The Judge's secretary led her to a nook off the reception room with walnut paneling, walnut furniture, walnuts in a large glass snifter. A loveseat and two chairs created a conversation group, a coffee table between them. The tall table lamps were brass with green glass knobs midway up the stem. French doors opened onto the reception area. The secretary motioned Delia into the room then closed the doors behind her.

Delia nearly disappeared into the cushion of the loveseat. Nestled in the small couch, she considered her next moves, not that she had any. Just a mother on a mission to save her brave, brainless fledgling. She worried Dr. Chaudhary's advice about Grieg and living up to his father. Ray moved quickly, assuredly, and without worry about his physical safety from one success to another. He was an icon to the big oil companies and to his son. A son who spent his young manhood under the weight of a felony conviction, the deaths of three people, and the disappearance of another. One who couldn't go out alone, who couldn't date, or, she presumed, even be with a woman because that happened unchaperoned in the dark. She slumped into the cushion as she had as a girl trying out for chorus lines competing with others who were prettier, more experienced, and better dancers.

The French doors rattled as Judge Burridge whizzed by to his office. The next moment he roared out and into the nook. Delia dragged herself from the loveseat, she swore she heard a sucking sound as it released her. Burridge gathered her into his arms.

"Well?" he asked.

"David John Willard is alive. He lives in Fisher, Indiana, under the name Wygart. He is a bus driver and has been for nearly five years."

"And you know this because?"

"I emailed the information to this office."

Judge Burridge stuck his head out the door. "Jane, check my emails and print out anything you find about a Wygart. You're sure it's the correct David John."

Delia nodded her head. "His mother was from Indiana. The ex-Mrs. Willard went back after the divorce was hashed out in every newspaper in Suffolk County. The kids followed her. DJ had a little sister. I don't remember her name, just the brouhaha."

"What are you implying?"

"Willard was the first responder. Remember him crying for the cameras, lamenting that his son had been crushed and incinerated by the subsequent fire. Willard whimpered that there was nothing to bury. He was the chief witness against my son, gave him the breathalyzer test, swore that Grieg killed his son. It was the trucker driver's death that convinced you and the jury to convict Grieg of felony manslaughter." Delia stopped, her fingers clutching the Judge's robe. "My poor Griegs!"

Burridge leaned out the double doors. "Jane, get the Suffolk County Chief of Police on the telephone, send the call to my office!" Jane pointed toward the courtroom. "They can wait, damn it. Get the Chief."

"What are you going to do?"

"Grieg swore from the start something was off. That the accident was staged. How did you locate Wygart?"

"A friend with magical powers, all I did was verify his location and identity. If you need to talk to me, ask me to meet you somewhere loud."

Burridge wrinkled his brow but nodded his consent. "While you're here, Sally Purdy left a package for you."

"Why here?"

The Judge shrugged. The only answer was that Sally knew the Meremer was under siege.

"When this is over, I want a cover story in every newspaper on Long Island proclaiming my son's innocence."

Judge Burridge patted her on the shoulder. "Delia, my dear, if this checks out, I promise the dead will come to life, Grieg's record will be expunged, and the guilty paraded in the town square. How's that?"

"What if…"

"Now, Delia, what if nothing. Willard is no match for a Washburn."

"Can I open the package here," she asked. He motioned her to a small desk in the corner of the nook. Delia planted a kiss on the Judge's cheek. Jane returned with a brown-paper-wrapped package. Years ago, while keeping Ray's books, Delia found the evidence that Hugh was skimming money to offshore accounts. She showed her findings to Ray. Ray made copies and sent the copied pages to Larch Swale. The proof was lost with Larch. She was hoping the pages Ray had copied were in the records she'd requested.

She discarded the brown paper and tore into the box. Instead of ledgers, it held photocopies of the ledger pages, not all of them, some of them, the wrong some of them. Delia rested her chin in her hands, elbows on the desk.

Finding a clean sheet of paper, she fumbled in her purse for her pen and printed Grieg's name. Around his name, she wrote Felix, Hugh, Doug, Sally, Judge Burridge, Willard, Delia, Ray, Larch, and Calypso. At the top of the sheet, she listed the issues: patent, skimming, succession, murder, blackmail. Jealousy? Jealousy popped into her head from left field, she added it to the list.

Why jealousy? With Ray gone, it was clear Doug wanted to be CEO. To ascend, he needed Grieg out of the way. If WET was dry, Hugh was relying on the percentage of WashEx profit allotted to WET to pay dividends. Sally had always assumed that Grieg would marry her, handing her and her father WashEx on a platter. When he hadn't, she attached herself to Gilft, who would benefit from marriage to a Purdy. On Sally's recommendation, Hugh asked Gilft, Dummer, and Toff for an

IPO prospectus to fund WET and to get WashEx back on track. Put that way, it made so much sense.

As for CaMP, Calypso Swale created chaos with her disruptive technology. Handled by the wrong organizations, it had the potential to collapse the world economy, WashEx with it. New lease by new lease, Ray and Grieg had ensured WashEx's future health, even as they jeopardized Exxon Mobile, Aramco, and all the other behemoths. Now the only way Big Oil could control the future was to dispose of CaMP and destroy WashEx. Which meant Doug Purdy had Big Oil's blessing if he wasn't on their payroll.

Delia ran her hands through her hair and stared at the lines and circles on her page. At his hearing, Grieg swore he'd seen Doug Purdy talking to Chief Willard as he drove through the gates of Meremer in the one car ready and idling, Hugh Highland's. She circled two names, Calypso and Larch Swale. If Callie and Larch had died in the accident, Callie's invention would have languished at the patent office until it expired, Hugh would have been freed from paying Larch blackmail, and Grieg would have been jailed paving the way for Doug to assume leadership of WashEx when the time came.

But that hadn't happened. Hugh must have killed Larch Swale and proceeded to suck the life out of WET until Callie's car was found. He owed Callie money, lots and lots of money. Now, he needed Callie dead, or he needed an IPO, and there was no IPO with Grieg alive.

Had her son come to the same conclusions? She prayed so for his sake.

XXI

Ensconced on the porch bench, Rafe whittled an amorphous blob from a perfectly good piece of manzanita. The shavings piled up between his legs. His rifle leaned against the cabin within arm's reach. His knife lay unsheathed by his thigh. His bow hung on a hook, a full quiver beside it.

Callie scanned the tree line, the stamp mill, the chicken coop, the pasture, nothing stirred. By the happy clucking of the chickens, Grieg had vacated the coop. Rex nickered. Rafe glanced toward the stable.

"Horses seem jumpy, don't they?" Rafe commented.

"It's Willoughby." She pointed to a fence post. The rooster sat atop it, feathers ruffled, and gave a long, heartfelt crow. The girls chattered in response.

Rafe whittled. He nicked his finger, a touch of blood bubbled.

"Do you need something for the cut?" Callie asked, an idea blooming.

Rafe squeezed the wound, it bled a bit more. "No. It's fine."

Rex whinnied. Frisco kicked the stall. Rafe stood.

"I'd feel better if you stayed nearby," Callie simpered, hating herself for doing it but fearful of what would happen if he encountered Grieg. Rafe nodded, sat, and took up his whittling. It wouldn't be long before he'd need another chunk of wood to demolish.

"I'm going to check on Bobbi." Callie entered the cabin and crossed to the bedroom. She placed a hand on Bobbi's forehead, Bobbi's eyes flew open. Callie gave a reassuring shush then went to brew Bobbi a cup of the herb tea she used for fevers. Returning, she helped Bobbi sit up, stuffing pillows behind her back. Bobbi held the mug of tea between shaky hands and sipped gratefully. When the girl nestled back against the angled pillows, Callie covered her with a quilt and returned to the kitchen to begin the chore of food preparation.

She hadn't considered it a chore before, it had been part of the now shattered rhythm of her days. She was sick to death of eating rabbit. A ham of dried boar wrapped in cheesecloth hung in a small vestibule out the back door. Callie unwrapped it slicing off enough to feed three. A basket of red rose potatoes occupied a shelf jammed between the 2x4 studs of the small room. A bunch of carrots hung by the greens. She selected several large ones. Ham, potatoes, and baked carrots, yum.

An hour later, she checked on Bobbi. Rafe heard her and joined her in the bedroom. Bobbi's hands rumpled the nightshirt Callie loaned her. The quilt bunched around Bobbi's ankles tossed by jittering legs. Fresh bloodstains wormed the surface of the nightgown and the mattress. Callie shook Bobbi. No response, not a flutter of her eyes. Callie placed the back of her hand on Bobbie's brow.

Callie swung towards Rafe. "She needs help now!"

"I'll make a travois for Rex and ferry her down to Washburn's Jeep. I hid the battery nearby. I'll hook it up then drive her into town. You bring the horses back here and wait for me and the police. Meantime, lock yourself in and don't open the door until you hear my whistle."

Callie shot a look at the stable. The horses were quiet. The chickens waddled happily stuffed with feed. She squeezed Rafe's right hand as though her clever plan hadn't backfired with a smoking belch. "I knew I could count on you. You make the travois. I'll prepare Bobbi for transport."

Rafe grasped the hatchet used for kindling and trotted to the stable. A breeze shuddered the trees. Rafe scanned the line between the timber and the farmyard, hunched his shoulders, and entered the stable returning to the yard with a hank of rope and a horse blanket. He selected two long thick branches from the woodpile nearest the house, set them on the ground so that they crossed at the top and tied them together, creating a triangle. He used the folded blanket to set the distance between the two poles, then went into the timber.

Callie returned to Bobbi. Bobbi's hands were slack on her stomach, her head lolled to one side. Callie rubbed her upper arms with lye soap coarsened hands. The chill she felt subsided, but not the sense that she was being watched. She fingered back the curtain on the window, no one was there.

Rafe returned from the timber with one thick branch and several flexible branches. He tied the thick branch well down the two long poles to keep the angle rigid, then wove the flexible branches into a litter, securing them to the pole frame with the rope. He weight-tested the web of boughs. When it held, he spread the blanket over them, lashing it into place.

"Bobbi's dead, Rafe," Callie said, one hand on Rafe's right shoulder. A movement at timberline caught her attention. Rafe followed her eyes. From his knees, Rafe roared to a sprint bringing Boomer down like a mountain lion on a deer. The thud of the two hitting the ground reverberated.

Rafe dragged Boomer to standing. "One down," he said, felling Boomer with a fist to the side of his head. Boomer dropped like he'd taken a bullet.

"I think you killed him! Why, why did you do that to him?" Callie screamed, clenching her fists, her stomach knotted.

"If I did, it's a blessing." Rafe tied Boomer's slack body hand and foot then dragged him to the stable, dumping him next to the travois. "He kidnapped Bobbi and for all we know killed her, just now, while you gathered eggs and I rocked on the porch. How could we have been so stupid? Change of plans. I haul Boomer to the cops. Don't let Washburn near the girl, he's around here. Boomer came back to meet him, bet on it. You bunker up until you see the whites of my eyes." Rafe took her chin in his hands, stared into her eyes, and said, "Got it, girl."

Callie saddled Rex anxious to return to Bobbi's body. Rafe positioned the apex of the travois over the saddle horn. He checked his knots then hefted Boomer onto the blanket and tied him to the rig.

Rafe swung into the saddle. Rex stood stiff-legged unsure what was expected. Callie smacked Rex' withers. The big horse took a step, stopped, took another step, shied at the weight of the travois and the raw poles rubbing his flanks, then settled on the path to the entry gate.

Callie sat on the front porch until Rafe disappeared. A doe with a wobbly fawn high-stepped in the tall grasses of the meadow. The doe's ears pricked. She nudged her baby away from the shadowed woods. A gust of wind whistled through the tops of the pines and redwoods, setting the crowns shuddering. The doe kicked up her heels. The little one trotted knobbily kneed to its mother, nudging its way to a teat. Tail wagging, legs trembling, it slurped.

The chickens muttered like gossiping friends. Frisco nickered. A door slapped. A rifle shot boomed in the timber. Callie ran into the yard, chickens scrambled out from under her pounding feet. She threw open the chicken coop door. Elsa squawked. Willoughby scurried out the window, done with his rooster duty until sunset. Otherwise, the coop was empty.

Callie slammed back into the yard. Chickens clustered around her feet, scampering away with disgruntled clucks like old ladies caught playing craps. Something scared them, something other than her.

"Grieg, Washburn! Goddamn it!" She hissed as loud as she dared, fear disfiguring her words. Rafe didn't miss when he shot, and he didn't waste ammunition.

Grieg rounded the stamp mill. Callie sat on a stump, her hands shaking. Grieg stood her up. Callie rested her forehead on Grieg's chest, feeling undone. "Rafe hit Boomer. Blam. Fist in the ear. Rafe's taking him to your car then to the police. He won't be back until morning. He'll bring the cops for Bobbi, but…where were you…we have…? I heard a shot. I thought…"

"Whoa."

"Whoa as in *Oh my God, you're right* or as in *rein it in*?" Grieg slipped his hands down her back. His touch sent waves of comfort and sensibility through her. "I'm afraid to lose my mountain," she said, ducking her head.

"You're not afraid of anything, Calypso Swale."

"Don't mock me." Callie huffed, turning for the cabin. He followed her sway through the gabbling chickens. She pointed out the doe in the pasture. He took her offered hand. She led him into the cabin then to the bedroom. "We need help."

With one glance at Bobbi's unconscious body in the bloody bed, his admiration for Callie grew. Callie slipped a teacup off the table.

"A natural sedative. I use it for Frisco when he gets too nervy. I worked for Bobbi, too. I doctored the place up a bit with rabbit blood. We keep it for soups, this had gone sour. Bobbi's fine. It was all I could think to do. The alternative was to let Rafe take her down the mountain. I couldn't let that happen. Now he has Boomer. You've got to stop him…from whatever he…he said Boomer came back to meet you."

"Remember, I sent Boomer out to Tenaya for his own safety. I told him to stay put. He must have seen or learned something that sent him back. If I go haring after Rafe to save Boomer, you, Bobbi, and your damn engine are unprotected. They grab you, grab me, grab the schematic, grab the money."

"So, we do the unexpected."

"Easy breezy, heh, just like that? You wouldn't happen to have a spare weapon. I'm pretty good with everything from bolas to bazookas."

"And after the letter b?"

"I punt. Can you hide Bobbi where no one can find her?"

She grinned, "Does a bear poop in the woods?"

"Well, I know you're working on pissing. Are you familiar with Boomer's alternate address?"

Callie nodded.

"Go there. Stay put. I'll figure something out."

"Why does that scare me? You who hared after a girl in a stolen car just to embarrass her."

"Thanks. I needed that."

"Whatever you do, don't endanger Bobbi, okay? And, Rex has never been harnessed, he'll fight Rafe every step of the way." She twitted at his shirt, "I think it's time to blow the engine. Can you set the timer, while I get Bobbi ready?"

Grieg jogged to the stable. Frisco greeted him by slamming his back hooves through the stable wall. Callie listened to Grieg soothing the small horse. Washburn chose the bit-less hackamore and pocketed a screwdriver. Frisco lowered his head and allowed Grieg to slip on and buckle the hackamore.

He ran a steadying hand down the horse's withers then with an ease Callie had never witnessed in another rider vaulted onto Frisco's back and reined the horse toward the mine. A shiver at the perfection kept her entranced until the two merged with the shadows.

Callie ran back to the bedroom. Bobbi was awake. Callie cleaned the bed, stuffing the bloody bedding in the burn barrel next to the root cellar doors. Meanwhile, Bobbi dressed in a pair of loose-fitting jeans, a flannel shirt, and enough socks to fit into Callie's spare boots. Callie pulled together a few supplies, tied them hobo style in a towel and laced the knotted end over a pole.

She eased Bobbi to standing. Bobbi wove, nodded, and took a step.

Grieg led Frisco into the mine shaft. Fifteen-feet in, he threw the reins over a post and stroked between Frisco's eyes until the horse's head drooped, then whispered, "Back in a jif."

A crude lantern made of a rag held by a jaw clip in a tuna can filled with bacon grease sat on a shelf by the first support beam. A box of utility matches provided a means to light the rag wick. The flame wavered then caught spangling the mica surfaces on the granite walls.

Following Callie's directions, Grieg worked his way down a newly reinforced tunnel, past old pickax and chisel marks, stopping to finger a deep scar in the rock. Boomer lied, there was uranium in this mine, too much of the right kind of granite. He doubted iron had been mined at all. A vein of quartz made him suspect gold.

As he slipped through the crevice, LED bulbs flooded the tunnel with light. Twenty feet on, a poorly constructed wooden door hung lopsided on repurposed hinges. Screws held it shut. Using the screwdriver from the stable, Grieg opened it. A soft thrub pulsed behind the door. Grieg used the key Callie had given him on the padlock. The wooden door screeched over the chunk of stone that served as the threshold.

Grieg stepped over the rock into a ten-by-ten dugout heavily reinforced with log uprights and hand-hewn eight-by-eight beams. The only way in or out was through the handmade door then the crevice. A trestle table occupied the center of the room.

A two-cylinder 1950 vintage John Deere tractor engine monopolized the tabletop chugging the distinctive Deere rhythm. A belt ran from the motor to a generator, which powered the lights activated by a motion sensor mounted just outside the door. Grieg placed a hand on the crankshaft case; it was warm, not hot.

A chart on a wooden shelf that served as a desk indicated that the engine had sung day in and day out, generating power for nearly three years. Small labeled canisters on the shelf contained the minerals, metals, and chemicals Callie needed. A soldering iron, a set of screwdrivers, a pair of gloves, work glasses, a little canister of lubricant, the spray kind, and other tools were strewn on another shelf. A workstation jutted into the room at waist height.

Wires coursed around the walls, some fed the lights, Grieg chased down the others until he came to a homemade but deadly fertilizer bomb attached to a digital clock on a shelf near the entry door.

Grieg searched on and under the shelves, beneath the purring engine for anything Callie may have squirreled away and might need. Nothing. The arch of rock that framed the entry door gleamed. A vein of gold ran across the span and down the roofline to the granite floor. He touched it for luck.

He wound the twenty-four-hour clock, set the alarm for 0800 the next morning, prayed the clock kept accurate time and rejoined Frisco. Frisco scuffed the granite floor with a hoof at his approach. He gathered Frisco's reins, led him from the mine before mounting, then kneed the horse gently to a lope down the path toward the gate, hoping to catch up with the travois, unsure what he would do if he did. Rafe was armed; Grieg had arms. The similarities ended there. And, he couldn't lose sight of the fact that Boomer and Rafe might be in this together. In which case, both men could be waiting to jump him.

If Boomer had connected with Moms, had she answered Grieg's questions? Moms wasn't easy to fool and where Grieg was concerned nearly impossible. Though occasionally, she trusted the damnedest people. He must have inherited that trait from her, he'd bought Boomer's story.

But if he was wrong about Boomer, then Boomer and now Rafe knew that the reward for Callie's return was small potatoes. The real money was in finding the engine and schematics and either heisting or destroying them, then Callie.

The engine spelled doom for the oil-producing nations. Oil would lose its value, the stock market would drop like a rock, followed by a worldwide recession. Without oil royalties, the Arabic Peninsula would be thrown into chaos and poverty. Russia, rich with rare-earth chemicals, might rise again able to refuel communism. China, as well. The heavens and the waters would heal, and WashEx would prosper.

It wouldn't happen overnight. First, there would be a scramble for patent rights, then designs, not of the engine, but of the vehicles and objects it powered. Finally, consumer purchase. Five years, ten. The attacks on WashEx would come from every direction. Those after the patent, those after the licenses, those after…without him, there would be an IPO, Doug would be CEO, and Big Oil would take over WashEx.

A breeze rattled through the pines. Frisco shied with each puff of the wind, each clack of branches. Grieg ran a reassuring hand down the horse's withers. Each time he did, Frisco huffed. Not this time, a shiver worked its way croup forward. Grieg knew the feel of muscles preparing to move opposite forward momentum. He readied to be bucked.

Frisco threw his head, reared, spun and slammed back to earth, then kicked. The object of his ire a pile of brush off the path about a half-mile from Boomer's lean-to. Grieg rode out the bucking. Frisco threw his head. Pawed. Snorted. A booted foot appeared from under a haphazard collection of branches.

Grieg dismounted, throwing Frisco's reins over a low hanging branch. Frisco cocked his head. He was a pretty boy with his brown and white patches and curly forelock. Solid, too. He might have made an excellent polo pony, he might still. Frisco nudged the exposed boot with his nose.

It wasn't a new boot, scuffs showed, the laces were worn. Grieg tossed branches and an armload of brush aside.

Special Agent Kyle Dempsey stared out of his hastily assembled grave. He hadn't moldered alone. From the scat, there had been a possum, from the tears in his flesh, a big cat, from the maggots around the wound at his throat, flies, and from the smell, skunk.

Dempsey's throat had been slit from behind right to left. The dreaded left-handed killer. There were no defensive wounds on his hands. Dempsey was Grieg's height, in excellent shape, and well trained. Either his attacker had been stealthy and powerful, or Dempsey had known him.

The khaki jacket Dempsey wore to Pete's Place was missing as were his sunshades, the kind cops wear, otherwise, he was dressed as Grieg had last seen him. Grieg sat in the loam, pursed his lips, and scratched the nose Frisco offered as he realigned everything and everyone. Dempsey and Ramirez had searched Callie's cabin before meeting at Pete's Place. Dempsey recognized Grieg at Pete's, Grieg was sure of that and chose not to point him out to Willard. Grieg trusted Dempsey and his instincts. He'd either followed a suspect onto the land or come to meet Grieg and been murdered. The only person Grieg could rule out was Boomer, who was too small and right-handed. That left Rafe, Ramirez, Willard, Purdy, someone from Aramco, the unknown man from Pete's Place, another squatter, drug growers, the list seemed endless and time spent ruminating on it pointless.

Grieg added new sticks and sprinkled pine needles over Dempsey's burial mound. He snapped a branch overhead marking the location for ease of return then led Frisco to a fallen log and mounted. He reined the horse back onto the path, checking the timber for similar piles of wood, worried he might find Boomer under one, equally worried he wouldn't and what it might imply.

At a nicker to his left, Grieg drew Frisco up. The pinto drooped his head and huffed expressively. In the subsequent silence, a branch cracked. Grieg urged Frisco forward. The horse balked, reared, then pivoted.

An arrow twanged into a nearby tree. Grieg slid to the ground. The second arrow ripped through the right sleeve of his coat, searing through the bullet wound. A third arrow sank into the bark of a tree inches from Grieg's left shoulder. Grieg swatted Frisco on the rump, flopped to the ground, played dead, and bled.

He listened for Rafe's approach. It never came. When a soft nose nudged him, he rolled to his left side and elbowed himself to sitting. The wound in his arm ached, unnaturally, blood had soaked through the coat sleeve. He ripped off a hank of cloth from the T-shirt he wore and bound the wound. It bled through. Lightheaded, he led Frisco to a rock where he could mount one-handed.

XXII

Callie coaxed Bobbi through the quaking shadows toward the rocky outcropping that disguised Boomer's hideaway. Smoke rose from the chimney. Someone was or recently had been using Boomer's crevice, and it wasn't Boomer. Callie seated Bobbi on a convenient tree stump and checked their surroundings. There was one place close by they could go until Grieg showed.

She drew a circle then a line through the edge, hoping Grieg would understand the old hobo sign she'd relied on to mark her way back to the cabin before she knew every tree, crevice, cave, and promontory on the property. She heaved Bobbi to standing and sidetracked to a rickety line shack of aged gray board planed at a sawmill that had since collapsed of its own weight, the saw, and planes still rusted in the undergrowth.

The shack listed to the left while the roof clung on by memory. Fallen branches filled in for missing shingles. It wasn't much, but it was out of the weather. Callie helped Bobbi into the back corner where walls, shielded by a rocky grotto, offered the most protection. Bobbi sat on a splintered hand-hewn bench then lay on it. Callie unfurled a thermal blanket from her hobo pack and covered the girl. She touched Bobbi's lips with a finger and squeezed one of her shoulders. It was a silent promise to return. Callie left the pack with its tins of food and goods.

Callie pocketed her multi-tool with its screwdriver blades, knife, can opener, bottle opener, awl, and scissors; it was a wood person's delight. Once while lost and desperate, she'd opened the long blade, plunged it in the ground, found the sun, direction, and time. Handy. By the cant of the sun filtering through the trees, Grieg had ridden off well over an hour ago. More than enough time to intersect Rafe and Boomer. With a reassuring smile cast Bobbi's way, Callie ducked out of the line shack.

Rather than wend her way up, over and around boulders thrown willy-nilly when the mountains formed, she followed a rivulet down to a streambed. Boomer's crevice lay uphill opposite a ring of redwoods. Hoofprints marred the dirt in front of the rocky opening. Smoke clung to the trees. She nickered for Frisco. No response. She smacked her lips. Rex responded, as did Rafe.

Callie postured, her legs at shoulder width, her fists on her hips. "Thank heavens, you're here!"

Rafe laughed, "Like a bee to the honey. How stupid do you think I am? I know dead, that girl wasn't. Where is she?"

Rex grazed nearby on the few hairs of grass breaking through the duff. Rafe's rifle hung from the saddle horn, as did his bow, the quiver tied to the saddle strings.

"I left her at the cabin. Where's Boomer?" Callie asked.

"At the Jeep. Still tied. It's just us, girl."

"Thank god!" If she played this right, Bobbi might survive the night.

But where was Washburn? All he had to do was set the charge then meet them here. She twisted away, Rafe pulled her to his chest and kissed her hard enough to bruise her lips. She tried to yield. He held her harder. She gasped. He kissed her again, this time there was nothing hard about it. When he was done, he pushed her toward Rex.

Rafe mounted first, without Grieg's grace. When Rex spun, Callie ran. Rafe cantered Rex after her, pinning her against a rock. How could she have been so stupid? How? Rafe reached down and pulled her up behind him on the saddle. His back muscles tensed at her shivering touch.

She laid her head against his neck, trying to relax him, her eyes locked on his quiver. "Three arrows missing."

"Killed a pig," Rafe answered, kicking Rex' flanks. Rex danced. Callie tightened her arms around Rafe's waist as Rafe intended.

Rex picked his way down the rough terrain toward the Jeep and Boomer. The travois leaned between boles of a centuries' old redwood tree, Boomer tied and bound to it. His bloody head lolled forward.

Callie slid off Rex. She touched Boomer's bloody temple. When he didn't respond, Callie felt for a pulse. It wasn't until she put two fingers to a vein in his neck that she got a thump. He whimpered. One eye pulsed.

"What have you done to him? Rafe, why? He's defenseless."

"You can't care. The man's a murderer, Callie. I found proof in his lean-to." Rafe kicked the bottom of the travois, it rocked but stayed upright. "I'd kill him if I didn't need him alive. You stay here, keep an eye on him while I put the battery in the Jeep."

As Rafe bent his head to the task, Callie tipped an open bottle of water to Boomer's lips. It ran off and down the front of his rasty fishing vest. She tried again. Giving up, she lifted his head, squeezed his lips until a small opening appeared then drop by drop fed him the water.

"Help me," Boomer begged through parched lips.

Callie glanced up, Rafe was still working. "Did you kill those women?"

Boomer shook his head. Though, it might have bobbled on its own.

"Did Rafe?"

The nod was more definite. "Mementos. Box. Things. Planted. My lean-to. Cloud curtains your place?"

"Rafe gave me the fabric, he said to cheer up my vegetables."

"Amy's. I found her naked. Grieg knows about pajamas. Untie me."

Boomer's eyes bulged. It was her only warning. Rafe ran his hands down her arms, spun her, then locked his lips on hers. She tried to back away, he walked her backward until her back met the Jeep. With one hand, he lifted her chin, forcing her head against the canvas top. He grasped her right wrist with his left hand, the feeling raced out of it. She tried to kick. He kneed her in the stomach. The day dimmed then faded to black.

Rafe lifted Callie into the front seat of the Jeep. Sitting her upright, he cinched the seatbelt and bound her hands and ankles. Satisfied, he returned to Boomer and kicked the travois to the ground. Boomer huffed air. Rafe placed a booted foot on the injured side of the small man's face until signs of respiration stopped. He knelt and put a cheek to Boomer's mouth and nose. When there wasn't a breath of wind or moisture, he lifted the travois onto its side and rolled it face down into the suffocating duff.

Grieg looped Frisco's reins over a branch at the entry to Boomer's hideaway, thought better of advertising his whereabouts, and walked his spotted buddy down the streambank until the horse was out of sight. He begged Frisco not to whinny as he tied him to a branch then scratched a scar on Frisco's right flank. Frisco nickered and butted. Grieg put a finger to his mouth and backed away. Frisco watched until he discovered miner's lettuce poking up along the banks of the stream.

Grieg snaked up to the granite crack that opened into Boomer's stone dwelling. He whispered Callie's name. When there was no response, he wormed through the crevice into the empty cave. Ashes smoldered in the makeshift furnace. The shelves had been tossed, bottles of water were scattered, some stomped. Water puddled on the rocky floor and muddied the dirt. The cot and bedding were heaped in the middle of the floor.

Grieg grabbed one of the unopened bottles of water, unscrewed the top and gulped it down. He jammed a couple of bottles in the hip pockets of Rafe's barn coat, grabbed a small bowl from the litter then worked his way down the streambed to Frisco.

Callie must have noticed the smoke and gone on, but where?

Grieg dipped the bowl into the stream. Frisco was only too happy to wash down his lettuce with mountain water. Grieg slurped down more bottled water. Frisco munched unconcerned about the babbling brook, the wind, and his own crunching.

Grieg got the message and circled back up to the crevice hoping for some sign of Callie. A circle drawn in the dirt with a line pointing to the northwest caught his eye. He'd seen a similar mark on a wall in Afghanistan, his guide trundled off following the direction of the line. In this case, uphill.

After a scramble up, a crumbling structure appeared on his left. He peered through a half-inch gap in the dried planks of the exterior wall. What light entered did so in thin bands through the rotting wood. He rounded the fallen side and inched open the door. A gasped breath responded. It could have been a possum. He'd shared an outhouse with one once. It hadn't worked out well for either of them. He clutched. The possum played dead. It went on for hours. He didn't have that kind of time now, he needed to link up with Callie. He whispered his name then waited for the arrow to bite into his chest.

"Over here," a small voice called, followed by a sniff that might have been tears or allergy. The structure smelled moldy.

"Bobbi?"

"Callie left me. I counted to 1200, so it has been around twenty minutes. I dropped some time while I drank water, so maybe twenty-five minutes, no more."

"Where…where did she go?" Grieg crawled under a fallen roof beam bumping his bleeding right arm against a fallen timber. Pain shot down to his fingers. He clutched the soaked bandage, blood leaked between his fingers.

"To meet you. Don't come any closer, please."

He stopped, swaying on all fours. "I came from Boomer's hidey-hole. She's not there. I need to find her. Are you okay here?" He thought she nodded, "I need a verbal."

"Scared," she shivered.

"You have a right to be, anything I can do?" Grieg crawled close enough to touch one of Bobbi's feet. He squeezed her toes. She didn't retract her foot.

"Be who I think you are?" Bobbi challenged.

"Which is?"

"The guy who gets dropped into the middle of a mess and saves everyone. That guy."

"Sorry, to say, I'm more the guy that drops in and leaves the mess." Grieg grinned, hoping she could see it in the light filtering through the boards.

"Find Callie, please, she'll know what to do." Her voice quavered, "Why, why me?"

"Because Rafe can't have Callie, not the way he wants."

"What if he has her? Right now!" Grieg squeezed Bobbi's hand. He tucked her under the thermal blanket, bundling her as his mother had so recently bundled him. "Is there anyone on your side?" she whispered.

"Just Frisco." He reached for one of her hands. "You're sure you'll be okay on your own. I'll be back as quickly as I can."

"With Callie," she whispered, linking her fingers in his. Her hand was hot to his touch. "Your hand's hot," she said to him. Not a good sign for either of them.

He left her in her bunting, crawled until he could stand, his right arm throbbing, and exited into what remained of the day.

Grieg grabbed a hank of Frisco's curly white mane in his left hand and vaulted onto the tobiano's back. Frisco's dark head rose with a snort producing a cloud of condensed air.

The day was cooling as dusk intruded, confirmed by the warmth of the horse between his legs. Grieg pressed his knees into Frisco's flanks. The horse responded with a trot. Grieg directed Frisco toward where he'd left the Jeep. The gate was open, the Jeep was gone. Fresh tire tracks through the grass marked its trajectory down the mountain.

The travois lay inverted, angled down a small decline. Frisco stopped stiff-legged next to the upended travois. After a moment, he poked at the travois, trying to lift it with his nose. Grieg dismounted and heaved it over, clutched his right arm and sat on his butt rocking in the duff. Boomer's bloody head lolled his direction. One eye opened. The two men stared at each other.

"Rafe has Callie." Boomer croaked between swollen earth encrusted lips.

Grieg crawled over to him. "You wouldn't have a knife on you, would you?"

"The grotto."

"Someone tore it apart. Same as your lean-to."

"Rafe back for his mementos. He needs them to screw me."

"Callie?"

"Unconscious. Tied." Boomer ran his tongue over a crusty slit in his lips.

Grieg fumbled at the knots. His right hand barely responded to the commands he sent it. "Rafe nicked me with an arrow, does he tip them when he hunts?"

Boomer nodded. "Rat poison. High octane. Shitty way to kill a deer."

"Shitty way to kill a human."

Boomer was laced to the travois, his arms, and legs under a tightly bound rope. Grieg managed to untie the only knot he found then unlaced the line from the long side branches. Boomer attempted to move. His eyes closed from the pain. Grieg hesitated, worried he might hurt Boomer worse than he already was.

Boomer stirred. "I'm not going to be much help. Something or things are broken." Boomer ratcheted himself to sitting relying on the trunk of the redwood, hefted his butt back until he leaned against the bark.

"What the hell are you doing here?' Grieg balanced his left fist on the ground riding out a wave of dizziness.

"The guy from Pete's Place, Willard, and another man, not Dempsey, are all at Tenaya. Talked to your mother, Khalil and his prototype are both whacked. His message at the cloud site was that the engine worked. The bad guys don't need to come for you, they sent Rafe. You're dead, Callie's dead, the patent is burned, the mine blows, Rafe's hauled in for killing those women, and nobody is the wiser."

"Except you." Grieg handed Boomer one of the bottles of water from his jacket pocket. "Dempsey's dead. Bobbi's at a fallen line shack. She'd welcome some company and some protection, though the condition you're in, I'm not sure who will protect whom."

Boomer rolled to his knees.

"It's a long crawl." Grieg jibed.

"Get!" Boomer muttered, creeping on hand and knees toward the gate, concentrating all his strength on reaching the line shack.

At Grieg's urging, Frisco exited through the gate. His ears pricked up. He refused Grieg's direction; instead, he picked his way down a steep slope, winding between trees, chunks of granite, and buckeye bushes until connecting with the tire tracks at an S-curve a hundred feet below the gate.

Stopped, Frisco checked his rider, waiting for direction, getting none, he took the next fifty-foot drop as sure-footed as an endurance horse, then another similar drop, intersecting the road each time.

After the last descent, Frisco's head bobbed up, his ears twitched, he broke into a canter on a straight stretch of the road. Grieg wrapped Frisco's mane around his left hand and concentrated on centering himself, his knees tight to the horse's girth. His right thumb tucked in a belt loop of his jeans, the lazy man's sling.

A half-mile later, Frisco veered left and plunged down an embankment. Grieg leaned back, disengaged his right hand and wrapped his fingers around the dock of Frisco's wavy tail for stability. They bounded through the trees. Branches twanged overhead. Bushes whisked by grabbing at Grieg's jeans.

As they met the tire track road, a blob of red made a corner less than a mile ahead. Frisco threw his head, thundered down the next embankment, catching the Jeep at the final turn before the road straightened into a long downhill slope.

Rafe drove with care over pot-holes, rocks, and tire tracks, anticipating the hazards in the dirt road. The rough road offered nothing to slow Frisco, the horse galloped to reach the Jeep. Grieg did as Frisco expected. He rolled to the right, got his left foot on Frisco's back, and leaped for the Jeep.

Rafe veered away. The car barreled into a well-established multi-stalked manzanita shrub. A rain of leaves and berries followed.

The force of the crash ejected Callie from the passenger's side. Rafe climbed from the Jeep, grabbed his weapons, and trotted to where Grieg lay on his back, the wind knocked out of him. Without hesitation, Rafe finished him with a savage kick to the head then tore downhill, crashing through the brush. Barely conscious, Grieg played dead, just possum-ed up counting the minutes, expecting an arrow to bring him down the moment he showed any life.

At a count of five minutes, Grieg crawled on his elbows to the Jeep, waited, then leveraged himself to standing. He scanned the brush for any sign of Rafe. There was none, but he could feel Rafe's eyes, almost hear his thoughts as the hunter studied his game considering his next move. Whatever it would be, Grieg was sure it wouldn't come on a road traversed daily by campers and residents.

Frisco whickered.

Hearing a vehicle on a curve below, Grieg relied on the Jeep to navigate to the passenger-side then his own wobbly legs to reach Callie. He knelt on his scraped knees next to her inert body and checked for a pulse.

As soon as Grieg's fingers touched the base of her throat, Callie flipped to her back and hit him upside the head with her bound hands fisted together. He tried to weather the blow, made the mistake of relying on his damaged right arm, and dropped like a rock in the grassy middle of the road. He rolled to his back. All he needed was another blow to the head.

A gray tinge washed the sky, darker on the left than right. A face appeared, one side bloodied, hair tangled and matted, hazel eyes intent on Grieg's blue ones.

"Sorry. I…never mind. Untie me," Callie demanded. "You okay?"

He chose not to answer the rote question. "Rafe took off into the bush armed to the teeth. We need to get Bobbi and Boomer somewhere Rafe-proof for the night."

"How did you find us?"

"Boomer, then your buddy Frisco. I'm buying him from you, any amount. I'm in love."

"He's a mustang, a Curly, and a pinto, they'll sneer at the polo grounds."

"Your point?"

"He's yours if you just effing untie me."

Grieg elbowed his way to sitting hampered by the wound in his right bicep and his tenuous grip on consciousness. Unmoved, Callie shoved her bloody bound wrists at him. The tightened rope refused all thirteen of his fingers.

"I have a pocketknife in my jacket pocket if that would help?" she grinned, splitting open the cut on her lip. She wiped the blood off with her fisted hands then held her wrists out to him.

He fumbled for the knife locating it by the lump in the left pocket of her coat and managed to finger out the big blade. He sawed as she kept the ropes taut. As soon as her hands were free, she grabbed the knife and used it on her ankle bonds.

Unbound, she pinned him to the ground and gave him a big wet kiss. "You're adorable beat-up and bloody."

"You're formidable and always have been. I loved you the minute you dissed me."

"I know." She ran her right hand down a scrape on his left cheek and pecked his nose.

"You know?"

"Why else would you chase me, kill my parents, and track me down."

"For your engine."

"Oh, that!" She stood, swaggered to the Jeep in her torn blue jeans and ripped flannel shirt. "Nothing useful. The only reason he didn't kill you, us, here is, it's too public. They'd find our bodies before dark."

Grieg held a hand up, she yanked him to standing. She fingered the sopping bandage on his right arm, sniffed then whistled. "That needs cleansing as soon as, there is already some tissue morbidity. Rafe no doubt, how'd he miss?"

"Technically, he didn't."

She fingered the boot bruise on his left temple. "Why aren't you dead?"

"Frisco zigged when Rafe expected him to zag."

"Looks like you should have done the same." She bent her knees to peer into his eyes and must have been satisfied with what she saw. She whistled for Frisco, his head popped up, a mouthful of grass hanging from his lips. If ever a horse deserved a nosh, Frisco did.

Callie led Frisco to a fallen log and gave Grieg a leg up. He put his left hand down for her, she vaulted on behind him and put her hands around his waist. He made a popping sound with his lips. Frisco stepped out. Grieg, to Frisco's disgust, insisted on following the road.

"What convinced you Rafe was the bad guy?"

Callie rested her chin on Grieg's left shoulder. "Bobbi flinched whenever he was near, swooned for you, and smiled at Boomer. That was enough to sway me."

"He's not through with us."

"You." Her chin bounced on his shoulder as they rode. "I'm going to bite the tip of your ear, then lick it."

And, so saying, she did. Frisco thought it was Christmas in spring when Grieg directed him off the road and into the timber.

XXIII

They reached the line shack Frisco's way clattering up what seemed an impenetrable granite wall then skirting a narrow chasm to sneak in along the bed of a small stream. The air had chilled. Frisco sent smoke signals with each breath.

In the smoldering light, the gray wood of the tumbled-down building merged into the granite surrounding it. Callie slipped off Frisco, followed by Grieg. She signaled her intent then crawled up the streambed, entering the shack through the door.

"Bobbi? Boomer?" No response. Callie crawled to where she had left Bobbi praying her hand wouldn't meet dank flesh. When it didn't, she sat on her haunches. "Boomer? Are you here?"

"They're gone," Grieg answered.

"There's only one place left they could be."

"Does Rafe know the place, because it's for sure he's stalking us, right now."

Callie bobbled her head. "We got here on horseback. He's twenty or thirty minutes behind us, maybe more in this light. Dusk is tricky in the timber. It will slow him down. Not to mention Frisco's off-roading through streams and over rocks."

Callie scrambled out of the shack into the fading light. Grieg stumbled after her. She grabbed Frisco's reins, led the horse to a boulder then signaled Grieg to mount. He threw his chest across the horses back, adjusting his legs with Callie's help. She garnered points for not taunting his weakness. Satisfied Grieg was aboard, Callie urged Frisco up the incline behind the shack. Frisco stepped lightly.

A breeze rose, leaves waggled, branches shook. Grieg grabbed a chunk of mane. Frisco danced between trillium, pranced by a nodding bush, and bucked at a fallen log. Grieg's bleeding arm ached. His head swam. He wound his fingers deeper into Frisco's curly mane and prayed he could stay aboard the anxious horse to their destination.

Frisco neighed. Rex responded from where he grazed on grass growing between man-sized boulders. Callie dropped Frisco's reins, skirting trees, cooing until she was close enough to grab Rex's reins. She handed the reins up to Grieg. Grieg tied them to a belt loop on his jeans. Rex fell in line behind Frisco. Callie continued to lead the horses up a narrow winding track.

Eventually, the path edged around a massif of granite so close Grieg's left foot grazed rock. The spine of the Sierra Nevada ran the length of the eastern horizon. Granite peaks blazed in the gilded light of sunset, weaving crazed shadows across crevices, cracks, and ledges.

Around the next corner, the lights of a small city twinkled in a distant valley. The hazy yellow glow invoked warmth and four walls, both of which Grieg needed. Callie dropped Frisco's reins then disappeared through a crack in the ridge wall. Grieg slid to the ground and leaned heavily against the warm horse.

"They're here." Callie held out a hand for Grieg. He took it, she pulled him through the crack into a cave. Fallen man-sized granite blocks created a roof over an eight-foot-high cave. Boomer lay on a self-inflating hiker's mattress to one side of the cave under an overhanging rock. Bobbi tended him. A lit lantern flickered spectral shadows on the uneven walls.

"How'd you get here?" Callie asked.

"Rex and the travois. I found them by the gate," Bobbi said, "It took us a while. I had to stop and rest. But Boomer insisted we come here."

"Good job!"

Callie rooted on shelves made of rough-planed boards. Finding what she sought, she motioned Grieg to a stone ledge that passed for seating. She fingered the wound in his arm, unwrapping the blood-soaked bandage, then helped him out of the layers he wore.

The exposed wound smelled. Callie uncorked a bottle with a handwritten label, the smell was distinctly that of distilled alcohol. She poured some onto a clean cloth, and, as Grieg whimpered, dabbed it deep into the graze. Callie finished her doctoring by spreading something involving petroleum on a pad of leaves and slapping it to the wound. She bound it with the hem of her shirt. When Grieg's head bobbled, she shoved it between his knees.

"Homemade drawing out salve of yarrow," she said, taking her hand off the back of his head. "It should pull the poison from the edges. The arrow tore a deep trough and reopened the bullet wound. Nasty."

The pain edged away from his bicep. Grieg clenched his right fist, wobbled, then stuck his head back between his legs, and croaked, "How's Boomer?"

Callie crossed to the small man. Black and blue eyes peered over a wool blanket with yellow stripes at the edges. Boomer's lips were swollen as though he were recovering from bungled plastic surgery.

Bobbi answered, "Okay, not great, but he's drinking water, and I managed to get some jerky into him."

"And you?"

"I can sit a horse," the girl responded. "We can lash Boomer to the travois. You promised I'd see my folks tomorrow."

"Help me build a fire, dry wood only, we stay here tonight. If we try to pack out in the dark, they'll find us shriveled up with rictus smiles at the bottom of some canyon." Callie made a good case. "Grieg, can you bed the horses?

"Can a girl piss in the woods?"

Callie laughed. Maybe, just maybe they could survive the night to make it out in the morning.

Grieg wiggled out the opening into the cold night and led the horses around the next bend, which curved into a cove under a slight overhang. He located some brush and constructed a barrier, corralling the horses into the granite bay. He apologized to Frisco for having no feed. Both horses whickered, positioning themselves nose to butt for the night.

Inside the cave, flames created a ring of warmth circled by pine boughs meant for bedding. Callie pulled Boomer within in the fire's warmth then gestured Grieg to a thick pile. He snuggled down, the scent of fresh cedar wafting from crushed boughs. Moments later, his eyes grew heavy, his stomach growled, a soft burble indicated he slept. Callie checked Boomer for any open wounds. Discolored bruises covered his skinny body.

When Boomer slept, she searched the pockets of his fishing vest. In his left chest pocket, she found an envelope addressed to him General Delivery and a check signed by Ray Washburn. Her butt hit the boughs gathered for her own bed.

Over the years, she wondered at Rafe's attachment to her and to the mountain when he could so easily have gotten a job and lived in town. Not once had she wondered the same about Boomer Bognavich. Damn, Boomer was good at what he did. When he trekked out to civilization, did he buy cigars, have a big meal, and contact his employer passing on Callie's latest secrets and successes. She had confided in Boomer, she shouldn't have.

Grieg liked the little man, there was a connection between them. If she told Grieg that Boomer worked for his late father, would he believe her? Probably. For all she knew, Boomer had already come clean with the boss's son. What a game, what a goddamn game. They'd played her like a fiddle! Well, they had nothing without her. If they wanted the damn engine, they needed her alive…for now…until someone like Khalil explained in layman's terms that the motor, as sophisticated as it was, either ran or didn't. Once started, it would run forever, but day to day driving, day to day use, meant stopping and starting. It needed a propellant to jar it to life. One that produced the same Newton meters each time.

She theorized one. But the chemical was rare, dangerous, and challenging to work with as anything that erupts is. She discarded that idea. The easy solution was gasoline. Which is what everyone wanted, a motor that didn't require a battery but still needed a gas fix like most electric cars. Ugh.

So, she moved onto the physical quirk that produces voltage when the temperature of a thermocouple differs from those on either side of it. She'd been unable to conceive a way to sustain the temperature differences. She posited a thermal resonator that generated electricity based on small temperature fluctuations to provide an energy source capable of persistent operation and of producing the current needed to start and stop the chemical reaction in her engine. Even on paper, it wasn't as consistently responsive as she'd hoped.

After months of theorizing, delving into various chemical components, she identified three commonly available chemicals whose reactions would consistently produce a spark, a touch of the foot on the accelerator pedal and bam, like a rocket. Between Boomer and Rafe, the needed chemicals were located. Each man had a separate task. She should have wondered when Boomer's material was top grade, and Rafe's off the shelf. She hadn't, but she did convince them she'd used the chemicals to boost the electrical output of the windmill when, in fact, the chemicals went to revamp the design of her engine. It was still in the testing phase. She itched to give it a try in the world. Instead, she whisked Bobbi away from the cabin and sent Grieg to destroy it.

Why hadn't it blown?

Simple, Washburn hadn't set it because he wanted it as much as the others. He bet his business on it. He'd told her as much.

Why hadn't she listened, really listened?

Callie built up the fire, forming a plan for the morning, returning to the mine at night was out of the question.

T**here** was no moon. It was overcast, and the power had gone out. The hum of the generator and the filminess of the browned-out lights added to the whole gothic-ness of the scene.

Felix Highland stood, one elbow resting on the marble mantle of Meremer's drawing-room fireplace. The casualness of his clothing spoke volumes. He had rushed over the moment the power failed to check that Delia was safe. Dressed for an evening out with Patty, her black pantsuit coupled with a pair of spiked heels, and a choker of diamonds around her neck made it clear Felix wasn't welcome. He hemmed and hawed. Delia, delighting in his show of discomfort, snapped, "I'm going out, make it quick."

"I don't think it's wise."

"You who-who and what pirate captain?" She asked with a jaunty bobble of her head.

"The night is foul."

"I'm going to dinner with a friend. We intend to gossip, eat, and wait for the end of this debacle. I tell Patty everything. For instance, it was she who first suggested given that Ray's wedding ring hasn't been found, though I sifted his ashes, that Ray is alive. And, if he is, where, the hell, is he? Times up?"

"This time of day, on Bondi Beach in Sydney," Felix answered, snaking an arm around Delia's waist.

Delia stomped one five-inch heeled shoe leaving a divot in the drawing-room floor. "Patty and I figure that when Calypso showed up in the Sierra four years ago, this Boomer was tasked with keeping her work a secret and her safe from all comers. In Boomer's defense, he claims no contact with Ray other than the occasional paycheck. Khalil knew the engine didn't work. He kept after a solution…something that would unfailingly break inertia. He couldn't find it. But she has, hasn't she?"

"Well…" Felix grinned. Delia growled. Viper trotted into the room, smelled Felix's freshly polished shoe, and lifted a leg. Felix kicked the dog away. Viper grabbed the cuff again, pulling and growling as though at 5.3-pound dog could drag a hundred-eighty-pound man out the door. "Stop him, I just bought these."

"You should have saved your money. You look ridiculous in jeans, you're a gray flannels man, you know, with pleats and cuffs."

"These jeans make me feel snappish and young." Felix kicked the dog away. Viper whimpered. Delia picked Viper up. "He's not hurt," Felix snapped

"I am. I am furious with you and with my husband. If anything happens to…"

"I suggested sending a helicopter in after Grieg and Calypso. Ray said no." Felix shook his head and scuffed one Cole Haan clad foot. It would have been endearing if Delia hadn't wanted to clobber him. "No one is closer to his boy than Ray, you know that, but Grieg's life was so interrupted by the damn accident that your son weighs everything against that scale. The left side of the scale is so loaded with lead that he could spend his life piling gold onto the other and never reach a balance."

"Get my son off that mountain!" Delia ordered.

"Not to mention his beloved helicopter mom. Delia, you aren't responsible for the original accident any more than Grieg. You've cosseted Grieg, protected him, excused him, fought for him. It's time for Grieg to fledge; show us how high he can fly."

Delia narrowed her eyes, stomped her foot again, and pulled out of Felix's arm. "You tell that sniveling son of a bitch husband of mine that he could have faced me and said the same thing. Instead, he sent you to do his dirty work!"

"Delia, it is going to be okay. But Ray won't stop the play before Grieg gets a chance at MVP."

"Does Grieg get a vote? He thinks his father is dead, that he is being forced from WashEx. For god's sake, he wasn't over the Dengue. Dr. Chaudhary warned him."

"Grieg's smart and tough. Ray may have underestimated some of his son's internal enemies. For instance, Willard nicked Grieg's bumper. The SUV was found in the police impound lot. But Ray knows that Purdy has peddled WashEx secrets to Aramco in the last year with the promise of a takeover. Ray staged the bombing. Everything since has been Doug trying to grasp control."

"With Sally riding shotgun?"

"How do you figure that?" Felix' elbow returned to the mantle, his head cocked, ready to listen.

"She no more wants to marry Chris Gilft than I would. She wanted Grieg. Always has. When they were six, she announced she was his lobster. Well, her wants exceeded her claws. She waited. Grieg never caved, so I surmise from her position as General Secretary she provided all the proof and impetus her father needed to derail my husband, son, and WashEx. And, Sally knows about the ledgers Ray sent Virginia. She knows Hugh is still embezzling and is blackmailing him just like Larch Swale did until Hugh murdered him. When are you going to stop your son, Felix? When?"

"Hugh has stashed the money in off-shore accounts. It's all there but a few million. WashEx is in great shape, Delia. No worries."

"Grieg?"

"Give him this chance."

"Did Ray tell you that Virginia promised Calypso to Grieg the day she was born. She and Ray locked pinkies on it. Then fate intervened. First, Calypso found Grieg repulsive. Second,

Grieg destroyed Calypso's family and sent her on the run. Third, don't underestimate her."

"I know, isn't it marvelous!" Felix grinned happily, nothing jaunty, nothing prescribed, nothing faked, just a great big sloppy smile.

Delia slapped him as hard as she could and tromped from the room. Ray Washburn would soon discover... No, he wouldn't; she'd grab him, hug him and drag *her* lobster upstairs to her boudoir. Then let him have it for endangering their son, assuming Grieg survived, and for underestimating what his son and his wife could accomplish. If he had?

No matter, the neighbors were in for a surprise. Should she return the charitable contributions made in Ray's name?

Frost lipped the edge of the cave. Grieg snuck out early, collecting twigs and branches to dry in front of the banked flames within the cave. Boomer and Bobbi slept, one snoring, one making puffing noises as though smoking a thin cigarette. Calypso mended the travois with a coil of handmade rope kept in the cave for just in case. Callie smiled at Grieg as he set the wood in a circle around the flames then rubbed his hands together for warmth.

"There's water over there, a tin of coffee, and my discarded coffeepot. You could try your hand at boiling water."

He gathered the items. The pot had a metal basket with a lid and glass nob in the tight-fitting top, like the percolator Moms used in Alice Springs. He poured coffee into the metal filter, suspended it on the pump stem, poured water to the fill line then balanced it on two flat rocks over the fire.

"Tell me about Sally Purdy," Callie whispered. "She always had the hots for you. What is she up to now?"

"She's WashEx's General Secretary. And, what's she up to? I think she's been funneling information to our competitors about our finances and blackmailing Hugh in your father's stead. She is engaged to Christian Gilft. He played polo for East Hampton. He dislocated my right shoulder during a foul back in the day. His father works for a Wall Street firm, they put together the IPO prospectus with privileged information. Sally and Hugh, I reckon."

"What are you going to do?"

"Get back alive."

"Sounds like a goal." Callie wrapped rope, cinching a branch to one of the main skids. "Mine is access to copper, nickel, and graphene."

"Conductors, thermal resonation…on-demand, self-generating electricity. Too damn bad that copper, nickel, and graphite are so accessible."

"Accessible enough to save the world?" She checked his face to see if he was kidding.

"I can get you all the copper, nickel, and graphene you need, Callie."

"Are you proposing?"

Grieg quirked his mouth in response then shook his head, puzzled. "Are you?"

"Nope, I'm marrying for love. I'm doing it once. And, it's going to last because the man I marry will be as strong-willed and as adventurous as me. He'll be someone who considers the world his home. Someone who has the guts to rescue me from myself and isn't afraid of what he's done, unapologetic if you get my drift. We're going to change the direction of the world, like Marvel comic heroes, and then we're going to pass the recovering climate on to our children. I'm thinking four, two of each, one of whom will be a frigging genius like his dad and one, a girl, I think, like her mom. There is one prospect who might fill the bill if he doesn't let the percolating coffee put out the fire."

Grieg yanked the coffeepot from the flames. Water bubbled out the spout onto his hand. He set the pot on the ground and poured bottled water over the scald. The fire kept burning. There was hope for him after all.

Grieg handed Callie a cup of coffee. "Bolt has us in his crosshairs by now. The only chance we have is to head straight over the mountain for the Lodge. I'm sending Boomer with you. We'll strap him on the travois…"

"Boomer works for your Pops."

Grieg nodded. "The first thought I had when I met Boomer was that if Pops had known Boomer's father, the man would be dead. Boomer chose to meet me over the men Highland sent. Loyalty is the only explanation. To Pops." When Callie didn't respond, he changed the subject. "Rex will do the pulling. Bobbi rides Rex and keeps the travois centered. You're going to have to lead them out. I assume you know the way?"

Callie wanted to smack a big wet kiss on Grieg's cheek. He was so damn adorable handing out orders, she could barely contain herself. She only hoped he understood that with each command he gave, he left his shame behind, that there was no going back to it, and no more hiding.

"Good. I'll take Frisco and draw Rafe away as long as I can. I'll meet you at Tenaya tonight. Do you need money?"

"Of course, do I look like the kind of girl that wears Stella McCarthy dresses and Louboutin shoes?"

Grieg shook his head, "No, but I bet you can…"

"That's so childish, get over it."

"Will you demonstrate for me someday?"

"How's your arm?" She crossed to him. He pulled his arm from the sleeve of his shirt. She admired the well-defined muscles in his chest while she checked the arrow rent in his flesh. The yarrow had helped, the inflammation was down, and the bleeding had stopped, but the wound was crusty and the edges red. He needed a doctor. He kissed her knuckles. She kissed the top of his head, then rebandaged his arm. "Don't get killed, okay?"

"My buddy Frisco and I are indestructible."

"Correction, your buddy and you are brainless and think you are indestructible."

He shrugged back into his layers of shirt. "No kidding, I feel good."

"I wish I had my thermometer. You look flushed."

Grieg checked his watch. "It's time we got going, it's early, but it might give us a head start. Do you need help with the travois?"

Callie tied the last knot, threw her hands in the air as though roping a calf and yelled, "Hell no. But I need a favor. I need you to go back to the mine."

"It's set."

She nodded. "I need to hear the concussion. I have to know it blew."

"You don't trust me?"

"It's just--no--yes--but until it's smithereens it's--we're vulnerable."

"I trust you have your schematics?"

"Does a girl...?"

"So, I hear. Your wish is my command."

"Just don't let cocky rule your brain, okay. I've lived with what your brain can do when it's juiced."

He caught her hair in his fingers and pulled her lips to his. "I can show you some cool stuff only boys can do. Stuff I learned in the better establishments while chaperoned."

Callie snorted.

The snort woke Bobbi, who put a pale hand to Boomer's brow. His brown eyes opened. Callie lifted the travois, managing it out the narrow entrance to the cave. Bobbi followed. Grieg got Boomer to his knees, with an arm under Boomer's armpit, he hefted Boomer to his wobbly feet. They joined the women on the ledge.

Bobbi spread a blanket across the litter. Grieg lowered Boomer first to his butt, then onto his back then centered him on the travois. Callie covered then roped Boomer on while Grieg went for the horses.

Frisco's soft nose greeted Grieg. Rex nibbled on nearby grass. Grieg haltered Rex and led him to where Callie and Bobbi waited. Frisco followed. Grieg had never fallen in love as fast or hard as with this horse, not even the granite he'd wanted for Christmas. Frisco butted his back knowingly.

Rex accepted first the saddle, then the travois, and finally Bobbi. Callie roped the travois to the horn and the poles to each side of the girth. Callie tested the ropes, kissed Grieg on the cheek, and said, "Tell Frisco where you're going so he can lead us to your body."

Grieg grunted then vaulted onto the horse's back to an admiring *wow* from Bobbi. Callie waved as she led Rex around the corner and past where the horses had spent the night. The view from the cliff in daylight spanned 245-degrees of the horizon.

A wispy trail of smoke rose to the southwest, perhaps a mile distant. Callie's cabin, someone had beat him there. He urged Frisco toward the smoke. Frisco shot Grieg a look, displaying the length of the white blaze down his nose.

"I know, old buddy. I'm counting on you to get me out of this."

Frisco didn't hesitate, he just galloped across terrain rougher than Grieg had ever ridden. When Grieg came unseated, Frisco stopped then walked, head drooping, to a log. Grieg checked to make sure the pinto was still sound, checked his hooves for stones, scrapping one out with his fingers. Frisco nudged him as he mounted. Grieg kneed Frisco toward home. Frisco wasn't one to take the beaten path, he headed into the timber and down the ridge.

His arm healing, his head working, and his fever down, Grieg relished the abandon of wending down cliff faces, between boulders, and around trees. As they neared the stamp mill from the tree side, Frisco cocked his head. By now, Grieg knew not to question the horse's instincts. He leaned forward and whispered. Frisco responded walking as delicately through twigs and rocks as a fifteen-hand, 1200-pound horse can. Frisco halted, legs straight. No one was visible through the brushy undergrowth, but Doug Purdy's favorite off-color, unrepeatable expression hung in the air.

"Now what?" Chief Willard asked, staring into the empty stalls. "The two horses Bolt told us about are missing. The way Washburn and Swale ride, they could be anywhere, including off the mountain. We'll never find them."

"Bolt will. He'll kill Washburn and bring us the girl, soon as that happens, we haul Bolt in for murder. Win/win," Purdy responded. "The girl is easy pickings. You heard Bolt, she'll come running to him. All we need to do is call in our chopper, grab the engine, get our asses out of here, and sell the damn thing to the highest bidder."

"One problem, where is it? We've searched all the structures but the coop."

Doug, dressed in workwear from head to boot as though he'd outfitted himself in a hardware store, headed for the chicken coop. Chief Willard, in uniform and blue windbreaker, followed his fledgling stomach. The back door of the cabin hung by one hinge. They must have forced their way in then trashed it. The kiln listed to one side. Strewn ashes darkened the ground. From the back of the cabin, Frisco picked his way downstream to the mine entrance, his brown and white coat perfect camouflage in the dodging shadows made by swaying trees.

Willard pushed his way into the chicken coop. Willoughby let loose a heartfelt crow at the disruption. An equally heartrending *Shit* rang out, proving that the big, brassy Australorp rooster would go down fighting before anyone made a stew of him.

Grieg took advantage of the gabbling chickens and the crashing boards to cover his mounted ride into the mine. He dropped Frisco's reins fifteen-feet in, then retraced his steps to the engine, opened the door with the screwdriver in Callie's pocketknife, and reset the clock. Five minutes.

He propped the lop-sided door open then trotted out to Frisco. Hearing voices at the mine entrance, Grieg mounted and urged Frisco forward. The horse gathered himself and roared to a gallop, his hooves striking sparks on the granite strata. They bolted from the cavern. Willard and Purdy jumped out of their way.

Willard drew his gun and fired. Frisco responded to pressure from Grieg's knees and tore across the open meadow into the trees. Once out of sight, Grieg reined the horse to a walk and waited for the explosion.

Willard entered the mine. Purdy stood with one hand on his hip, eyeing the tree line. The next moment, the ground rumbled. Purdy ran for the cabin. Willard burst out of the mine entrance.

The eruption belched rock and dirt twenty feet out the main shaft. Fire shot out a ventilation pipe. Trees ignited, burning out on the wet ground. The hill collapsed. Purdy and Willard stared at the resulting heap, hands on their hips, speechless.

Frisco cantered through the woods, around the massif, up another steep slope and onto the path Callie had taken toward the Lodge. The gelding broke into a smooth lope over the increasingly manicured hiking trail. The skids of the travois had cut two grooves in the mud left by the combination of rain and melting snow. The consistency of Rex' hoof prints and the straightness of the skid lines, reassured Grieg with each passing foot that Callie was unharmed.

Grieg should have asked Boomer how long it took to reach the Lodge, he guessed four hours on foot. Rex didn't change the equation, Callie was afoot, and the travois might slow them. At best, they had a five-mile head start.

Comfortable with the trail's surface, Frisco kept a leisurely pace. The warning was no more than a squiggle in the travois tracks, so slight Rex might have shied from a squirrel. Grieg waited for Frisco's take. The pinto's head bobbed. His lope became a walk. All Grieg needed to know.

Grieg dismounted, placing a hand over Frisco's muzzle. The horse stayed silent, hidden behind a small stand of scrub oak. Grieg lobbed the reins into the general bramble then crept forward into the brush.

The travois lay face down twenty feet below the trail. A pair of feet emerged from the blanket. There was no movement. Grieg crabbed sideways down to the wreckage. The left skid of the travois had snapped in the fall. Once that occurred, the tension on the ropes loosened, the supporting branches broke free. The blanket no longer stretched across the V-shaped litter draped on the hillside. Grieg worked his way to the head of the travois.

No need to check for a pulse. An arrow shaft angled from Boomer's neck. Poor bastard hadn't had a chance. Grieg gathered the blanket and draped it over Boomer's ruined head and neck, stifling the urge to rub Boomer's hands until they warmed.

Stupid, it had been stupid to go back to the mine, despite Callie's urging. He'd left Callie unarmed, unprotected, and undefended and Bolt an hour to track, subdue, and kill.

Grieg considered his options, there was only one, thunder in brainlessly as Purdy expected. Purdy wanted Grieg dead, Rafe was his man. Boomer's death was proof. Worse, Rafe craved Callie. With Grieg dead, Rafe would have all the time he wanted with Callie until he tired of her, as he had Amy. And Bobbi?

Frisco whickered. Rex responded. The buckskin appeared out of the brush to Grieg's left. A bloody gash on his right flank. Grieg caught Rex' dangling reins and checked Rex's wound, the right brace had torn his side as the travois broke free. Rex's ears twitched. The horse took a step up the hillside. Frisco screamed, the whites of his eyes showing. He reared, tearing free of the manzanita, and plunged downhill.

Grieg heard rather than saw the arrow. The barbed tip whizzed past, landing harmlessly in the thick layer of pine needles on the forest floor.

Once, in the mountains of New Guinea, his exploration party had been attacked by bow and arrow wielding natives. The tribesmen moved silently. Their arrows tipped with poison so strong, death followed in minutes, not some namby-pamby rat poison. The guide warned Grieg that they had passed the point of safety. In New Guinea, they had climbed into the dense canopy to escape the tribesmen moving silently below. Grieg didn't have the luxury; the canopy was gangly pine, and Bolt held the high ground able to lob arrows at Grieg until one hit home.

Grieg elbowed downhill to the flipped travois where it angled over Boomer's broken body and considered the tools at his disposal. Rex. Frisco. The broken branch from the travois. He searched Boomer's pockets for anything he could use as a weapon. Nothing, except the arrow lodged in the dead man's throat and Callie's pocketknife.

Grieg steeled himself then yanked the arrow from Boomer's neck. It was as awful as he anticipated, the front of his shirt and forearms were splattered with blood. He wiped the arrow with leaves, not questioning why it mattered given how he planned to use it, then fingered the two-inch blade out of the pocketknife. Armed, he cozied up to Boomer's cooling body for cover. A sharp whine descended. An arrow bored into the uphill side of the travois. Grieg counted the fletched shafts he'd seen in Bolt's quiver. Six, maybe seven. He'd lofted three at Grieg the day before. One in Boomer. Two now. One left? Then the knife or a bullet.

The next arrow pierced the blanket, lodging in Boomer's right shoulder. Grieg grunted for effect. The third arrow grazed Grieg's right calf. Okay, eight.

Grieg concentrated on the hushed footsteps sneaking downhill through the duff toward where he hid. He lay motionless waiting for Bolt, preternaturally aware that only speed and surprise separated him from death.

Rafe drove his knife blindly into the blanket. Grieg roared to standing, the arrowhead pointed up, the two-inch blade open at his side. Bolt yanked his skinning knife free. Howling, he raised the drop-point blade over his head. Grieg lunged.

Frisco roared past jolting Grieg to the ground. Rearing, hooves flailing, lips curled, the horse pummeled Bolt's chest and head. When Rafe hit the ground, Frisco thrust his front hooves into Rafe's chest, screaming and plunging until his pasterns were saturated in blood. All sound stopped. Frisco stood stiff-legged, smelling the air, his nostrils flared.

Grieg crabbed to standing. Frisco presented his blood-splattered muzzle. Grieg stroked the velvet softness, wiping the blood from his hands onto his jeans. With a last look at the pulp on the forest floor, Grieg tied Rex' reins to a belt loop on his pants and mounted Frisco.

Frisco picked his way up the slope. When they reached the trail, the pinto threw his head, swung a backward look at Grieg then broke trail. Grieg reined him in at a snapped branch, then followed the trail through the undergrowth. Two minutes later, Frisco stopped, his head pointed toward a tumble of stones. The sound of trickling water led Grieg to a wedge-shaped opening. He ducked in fearful of what he would find.

It took his eyes a moment to adjust in the filtered light. When they had a body, curled in the fetal position emerged in the shadows. He stepped toward it. The head bobbed.

He kneeled. Bobbi, eye's wide, was gagged, tied hand and foot, her teeth back, holding a scream she needn't use. Grieg removed the gag then her bindings. Bobbi stared, not at him but across the cave, incanting, "That son of a bitch. Son of a bitch.

Grieg followed her eyes as afraid as he'd ever been.

Callie's hands were tied to a root well over her head. She was blindfolded and gagged, as well. She cocked her head, trying to see under or through the blindfold. Relief washed over him. Her field coat lay on the ground, her flannel shirt and the Henley beneath were sliced open. Her skin was translucent with the cold.

"Calypso," Grieg whispered, crossing to her.

She raised her blindfolded head. Two buttons remained on her blouse, he buttoned them. When she was covered, he used the pocketknife to cut her down. Her hands slammed to her sides. She buckled to her knees, tore off the blindfold and gag, and muttered, "Rafe?"

"Dead," Grieg answered.

"He couldn't be dead enough," Bobbi responded.

"Both of the horses are here. Can either of you ride?"

Bobbi sobbed a yes, he thought. Callie held out a hand. Grieg supported her to her feet. "Can a girl…?"

"You can, Callie," he answered, brushing a strand of her tousled hair over her shoulder.

"He's really dead?"

"Most sincerely dead."

"You?"

"Frisco. Which makes Frisco mine until I save him back." Callie grinned; the cut in her lip started to bleed. Grieg wiped it with the cuff of his grimy shirt. She put her head on his shoulder. "Let's go, ladies. The sooner we get out of here, the sooner we can get you both to a doctor."

"I just want a bath," Calypso said.

"The last thing Callie said before Rafe gagged her was that no matter what happened, you'd find him and kill him," Bobbi offered.

"In retrospect," Callie responded, "It wasn't the smartest thing I've ever said. But then, here you are."

XXIV

Grieg tied the horses to a tree outside the tall double entry doors of the Lodge. Filthy, bloody, and tired, he limped into the lobby. The whoosh of people turning, and the hush of sudden silence greeted him.

He strode to the front desk as though he owned the place, as though he didn't stink, wasn't bleeding, and hadn't killed. He demanded three rooms, two adjoining. The clerk stuttered. Grieg yanked his battered wallet from the front pocket of his jeans and slapped his identification on the counter with blood-encrusted fingers. The clerk typed on her computer, a moment later, all smiles, she addressed him as Mr. Washburn asking if suites would meet his needs. He pulled out his WashEx credit card.

"I have two women on horseback who need assistance. We've been chased for over a day through the mountains. One of our company was murdered. I'm afraid the murderer is dead, as well. Call the police, I can accompany them to both locations, sooner rather than later, given the wildlife. They also need to pick up Chief Willard of the Suffolk County Police Department and Douglas Purdy, interim CEO of WashEx, for attempted murder, theft, and any other charges I can dream up. Oh, and I started a fire at the old mine on the Yellow Sky Holdings property about eight miles south-southeast. I suspect the Forest Service has responded by now, but it was burning when I left."

The manager gasped. An assistant trotted across the lobby and out the door. Moments later, Callie and Bobbi made their entrance wrapped in blankets. A man crossed the tile floor in long strides headed for Bobbi. Grieg's hands fisted. With a final brisk step, the man reached out. Bobbi ran into his arms. Her father. She laid her head on his shoulder. A woman joined them smoothing Bobbi's hair with her right hand, before wrapping her arms around both her husband and her daughter.

Bobbi looked up. Wiping her eyes, she said, "I'd like to introduce you to Miss Calypso Swale and Mr. Grieg Washburn. They got me out alive."

Grieg offered Bobbi's father his right hand. Her father stared at the dried blood, then shook. "Thanks, thanks for our daughter."

"I've reserved a suite for her," Grieg said.

"We have a room," her father responded. "She'll want to go home as soon as she can."

"I suspect the authorities will want her to stay around for a few days, why not be comfortable? Please, accept the suite. I'm paying. She'll need a doctor, and I'm glad to pay for any therapy."

"Who are you again?"

"Grieg Washburn. They were on my property. I'm the CEO of Washburn Exploration. I'm sure you've never heard of my company, but trust me, I can afford this gesture."

Her father chuckled. "I'm in oil. I've heard of WashEx."

"Good things only, I'm sure," Grieg bantered.

"Heard about you, too." Grieg raised his dark eyebrows. Bobbi grinned. Her father said, "We'll take the suite."

"A doctor should be here soon," Grieg responded with a nod. "By the way, I recognize you from Pete's Place two days ago."

"I was hoping to track down a lead I had on Bobbi. Thanks, thanks again."

"I see the stableman at the door, I need to see to the horses. Maybe we can catch up later."

The moment Grieg walked outside, Frisco nickered. Grieg rubbed the brown tip of his nose. The stableman, holding both sets of reins, asked, "Any special instructions, sir?"

"Call a veterinarian and see to the buckskin's injuries. His name is Rex. He's a big lug, but a good boy. As for my buddy Frisco, make sure he gets a good scrubbing, groom him until he purrs and feed him as much as he can eat. Believe me, I'd stand him to a beer if I could."

"What about their tack?"

"Frisco hasn't any other than the hackamore. But clean up the gear on Rex."

A tall, redheaded cop swaggered up to Grieg, another in tow. Grieg didn't know whether to hold his wrists out for the cuffs or answer like a CEO. So, he offered his right hand, "Grieg Washburn. I understand you have a warrant for my arrest."

The older of the two men smiled, "Patrolman Hager. Nah, that's been straightened out. Got a call from back East a day ago. A Judge Burridge said you were a free man, but if we caught up with Chief Willard, we should detain him for questioning. We got a tip that he was out hunting you down."

"Last seen, Willard was with Doug Purdy at the Yellow Sky Holdings property watching the forest burn."

"You look done in and smell the same."

"If you've got a camera with you, you might want to take photos of the pinto's hooves. Frisco's the real hero. He killed the man who's been preying on those young women, Rafe Bolt. Horse saved my life in the process."

The younger patrolmen returned to the car for the camera. Hager said, "Ramirez will snap some shots. You say the smaller horse got the killer."

"I can show you Bolt's body. Today would be better than tomorrow, it's exposed and torn up. Carnivores will be hot on him by nightfall."

"Give us the location. We'll find it, call you in if need be."

"He's just off the trail, there's a stone grotto nearby. He held the women there while he hunted me. It's about four miles in, based on the time it took us to reach the Lodge."

"I know the place," Ramirez noted, joining them. "We figured it out, you know. Once we got suspicious, we searched Bolt's place, found all the evidence we'd ever need. We boxed it and hauled it out."

"I got separated from the women and Boomer Bognavich. Something I'll regret for a long time. Bolt killed Boomer, beat him near to death, then shot or plunged, hard to tell, an arrow through his throat. Boomer's body is under a travois." Grieg realized he still carried the broken arrow. He pulled it out of the pocket of Rafe's borrowed coat. "Here, it was the only weapon on hand. Sorry."

Hager took it from Grieg's hand and studied it. "Anything else?"

"Special Agent Dempsey. I marked his grave. No idea who killed him, but I suspect it was Bolt. He tipped his arrows with rat poison, and he had a rifle. Expert at both. And, he had a skinning knife he wasn't afraid to use."

Ramirez shook his head. "Dempsey didn't buy Rafe's line about the woman's clothes at the old iron claim, told me he wanted another look there and at the lean-to by the gate. He was looking for the girl. Good man. Anybody else?"

"Just Willard and Purdy. Somebody needs to arrest the bastards. They tore up the property, sent Rafe to kill me, and that's just here. They got the money to disappear in a blink."

"We're on it. We'll need a full statement, but it can wait. So, officially I'm asking that you stay nearby until all the bodies are found and the investigation completed. If for some reason you need to leave, give us the word."

"No, problem. I plan on being right here."

Grieg glanced into the lobby as Callie entered the elevator. He longed to be with her, knowing this was the inexorable finale to what they'd started five years, four months and twenty-five days ago.

The hotel in Oakhurst sent Grieg's suitcase by taxi to Tenaya Lodge. The bellboy put it on a cart and headed for the elevator. Grieg sauntered into the gift shop through being embarrassed by his appearance. Lacy greeted him with a huge grin and a hug.

"It's all over the Lodge that you caught the man who killed all those girls. Too bad he's dead, I mean their parents may never know where he buried them. Good job, though."

"They'll be found. He kept mementos, it's likely they're all interred near his cabin. I'm sure the police will be searching the area tomorrow at the latest."

"You look like you could use a doctor." She touched the blood on his sleeve and pointed at the blood staining the calf of his jeans.

"I'm okay. Better than okay. I'm good. Do you sell champagne?"

Lacy shook her head. "Not here, but you can order it from room service. They have Dom Perignon for people celebrating anniversaries and weddings and such." Her eyes kept glancing over his shoulder. He followed them. "You know what I'm going to do?" she asked.

"Take down some pictures? Not before I check something." They crossed to the Bulletin Board. Girl number three had been practicing for a cross-country endurance run on a Curly pinto named Toby. Rafe had abducted her and left the horse to forage and survive on his own. Grieg could only imagine Rafe's surprise when Boomer brought the pinto in for Callie to heal. Grieg would let the police know.

Lacy pulled thumbtacks from the corners of Amy Dunstable's pictures as shoppers gathered around her. Grieg left them to their celebration. Crossing to the front desk, he thanked the clerk for her help then asked how to contact the stable. The number in hand, he took the elevator to his floor.

Callie was in her room arguing with someone, audible through the half-closed door to her room. "Damn it, go next door. I'm telling you the man there needs attention. I'll be fine. Just leave me a bottle of disinfectant. I'll bath and apply it where it needs application. Right now, my brain is obsessing over hot water and bubbles."

Grieg slipped the magnetic key in the lock to his suite and entered. At a sharp rap on the door, he opened it and ushered in the doctor.

"I see what your neighbor means," the man said, touching Grieg's right sleeve. "Any specific place you want me to start, or should I just bandage your body."

It was meant as a joke, Grieg thought.

The doctor worked his way efficiently over Grieg's rips, tears, and seeping wounds. He cleaned, stitched, and dressed the gunshot cum arrow wound with one eyebrow arched throughout the proceedings as though expecting Grieg to explain. The doctor administered two shots, an antibiotic and a pain killer. One of them made Grieg woozy. The doctor helped him into a chair, suggesting Grieg eat something substantial and drink an ocean of water before attempting any further feats of glory.

Grieg ordered a huge meal from the room service menu, sriracha fried shrimp for starters, French onion gratinée, two filet mignons with horseradish mashed potatoes, and a bottle of Dom Perignon envisioning sharing it with Callie while wrapped in bathrobes.

He lifted the receiver to invite her over then returned it to the cradle. He had waited so long for her forgiveness a few more hours were nothing. Besides, it had to be her choice. She would come to him when and if she was ever ready. He prescribed patience but didn't like his own medicine.

So, he tried staring at the adjoining door. He checked to make sure it was unlocked on his side. After ten minutes, he gave up, sat in a plush chair in his shorts and bandages, and dialed Moms. She answered on the first ring.

"Griegs?" she cooed; her voice relaxed him.

"Moms, I'm afraid I've made another mess of things. I started a forest fire, got a man killed, abetted a horse in killing another man, and offended pretty much everyone at the lodge where we are staying."

"Oh, Griegs! It is so good to hear your voice." He could see her in skinny jeans and a tunic top, her hair wrapped up in a scarf and five-inch spikes on her feet. Her brilliant gold hair, her dazzling blue eyes, coupled with the new wrinkles he'd added to her years.

"Anything popping back there?"

"Not much. Felix and I had a good long talk. We agree that Doug and Sally Purdy and their little buddy Chief Willard are ready for long supervised vacations."

"Has Pops shown up yet?"

"You beast! You knew. How could you, I didn't. Not until yesterday."

"Once I thought about it, I realized Felix was the only person Pops would entrust you to in his absence. Things started to make sense after I made that leap, regarding good guys and bad. You do know Callie's engine doesn't work."

"Dr. Khalil posted it on the Yellow Sky dropbox."

"Ah…and that Willard and Purdy worked for…"

"Aramco. Exxon claims total ignorance, though…"

"Though."

"And, you're a big hero. Because you didn't have enough on your plate, you just happened to catch and kill a serial rapist and killer. It's all over CNN. What did you use on him?"

"A twelve hundred-pound, fifteen-hand hammer. You'll meet him, his name is Frisco if I don't lose him to his original family."

"And this Boomer?"

"Dead. Bolt killed him. Thing is Moms, he was the real hero. He took so many risks to keep Callie safe and protect her patent. I wish I knew more about him."

"He met Pops in Bakersfield as a boy. That's all I know, except he was a loyal fan of Ray Washburn. Pops will have to fill you in when he gets stateside from Sydney."

"How's the Board taking it?"

"Sally and Gilft had a huge row. I guess she made promises she couldn't deliver. Hugh is skulking about waiting to be arrested. Jones and Fred are delirious, running around bragging about your adventures. Tom nailed the contract in Australia, then flew to Samoa. I think he's your new wingman. There's a symmetry to it. If I were you, which I'm not, I'd fire both Doug and Sally by email. Then have Judge Burridge arrest one or both."

"I think I'll keep ol' Sal on, Moms. As for Doug, he and Willard staged the accident five years ago to kill Larch. Poor Virginia was the only one to die. Hugh killed Larch. Willard deep-sixed me for Doug's money and other considerations. And, Larch told Callie to run. She did. Five years of our lives!"

"When will you be home?" Delia asked, hearing only *our lives*.

"When I am."

"But…"

"Moms, I'm okay."

As happy as she was for her son, she already mourned his loss. She was that helicopter mother Felix had accused her of being, but Griegs had needed her, he'd bourn his guilt and hurt on his sleeve. Now, his trajectory had changed overnight. She heard it in every word he uttered. Delia sighed.

"Moms?"

"Sorry, that was more an exorcism than anything, Griegs. Hang up and go to Callie, okay?"

"Moms, I got this."

"I'm floating on air."

"Love you, Moms. Always will."

"Oh, Griegs!" she squalled and hung up.

Grieg knocked on the adjoining door. Callie didn't answer. He tried the knob. It was open. He called out. No response. Steam flowed out the bathroom door. He tiptoed in. She lay in the Jacuzzi tub, her head resting on the edge, her eyes closed, humming.

He sat on the edge of the tub and asked, "The work glasses, tools, soldering iron, all yours?"

"Mine."

"Anything else I should know about you."

"I can't shoot for shit."

"I bear the wound. And?"

"Shave. You are positively scruffy, adorable, but scruffy. I need to see that cleft in your chin before I can eat the outrageous amount of food you ordered. They delivered it to my room by mistake, or was it?"

He held two fingers to his lips, then folded one. Callie's eyes lit. She flipped a dial on the edge of the tub. Bubbles pulsed. Grieg got one up his nose as he bent in for a kiss.

A real kiss, the kind filled with promises.

Acknowledgments

The mountain towns described in Saving Calypso exist and are lovely though being in California occasionally beset by forest fires. California Highway 41 runs from Fresno, through Coarsegold, onto Oakhurst, then Fish Camp and into Yosemite National Park. The mountains are beautiful, the land filled with wildflowers and elegant redwoods. I hope I've done it justice.

Pete's Place exists as does Tenaya Lodge and the wee general store in Fish Camp. All the people and occasionally the descriptions are from my imaginings. For instance, the bulletin board in the store in Tenaya Lodge.

I would like to thank Janet Dawson, author of the Jerry Howard and California Zephyr series, for being my first reader. She has a great eye and a need for commas, which is a wonderful fit because sometimes I find them a nuisance. I try to heed her advice. As a result, if you feel that there aren't sufficient commas, I take responsibility.

Most of all, I hope you enjoyed *Saving Calypso* as much as I enjoyed writing it. If you did, please leave a review, or even if you didn't, I like hearing from my readers, it helps me improve.

And:

Reviews help keep authors writing and publishers publishing them. Please take the time to post a review of this book at its site on Amazon. Every little review helps.

For more information about this book, please visit
www.dzchurch.com

About the Author

D. Z. Church has lived in the Eastern, Mid-Western and Western United States. Writing wherever she was, gathering characters, finding joy in foul weather, and wondering why she only managed one month living in the Deep South. She has been on her way to Australia and Ketchikan since high school. She did live in Barbados for one glorious long summer. She found out firsthand that Leech Lake in Minnesota is well named and that you can too walk across the Mississippi River. Along the way, she discovered that people aren't always as they seem and that their stories are best served in a whopping good tale. The kind people like to read with a little history, some foul weather, and an absorbing plot laced with adventure, romance, and suspense.

Perfidia

"In Church's debut thriller...Church manages, quite impressively, to maintain a sense of a hidden but perpetual threat...Overpowering dread and a leery protagonist make this a suspenseful read." ...Kirkus Reviews

One August night in 1974, a California schoolteacher overhears her father whispering into the telephone. The next day, he's gone.

Soon, two DEA agents appear claiming her father, Del, was last seen retrieving the wave-battered body of a drug-running buddy from a rocky cove in Barbados. Witnessing the agents grab the key to her father's safe deposit box, she outruns them to the bank, finding a .45, and a rusty key stashed among other secrets her father kept.

When she receives a couriered note demanding that she bring the key to Barbados, followed by a telephone call from a glib Barbadian lawyer, she accepts the duel challenges or were they threats. Grabbing the next flight to Barbados, she lands in the middle of a tug of war over a historic plantation, a hunt for rumored pirate treasure, and the men who stand to inherit.

Now, everyone sees her as a threat.

It will take all of Olivia's wiles and the skills her father drummed into her to survive Perfidia.

Perfidia

Available at Amazon, Kindle, and Kindle Select

Dead Legend

Cooper Vietnam Era Quartet: 1967

First Sergeant Laury Cooper and LT Byron Cooper have two things in common, a legendary dead father, and the war in Vietnam. Since their father's death, they've been on opposing trajectories. Now, from the moment Byron's squadron suffers higher than average loss of jets on Yankee Station, and Laury, home with a career-ending wound, finally opens his father's box of effects, the estranged brothers are in peril.

From aerial combat to the tumult of a country at odds over the war, each brother must face down the part he played in their father's death before more pilots are sacrificed, and the innocent die.

Dead Legend is the first novel in the Cooper Quartet, the story of a military family set against the turbulence of the Vietnam Era. It is 1967, the war is escalating as the protests at home gain traction.

Dead Legend

Available at Amazon, Kindle, and Kindle Select

Head First

Cooper Vietnam Era Quartet: 1972

For Jolie Minotier, the stakes couldn't be higher, adrift in the town where her mother, terrorist Chloe Minotier, abandoned her, fearful her mother will resurface, rejected by her father, she does the one thing she can think to do--- run. She doesn't anticipate being kidnapped or that her father, now CDR Byron Cooper, her uncle, Laury Cooper, or her aunt, LT Robin Haas, will care. But they do. Enough to risk their lives and careers in their headlong rush to find her.

Jolie's disappearance sets off a chain of events from kidnapping, to heroin smuggling, to an unsanctioned insertion into Vietnam that will change the landscape of the Cooper family forever.

Head First is the second novel in the Cooper Quartet, the story of a military family set against the tumult of the Vietnam Era. It is December 1972, President Nixon has ordered carpet bombing of Vietnam, and public opinion has turned sharply against the war.

Head First

Available at Amazon, Kindle, and Kindle Select